THE DAYS
TO COME

THE DAYS TO COME

A Novel

TOM ROSENSTIEL

ecco

An Imprint of HarperCollinsPublishers

THE DAYS TO COME. Copyright © 2021 by Tom Rosenstiel. All rights reserved. Printed in the United States of America. No part of this book may be used or reproduced in any manner whatsoever without written permission except in the case of brief quotations embodied in critical articles and reviews. For information, address HarperCollins Publishers, 195 Broadway, New York, NY 10007.

HarperCollins books may be purchased for educational, business, or sales promotional use. For information, please email the Special Markets Department at SPsales@harpercollins.com.

Ecco® and HarperCollins® are trademarks of HarperCollins Publishers.

FIRST EDITION

Designed by Angela Boutin

Library of Congress Cataloging-in-Publication Data has been applied for.

ISBN 978-0-06-289264-5

21 22 23 24 25 LSC 10 9 8 7 6 5 4 3 2 1

For my mother and all her friends on the hill

In every dark hour of our national life a leadership of frankness and vigor has met with that understanding and support of the people themselves which is essential to victory.

—FRANKLIN D. ROOSEVELT, FIRST INAUGURAL ADDRESS

Frantic orthodoxy is never rooted in faith but in doubt. It is when we are unsure that we are doubly sure.

—REINHOLD NIEBUHR

CAST OF CHARACTERS

RENA, BROOKS & ASSOCIATES

PETER RENA, *partner*

RANDI BROOKS, *partner*

ELLEN WILEY, *head of digital research*

ARVID LUPSA, *digital researcher*

HALLIE JOBE, *investigator*

WHITE HOUSE

DAVID TRAYNOR, *president of the United States*

WENDY UPTON, *vice president of the United States*

QUENTIN PHELPS, *White House chief of staff*

STERLING MOSS, *political counselor to the president*

GIL SEDAKA, *chief of staff to the vice president*

KIM MATSUDA, *counselor to the president for environmental affairs*

THE SENATE

TRAVIS CARTER, *Senate majority leader*

AGGIE TUCKER, *chairman of the Senate Judiciary Committee*

LEWELLYN BURKE, *senior senator from Michigan*

BATTERY COMPANY EXECUTIVES

KUNAI SREENIVANSAN, *founder, Ignius Corp.*

BILL STENCEL, *founder, Helios Corp.*

VENTURE CAPITALISTS

JAMES WEI, *partner, GCM Investments, investor in Helios Corp.*

ANATOL BREMMER, *founder, Global Partners, investor in Ignius Corp.*

OMAR ABBAD, *partner, BFP Investments, investor in Tolle Industries*

OTHER CHARACTERS

VICTORIA MADISON, *friend of Peter Rena*

JASDEEP BHALLA, *FBI Special Agent in Charge, Palo Alto Office*

DAVE POLANSKY, *FBI Deputy Special Agent in Charge, Palo Alto Office*

KATIE COCHRAN, *former wife of Peter Rena*

MATT ALABAMA, *friend of Peter Rena*

STEPH MEYER, *a seventh grade teacher*

JAMES NASH, *former president of the United States*

JEFF SCOTT, *governor of Michigan*

THE DAYS
TO COME

PROLOGUE

Kunai Sreenivansan liked to visit the farm in the last fading minutes between night and morning. Astronomers call that moment civil twilight; the sky is lightening, but the desert is still asleep. The sun is six degrees below the horizon.

In summer, the valley at this hour was still a gentle enticement, not yet the angry mystery it would become a few hours later. By midday, temperatures would exceed 120 degrees Fahrenheit, and after a few minutes the searing desert would become uninhabitable for humans. In winter, the same valley was a frigid moonscape. Last winter, the earth's temperature below the cactus here registered the same Celsius as it did in the Arctic—a new alarming record.

Kunai knew only that these changes were unnatural. To be precise—and Kunai was always that—for each of the last fifteen years, the hundred acres he had just leased in this part of Nevada were hotter than any years recorded before 1950. And every one of the last five summers had been the hottest ever.

The desert flowers had begun to bloom at the wrong time of year; then they would stop and slip back under the earth again because they recognized they had come too soon. Everything was confused: the lizards, the plants, the Earth itself.

Kunai's meticulous crop of shiny flat silicon panels—sand converted by heat into crystalline silicate—jutted out into the desert farther than he could see. The panels were canted at forty-five degrees so they would smile into the rising sun. He checked a few each morning, but he was not really here for them. The panels themselves were simple, self-monitoring devices and rarely failed. He was here for the boxes that sat behind each panel.

Sreenivansan was dark skinned and broad shouldered, especially for a Maithil Brahmin from Northern India. He wore dirty blue jeans and a black tee shirt, and he was often mistaken for a student, which he hadn't been for many years since he had moved out of his crammed apartment with his doctorate from MIT.

And though he was young, he thought his face was blighted by a strange crease, a worry line that ran from his eyebrows to just above his nose. The mark had appeared one day when he was sixteen. He wondered if he had dreamed something terrible while asleep and that the nighttime terror had left a scar. He wondered what it portended about his life. He worried he had committed a sin against God for which he was being punished. Fifteen years later, the crease was unchanged. Time had neither softened nor deepened it, though now he was more worried about the Earth than about religion.

His English was more American now than British or South-Asian. He credited that to his grandfather, an ascetic monk. Grandfather had wanted Kunai to be a monk, too, and a singer of sacred music, and he had made the boy wade into winter lakes to practice singing in the belief that the cold water would improve his voice. Instead, the freezing water and the family's looming demands drove Kunai away from Grandfather's asceticism toward science. But singing while his twelve-year-old body was rapidly dropping in temperature also had the effect of somehow changing his English public-schoolboy accent. The only way to sing the words to the spiritual songs with his body so tense was to flatten and quicken them out, like an American pop star.

He looked at the boxes connected to the panels. There were thousands of them, each a little bigger than the size of two car batteries. He opened up five of them, just for a glance. Then he stacked those five on the hand truck he had brought with him and rolled it to his pickup. He would look at them more closely back in the city. But he already knew what closer examination would show.

They hadn't lasted. The liquid metal had failed after four days. That was eight times better than the lithium-ion battery the world used now. But it isn't what he'd theorized. It wasn't good enough.

PART I

Defining the Problem Is
Half the Solution

1

PETER RENA

The quarrel started in the hotel. Now it was continuing in the car.

"That is exactly what you said, Peter. You should listen to yourself."

Peter Rena felt like a swimmer knocked backward by the surf, head suddenly underwater, feet thrashing above him. Vic was right. That is what he'd said. He'd forgotten—not quite believing he had said something so thoughtless—and then denied it.

Vic was staring straight ahead, driving. Now she turned to look at him.

Her eyes, the color of smoke flecked with gold, were the first thing Peter had noticed about Victoria Madison when they met three years ago, the first thing about her he had fallen in love with. Now they were filled with accusation.

"You need to say something, Peter. This is not a time for one of your deep silences."

But Rena didn't know what to say. His mind was flooded, the swimmer scrambling to regain purchase. The woman he loved had just asked for his true feelings. Why did he not know them?

A few minutes earlier they'd been laughing. They were at the hotel getting ready and Vic was talking about how strange the evening was going to be. She was looking in the mirror, putting on earrings, using her free hand to pull her hair away from her face. Her hair, which was straight and dirty blond and which she always wore short, reminded him of summer.

Her reflection in the mirror looked back at him. He needed to make his mind up about something, she said. About whether he had to work tomorrow or would spend the day with her. She had upended plans to be here, and she wanted to talk about something.

Tomorrow? He'd forgotten to tell Vic: the vice president-elect wanted to meet with him.

Rather than answering, he'd tried to lighten the mood. "It isn't fair to give me ultimatums when you look so good."

It was a joke, but Vic's expression had frozen.

"Make up your mind for once in your life," she'd said sharply.

Her vehemence had surprised him.

"Babe, I don't understand what the problem is."

That was the truth, but he wasn't thinking—and in an instant this had become serious. She had never given him an ultimatum, not once in all the time they'd known each other.

IN THE CAR ON THE WAY TO DINNER VIC WANTED TO TALK MORE about why she was angry.

"This isn't just about tomorrow."

A year earlier Vic had asked him to move to California to be with her, or she could move to Washington with him. This afternoon she'd brought up having children again. He had missed that cue, too. And tonight he had made a joke about ultimatums.

He watched himself being stupid, hurting her.

She was crying as she drove. "Go to hell, Peter."

This was Vic, who never lost her temper, who helped everyone else manage their moods, who Randi Brooks, his friend and business partner, said made everyone around her better at life.

Rena was supposed to be good in tight spots; that's how he made his living, helping people in trouble. A cool head and a slow heartbeat, even in combat. But he was *this* person, too. A fuddled man in a car having a fight with the woman he loved, understanding nothing and making it worse.

He and Vic had flown in that morning from different ends of the country, Rena from Washington and Vic from California. They had come to Aspen for dinner at the home of the next president of the United States. The evening would be "a small personal and professional gathering," they'd been told. "About a dozen people. A semi-working dinner." The invitation had come only a few days before, a surprise.

Rena only glancingly knew president-elect David Traynor, the tech entrepreneur and Democrat who a month ago had won the presidency on an improbable bipartisan ticket. He and Randi had done work for Traynor's running mate, a Republican senator from Arizona named Wendy Upton. Someone had threatened to destroy Upton if she accepted Traynor's supposedly secret offer to join his ticket. Rena, Brooks, and their small consulting firm of background investigators found the person behind the threat and ended it. The episode had probably pushed Upton toward accepting the offer to run—not away from it.

In the months that followed, Upton by most estimates helped tip the razor-thin election to her running mate. While Americans wanted change, a good many had doubts about Traynor—a new-economy billionaire turned populist outsider—just as they did about his Republican opponent, a charismatic, ultraconservative war hero from Michigan named Jeff Scott. Having to choose between two macho disruptors, a growing number of voters found something reassuring about the shy, tough, western woman senator who crossed party lines. In the odd alchemy that happens between TV screen and voter, Wendy Upton made the daring David Traynor feel more trustworthy.

The mysterious dinner invitation was not the only odd element of the day. There was also the magazine story. A Washington policy publication called *The National* had published a lengthy profile that morning about Rena and Brooks as Washington fixers. The headline had been embarrassing: WASHINGTON'S SECRET PRIVATE EYES: THE ODD COUPLE BOTH PARTIES TURN TO WHEN THINGS GO WRONG. Peter and Randi had only cooperated because *The National* would have done the story without them—and it was safer with them. But the article struck a sensitive chord with Vic. A year ago, in the middle of the whole Upton probe, she'd asked Peter flat out: How can you keep doing what you do when politics has become so grotesque? He had answered in a way he thought at the time persuasive. All the things wrong in Washington were a reason to stay, he said, not leave.

In the year since, he saw more clearly their relationship had drifted into a state of suspended animation. They talked every day, saw each other often—one or the other making the trip across the country each month or so. But they had fallen into a pattern avoiding all difficult questions, until tonight. Vic was thirty-eight and Rena forty-three. It was time they decided where they were headed.

The magazine article talked about Rena's "detective's intuition," about how—when he developed a theory about a case—he could fall into deep silences, pondering what the article called "thought experiments": *What if?* His mind would drift into the *if*, and he would mull by himself, until all the pieces in a case were examined against the possibility of the *if*.

Detective's intuition? Vic was the most important person in his life. And he had no idea what she was thinking. He was the master of oblivion.

What was frightening him? Failing at marriage a second time? Failing Vic?

She had stopped crying. "I told myself I wasn't going to bring this up tonight," she said. "I was going to wait until tomorrow." She wasn't looking at him. "I've started to see someone else."

Rena thought he hadn't heard her right.

Not Vic. She wouldn't do that. He tried to process the words. He looked through the windshield at the dark night. There was little moonlight and clouds masked the peaks of the jagged snow-covered mountains, as if the tops had been cleaved off by the sky. What remained looked like white elephants.

His phone rang.

Don't answer it.

Then a text message. Then the phone rang again.

He stole a glimpse at Vic. She was reading his mind, sensing his panic, understanding everything better than he did. She was still angry.

Then came another text. "Look at it," Vic said.

It was from Arvid Lupsa, one of the computer experts in Rena and Brooks's office. Urgent. Read this! Something from the social platform Y'all Post had been copied into the message:

Peter Rena is a liar and a fraud. He is a wife beater and a baby killer. He is no one to judge others. Or investigate anyone.

I have the proof.

It was signed by someone using the screen name *Out of the Past.*

"I'm sorry," Rena said to Vic, "for being an idiot."

2

DAVID TRAYNOR

Everyone kept eyes on David Traynor and pretended not to. Traynor could feel it. He swept the two dozen faces seated around the long table set up for the night in the great room of the Aspen house. Then he rose. He was more nervous than he would have liked.

"I promised Mariette I would wait till after dinner before I did this. But I can't wait. Sorry, Mar." A sheepish grin at his wife. Her sky-blue eyes looking up at him, her broad swimmer's shoulders, that confident Stanford smile, they gave him strength.

He didn't crave attention, not the way sneering strangers on cable and social media thought he did. They'd be shocked if they knew the truth, the talking heads who had never met him but made their living opining about him. He'd read about how basketball master Bill Russell suffered paralyzing migraines before NBA games; how the most famous actor of the twentieth century, Laurence Olivier, would feel his throat constrict so tightly from anxiety before walking onstage he couldn't breathe. Though Traynor had been famous most of his life, and had profited from that fame, the attention still at times made him ill.

David Merrill Traynor, the president-elect of the United States, "the bro billionaire," who had risen in a blink to the top of American politics, kept his secret terrors to himself. Never show weakness: that had been his vow to himself, ever since his senior year in college when he founded his first company—custom-made personal computers sold online for less—and the marketing people found that photo of him in his dorm room clowning around with the computer boxes and put the picture in the TV ads. He hadn't wanted to be the face of the company. He despised those idiot CEOs who starred in their own commercials for pillows or electric shavers. But marketing said the picture told the story—how a kid dreamed up a better way to sell the one thing everyone wanted. "You are the story." He had Dumbo ears and thick curly hair that wouldn't comb, and he was loud even though he was shy. One of the ad people called it "awkward authenticity," and someone said "that's the thing," and it became the thing.

He had never revealed to anyone, even Mariette, how uncomfortable fame made him. They wouldn't have believed him.

The bigger his fame got, however, the more it became a responsibility—to his company, his shareholders, his employees, the marketing plan, the projected earnings. He began to amuse himself by owning sports teams and being on reality TV. They were good for the brand. And, by then, he had learned to appreciate the attention; it made him richer, after all. But fame had become its own career, its own obligation, and the meaningless influence it brought him eventually began to feel like a corruption. He needed to do and think about something more consequential than amusing himself and making more money than he could possibly spend.

He wasn't a pure engineer like his friend Bill Gates. He didn't have that intellect. He wasn't a visionary like Steve Jobs. He was an integrator, a storyteller, a guy who could diagnose what was wrong and spot new markets. When he began to think about how to use his influence beyond business and games, Mariette urged him to turn his attention to public problems. He didn't want to start a foundation—that sounded like fatal boredom. He wanted to work on public problems the way he and his partner Quentin Phelps thought about business problems—looking at systems failures, using change management techniques, and seeing what old ways no longer made sense. And before long, he had been tapped by Democrats to run against Phil Albin, the wing-nut senator who was embarrassing Traynor's home state of Colorado. He not only won the seat. He also seemed to have a rare appeal to the kind of voters Democrats struggled with, especially young white men. It was "the thing," all over again. And the day after his election to the Senate people started talking about the White House.

He and Quentin hired consulting firms to develop plans for tackling the problems the government had failed to address: the budget, health care, manufacturing, infrastructure, climate. The gap between what could be done and what hadn't been was staggering. But when he got to the Senate, he was even more appalled. He finally understood how these old men had neglected the country's problems for so long that the problems had become crises and then emergencies. If he'd hired these people at his companies, he told Mariette, he would have fired them for not doing their jobs. It took just one miserable year in the world's most deliberate body for him to decide to run for president. Better that than becoming one of these bloviating knuckleheads, which is what would have eventually happened.

In five weeks he would take the oath and become the most powerful human on Earth. The prospect felt a hundred thousand times bigger than any fame or responsibility he had known before. Bigger than he ever imagined. Bigger every day.

In Aspen, he scanned the faces in the room again and began.

"My problem, our problem, the country's problem, is this: How do we launch a successful presidency when the government and the political system are broken?"

This question was everything, he thought, and he sought the

answer the way he would have approached any disrupted industry. What was the system failure? What core factors created the
dysfunction? What mistakes had predecessors made that he should
avoid? How could the government for thirty years have let the infrastructure crumble, jobs vanish, the planet overheat, the health care
system and education fall behind, all because the stock market was
going up?

He glanced at Wendy Upton, his vice president-elect, the strong,
quiet woman who had risked everything to join him. He owed a
good deal to her, he thought, and he was beginning to trust her judgment more than he expected.

The country was split down the middle, and the two sides despised each other. Republicans had learned to simply block everything his predecessor, Jim Nash, tried to do. Their increasingly
furious base punished them for doing anything else.

"We've looked pretty hard at these questions," he told his guests.

And they had. He and his inner circle had talked to former cabinet members and presidential aides, former senators and historians,
and every living president. The press and his enemies had mocked
this "cram course" in presidential leadership as maybe too little too
late. But no one had been able to penetrate the nature of these conversations, only that they had taken place. The meetings were not
for show. Everyone, even the former presidents, was asked to sign
one of Traynor's famous NDA agreements, a holdover from his
paranoid technology past. Each guest at his home this evening had
signed one, too, and left their phones in a box by the door.

"Tonight I want to share with you my plans and get your reactions."

It was a good start, he thought, but he was still nervous.

Tonight, he wanted to debate with smart people the strategy he
planned to use to avoid those mistakes. To the outside world this
was just a social dinner at his home in Aspen, the one he had fa-
mously made look like a cowboy ranch house, the only one of their

six houses Mariette had allowed him to decorate. He'd assembled what some might consider an unlikely group for the evening. But Traynor liked friction and craved debate. He thought they helped avoid mistakes.

His small inner circle was present, of course—Mariette and his best friend and longtime business partner Quent Phelps, who had been his roommate at the University of Illinois and who was about to become the first Black man to be White House chief of staff. He had invited his political strategist, Sterling Moss, the ultimate pragmatist, and his budget guru, Carol Serrano. He had stolen her from one of the consulting companies he had hired. There were also a few old business friends from outside politics.

In addition to them, Traynor wanted people at the dinner he didn't know well but found interesting—if they could keep a secret. So he had invited a former moderate Republican lawmaker who now ran a foundation looking for a "third way" in politics; a systems analyst who had studied political polarization; a scholar who thought democracy had run its course; a Harvard presidential scholar he had met on the campaign; and her husband, an economist from MIT.

There were no lawmakers, no senators, or members of the House, he'd been adamant about that. This was a night for pressure-testing strategy, not selling product. A night for people you could trust, and he didn't trust anyone in Congress to keep any secret. The two legislative chambers were run by the opposition party—Wendy Upton's party. The Senate majority leader and Speaker of the House were both members of what was now called the "firm right," a term the new conservative leadership had think-tanked and market tested and preferred over "right wing" or "far right" or even "conservative." And the "firm right" opposed Traynor on all matters. It especially despised his vice president, Upton: it considered her a traitor.

Traynor had given Upton two criteria for deciding which guests she could invite tonight. They had to keep his plans secret and they had to be capable of leveling with him. She had chosen the two political fixers Peter Rena and Randi Brooks, who had helped save her career. She now wanted them to help with the transition.

They ran a small consulting firm, one of the last bipartisan shops in Washington. They were relentless, clever, and discreet, and their bipartisanship—Brooks was a liberal and Rena a Republican—made them more objective than most, which Traynor considered a rare trait in Washington. Above all they were notorious for their bluntness; there were stories, perhaps apocryphal, about their telling one client, a governor, that his best option was prison or suicide. When she hired them to investigate threats against her ten months ago, Upton had told Traynor, the two fixers had confronted her with secrets she never imagined anyone could know—secrets she had barely confronted herself—among them conflicts with her sister, Emily, whom Upton had raised after their parents died; another was Upton's own closeted sexuality—the fact that she was attracted to women more than men, an attraction that she had largely repressed when she entered public life.

Brooks was quick, loud, and savvy; Rena was reserved and observant, and Traynor could tell Rena didn't much like him, which intrigued him all the more. But he noticed the moody Italian hadn't made it to the dinner. He was supposed to be coming with his girlfriend, Victoria Madison, the daughter of the Supreme Court justice Roland Madison. Maybe they were late. Who was late to dinner with the president-elect?

Traynor kept on. "We got elected arguing *the government* was broken—not the country. And we would fix it by putting government to work on the country's biggest problems. Reform the government, not tear it down."

That had been the crux of his campaign message, positioning him as both moderate and disruptive reformer: he would retool and shrink government and, at the same time, restore faith in it. And by twelve votes in the electoral college, the nation had narrowly decided to gamble its future on a rogue figure from business rather than on the dashing right-wing war hero who seemed perhaps more taken with martial law than with civil government.

"In my old career—inventing new businesses—there's a saying: defining the problem is half the solution."

He smiled skeptically. "Like most old sayings, it's about fifty percent bullshit. Which means fifty percent right." A pause, his timing deft as ever. "So the question is: How do we launch a successful presidency when Washington is broken? To know how to fix it, we need to know why it's broken. And what we should do differently.

"I've received a lot of contradictory advice. Old hands told me to go slow. Prove myself first. Make good appointments. And most of all, get one big win." Here he mimicked a former secretary of state with a recognizable European accent, capturing the voice perfectly: "Yourrr presidential apprrroval nuumbuh isss like your credit score. It tells you how much pawlitical capital you have een the bank and how much you owe. Get one big win. Rrraise your crrredit score. Put more capital in the bank."

The impersonation had been a mistake—he realized it instantly. He was met by nervous laughter and some awkward silence. He plunged on.

"It wasn't bad advice. Appointments matter. So does a smooth transition and scandal-free confirmations. Like a good supply chain, they're essential. But insufficient. We could do all those old things right and still fail." A smile. "The road ahead could still be blocked. Unless we know what's blocking it."

This, he knew, was one of his true gifts: telling stories that defined problems. That was how he got venture capitalists to give him money to create companies that existed only in his imagination. It was how he'd won the election.

In the last debate, he had told a story about his opponent, Michigan Governor Jeff Scott. The story flattered Scott, telling of the man's battlefield daring, the risks he took and the people he killed.

Afterward people liked Jeff Scott, but they liked David Traynor more. He had assumed the role of narrator of the race. He had taken ownership of Scott's story, and in his praise of Scott, which was sincere, he had made the colonel sound just a little too ruthless—and a little more risky than Traynor. There were ten days left in the campaign; Scott never quite got his rhythm back.

Now Traynor was about to tell the story of how he could make the government work and heal the country. In Silicon Valley, you faked it till you made it. You took your investment money and only then tried to actually build the thing you had talked about in your story.

"So what is blocking the road ahead? What have we learned from our cram course? How will we succeed when, to be honest, the government hasn't really worked in twenty years?"

He could feel himself gaining momentum.

"One mistake is thinking we have more time than we really do. There is no honeymoon anymore. We have sixteen months to succeed. Maybe eighteen. That's all. And the other side will not work with us, even if we give them what they want. Politics is no longer the art of compromise. It is the art of war. And the point of war is to force your enemy to submit to your will."

He paused now. All that training for talking to shareholders and boards and product presentations, his timing honed by years of practice, was almost by now muscle memory.

"If half the solution is defining the problem, I define the problem we must solve as this: we will have only sixteen months to accomplish anything—to show government can actually succeed at solving problems. Then the window closes and the next election starts. In those sixteen months, we must outthink, overwhelm, and divide our opponents. How do we do that? After twenty years of dysfunction and polarization, how can we, in less than two years, outwit our opponents and get quick wins? How can we begin to meaningfully address problems that have been ignored for as long as half the American public has been alive? How can we move that fast and that well?

"Seems pretty daunting, doesn't it?" A smile.

"My answer has nothing to do with policy. And it comes in four parts, so listen closely."

3

WENDY UPTON

There were moments when Wendy Upton wondered what she had done.

How was it she had lashed her future—and the country's—to this man she barely knew?

In more rational moments, of course, she knew the answer. The presidential campaign had been a months-long nightmare of fear-mongering and promises. She was genuinely anxious for the country's future. Her own party seemed to have gone mad. When Democratic presidential candidate David Traynor, an outsider who didn't like party orthodoxy and promised reform but not revolution, had asked whether she would consider being his vice president, she had allowed herself a day to entertain the hopelessly naive and politically suicidal idea: perhaps, just perhaps, a bipartisan ticket might heal the country.

Gil Sedaka, her chief of staff and closest friend, had encouraged her, thinking the rumors of her being sought out would help her politically, never imagining the offer would actually come through.

Then she'd been threatened by a conservative billionaire who'd gotten wind of the offer. Through intermediaries, her unknown antagonist promised to destroy her career if she accepted the vice presidency. The person making threats should have done his homework better. Once challenged, Upton was unlikely to back down. She said yes to Traynor out of defiance more than reason. And it had made her vice president.

This evening, about a month after the election and a month before taking office, she was full of new doubts. Buyer's remorse? Was her optimism, she wondered now at stray moments, an act of political vision or epic delusion? History was littered with people who had once been considered serious and had made themselves ridiculous.

Sitting in the middle of the huge dinner table at Traynor's magnificent Arts and Crafts–style house in the Colorado mountains— the enormous outdoor chimney was a climbing wall—she watched the president-elect. If they won, she had told him during the campaign, her role would be to watch, listen, and advise him honestly. And she would remain with him as long as he would take her advice seriously. If he were sincere about trying to realign his party and reshape the country—and would listen to her—she would join him. If not, she would resign. They both knew that would wound his presidency.

Now he was going to reveal his plan, outlining it for the first time, even to her. She was irked not to have heard it sooner—but not entirely surprised. For all his promises to treat her as a partner, Traynor kept things to himself. Upton now knew that he was a complicated amalgam of obsessive-compulsive, insecure, and improvisational; he may not have entirely finalized all he had to say tonight until an hour ago.

In that way, as in so many others, they could not have been more different. She was methodical, a planner, a list maker. She not only worked out her plans ahead of time. She also studied how each different person in the room might react to what would happen and prepared answers to them on index cards. Though she appreciated the value of surprise, she found Traynor's manic style and bold instincts bewildering. Yet she had to admit there was something exciting about it—even if she sometimes worried he was part illusionist.

"First, unlike others, we're not gonna go for one big win," Traynor said. "Instead we're gonna do the opposite. We're gonna do all the things the American people hired us to do, all at once—and faster than any one has ever tried before. The reason is simple: if we move fast on everything, our enemies will be unable to concentrate their opposition in one place. That's what they've done before to stop presidents trying to make change. Now they won't know where to turn.

"And as we succeed, the public will gather to us." He paused, his eyes moving across different faces around the table.

Upton felt a creeping sense of doubt already rising. This idea, which she'd heard bandied about but not settled on, struck her as foolish. Moving on everything at once could easily mean failing at all of them and quickly dooming Traynor's presidency before it had begun. She knew the Senate far better than Traynor. It was a place designed to never be caught off guard and to easily stop things in their tracks. Why not move more carefully, taking time to learn first? Test the waters? A couple of quick failures could be fatal.

"How do we do everything at once? We start with a list of the biggest problems facing the country. For each, we will identify two or three things we can make progress on immediately. Start small and move fast. Franklin Roosevelt didn't solve the Great Depression in a few months. But he made people feel the government was finally doing something. And he did so almost immediately."

Traynor paused again as he moved on to the next point.

"Second, we're gonna write laws differently than before. Government usually fails because it tries to solve every damn thing around a problem in a single massive god-awful bill. Everyone marshals their complaints. The bill gets watered down. It takes years to pass. And it's obsolete on day one. We're not gonna do that."

Traynor moved his eyes around the room again, stopping briefly on Upton.

"How do you solve problems in real life? You start small, go one step at a time, learn as you go, fail, and get better. And delegate.

"That's how we're going to write laws and make the government work again. Tell Congress which problems to solve but not precisely how, mandate they start small and move fast. We're gonna build in frequent checkpoints and require that progress be proven before any new money is provided. And we're gonna do things in months, not years.

"What do I mean? Find a broken bridge. Rebuild it in a month. See it's done right. Fix anything done wrong. Then take what you've learned and rebuild another bridge. And don't go big until you know what you're doing."

This, Upton recognized, was agile management brought to government, ideas from Scandinavia and China that had gained popularity among academics.

The Scandinavians charged their bureaucracy with solving problems, but did not dictate precisely *how* they do so. Their laws were written in brief and described needs without detailing every aspect of the solution. And no new money was spent unless the agency could prove concrete progress. The approach developed accountability, saved money, and avoided prolonged political fights up front. It was massively different from the rule-laden way American legislation was written.

The Chinese, meanwhile, used huge work crews to get work done with impressive speed, constructing bridges or erecting buildings in weeks rather than years.

"Third, we're gonna tell Congress if they can't do it—if they don't pass these bills by a certain time—we will declare national emergencies on any of the issues on which Congress failed to take action. And we will make sure they are blamed for the failure. This will not be executive overreach. It will be the executive branch rescuing the country from a broken legislature. And we believe we have sound constitutional arguments that will prevail in court."

The doubt Upton had been feeling was hardening into dread. This part, about threatening to declare national emergencies, was new; she had not been consulted on it. Congress would consider it a major threat to congressional independence and a massive overreach of executive power. If Traynor did this—used the threat of declaring multiple national emergencies to grant himself extraordinary powers to evade Congress—it would change the presidency forever. It would also threaten what little was left of balanced government in the United States.

She glanced at faces in the room. Friends, but also many outsiders, sat transfixed. And Upton began to feel more alone than before.

Traynor wasn't finished. He had saved, she saw, the most dramatic parts of his plan for last.

"Fourth, I'm gonna bring these guys from Congress to me—the Senate majority leader and the Speaker of the House—and I'm gonna tell 'em they have to change their rules. They both have these little internal party rules that they won't bring a bill to the floor unless a majority of Republicans supports it. The 'majority of the majority' rule they call it in the House. But what it really means is that they're practicing one-party rule.

"I believe this practice is unconstitutional. If the majority of members of Congress support something, I believe they have an obligation to let the people's representatives have a vote on it on the floor. If Congress doesn't voluntarily abandon these little tricks that ensure party unity, I will direct the Justice Department to bring suit. And I believe—based on the interpretations of scholars we have consulted—we will win.

"More important, I will lay all this out to the public. They don't give a damn about internal congressional rules. They just want their government to work again."

This, too, was an unprecedented act of war that crossed historic lines. No president had ever sued Congress over the constitutionality of its internal rules, let alone private internal party procedures.

And she had most definitely not been consulted on it. She would have opposed it.

"Oh, and one more thing," Traynor added.

This, Upton recognized, was the old Steve Jobs phrase. At the end of his annual presentations, the Apple CEO used to announce the year's biggest product with that modest phrase, "oh, and one more thing."

"So maybe I have five points, not four," Traynor said with an apologetic smile, as if he had just realized it. "If they agree, if they pass these laws in new ways and abandon their obstructionist rules, I will promise to serve only a single term."

Traynor let that sink in.

"But if they resist, not only will I sue, I will promise to serve eight years and dedicate myself to ensuring that Congress and its leaders are blamed for the failures of the government. And I will use all my power to see them defeated.

"That will be my deal with them. Do this, work with me, make the government functional, and I will be gone. Resist, and I will dedicate my presidency to ending their careers and replacing them with leaders who can make the government work. It will be very, very personal. They can submit or go to war."

The room was quiet. The pledge of serving a single term as chief executive was unprecedented. So was the idea that it was a bargain in exchange for legislative cooperation. And if Congress refused, the bargain would be replaced by a personal vendetta and a massive assertion of the power to declare national emergencies.

Traynor was proposing that he would creep further out on the edge than any president in history.

He also had not warned her in advance. She had been blindsided by this.

Traynor, a galvanic smile lifting his whole face, studied the room one more time.

"What I have told you must be confidential. I want your reaction and your thoughts. But, for obvious reasons, I cannot let this be known until after I have been sworn in. I have taken you into my trust."

How did she feel about all this? She was angry about being left in the dark. But she was also intrigued—and a little enthralled—by the boldness of Traynor's plan. A promise to take action on all of the country's biggest problems immediately, to make progress one decrepit bridge at a time. A plan to write laws in new ways that started small and pushed responsibility down. And this bill writing would include triggers where no new money was dispersed unless real progress was made—the equivalent of agile management applied to government. And if congressional leaders continued to insist on internal procedures that amounted to one-party rule, Traynor would threaten to sue. But if they relented, he would agree to serve only a single term.

It was complex and hard to fathom. A little despotic perhaps. Daring and disruptive.

And it would impact her. If in four years he stepped down, would she be a political orphan? Or a national figure in line to run for the presidency? It was too soon to have any idea.

Upton had seen parts of the plan floated as ideas over the last few weeks. But she had not seen the whole. She wondered who in the room had.

A month before they took office and she was already being kept at some distance, already wondering if she was losing Traynor's trust. It couldn't be just Traynor keeping her in the dark, it had to be his people, too. Sterling Moss, his strategist. Almost certainly Quentin Phelps, his friend and partner. They might feel threatened by having to share the role of being Traynor's close confidantes.

She had always been an outsider. An orphan since sixteen, when her parents had died in a car crash, she had acted as a teenage parent to her younger sister, Emily. She'd even sued the state in order to be an emancipated minor and run her parents' restaurant tavern.

She missed the rest of high school and had taken the GED for her diploma; then she'd rushed through college in two years, then law school and the army. She always did things on her own terms. She would be an outsider here, too. She hadn't felt the whole full weight of it until now.

People around the table looked a little shocked, trying to process, too, wondering if Traynor was about to set off a constitutional crisis.

"Questions?" Traynor asked, smiling. At first, no one seemed to want to ask one, perhaps stunned or afraid. "Come now," Traynor scolded.

"Doesn't your threat of national emergencies set up a constitutional crisis?" asked the scholar who, in his books, argued democracy had played itself out.

"I'm not going to tell them what to do. Just declare that these are emergencies and they must do something—if they haven't acted already."

"What are these problems?" asked the presidential scholar from Harvard.

"You know the list, Nina. We campaigned on it. Rebuild crumbling infrastructure. Fix taxes so big corporations actually pay what they owe. Reform entitlement funding. Get serious about climate. Rebuild manufacturing. Criminal justice reform."

It was mishmash, a wish list, Upton thought, two generations of problems deferred, tossed off now by Traynor as if they were easy. She liked the list, but she wasn't sure what came first or how sincere he was about any of it. Besides, it was a list many candidates from both parties had used for years in different combinations. David's flavor mix had been unusual—a populist businessman, but pro tax and pro union at the same time, embracing regulatory reform and tariffs—someone hard to classify.

"You're going to propose all that in ninety days?" the Harvard professor asked.

"And more. A hell of a lot more. There are thousands of good ideas in the can and money to spend. We've identified almost twenty-five billion we can redirect on Day One. And if we start small, we can make progress on all of them, meaningful visible progress, in three months. That much is clear."

Really? She had been involved in the conversations about how quickly they could make progress on different fronts. The answer was hardly "clear." Hearing him now, she felt various words were better choices: *idiotic; naive; visionary.*

There was a vocabulary for this kind of magical thinking, a vocabulary that Traynor knew well. Martin Luther King Jr. had called it "the audacity to believe"; those words were carved on his memorial back in D.C. People around Steve Jobs called it his "reality distortion field," an ability to just say things were possible that had never been done. Ronald Reagan confused old movie scenes with reality and believed the Star Wars defense umbrella his scientists dreamed about had already been built.

"There is more I can't tell you," Traynor said. "Some of it will not be legislative." He took a deep breath. "Now, I asked you here tonight to tell me what was wrong with this plan. So I expect harder questions."

$$=== 4 ===$$

RANDI BROOKS

Where were you?

Randi Brooks pushed send on the text.

There were only a couple of reasons Peter Rena might have missed that dinner. He and Vic were either dead by the side of the road. Or . . .

She couldn't think of another reason.

She was outside Traynor's house, just past the Secret Service and police perimeter, and finally had her phone back and turned on. Traynor's people had collected them at the door so no one could make a secret recording.

The damn thing was full of new texts, but none was from Peter. He wasn't answering her calls either.

She checked the mountain of messages that had built up. Several were from Ellen Wiley, their firm's chief computer sleuth back in D.C. From what she could decipher from Ellen's shorthand texting style, Peter had been flamed in a series of posts online. It appeared to be bubbling up from some dark random military chat rooms. What the fuck?

And then there was the bizarro dinner she'd just attended. Either this was the beginning of American political renewal or the country had just put a cartoon character in charge. She wanted to talk to someone about what she'd just heard. Peter and Vic had never shown up. But at least they'd already had to sign one of those ridiculous NDAs that Traynor loved, so Brooks figured it was sort of okay to tell Peter and Vic what happened and get their reactions. Technically, that had to be kosher. They'd been invited, too, hadn't they?

Traynor's opponent, the Republican nominee Jeff Scott, had been a scary, hard-right born-again mansplainer who thought America had lost its moral way and the path to redemption was to revoke everyone's civil rights and make America Christian and white and armed. At least Traynor was a technocrat rather than an ideologue, a guy who thought about problems pragmatically. His solutions, though, could be massively wrong. A rich, dorky, helplessly naive president? Great.

Where was Peter?

She found the car she had ordered on her now liberated phone and began the short ride back to her hotel. Aspen was the size of a matchbook. There were more face-lifts in this town than there were houses. When she reached the Aspen Meadows resort, Peter still hadn't texted her back.

She called him and got no answer. Then she delved into some of the awful things being said about him online. "Baby Killer . . . Disgraced Soldier . . . Proven Liar." This shit was out of control. Then she called him five more times. Finally, past eleven, he called back.

"What the fuck in hell is going on, Peter?"

He was silent for a second before he said, "Vic has gone back to Denver."

So they had some kind of fight.

"Have you seen what's online?"

"Yes."

He sounded awful, almost woozy.

She offered to come down to his room to talk. He refused. He would see her in the morning, he said. He was joining her on the early flight back to D.C. He had scrapped plans to stay a day for a meeting with the vice president and spend time with Vic.

"Okay, but I totally need to talk to you about what the hell is going on with you. And I'm worried about the state of the freaking Republic, too. So you better get your shit together. Because I know we're gonna get dragged into something."

He wasn't in the dining room for breakfast. He'd probably gone for a run. She didn't see him until the second before their cab showed up to take them to the airport.

"Vic and I had a fight," he said.

And, of course, that was all he said.

"I figured that much, Sherlock, when you told me she'd left."

It must have been a hell of a fight. Brooks could imagine what it was about. Victoria Madison was thirty-eight and the most sensible person Brooks knew. Peter was forty-three and the most stubborn. If they were going to make a life together, they should have started like a year and a half ago. She had seen this trouble coming forever, like a long, slow-moving train snaking out of a tunnel. She wanted to shake Rena by his thick black hair until he came to his senses and married the woman, who, by the way, was like four points out of his league emotionally, as good-looking as Peter was.

And now Peter was being flayed online.

She had stayed up late last night trying to parse the attack on him and see the reaction. And just this morning she'd seen another one.

Another message on Y'all Post, the country's biggest social media platform. It was the New Jersey Turnpike of the web, a thing everyone hated but no one could avoid. The post appeared to be a copy of a message from another place on the web, a discussion forum called 5Click, which appeared to be a weird, harsh, quasi-dark place for chat messages. This one read: "My law enforcement source says the details about Rena's abuse of women are more vile and shocking than what's been public. We're talking about an emotional

THE DAYS TO COME

terrorist here, who abused his wife and killed his unborn baby. Maybe criminal."

There must have been more overnight she hadn't seen. She felt like she had entered the middle of an angry, paranoid argument but missed the beginning. A lot of the web read like that to her, as if it were a half-crazy cult code.

This post was signed "Camilla Goldberg." Her profile said she was from Peoria, Illinois, and practiced law.

When Rena got in the cab, she handed him her phone. He looked at it, drew a breath, and handed it back.

On the short trip to the tiny Aspen airport, Brooks scanned earlier Y'all Post offerings from "Camilla Goldberg," whoever she was. There were a lot of them. Goldberg claimed to be a small-town lawyer who loved guns and worried about kids and believed in LGBTQ rights. Hard to classify. Was she a real person? Or a Russian bot? Who the fucking hell knew anymore?

Rena, who was staring out the window, pulled out his phone and started looking at the hate that was bubbling up at him from the Internet. Brooks looked at him. She could tell they were thinking the same thing.

"You think this might be a former client?"

He didn't answer.

Who would want to attack Peter, and why? They were not really public figures—even if they had been on the cover of *The National* yesterday—something she now regretted. Peter wasn't even all that political, and only a handful of their clients were. If anything, Randi was the political animal. Maybe the person behind the attacks was trying to get at someone they worked for or an ally of theirs. Maybe Llewellyn Burke, the senior senator from Michigan, who chaired Armed Services. Burke was Peter's mentor and protector. He had swept in when Peter was run out of the military ten years ago; he'd added Rena to his Senate staff to signal to the world the young army major had done nothing wrong. But it was unlikely Lew Burke was the target. Though one of the last surviving moderate Republicans still walking the earth, Burke was well liked and trusted by everyone, including the flesh-eating zombies who now called themselves the firm right. Even Jeff Scott liked Llewellyn Burke. They were both from Michigan, and for at least a little while longer Scott had to kiss Burke's ring or seniors would turn on him. But people like Lew Burke were becoming an endangered species. The same could nearly be said for Rena and herself. They were virtually the last consultants in town who worked for both parties. They'd done work for the outgoing president James Nash, a Democrat. Now they, especially Peter, were becoming close to the vice president, Wendy Upton, a sort-of, kind-of, used-to-be Republican.

So disgracing Rena didn't carry a heavy partisan echo, at least not one she could see. Or was she missing something?

The attacks had to be personal, she thought. Who bore Peter a grudge? Over what? She was already thinking like an investigator.

Now they would have to look into it. When they did, she and Peter would look for the answer by different paths. That was part of Rena, Brooks & Associates's success. Peter solved problems by starting from a distance, like a person in a spotter plane, looking across wide expanses for something that was not yet apparent to him, some break in a pattern, something that didn't belong. Then he would double back and dive in for a closer look. When he interviewed people—with his famous and patient method of "careful listening"—he could sense things about them, a fact out of place, something in their voice or body language. Peter could talk to someone for an hour, say almost nothing, and know things from listening about their hidden anxieties, their childhoods, their parents, their fears. He could read people. It was eerie. Except, of course, when it came to his own life.

Randi's own brain was different, more linear. She began any problem by listing her concerns about what she didn't understand. She would catalog the gaps, the unknowns, all the things that could go wrong. And just when her list of worries seemed to push her near the brink of thinking the problem was hopeless, the other part of her brain, the rational left side, would take over. Her father called it her "turbocharged V-8 logic engine." At the last moment—at a pace she knew few people could match—her turbocharged V-8 logic engine would fill in the missing parts of the map her anxious heart had helped her draw, document by document, data point by data point, file by file. She loved documents. She loved the pure truth of them. The fact that they didn't bat their eyes or talk sweetly. They were written down; you could see what was missing; you could see how the people who had written them had tried to make them lie.

Now she wondered if Rena, her partner, would be the next client.

They had arrived at the airport.

"Peter?" she said. Her voice pulled him out of his thoughts, and when he looked at her Brooks thought she saw something she had not seen before in her partner. At moments of crisis he usually became calmer, his heart beat slower, his perceptions became keener. Now she only saw hurt and confusion, like a door had opened in Rena's life and it was dark on the other side.

During the presidential race, when they were helping Upton, she had seen a growing ruthlessness in Peter that worried her. She'd attributed it to the ugliness of the campaign, which had devolved into pandering to people's fears, to a gnawing sense of the new Rome in decline. But it had seemed to take something out of Rena, the Eagle Scout soldier who believed in all the trappings and symbols, all the rules and oaths—all the stuff about which she was skeptical. She worried that whatever was eating him would spill over into the growing tensions with Vic. Maybe it had.

Peter often took personally what they worked on—what their clients had done, the shit they saw, what was happening in the country. That was both his superpower and his kryptonite. The boy could be scary cunning and coldly strategic. At heart, however, he was an idealist. He saw the world, or at least good and bad, in clear contrast, with people caught between them. Very old-world, she thought. A little of the child from the hills of Tuscany. That idealism is why he read all those history books, she thought. He was looking for an explanation for all the crap in the world, a unified theory of the human psyche.

But that idealism was also, of course, his weakness. He was drummed out of the army for digging into things others would have let go. And that had pushed him, ironically, into politics and private consulting, a world where very little was black and white. She and Rena made their money in the gray.

Maybe after a decade, all the gray was catching up to him.

She thought about the insane all-in poker plan she'd heard from Traynor last night: I want to fix everything at once. "Cooperate and I will go away. Resist and I will destroy you." She looked over at Peter, whose world appeared to be blowing up online and in real life, too. Somehow, they were going to get pulled into Traynor's craziness. She knew it. Why else would they have been invited last night?

It seemed like the last thing Rena needed.

5

WASHINGTON, D.C.

Thursday 17 December

PETER RENA

When they arrived in D.C., Rena and Brooks headed to their office at 1820 Jefferson Place, a narrow town house on a block-long street near Dupont Circle.

Ellen Wiley and Arvid Lupsa were waiting for them, laptops open, at the small worktable in Rena's office under a bay window. When he saw the two cyber experts, Rena felt a sudden urge to go home and disappear into a book.

"How are you?" Ellen asked him, a glance at Brooks.

"Lovely."

She looked back at him doubtfully. "Then let's get to the bottom of this," she ordered, opening a tab on her machine. "You should have answered my calls last night, Peter, when we first got wind of this."

He didn't need her guilt. He'd spent much of last night and the flight home this morning supplying his own, as he sorted through the trilogy of shocks: Vic's anger, his shame at his obliviousness to her feelings, and the public hate suddenly rising up about him online. After their fight and the texts from Lupsa, it seemed too much to go to Traynor's dinner. Vic had wanted to go back to the hotel; once there she announced she was driving to Denver and flying home to California. Before she left she wanted to tell him more about the person she was seeing. She felt she owed him that. His name was Robert Alter, a lawyer, a friend of a friend; they had been seeing each other a few weeks. She didn't know where it was going, but it didn't matter. What mattered was that she felt the need to be with someone, date someone. She didn't feel guilty about it, she said, but she no longer wanted to keep it from him. Had the day gone differently, she said, had *he* been different, she might have told him she was ready to stop seeing the man. But the day, and Peter, had not been different.

Rena had been replaying the conversation over in his mind ever since. He'd made the same mistakes with Katie Cochran, his ex-wife—burying himself in work, becoming almost willfully oblivious to Katie's needs.

When not pondering all of his mistakes with Vic, he'd been absorbed in the paranoid fantasist posts swirling about him online. On the flight home, lost in dozy exhaustion, his mind had begun to spiral. He was fighting self-pity and déjà vu. He felt brittle.

"You're flaming me now, too, Ellen?" he said.

"Peter!" Randi admonished him.

He sat down next to Wiley at the small table by the window. She put her hand on his arm and said, "We'll sort this out."

Strangers were more likely to take Ellen Wiley for a sweet-natured grandmother than a master cyber sleuth. She favored artisan craft-show clothing. Wire-rim reading glasses hung on a gold chain around her neck. But as a graduate student at Berkeley in her twenties, she had been present at the birth of the web and was one of Silicon Valley's pioneering experts in cyber security before most people had heard the term. She'd fled California in the 1990s, when, as she put it, the capitalist class began pushing out the inventor class. She became chief librarian of the *New York Times* Washington bureau, and then—when the Internet began to make things like newspaper libraries unnecessary—she was Randi Brooks's first hire at the firm.

"If we could have asked you some things last night, Arvid and I might have been able to track more of this down by now," Ellen said.

Lupsa, Wiley's deputy, was a thin, bearded man in his thirties who resembled a beat generation poet in his black turtlenecks and Van Dyke beard.

"Got it," Rena said.

Brooks joined them at the table.

Wiley normally had a look of playful intrigue when she dove into what she called "her digital looking glass." But as her fingers skated across her keyboard now her expression was fretful.

"Here's what we know. Three days ago, someone calling himself BadgeAnon had hosted an anonymous 'Ask Me Anything?' Forum on 5Click."

Rena had only vaguely heard of 5Click. It was a message board on "the semi-dark web," Wiley explained, which was divided into "channels" where people talked about very narrow topics, hobbies, or grudges.

The semi-dark web. Rena's mind lingered on the phrase. They rated gradations of the darkness of the human spirit online, he thought, like different levels of cocoa in chocolate.

Rena's name, Wiley said, came up in a channel where cops and other law enforcement people aired grievances. BadgeAnon was the screen name for someone claiming to be a "high-level analyst and strategist" for the FBI. BadgeAnon claimed he was leaking government intelligence online out of "love for country." BadgeAnon for Anonymous Badge. Wiley was reading from notes she had made in a document on her computer.

She quoted BadgeAnon:

"I've uncovered hidden information about this fixer, Rena. You can ask me anything."

Readers then had posed an array of hair-raising conspiracy theories about Rena's life, asking BadgeAnon to verify. There were questions about his "reckless behavior since he was forced out of the service"; how he helped a "weirdo" get on the Supreme Court and covered up connections between "terrorists and the Nash Admin." And, last year, how he "extorted the Jeff Scott campaign to remain silent on 411 that would have tipped election and saved USA from Traynor/Upton."

BadgeAnon agreed law enforcement "had many questions and were pursuing many leads about this man Rena."

"Jesus Christ!" Brooks exploded. "What kind of exorcist batshit world have we made out of the Internet?"

Her anger roused Rena out of his stupor. They had seen clients attacked online before. But this felt different. This was his life. And whoever BadgeAnon was, they had inverted the details into a kind of film negative, black reversed to white, white to black.

"Of particular interest," BadgeAnon had written, "is the real story behind why Peter Rena was tossed out of the army and what caused his divorce."

So these people were dragging Katie into this, his ex-wife? Katie had a new life, a new husband, and a baby. And they were dredging up the story of General James Stanhope, the man whose military career Rena had ended at its pinnacle, which then triggered the end of Rena's own army career.

What Wiley and Lupsa had unearthed was worse than what Rena had read on his own last night in the more sanitized parts of the web like Y'all Post. He had a sinking feeling.

Wiley touched Rena's hand again. "We also found traces of a second campaign against you starting around the same time, maybe a few hours later."

Just after BadgeAnon showed up on 5Click, she explained, postings began to appear on something called TheRant, which described itself as a "candid" message board for U.S. military personnel. "But it's all anonymous, so it's likely a mix of professional conspiracy peddlers, bots, and real people," Wiley said.

Someone using the screen name AngryCptn announced he had a "hot rumor" that Rena had pulled DOJ and FBI strings to bury a sex scandal about vice president-elect Upton.

"Unbelievable," Brooks muttered.

Wiley made a face that suggested what came next would be worse. "But the irony runs deep," AngryCptn had written. "Rena has history of alleging sex scandals about other people—as a smoke screen to cover his own." Minutes after this post appeared, another account, calling itself EagleSquad, said it had proof of allegations of Rena's own sexual misconduct. Rena, EagleSquad wrote, had accused a general in the army of sexual harassment to cover up the fact that Rena had abused his wife and killed his unborn child.

Rena closed his eyes and took a deep breath. This is insane, he thought. The story wasn't entirely invented out of whole cloth. There were fragments of facts here, just enough to make everything more complicated; but the context was a distortion, and then lies had been added to make a story so complicated it was hard to think someone had invented it.

"A few hours later someone posted a version of that allegation on the public web on Y'all Post," Wiley said.

"So it's an orchestrated campaign?" Brooks said.

"It has all the earmarks," Wiley agreed.

"Which are what?" Rena asked.

Orchestrated troll attacks like this, Lupsa explained, usually started with someone on the dark web planting a malicious lie posed in the guise of a theory or a suspicion—not a fact. "But these planted theories," Arvid said, "always contain just enough true things to be possible. And often they are posed as a question. Could this be true? Does anyone know?

"Then someone else in the network responds with some answer like, 'there should be an investigation.' But it is all prearranged," Lupsa said. "Like theater. Or a flash mob."

"And at first," Wiley added, "this conversation is not supposed to get too large. They're just laying down a baseline. Let it simmer and bubble at a low heat for a while, especially in chat channels like 5Click or TheRant."

"How do they get it to spread?" Rena asked. Even though he had heard about such orchestrated attacks, he had never looked at the detailed mechanics of how they spread.

"Have you ever heard of the terms 'shepherds and sheepdogs'?" Wiley asked.

He hadn't.

"Shepherds and sheepdogs are different kinds of digital accounts used to grow malicious campaigns," Wiley said. Shepherds were accounts that had a large number of followers. Sheepdogs were the followers.

"All these are fake accounts, not real people. The shepherds are usually managed by someone to look real. The sheepdogs are usually automated. They're bots, which repeat the posts their shepherds send them." That was how the rumors and attacks that the shepherds produced about Rena got wider distribution online.

"Once the shepherds and sheepdogs have spread something, they wait for a real person to find it. A frightened old lady in Iowa. A retired soldier in San Diego. Someone who's worried the country's going to hell," Wiley said.

Rena was nodding. He now recalled reading about some of this. And the posts that these real people published, Wiley said, were often very emotional, very human, very alarmed. That alarm was what the organizers of the smear were looking for. They wanted a reaction that looked and felt genuinely afraid.

In the art of spreading malicious lies, Lupsa added, this is called "the moment of human touch," or "the fingerprint."

"Christ, this is sophisticated," Brooks said.

Wiley gave her a look that said, you have no idea.

"After a real person has added the human touch, that's when the shepherds and sheepdogs really kick into action," Wiley said, amplifying the real person's post all over the place until it takes off.

She paused to see if Peter was following what they were saying.

"What we have here, what we sent to you last night, when we became alarmed, was the moment of human touch," she said. "In the next twenty-four to forty-eight hours, it is quite possible this may explode on you. If it's orchestrated, rather than random, someone will go on a conspiracy podcast and be asked to comment. And you will be in the crosshairs. And it will get very intense."

There was silence for a moment before Brooks asked what they should do. Wiley sighed, which didn't strike Peter as a good sign.

"We find where this started and try to be ready to prove it's false before it gets too big. That's why you should have called me sooner. There were some questions I would have liked to ask you."

She gave him another pat on the back of his hand.

"For now, Arvid and I are going to go back to our office. Go live your life. Do something fun. And give us the rest of the day. Maybe less, if we're lucky."

"I should seriously just do nothing?" Peter asked.

That sounded to him like the worst possible plan. Like exactly what whoever these creeps are would want him to do.

Wiley gave Peter a maternal look—half sympathetic, half warning. "Please, Peter. Let us hunt."

Hunt. The term soldiers used when they went on a patrol looking for enemy to kill.

Rena tried to work. When he got nowhere he went for a run, but apparently there were no endorphins in his wretched body to be freed and the run only left him feeling low. He fretted over Vic, felt helpless about the web, and by day's end Wiley and Lupsa did not yet have enough to report anything more.

Going to take more time than we thought, Lupsa emailed around five-thirty.

At home he was rescued, momentarily, by Nelson, his cat, the British Shorthair Vic had given him last year. "To help you start with your commitment issues," she'd joked. Yet another message he had ignored. Carrie, the neighbor's daughter, took care of Nelson when Rena was away.

At the door, Nelson rubbed a grateful face against Rena's legs and let out a soft purr that was quickly overtaken by a great face-wrenching yawn. Peter had named him Nelson because the cat's round head and enormous jowls resembled Winston Churchill's; Churchill's favorite cat was named Nelson, in honor of the Lord Admiral of the British Navy. The logic was hard to explain.

"Hello, Admiral."

Nelson blinked and again rubbed his head against Rena's leg. Then Rena sat down in the brown leather Morris chair in his den where he did his reading. Nelson executed a silent leap into his housemate's lap. He had bright golden eyes with the slits like daggers in the center.

"You're not behind this, are you?" Rena asked him.

Nelson's fearsome eyes closed in pleasure.

"Someday, I'll make you crack."

The phone rang. It was Matt Alabama, the TV correspondent and Rena's friend. Matt had a late-evening discussion program on one of those cable news channels, but it didn't fit with its network. It was a rare half hour of historians and writers, what you once saw on public television and never on cable.

"You okay?" Matt asked.

So he knew about the cyberattacks? Great.

"Sure," Peter lied.

"You sound tired."

"Totally wrecked."

"That can be your screen name on TheRant," Matt said, coaxing a rueful laugh from Rena.

The men were twenty years apart but tethered by other bonds than age. They shared failed marriages, military backgrounds, and something deeper, a kind of romanticism about the capital city that was not as rare among Washingtonians as people in the rest of the country imagined. Alabama saw a younger version of himself in Rena. Rena in turn found a mentor who wanted nothing in return. He may never have had a closer friend.

"This is the worst of it," Matt said. "In no time, the Internet will have moved on."

Matt liked to call most nights and always preferred to talk rather than text. He asked how Colorado had been. Rena hadn't told him about the private dinner with president-elect Traynor. The two men were careful to keep their friendship and their work in separate compartments. Matt thought it was merely a quick rendezvous to see Vic. "Complicated," Rena said. "I can't tell you yet. Later. When I can."

Matt said nothing for several moments. The two men were content in their silences together. Eventually, Alabama said, "I look forward to hearing about it—when it's gotten simpler."

When they had said goodbye, Rena texted Vic. Can we talk? She didn't answer. He waited. Nothing.

Then he began to compose a message to Wendy Upton. The future vice president had invited him after the election to offer her advice privately. "I'm largely alone here," she told him. "I could use a friend. And you already know all my secrets."

The vulnerability of her message was striking and unlike her, Rena thought. He had proposed that they set up a back channel to congressional Republicans—from Upton to her party with Rena as intermediary—a kind of bridge of trust over which private messages could cross, where the two sides could understand each other and be candid and not be punished for it. Traynor would have to give it his blessing.

Rena and Upton were going to talk more about it today in Colorado. That meeting was part of what had triggered the fight with Vic. But after the cyberattacks, Upton's chief of staff, Gil Sedaka, had canceled the meeting.

Randi Brooks had filled Rena in on what had happened at Traynor's dinner last night. He composed a message to Upton now based on that, along with his apologies for not showing last night. "Find a way to pass along some of the plan to the GOP," he urged. "To soften the blow. How can you persuade Traynor to let you pass info along to them so they feel respected rather than blindsided? Let me know. I am still happy to be intermediary."

Some kind of back channel was vital, Rena thought. Surprising the GOP would antagonize them, but this bridge could be a lifeline to compromise. He did not know if Upton would do it or persuade Traynor to go along. That was what they had been going to discuss today before the cyberattacks scotched the meeting.

Emails written, he tried to sleep. When he couldn't, he got up and drank, a martini of Gray Goose vodka he kept in the freezer and chilled Dolin vermouth. Then for several hours he read.

6

GREENBRIER RESORT,
WHITE SULPHUR SPRINGS, WEST VIRGINIA

Friday 18 December

TRAVIS CARTER

The majority leader of the United States Senate was trying to light a cigar. The intelligence just offered by Aggie Tucker, the senior senator from Texas, however, had caused him to hold the match too long, and it singed the tip of his finger. He wagged the flame out with a curse.

"He plans to what now?" the majority leader, Travis Carter of Idaho, demanded.

"The president-elect, after inauguration, plans to go to court to challenge our internal rules as unconstitutional," Aggie Tucker repeated.

The two Republicans were sitting in the majority leader's magnificent suite overlooking the eighteenth green at the Greenbrier resort. It was the night before the opening of the Republican congressional retreat, the gathering before a new session of Congress to plot strategy and offer the newly elected House and Senate members a little basic training.

Aggie said he wanted to see the majority leader in private for a pre-festivities chat, before the others came for a briefing on some new polling data. Aggie said he had some "intel" to share about "the prezidunt eelect, Mistah. Traaynuh."

"Go through it again," the majority leader said.

"It's a whole plan," Aggie said. "When he's got somethin' he wants Congress to do, he's gonna promise to come to our party first and ask our members what they want—before he goes to his own party. And he plans to make sure we get what we want."

The majority leader made a sour face, which was something, since his usual expression, as his grandkids told him, looked like he'd spent the day sucking lemons.

"And why would he do that?" the majority leader asked.

"In exchange for our cooperation. We get what we want. He gets what he wants. The Democrats have to go along."

'Course it was a trick, the majority leader knew, like the first price you get from a grain salesman back in Idaho. You never see that price again.

"But then there's the hitch," Aggie continued. "In exchange, he's demanding we change our internal rules—end the majority of the majority rule."

"Which is none of his damn business," Senator Carter replied.

"No indeed it is not," Aggie agreed.

"And why does Mr. Traynor think we would do that?"

Mr. Traynor of Silicon Valley. Mr. Traynor who made his money from software for tracking sales and shipping information, software that the world got along without just fine before.

Aggie smiled dryly. He seemed to be enjoying his role as telegraph delivery boy a little too much.

"It's more a carrot-and-stick thing," Aggie said. "If we don't agree to do business, he's going to go to the Supreme Court and argue that the majority of the majority rule violates the Constitution."

The majority leader felt that feeling building up, when someone thinks they're being sly but they're really just being an asshole.

Not Aggie, who was genuinely sly but harmless. He meant David Traynor.

"I assume that's the stick. He got a carrot?"

Aggie was hiding a grin like he'd stolen candy.

"If we go along, dump our rule and cooperate on legislation, he'll promise to serve just a single term."

So that was the big reveal. The reason Aggie needed to see him in private.

"And just how do you know all this, Aggie?"

"Let's just say I got it from someone who was there at the private dinner," Aggie said.

Handsome, sly, and charming, "Wily Aggie" always seemed to have "someone" just about everywhere.

Aggie had started in Texas politics as a Democrat—back when that was about damn near the only way to get elected to anything. For a time, he was even at the far-right edge of the Republican Party, but the edge kept moving on him. Now he survived by having friends in all places—even apparently in the Traynor White House.

The majority leader was different. No one accused him of being either handsome or charming. His first wife said he had the look of a priest who had heard too many confessions.

But Travis Carter was more genuinely conservative than Aggie was, and he didn't suffer from what he considered Aggie's weakness: Aggie liked to be liked, which made him fond of making deals. The majority leader didn't believe in deals. Deals always revealed your weaknesses.

He had succeeded in politics not through charm but through a careful study of human psychology. If the history was ever written, he believed he might be the most avid student of the human public mind to ever rise to such a high position in American politics. He consumed every study and survey on the question of the American public he could get his hands on. He used PAC money to commission private polls of his own design for his eyes only. He pored over raw top-line data at home at night for pleasure and kept a spreadsheet of his own making of the American voter, which tracked the trend lines on a dozen different attitudes and behaviors—everything from church attendance by denomination to what kinds of TV shows people watched—along with their attitudes on a dozen key political and social issues—broken down by state and county.

And from all this the majority leader was convinced, in his insurance lawyer's mind, that a third of the American people fundamentally did not believe that democratic institutions worked. Either because the rules seemed stacked against them, which explained their failures in life, or because they exploited the rules to get rich, which explained their success. Either way—victims or wolves— these people thought democracy and most government was for suckers. They were nihilists. And if you engaged in expensive legislation designed to help people and solve problems, they thought they were going to be ripped off.

He had ridden his understanding of the human mind to the top of the Senate, dethroning eighteen months earlier the previous majority leader, Susan Stroud, who was, like Aggie, prone to making compromises.

The nihilists would dethrone him, too, if he wasn't careful. And if he compromised with the new president, Mr. Traynor.

Most people tended to attribute his success to a more mundane skill he had mastered. He knew the rules of the Senate better than anyone who breathed air. And he would discuss these rules with reporters. But his views on the American people he kept entirely to himself.

The majority leader looked away from Aggie and took in the magnificent hotel suite. It gave him pleasure. He had returned the Republican retreat to Greenbrier in West Virginia to make a statement. For the last several years the gathering had taken place at the Inner Harbor in Baltimore. The Greenbrier resort spoke of old rich privilege, of black waiters in white coats, and for a time the party had wanted to expunge that image. Carter hated political correctness, and he wanted the public to see it, and for Democrats to be enraged by it. And his goddamn suite overlooked the eighteenth green.

"So you have a mole inside Traynor's White House?" the majority leader asked. Straight out. Nothing subtle about it. He liked to be direct. He would leave the subtlety to tangly men like Aggie Tucker.

"Now, I wouldn't say it like that. They don't work for me. We're not talking double agents in a spy novel, Travis. Just people who want us to be informed. Who think that's good for the country. Who want a bridge."

A bridge to what? the majority leader wondered. Their job was to stop the president. To weaken him. Just as they had weakened Jim Nash, at least after Carter took over. To pave the way for a Republican successor. That was the message he would convey at this retreat, without, hopefully, ever saying it so plainly.

His majority in the Senate had shrunk. And the strongest figure in the party now was Jeff Scott, the Michigan governor who came out of nowhere to win the GOP nomination. Those were other complications.

Scott frightened him. The young Iraq war hero was using Michigan as a test lab for what he would do in Washington—closing borders with Canada, stomping on norms, and rewriting the state constitution. And that base of nihilists Carter kept his eyes on, they loved Jeff Scott. Jeff Scott was the future, and the future worried him.

In a few minutes Scott would be arriving in the suite, along with some party leaders, including the Speaker of the House. They were gathering to get a preview from Drex Hicks, the new "It Boy" pollster of the GOP, on new language Hicks had tested about how to defy Traynor.

They were planning total resistance. "Not one bill, not one dollar" had tested particularly well.

Aggie Tucker had asked if, before everyone else arrived, he could come up early to talk. He had some news, he had promised.

"Is this supposed to be secret? This one-term proposition?" Carter asked.

"I believe that's Traynor's intention," Aggie said. "But it don't matter much either way. We can't let it be known we know about it. We can't even warn our members to be wary of Traynor coming to them. That would give away something we do not want to give away: that we have ears inside Traynor's circle."

The majority leader made a disapproving face.

"All we can do is wait, listen, and think ahead," Aggie said.

"Why would one of Traynor's people let you know these things? Who is it?" the leader nudged.

Aggie shook his head. "Sorry, Travis. Let's just say, people hedge their bets."

He would get it out of Aggie eventually. He just needed to be patient.

There was a knock at the door, and Carter looked down at the unlit cigar in his hand. He placed it in the ashtray on the coffee table in front of him and signaled to his aide to let the annoying child pollster, or whoever was at the door, come on in.

7

BOULDER, COLORADO

Saturday 19 December

DAVID TRAYNOR

Most people measured life by pleasure: "How was your day?" Some measured it by accomplishment: "Get a lot done?"

David Traynor measured life in time wasted. A good day wasted as little of it as possible.

Life was time—an indisputable fact most people put out of their minds—probably, Traynor thought, because they weren't sure what they wanted to do with theirs. Not Traynor. His father had died at forty-two. Heart attack. Traynor had been a senior in high school. That will teach you something about time.

Three days after the Aspen dinner, the president-elect gathered people at a private estate owned by a friend outside Boulder. The four-hundred-acre compound, complete with a twenty-bedroom main house and complex of fourteen cabins, was designed for retreats and lavish parties. It also offered maximum privacy for those inside the fence line.

The purpose of Traynor's gathering was simple: to confront one of the country's major crises he'd promised to tackle Day One. You just had to freaking do it.

Historians, he hoped, might mark today as significant: the moment the industrialized world finally got serious about combating
the crisis of a failing planet. The prospect adrenalized him. Audacity was a powerful inspiration. Henry Ford used to say: "Whether
you think you can or think you can't—you're right."

It wasn't okay to quote Henry Ford anymore, of course. The man
was a rabid anti-Semite. But many such aphorisms from people who
changed the world swam in Traynor's brain. When he was a boy,
they had ignited his imagination, and he had grown into teenage
awareness reading about the lives of such people, trying to squeeze
the secret juice of what made them different, collecting their words
in his frantic scrawl in notebooks, puzzling over the words again and
again, as if they were poetry. To Traynor, the lives and thoughts
of groundbreaking figures were keys to a secret universe. The first
such quotation he remembered was from Bobby Kennedy. It was
chiseled on his heart: "Some men see things as they are and ask why.
I dream of things that never were and ask why not."

Fucking A.

Even if he found out later Bobby had stolen it from George Ber-
nard Shaw.

By the time Traynor headed off to college, he had notebooks full
of aphorisms and had absorbed the life stories and ideas of scores of
dreamers, people who had risen from the pack and made the world
different from how they'd found it. He was determined not to waste
a minute of his time.

One such aphorism fit today: "Nothing is particularly difficult if
you divide it into small jobs." Henry Ford again. Today was going
to be one of those days. The impossible broken into small jobs and
thereby transformed into the possible.

Most of the people gathered in the room were scientists. A few
were military. Only a couple had been present three nights before
for the private dinner in Aspen—his chief of staff, Quent Phelps,
and the vice president-elect. It was time to bring her along. She had

asked for time following the dinner three days ago. He had told her to wait until after the group met today. Then they would talk.

Just after 8:30 A.M., Phelps called the last stragglers from the buffet and Traynor began. He had summoned them under false pretenses, he said. They weren't there to discuss global warming. They were there to decide how to solve it.

"Before we leave this room tomorrow, we will have a plan—which will lay out the immediate steps we can take to stop and reverse the warming of the planet. The time for debate is over. It's time to act."

They would choose two or three solutions that would make a material change in American carbon use, he explained, ones that could be accomplished in two years. "Ignore the cost. Ignore the politics. We're here to talk science." They had all signed NDAs when they entered the room, he reminded them. "I'm serious about those. Nothing we discuss leaves this room—not with your spouse. Not your best friend."

Then he explained how they would proceed. They'd hear five proposals to reduce or reverse carbon emissions. Then rank them—based on each one's impact, practicality, and time frame. Then they'd hear five more and vote again.

"We'll go until we have heard thirty proposals and ranked them all. From those thirty we'll get to ten. Then five. Then three." He studied faces. "I know it sounds arbitrary. But believe me, it works." A smile at Phelps. "Quent and I have done this hundreds of times."

This was not the David Traynor most people saw. Not the loud guy in a midnight-blue tee shirt sitting courtside, or the charming populist entrepreneur wooing the public for votes. This was the version of Traynor only his corporate deputies usually saw, and even they tended to be split over it. Some considered this version disciplined and visionary. Others saw a bully with a loose tether to reality. Traynor thought himself a little of both. He believed in duality, he would tell people, when the question sometimes came up.

He glanced at his vice president. He needed to win her over now. They were so close to the inauguration.

People introduced themselves, titles only. Most present knew one another, at least by reputation. They included advocates for particular solutions, general experts, and people responsible for national security who intersected with climate. Then Traynor framed the issue outside politics: "I consider global warming first and foremost a national security issue. Colonel Jackson, would you share what you told me yesterday?"

Marine Lieutenant Colonel Louise Jackson once had run something called the Strategic Research and Development Program at the Pentagon, which was responsible for ensuring the operability of weapons and bases.

"There are more than a thousand islands in the Pacific that will be uninhabitable in ten to twenty years. Among them are more than a hundred U.S. military bases in the Pacific atolls," she said. "That network of islands, hard won against the Japanese in war, is where we do most of our weapons testing and most of our monitoring of the oceans and scanning of space. Most people know little about them, but they are critical to our security." There was a billion-dollar radar installation on Kwajalein Atoll, she said. "It tracks the tens of thousands of pieces of space junk that orbit Earth. That is how we keep them from colliding with satellites and astronauts—or falling to Earth like meteors. There is junk up there the size of loaded eighteen-wheeler trucks.

"In three years, Kwajalein Atoll will be abandoned. We have no money or plans to build another installation, because we thought we had another twelve years. We were wrong." She paused for emphasis: "And the chemicals we detected in the water and the soil of the Pacific atolls ten years ago, we are now seeing in the water and soil of New York City. In fewer than fifteen years, portions of Manhattan will need to be abandoned. That information is classified."

Traynor watched the room react. He saw doubt and curiosity, but mainly concern.

Then he handed the duties of controlling the day to the person on his left.

"You all by now know Colonel Kim Matsuda," Traynor said.

A small, unsmiling woman with a coppery round face nodded. She was conservatively dressed, and her mouth was set in a vague expression of disapproval, a look that seemed to draw people's attention to her. It was she who had summoned them today on Traynor's behalf.

"We have today, and maybe part of tomorrow—not much time to make up for the last wasted forty years," she began.

She spoke in a bland monotone that suggested she would make sure they did not waste any more time than the world already had.

"Our task—your charge—is to provide the president-elect with the three best options to address the climate crisis before you leave this house tomorrow."

The confident words came in an odd package. Matsuda spoke with a thin, high-pitched voice; if one closed their eyes, it sounded as if a precocious nine-year-old were in charge of the government efforts to save the planet.

Traynor loved it.

She was a biogeochemist and a former air force colonel now working at the National Oceanic and Atmospheric Administration, NOAA, the federal weather agency and primary organization responsible for climate research. He had met her during the campaign, when he'd begun receiving security briefings. He'd known almost immediately he wanted this quiet, persistent woman to run point for him on climate—to invent a bold and secret plan to save the planet. There was something about her, he thought, a polite insistent quality that managed to persuade people to do things they normally would resist.

"If we do not succeed, some other group must begin to prepare to migrate four billion people to another planet. And no one in this room will be invited. Because we'll all be over the age limit for migration."

Traynor could only imagine what this woman's professional ascent had been like, this strange stubborn scientist rising in a military world dominated by men.

Her file told him more. Matsuda was a fifth-generation San Franciscan whose Japanese family had spent World War II interned in a camp in Manzanar, California. Her great-grandmother and a great-aunt had died in the camp. Her grandfather Tom had been drafted into the U.S. Army and died in Normandy protecting a bridge from a Panzer tank division with a bazooka. Tommy Matsuda saved his platoon, and thirty years later was posthumously awarded the country's second-highest award for valor.

The medal and its complex irony—that it took thirty years to be awarded, that Tommy's mother had died a prisoner in Manzanar while he was overseas dying for the country, the fact of the internment itself—had split the family into factions that still divided the Matsudas three generations later. The schism had become so public there was a newspaper clip about it in Matsuda's file. Part of the family believed the way to end racism against Asian Americans was to do one's American duty and succeed at the highest level. To that side of the family, Tommy Matsuda was a hero. Another part of the Matsuda clan considered the family's lethal internment an unforgiveable betrayal and Tommy a tragic figure. That side of the family had helped found a group of Japanese Americans that publicly demanded reparations and apologies from the U.S. government. Time had made the schism more complex, not more distant. The two sides of the family barely spoke. Kim must have epitomized the assimilationist camp, Traynor imagined. A scientist who joined the air force and even, for a time, the CIA. A climate radical who decided the way to make change was not just from inside the government but inside its most secret corridors. He was fascinated.

Matsuda walked the room through the basics of the climate crisis. Most guests already knew them. The planet was warming at six
times the rate NASA had estimated fifteen years ago. The amount of
carbon in the atmosphere had doubled since the beginning of the in-
dustrial revolution. The planet could be uninhabitable by 2070, perhaps 2050. By 2035, millions of people will already have had to leave
their homes because of rising sea levels, crop destruction, infectious
diseases and infestation. The streets of Miami now flooded nearly
every time it rained.

Two human activities, in roughly equal measure, made up two-
thirds of the carbon problem—vehicle emissions and the power grid.
All other human activities made up the other third.

The aging domestic power grid had become America's greatest
national security vulnerability, Matsuda said. Russia, China, North
Korea, and now Iran had all developed technologies to cripple the
United States with cyberattacks on the power infrastructure of major U.S. cities.

"And less than ten percent of our energy production is renewable. Consider, for instance, one statistic: the amount of energy from
the sun that strikes the surface of Texas in one year is equal to three
hundred times the amount of energy created by all the power plants
in the world during the same period." She glanced for emphasis at
the faces around the room. "But we capture almost none of it."

For these reasons, Matsuda told them, the solutions they would
focus on today would lean heavily toward automobiles and the
power grid. They needed to aim either at reducing future emissions,
or reversal—what some called "drawdown"—the prospect of re-
capturing and reabsorbing already released carbon into other materials, thereby letting the planet heal.

Following her introduction, the scientists and soldiers in the room
began to present their ideas. Five speakers in sequence offering solutions. Seven minutes per presentation, thirty-five minutes total. Then
forty-five minutes to debate the five proposals. Everyone was told to

rate each idea from one to ten for its viability and impact, either for reducing reliance on carbon or drawing it down. When that assessment was done, they would take a ten-minute break, then move on to the next five ideas, and the process repeated—presentation, debate, and score.

Matsuda kept things moving. Traynor admired her economy of words, and her impatience. She reminded him of the best teacher he had had in high school, Mrs. Ossoff, whose high expectations somehow lifted the expectations of her students.

Wendy Upton listened attentively but said nothing.

Each presenter had previously submitted to Matsuda a five-page memo outlining their idea. Packets had been provided to the full group a week ago, including each proposal's projected costs, estimates of the gigatons of CO_2 reduced by the year 2050, and estimated savings in dollars by the same year.

Traynor, who had read them all and considered some of the ideas pretty far-fetched, especially those focused on drawdown: shooting acid rain into the ozone to block the sun's rays; casting giant barges into the sea filled with filament to absorb the damaging elements of the sun; erecting millions of wind turbines buried into the ocean's floor; reforesting half the planet. Some of this stuff was bullshit. But the whole voting process got such nonsense out of the way.

Other ideas had the ring of plausibility: massive solar farms; extensive solar roofing; replacing refrigeration materials; improving energy storage by improving batteries.

An international team three years earlier had ranked eighty different solutions, Matsuda noted, which would have reduced carbon emissions to roughly zero in thirty years, at a cost of $27 trillion and saving, they estimated, $74 trillion. To put that into perspective, she said, the total U.S. economy was $19 trillion. A group of academics at Princeton a year later had distilled those eighty solutions down to seven. But that work was all theoretical. This meeting, assembled by the president-elect, was actually going to select two or three solutions and the government was going to pursue them, she explained.

They worked till ten that night before retreating to their assigned rooms or cabins to sleep. They continued the next morning, reducing the number of solutions to twenty, then ten, then five, becoming more uncertain as the number got smaller. Some complained they were just guessing. "Yes," said Traynor with an exasperated smile. "It's called deciding."

But he could tell their doubt was bending into commitment. They could feel what he could. The future was changeable. And that felt like leadership.

They broke, finally, just after lunch the second day—the list was narrowed to four options: onshore wind turbines, changing the refrigeration chemicals worldwide, solar farms, and developing a new kind of battery storage.

As people were leaving, Traynor tried to catch Upton's attention.

"What do you think?" he asked, summoning her to the open seat next to him.

She seemed caught off guard. "To be honest, Mr. President-elect, my head is swimming. Can I think about it? And write you a short memo. Something coherent?"

"Coherent would be good."

She was a "stabilizer," he thought, one of those people who in any situation worried about what could go wrong. He hadn't chosen her because of that. He had chosen her for political factors, and because he could see how pained she was by the turmoil in her party. There was something about her that made you trust her. But the way her mind worked, this stabilizing quality—identifying holes in things and thinking about them—might prove useful. Some people might find it a reassuring balance to his bold improvising.

"What do *you* think?" she asked him.

"Flow batteries," he answered quickly, trying to push her out of her caution.

"Flow batteries? Why?"

"Storage. Everything we talked about for the last two days depends on storage. The sun and the wind have all the power we need. We just can't hold it longer than a few hours."

"You know how much that would cost?"

"No," he said with a grin. "But money—contrary to all public rhetoric on the subject—is not what the government lacks."

"What does it lack?"

She was beginning to smile.

"The will to act. And the government is almost completely incompetent at execution."

"What does that mean?"

"The will to spend money differently," he told her. "To think differently. And the diligence, once we've started something, to find out whether it's really working and change it if it's not."

He offered a quote. "Vision without execution is just hallucination."

"Edison," she said with a wry smile.

Well, well, he thought. She's been studying up.

"Why not wind turbines?" she asked. "Or some of the others?"

"This first," he said. "If we can store the energy, then we can do the rest."

She probably thought he had the will, and maybe the vision. But he suspected that she doubted his ability to execute. People usually did. That's why he prepared so hard and tried not to show it. To prove it to himself as much as to anyone else—that he was not just lucky.

"If we're really bold, Wendy, we can shift everything."

"How?"

"People will see we're keeping our big promises and they will think it's possible for the country to accomplish great things again. We can heal the country with boldness. The public will want us to succeed. And that will be our leverage." He studied her reaction.

"The public will be our secret weapon. You see? You think today seemed crazy. But audacity will give the public hope. And if we can keep them, we can do so much more than people think."

She didn't see it. Not yet. Not really. But she would, he thought. He knew it.

8

WASHINGTON, D.C.

Tuesday 22 December

RANDI BROOKS

Peter was missing.

Not literally maybe. But the boy hadn't shown in the office for days, which was worrying enough.

With the crap now spewing out of the Internet about him, Brooks thought . . . well she didn't know what to think. "This vile animal should be put down," someone on 5Click who called themself Truth-Seeker had written.

"Die you motherfucking bovine piece of crap. I am coming for you. And I *will* be carrying." That had been written by someone calling himself Sheriff Jack.

Five days had passed since she and Rena had returned from Colorado. The attacks had not subsided; they'd grown and jumped from the semi-dark web into the public Internet. It was like watching cancer cells through a microscope metastasize so fast you could see them replicating.

The public bile was bad enough. Peter had also received dozens of private "direct" messages threatening his life: people who didn't even know him wishing him dead. The numbers had become hard to process. Thirty-five thousand posts in five days, half of that in the last two. Peter had become a notorious celebrity in an anonymous digital world of paranoia and conspiracy about which a week ago Brooks had only a passing awareness. Wiley and Lupsa were still trying to track it all down, but the viral spread complicated the task.

Rena, meanwhile, was not answering emails or texts. She'd dropped by his row house two days ago and he had seemed okay, promising to be back in the office Monday. But the pace of all the crap piling up online had accelerated, and he hadn't shown. Then since yesterday, radio silence. It was time to go see him. And bring Ellen Wiley.

He met them at the door. He was dressed, at least. He had been in his den, his little reading cave. Nelson, the cat, was keeping guard. His laptop was open on the library table, with an empty martini glass next to it. And four toothpicks next to the glass. So it was not his first, she thought. It was a little after 4:00 P.M.

She set herself down on his sofa and began to unpack her purse to show she was staying awhile. Suck it, fella. Ellen sat down, too. They had a plan. They were going to rouse their man by engaging Peter in the fight.

"I called a friend who works at Y'all Post," Brooks started. "A former Nash Justice Department guy. This nimrod lawyer is now making a million plus lobbying for a tech platform." She rolled her eyes. "He promised to look into the attacks on you. When I didn't hear back, I called him again."

Peter said nothing. He looked like he couldn't wait for them to leave.

"He told me he'd asked someone back in the Security Services division in Cupertino to check on the accounts threatening you. He said while they appeared to be real people—not robots—they didn't live anywhere near Washington, and didn't have many followers." She inhaled a deep breath of frustration just even thinking again about this useless Y'all Post dude. "I pointed out to my friend that these lunatics don't need many followers. It only takes one."

"What did he say?" Wiley asked, trying to bring some enthusiasm to the conversation.

"That people had a constitutional right to free speech." She scowled. "That's when I really lost my shit." She glanced at Peter and hoped, in vain, that might nudge a smile out of him. "I told him he worked for a goddamn private commercial billboard company, not the Supreme Court, and he wasn't protecting anyone's constitutional rights. Just maximizing their fucking revenue."

That got a smile from Ellen at least.

"I may have added that they were using the Constitution as a loincloth, too, which meant putting their dicks in the Founding Fathers' sacred text."

"What did he say to that?" Wiley asked.

"Some shit about 'the Open Web being a foundational value of the company's civic philosophy.'" She added a frown. "And I said something along the lines of 'Fuck you, Ted. Your only philosophy is greed.'" She gave a little shrug. "I hadn't meant to say that. But then I hadn't planned on his puking corporate PR goo all over my shoes, either."

Wiley laughed. Peter was still quiet.

"So then I said, 'If someone were doing this to your CEO, what they're doing to Peter, is this how you guys would react?'"

"And?"

"That's when he said fuck you back to me."

Wiley laughed harder this time, and so did Brooks. Peter finally at least smiled.

Randi became more serious. "I told him if someone shows up coming after Peter, he could bet on his mother's grave I would come after him, and his punk-ass company and its thirty-five-year-old sociopath CEO. And I would bring the goddamn leader of the free fucking world with me. And his predecessor. And Ellen Wiley. And then he would learn something about foundational values."

Usually, when she told a story like this, about losing her temper, and telling someone exactly how she felt, Peter would squint at her in mock disapproval and make some tough-guy repressed-male-trying-to-be-cool remark. Peter loved Brooks's brazenness—that she had no filters and no fear, that she cursed and belly laughed and hugged and told everyone the truth. He thought people were drawn to her honesty like a hearth.

But he had no response to her story. Instead, he leaned forward in his chair toward Wiley. "Why is this growing?"

"Remember, Peter, what I told you about 'shepherds and sheep-dogs'?" Wiley asked. "And trying to get someone to provide the moment of human touch?"

Rena nodded.

"We know more about the shepherds now," Wiley said. "The account who said they had proof you abused your wife and killed your baby was an account called EagleSquad. It is almost certainly a fake account."

"How do you know?" he asked.

"The account's owner claims to be a former army officer, a woman, now living in Sarasota, Florida. But the account posts too often to be real—more than sixty thousand times in three years. And her photo is doctored." Wiley had a small notebook open where she had made notes. "But the account has a lot of followers—more than a hundred and seventy thousand. If you post that often, you get a lot of followers."

EagleSquad, she said, was part of a private group of accounts that shared and amplified political messages about national security. So EagleSquad was followed by some influential people who were real. "Senior Pentagon officials. Foreign policy types. Fringe na-tional security folks."

"Do these people think EagleSquad's a real person?" Brooks asked.

Wiley said, "Who knows what they think. But some of them probably do. And some of these officials are serious people." Peter looked a little stunned. "But then remember the post I told you about the other day?" Wiley asked. "That lawyer in Illinois who was appalled by what she heard about you, Peter?"

At the mention of it, Rena finally seemed to engage. "Camilla Goldberg," he said. "In Peoria."

Wiley nodded. "Yes. She is a real person. She was 'the human touch.' That's a real person who's so provoked by what she's seen, that she's commented on it and passed it along and given the whole thing authenticity."

"And she has no connection to the fake bots?" Brooks asked.

Wiley said, "Probably not."

Peter, so quiet a moment ago, began to offer details about Camilla Goldberg he had picked up. She was a lawyer in Peoria, Illinois, who supported gun and LGBTQ rights and had posted how angry she was to hear Rena had allegedly killed his unborn child. It was after she posted about him that the false rumors about Rena really went viral. "Her Y'all Post message was shared more than seventy-five thousand times."

And Brooks realized that for the last five days Peter had been living in the little corner of the world that hated him. That's what he'd been doing here, holed up in his row house. Reading shit about himself on the Internet, trying to understand it. And drinking.

"Peter, you asked what changed," Wiley said. "Why this got so much bigger? Well, Camilla Goldberg changed it. But then it got turbocharged after that."

"Turbocharged by what?" asked Rena.

"A podcast. By David Highsmith," Wiley said.

"Who the hell is David Highsmith?" asked Brooks. "Another asshole spreading lies about Peter whose First Amendment rights Y'all Post is protecting?"

He was a political activist who was big online, Wiley explained. He called himself "a self-employed private investigator exposing the 'New World Order agenda.'"

Brooks said, "The new what!"

"The New World Order," said Wiley.

"Weeping mother of Christ!" Brooks added as punctuation.

Ellen looked at Rena. "Highsmith claimed to have done more research on you, Peter. And then he was interviewed by TrueFlag about it for one of their podcasts."

This was like peeling a rotten onion, Brooks thought, and finding just more dark mealy paste inside.

She knew about TrueFlag. It was a conspiracy website with a huge audience—something like seventeen million followers—and most of them avidly shared what they heard there. TrueFlag's imprint was significantly larger now than any of the three old evening newscasts.

"I listened to the podcast, Peter," Wiley said. "It's ugly. Highsmith couches everything; they're just allegations; he's trying to sort out the truth. It's clever, legally. None of it asserted as fact."

Rena closed his eyes for a moment. Apparently, even if he had been diving into what was said about him online, he didn't know about the podcast. "What did he say?" he asked.

"The same lie. That you beat your wife, which killed your unborn child. And that's why Katie left you." Brooks saw Rena take a deep breath. He looked more vulnerable than she had ever seen him. "He also says you accused someone of sexual harassment so that when the army threw you out, you could say it was revenge against you."

All of this—the accusations against the general—had occurred before Brooks had known Rena. The general was being elevated to take over Central Command, the U.S. military's Middle East Theater. Rena, who was a military investigator, was tasked with the man's final vetting. He began to discover holes in the general's file, and three weeks later the general quietly retired.

A few months after that, Peter was gone from the army, too. That's when Senator Burke hired Peter as a staffer on the Senate

Armed Services Committee. Which is where Brooks and Rena met,
working for senators from different parties.

Ten years ago.

Wiley hadn't finished her story. "The day after Highsmith appeared on the TrueFlag podcast, Peter, the allegations against you
went viral for real." She leaned toward Rena. "The day before, your
name scored zero on something called the Composite Search Index.
The next day you scored a hundred."

"The what?" Brooks asked.

"It's a score of how often something gets searched online," Wiley said. "One hundred is as high as it goes."

Wiley hadn't had a chance to fully brief Brooks before they'd
made this trip to Rena's, and while she and Peter had dealt with bizarre venom on the net before, it wasn't her world. The goddamn
New World Order? She and Peter were about as far from whatever
the hell that was as you could get. They were just old enough to have
been pre-Internet adults and they'd had the nagging feeling for the
last twenty years of barely keeping up.

Wiley continued, "The Highsmith podcast got attention. Dash
Zimbalist did a show on it." Dash Zimbalist was a popular alt-right
radio talk show host and ran a series of websites that was now the
largest political talk empire in the country. "And then Zimbalist did
an interview with some ex-military officer who said he knew you.
Someone named Arthur Duke."

Duke was a character so dark, so amoral, it was hard to believe
he was real. But he was. He was a billionaire ex–Special Forces guy
who ran an infamous private security firm. He'd been blackballed
from contracting with the U.S. government after committing war
crimes. Now he worked mostly for notorious foreign regimes.

"Traffic about you doubled after Zimbalist's interview with
Duke," Wiley said.

"So this thing swirled in the semi-dark web till Camilla Goldberg, a real person, picked it up. Then these podcasts picked up the story, which really turned the gas up?" Brooks said, trying to get the trajectory right in her head. Wiley nodded.

Peter looked overwhelmed. He loved the military. He loved its commitment to duty and honor, the courage and sense of higher purpose of the people who served. Peter was Randi's cunning Boy Scout. But she was beginning to think that coming to his apartment had been a mistake. Seeing him now, she worried that, rather than engaging him, they might drive him deeper into whatever hole he was crawling into.

"It's all a pretty fairly familiar formula," Wiley said, trying to be reassuring. "Plant the rumors. Spread them with bots. Wait for the human touch, then when it comes, boost the conspiracy on websites and podcasts." She gave Peter a smile. "Lots of cases follow similar patterns."

If Peter had been trolling the web about himself for the last two days and didn't know about the podcast, his online wanderings must have been pretty aimless, thought Brooks. She had never seen him so low.

"I want to listen to that Highsmith podcast," Rena said. "And the Duke interview."

"They're garbage, Peter," Wiley said.

"I want to hear them."

"Let *me* listen to them, Peter," Brooks volunteered.

"Has to be me," he said.

Brooks gave Wiley a pleading look. They both knew, however, that Peter would never back down.

"I'll share the link with both of you," Wiley said.

9

PETER RENA

After they'd left, Peter sat down and stared across the room at nothing in particular.

His eyes settled on a picture of Vic, which sat in the place where he once had a picture of Katie. Next to it sat a picture of his father.

He and Vic still hadn't talked, only messaged briefly, though he had left voice mails. He told himself he didn't want to intrude, that she needed space and time. In truth, he didn't know what she wanted to happen next. He also still didn't know what to say or how to adequately apologize. Was the fight last week in Colorado going to get them through the inertia and bring them closer? Or was it a shove that would begin an unreconcilable drift apart? He needed a signal from her.

He was uncertain of so many things. He glanced at his laptop on his desk, which was now open to the podcast about him. There had been a couple of stories written about his becoming a target online. "Former aide to President Nash and VP Upton slammed in cyberattacks." The stories hadn't dug into the substance of the false allegations, but they had repeated them. Randi had denied any of it was true. The Pentagon had no comment on the allegations. President

Nash's spokesperson had dismissed the rumors as nonsense. But a couple stories had quoted people he knew from the military, former friends who were unwilling to defend him because they were frightened. More than a few people apparently believed that if something had gotten this big on the web, there must be something to it.

He couldn't articulate yet what he was feeling. It was too large, and he couldn't make out the boundaries of it. But he sensed that what was happening in the world revealed something deeper—a crack in the foundation that could not be repaired. Rena had seen the walls of civilization collapse before—seen men in war, consumed by fear, succumb to their most savage impulses. He'd seen soldiers engage in acts so terrible they would never forget them, never mention them, and never forgive themselves. He had seen countries fall into madness and collapse in a matter of weeks. But when the righteous wars ended and the soldiers returned home, even those who had committed awful acts usually sought to leave them behind—or went insane.

He was trying to connect that—his reference for when people abandoned their moral and civil norms—to what seemed to be happening nearly every day online, including what was happening to him. He knew talk on the Internet was different from people going off in wartime. These were just words, not acts. He was not dead, just defamed. But the impulses behind them felt familiar. He had seen them before. They both reflected hate born out of fear. Once the world had become connected and everyone could speak to everyone else online, why had people begun to treat each other so badly? What dark truth about the human psyche lingered in the hate-filled conspiracy-heated, misogynist, racist rants that filled the web? Even if that hate were manufactured—the product of Russian, Chinese, or Iranian state agents—governments only launched those operations because they worked; because the words touched something in people's souls.

The web was only a generation old. But in that tiny flicker of time, the delicate virtues of human interaction that took centuries to nurture seemed to have been overrun. Once we were all connected, the gossamer wings that held aloft the better angels of our nature apparently were no match for the private human weakness that connection unleashed. Rena tried to banish these thoughts from his mind. They sounded like self-pity. But they would only stay away for a while before wandering back.

He looked at the picture of his father, who had emigrated to America from Italy with Rena when Peter was a baby. Peter was told later that his mother had died when he was one. It was now just the two them. Even as a fairly young child in America, Peter had functioned as a kind of cultural interpreter for his father, and that role gave him the courage to sort matters out for himself when his father didn't understand their new country's customs. It was a strange way to grow up—maybe an immigrant's way—but most Italians had come so many generations earlier there wasn't much of a community for people like them. And in his mind, in the life story he told himself, he was most proud that, as a boy, he had developed a code for himself about what mattered. And he had tried to live by that code as an adult, when life was more complicated and always challenged by compromise. At the heart of Rena's private code was the idea that you told the truth. If you stuck to that, you also could learn what the truth was.

He could recall the day this code had begun to form as the germ of an idea in his mind. He was fourteen. It was the day he discovered that most of what his father and his grandmother had told him about his life up to that point was a lie.

In his memory of that afternoon, he is cooking supper, fresh tomatoes from the yard, sautéed in garlic. He would add the fresh basil at the last minute. The pasta is boiling. He remembers hearing the door and looking up to see his father. "Hello, Pietro." The old man's pants are covered in white dust from whatever stone he had chiseled that day working on the big American cathedral across the river in the city. Rena watches his father head to the bathroom to wash off the dust, to scrub it from his eyebrows, and mustache, and from inside his ears. Remembering it now, twenty-nine years later, Peter imagined his father was already beginning to look bent over, the first signs of the illness that would sweep him away. But mostly Peter remembers feeling resentment, even in the way his father said hello. There is too much affection in it, too much need.

Rena had been waiting to confront him. For that was the day he had puzzled out the secret he suspected Papa was keeping from him. Why had they moved to America from Italy alone when Rena was only eighteen months old? Why had Papa taken Peter away from grandma Nona and his cousins? Why had they come to this world his father didn't understand?

Standing at the stove, he can barely contain himself. His hands feel numb, and his veins tingle. But he is patient. He will wait until they are at the dinner table so his father can't bow his head in that stubborn way he had and walk away.

Why, Papa, did you lie? They had come to America in 1980, Peter had always been told, so his father could help finish building the Washington National Cathedral in Washington, D.C. The big church on Massachusetts Avenue was the only true European-style cathedral in the United States, his father explained, and the only people who knew how to build such buildings were Europeans. His father was a stone artisan, and he was needed for the work high above, for the spires and the high windows and the gargoyles lurking on the roof.

It was during the summers he spent with his grandmother in Tuscany that he had first sensed something was wrong. People whispered about the boy from America who was Italian but not quite. He thought at first they were whispering because he was different. Eventually he realized they were sharing secrets about him. He was accustomed to being alone and was good at puzzling things out for himself. In soccer, where he was beginning to excel, he had taught

himself to watch an opposing player and sense the other boy's weaknesses; how to mislead opponents by making deliberate mistakes
that would cover up his real weaknesses. By the time he was twelve,
he had learned how to interrogate his aunts without their realizing
it, to wrap his real questions inside innocent ones. He was beginning
to recognize when people lied to him. By fourteen, he had collected
enough clues, heard enough whispers, asked enough questions, detected enough lies, and gone through enough of his father's things,
to puzzle out the most important mystery of all.

Rena's mother was not dead. She had run off with another man
when he was a baby. She had abandoned her husband and her child
and fled to Rome. And Rena's father had gathered up Peter and come
to America in shame. They had not moved because his father's skills
were so necessary and rare. They had come so his father could flee.

"You lied about everything," Peter shouted at his father. "Your
whole life is a lie. And you made mine one, too, Papa." He was young
enough that his outrage was pure and quick. "But I am not ashamed.
I am only ashamed of you!"

His father did not bow his head or walk away from the table. He
said to Peter, "It was a secret I wanted to protect you from." Peter
remembered his father mumbling the words.

"No, they were just lies!" In his memory, Peter is screaming.
"You're a liar! Even to yourself. You can't tell the difference anymore!" And in his memory of it, it is Peter who gets up from the table
and walks away.

Two days pass before they speak another word. Peter is in the
garden working the tomatoes. His father comes outside. As Peter remembered it now, his father says, "You were so small, Peter. I meant
to tell you someday. I didn't mean to lie, only to keep something a
secret until you were old enough."

In his memory, Peter stands up—they were almost the same
height now—and looks his father in the eye. "They are the same
thing, Papa. As soon as you try to hide them, secrets become lies.

And all lies become conspiracies." Maybe he hadn't used those words. Maybe through recollection he had made himself more articulate. But after that day Peter saw his father differently, not as someone wise and exotic, but as a man outmatched by life and a country he didn't understand. A construction worker with a few skills, not an artisan. Most of all, Peter saw a man ashamed. Hiding. Of course, these things he thought were not the whole truth. They were lies of their own. But that's how Peter would see his father for a long time.

It would get better between them eventually, but not until after West Point, after he married Kate, after a lot of things. By then Peter was an adult and his father was sick.

That would all come later. That day, in the garden, Rena began to form a theory about how he wanted to live his life, in ways that would be different from how his father had lived. He was fueled by the absolute conviction that all secrets become lies and all lies were evil, and that if you made them part of your life, they would poison you. He was determined to live without lies. He knew, of course, that everyone told lies—and that everyone told themselves they wanted to live an honest life, too, as if those things went together. But he would be serious about it. Lies were like shadows, and he wanted to live in the light. He didn't know if he could do it or what it would be like. He didn't really know anyone who lived like that. But he was fourteen, and he thought everything was possible.

He liked organizations that had rules. He became the youngest Eagle Scout in the history of Virginia. After that, the army seemed like a good place to live the kind of life about which he dreamed. It had rules and codes of honor. It had historians who wrote the stories of battles to study what went right and what went wrong, searchers of truth in a world where facts saved lives and where too much faith in credo could get you killed.

He had believed it all. Even after the army broke his heart and banished him. He had believed it all.

Now, sitting in his living room, peering into the semi-dark web, he was beginning to doubt, to wonder whether maybe he had been wrong about almost everything he had believed and fought for. Lies and innuendo were being told about him by people he didn't know. A lot of these people were military—or they claimed to be. Maybe some really knew him. A version of his past was being written that was unrecognizable. And though they were lies, people believed them. And didn't that, in some way, make the lies real?

Maybe he had built his life around an adolescent grudge? Were lies of self-delusion the most damaging of all because you told them to yourself?

Then he brought his computer to life and began to listen to the interview of David Highsmith, the self-described private investigator into the New World Order.

10

PETER RENA

The podcast host's voice had the deep timbre of a heavy smoker.

It was a "special show tonight," he promised, which would shed light on "a new major story emerging online." A group of courageous veterans and law enforcement officials, working anonymously, were starting to raise questions "about a shadowy political operative who has become one of the most influential behind-the-scenes figures in Washington. You might say he is a fixer for the New World Order."

The host let that notion sit in his audience's mind a moment. Then he set the hook: "And if the allegations being raised about him are true, we might just have a chance tonight to correct a terrible injustice that he inflicted on one of America's most important military leaders."

Rena had seen reference to the podcast in his searching online but he hadn't realized how important it had become. Or maybe he hadn't had the stomach to think about it, until Ellen and Randi had visited.

He kept listening. The husky voice introduced his special guest: a man "who should be familiar to the TrueFlag nation, investigative reporter and private detective David Highsmith. Tell us about this man, David, this power broker behind the scenes."

"Thanks, Brandon. Glad to be with you. His name is Peter Rena, and the allegations about him are enormously troubling." Highsmith had an appealing catch in his voice, as if he were reluctant about what he was about to say.

"What are these allegations about him, David?"

Highsmith began to weave a tale about how Rena had brought down an army general in order to create a controversy to mask his own scandal.

"Just to set the scene, this man Rena, at the time we are talking about, ten years ago, he was one of the army's top investigators?" the host asked.

"Right, Brandon. And, according to what we're finding out, Rena's marriage was falling apart at the time. And that may have been the motivation behind the allegations that out of nowhere he brought against this general."

"Can you explain that?"

"Rena was married to a young woman named Katie Cochran, who by the way comes from a distinguished military family. Four generations of West Point graduates."

He had named Katie. That son of a bitch.

Then Highsmith talked about her miscarriages. Rena seethed.

"And reports were surfacing, from family and friends, that maybe domestic abuse was a factor."

"Oh my. What can you tell us, without betraying privacy?"

Highsmith paused, as if he were hesitant to say. "I'm still investigating. I don't want to say more than I can prove."

"Of course."

But friends knew they were having so many problems, Highsmith said. "There was a widely shared sense that Katie felt psychologically abused. And there was speculation about physical abuse."

"Would the death of an unborn child due to physical abuse be a crime?"

"Yes, it would."

They let that hang.

"And this man Rena was one of the army's top criminal investigators?"

"Yes."

"Who might have killed his own unborn babies by abusing his wife?"

"That's what I'm trying to pin down."

Rena stopped the audio. His hands were tingling. Highsmith had pulled all the random threads in insane digital posts into a single even more insane narrative. Rena got up and wandered into the kitchen. He needed to take a moment, move his body and breathe. He was angry, but he didn't know what to do about it. He began to make another vodka martini and then stopped. He went back into the den and restarted the audio.

The host was asking how this all connected to the fall of one of the military's top leaders.

"Around this time, Rena launched an investigation, largely on his own, that is so controversial it has remained sealed ever since."

The host pressed for an explanation.

"A general, one of our most gifted battlefield leaders, was about to be promoted to one of the most important jobs in the U.S. military." Highsmith wouldn't share the general's name, he said, out of respect for the presumption of innocence and due process.

"Of course."

"But Rena was asked to do a final vetting. Now understand, this general was a man whose record had been reviewed over and over and found spotless."

"Sure."

"But this time, Rena insisted he had uncovered proof of a terrible scandal: a secret history of the general harassing women," Highsmith said.

"And rather than going through the correct channels, Rena went

off on his own and conducted some kind of private 'investigation.'
One source I talked to called him 'hell-bent,'" Highsmith said.

"What happened?"

"Rena's colleagues at the Pentagon were shocked. He had gone
on a private crusade. Off the books. And, of course, there were never
any formal charges against the general."

"Hmm."

"Instead—and this is where it gets weirder—Rena went rogue.
He went to the general's house and threatened to make his allegations public if the general didn't step aside. In total violation of every
protocol."

The host said he was aghast.

"The general in question, who had a distinguished record of service to his country, chose duty and country one last time. Rather
than drag the military and his family through the mud to clear his
name, he chose to protect the service from what he knew would be
a controversy. He chose to retire. And there was no hint of the army
blaming the general for anything."

"What happened to Rena?"

"This is the part—if you know much about the army—that
probably tells the tale. A few months later, Rena was forced out of
the service. Not reassigned. Purged. And eventually, his wife filed
for divorce."

A pause and the interviewer asked: "Are you suggesting, David,
that Rena invented this scandal? That he manufactured allegations
against a general as a smoke screen to cover up the scandal about
himself—that he was beating his wife."

"That's exactly what I am trying to pin down."

"He knew the army was about to kick him out? And then he
concocted this tale about the general and sexual harassment so that
when the army acted against Rena for domestic abuse, as he knew it
would, he could claim it was revenge for his pursuing the investigation."

"That's the allegation."

The interviewer sighed. "It's so devilish, so twisted, it almost has to be true."

"All the pieces fit," Highsmith said. "I'm just trying to confirm them."

"God bless you, David."

RENA THOUGHT ABOUT KATIE. SHE WAS MARRIED NOW, LIVING IN the Hunt Country of Northern Virginia, the old money region near Middleburg. They'd been divorced five years. Her new husband worked in finance. They had a son.

He didn't want her involved. He had emailed her to tell her to stay out of it. It was his problem. He hoped no one sought her out. Her family, including Katie's brother, who was Peter's roommate at West Point, were angry enough with him. Katie's parents had never approved of him.

He looked over at Nelson, the cat, who seemed to be reading Rena's thoughts. He opened his eyes and looked at Rena and seemed to be saying, "Having a tough time, mate?"

Rena picked up his phone and typed a text to Vic Madison.

How are you? I hope you are well. It sounded stilted and lame.

He didn't hit send, but he didn't delete it either.

11

ROANOKE, VIRGINIA

STEPH MYERS

Steph Myers finished the podcast and shook his head. He knew little about this. But he knew the general they were talking about. He was sure of it. He had heard something about this when he was in the army. Dooley had told him. A good man taken out. Never got that last star.

He opened What's App and sent Dooley a message. CHECK THIS OUT. SERIOUSLY MESSED UP! He copied in a link. He couldn't wait to hear what Dooley would say.

He only recently had begun to get into this kind of stuff, these places on the web. What he couldn't figure out was what had happened. It was like an illness. America had gone from being the country that made the things that everyone in the world wanted to being a country that didn't make anything for itself. Americans had become sad, defeated, overweight.

STEPH HAD TO DO SOMETHING. HE COULDN'T KEEP TEACHING kids seventh grade social studies when the country was falling apart. He couldn't teach them about the American dream, the promise of liberty and opportunity, when the factories had all closed up and all the jobs had been shipped away. He couldn't teach it and not believe it.

How had it happened? How had the world changed so much since he was a kid? How had the country not seen it coming? How had he not seen it coming?

There were answers. But they weren't in the usual places. They weren't on TV or in the newspaper. He didn't believe in cover-ups and conspiracies, of course not. But there were people out there trying to find the truth. And he was beginning to discover who those people were and where they were talking to each other.

12

DAVID TRAYNOR

In five days he would become the most powerful man on earth.

"How do you feel?" Quentin Phelps asked him.

Quent had come out of the cabin they were using as an office. He sat down in a rocker on the front porch next to the president-elect.

"Not ready," Traynor said. "But better this afternoon."

"It was a good day," Quent agreed and smiled that familiar grin of anticipation they had shared over many years. It was good to be lost in the details again. This anticipation, however, was unlike any they had shared before, Traynor thought. The challenge more monumental. It was hard to grasp the geometry of it. You could break it down into smaller problems, but there were just so many pieces. You needed to divert people's attention from most of them.

They were back at his friends' estate in Boulder working—and hiding from the press. The Boulder compound had become his pre-inaugural headquarters. He had taken over one of the cabins as living quarters for himself and Mariette, and a second cabin for himself, Quent, and a few aides to use as an office. There was plenty of space at the estate's big house and other cabins for any number of staff and any number of visitors. They had rooms for meetings large or small, and they could hike, run, play basketball, do anything they wanted to without leaving the grounds. They could bus the press in when it suited them and bus them out when it didn't. The location was easy for visitors to get to, a half hour from the Denver airport, and a little less elitist than the Aspen house, which was not meant for anyone but him and Mariette.

He sat on the porch of the office cabin with a yellow legal pad on his lap, staring at the Rockies and the Continental Divide. He sat squarely in the middle between the East and the West of the country. It felt right.

"Yes, today was good," Traynor said, but he was nervous, and Quent could hear it in his voice.

They were running out of time to have everything ready. Today they had settled on one of the biggest agenda items of his new presidency. Traynor had reassembled the climate team from last month, and they had arrived at a secret plan to radically address climate without Congress knowing. It was brilliant, bold, and could make or break his presidency. But he needed Upton on board and he couldn't tell what she was thinking. He had asked her to stay behind at the big house after the afternoon meeting broke up so they could talk. But she said she needed to go back to her cabin to deal with something. She looked bothered. It worried him. He said he would come to her in a half hour.

So many details to worry about. He'd outsourced most of the inauguration day decisions to other people, especially Mariette, the most competent person he knew. Before they met, Mar had been an Olympian, a Stanford business grad, and had been the kind of competent executive whom bosses put in charge of whatever department was lagging. She'd run, at various companies, HR, Finance, Operations, and Logistics divisions and made them all better. That was how they met, when she was running one for him. She could handle his inauguration better than any of his staff. He knew the events around inauguration mattered, the galas and parties. "The spectacle of leadership," Sterling Moss called it. But planning parties bored him. He didn't have the patience.

He had much more to worry about. He had the first three months to accomplish a singular goal: how to utterly surprise his opponents the day he took office and not give them a chance to catch up. How to hit the ground faster than any president in history.

He and Quent had obsessed about it.

Franklin Delano Roosevelt had transformed the country in eight days. Height of the Depression, 1933. When Franklin D. in his inaugural declared "the only thing we have to fear is fear itself," his aide Tommy Corcoran said it was like Arthur pulling Excalibur from the stone. Everything seemed to change in an instant. A week later, when FDR gave his first "fireside chat" and told people to put their money back into banks—not take it out—people actually freaking did it. The country started moving in a new direction. He was learning more about FDR, thanks to the historian he had hired for the West Wing, a woman Upton had introduced him to, someone she knew from Arizona. The historian was trying to teach him more about government leadership. John Kennedy had had an in-house historian, too.

He needed something stunning, something transformative. Something like FDR had.

He had surprised people by picking Upton, a Republican, as his running mate and doing so early, at the height of the primaries. Washington insiders said it was a stunt, but the public got it. Now he was committed once he became president to keeping the surprises coming almost continuously. And they had to be real. They had to add up to something. That was how he would keep his enemies afraid and his supporters cheering.

A lot hung on his inaugural address, the official first public act of a president. Sterling Moss was already referring to it as "The Seven Crises" speech—for the seven major problems Traynor's administration would tackle on Day One. They hadn't used the term before, seven crises, at least not since two years ago, when he had announced his candidacy. And he wanted the speech's theme to remain a secret now—until the last minute. Only a few people knew about the speech's content: Moss, Mariette, the speechwriter Will Gersch, and Quent.

The speech itself would be shy on details—purposely. They had all agreed on that. It was both a sleight of hand and a way to keep the focus on surprise. Put another way, he wanted to mislead his critics by reassuring them that he was a fraud and an empty suit. His critics considered him a showman and charlatan, a man with no patience for details. They would excoriate the speech for its grandiosity of ambition and its paucity of specifics, because that's what they were expecting.

Seven crises? They couldn't imagine David Traynor developing a serious plan to handle one—let alone seven. He'd heard it all his life. He talked like a frat dude, not a world leader. He was an overgrown "adolescent with ADD," a man whose biggest strengths were "galling ambition and ruthless impatience," who knew "just enough about engineering, marketing, and accounting" to have gotten into the customer-tracking software businesses "at just the right time." But complicated global problems? Those were beyond his reach. Even if he made good appointments, the *Week Ahead* had editorialized last week, the country still needed a master at the helm, and "he was no master." Deep down, his critics liked to joke, David Traynor was shallow.

In business, the Ivy MBAs and the Stanford engineers who worked for him usually thought him a sloppy thinker because he didn't talk in jargon. They would come out of meetings wondering if he understood his own technology. Well, for all he could see, people in politics were even worse. He had never seen such arrogance, or so many people be so wrong so often. Maybe it was because politics was about belief and only occasionally about results. But most of the predictions he heard were ridiculous. People in politics, he found, tended to put way too much stock in their own rhetoric and too little on actual strategy. And they were often utterly out of their depth on execution.

He was counting on it. Just like he was counting on the spectacle of the inauguration Mariette was planning to help catch his opponents off guard. Everyone in Washington would be fixated on the day, the inaugural speech, the parade, the parties, the uber A-list celebrities, Mariette's gowns, the amazing lineup of musical stars slated to perform at the different galas. And it wasn't just the public. The press, too, always focused on the obvious, on what was arranged for it to see, and always imagined it could see more than it could. He was amazed that the press seemed capable of covering only one story at any given moment—a single plotline they shoved everything into, whether it fit or not. The media was a cyclops, a one-eyed monster.

That's why the inauguration presented a perfect magician's moment, a giant national sleight of hand, aired live on every news channel. While everyone was looking there, his presidency would have begun over here. And here. And here.

Everything had to be ready. At the moment of transfer of power, he wanted his administration moving at maximum speed. Bills prepared for Congress, meetings set, revised regulatory rules filed, and more. Much more.

His enemies would be irate; the news media shocked. Both drew their expertise and comfort from precedent. But their second reaction would be grudging admiration. And their third reaction would be the inkling of a new thought: maybe Traynor's administration would be cleverer than they had imagined. The people who'd backed him, hoping he might shake things up, would begin to love him. And the people who despised him would begin to be fearful.

The seven crises themselves were not new. They were problems that had been ignored for generations. He had plans for all seven— and he would put parts of those plans in motion the day he took office. And from then on, people who were opposing rather than helping work to solve these crises could no longer credibly claim to be on the side of the American people. Didn't matter which party you belonged or didn't belong to; Americans knew when they were being lied to.

The list was simple. Introduce a plan to radically simplify the tax system. Secure the future of Social Security by significantly reforming it (unheard of from a Democrat). Rethink federal regulations from the ground up so everyone played by the same rules (again, surprising from a Democrat). Confront systemic racial inequities in criminal justice and judicial systems. Renew American manufacturing. (It could be done and Traynor loved the ideas they had so far.) Fix the country's crumbling infrastructure (that, too, could be done). And attack the climate crisis as if it were a war to save the planet. The country, the whole damn world, would be reeling from the enormity of what they would send up in the first few days. No one would be able to keep up. They would think, finally, someone was doing something. Even those who thought him naive and certain to fail would have to admit it. Roosevelt hadn't fixed the Depression. But he had made people believe they had finally started beating it back. And that was enough at the beginning.

IT WAS THE LAST PLAN, TO SAVE THE PLANET, THAT FASCINATED Traynor most. It involved the most secrecy, but if it succeeded, it would be the most important. That was what he and Kim Matsuda had just laid out all day long with a key group of advisors. It was what he wanted to talk to the vice president-elect about now.

Upton had spent only a few days here in Boulder in the last month. They needed time to catch up. Traynor made the hundred-yard walk to her cabin. She was waiting on the front porch.

He looked at her as he came up the steps. She could appear lovely when she wanted to, and always did in public. But in private, she hid

herself in a hard shell of quiet intellect. He had seen that shell in the
Senate. She used it to signal to colleagues, the vast majority of whom
were male, not to push her around. She was like a lone redwood on
a California hillside, he thought, that had rooted itself at an eleva-
tion where all the other trees were oaks and elms. Out of place. But
a redwood would outlive them all.

"Everything all right?"

"Just a friend having a problem," she said. "But he's all right."

Traynor plopped himself down in the chair next to her.

"So whaddya think about our secret plan to stop global
warming?"

13

WENDY UPTON

Wendy Upton was tired. And dubious. Or maybe just tired. She and Gil Sedaka had just gotten off the phone. Gil was worried that the attacks on Peter Rena might damage Upton by association. She appreciated that Gil was looking out for her. That was his job. But she was irritated that they were contemplating distancing themselves from Rena rather than defending him. It felt dishonest and disloyal, but she was no longer in a position to make that judgment on her own. Her responsibility now was to Traynor.

She looked at the president-elect. What did she think about his secret plan to save the planet? Better batteries? That was it? Really?

No, she was definitely dubious. Not just tired.

Traynor was relentless as ever, eyes shining. And the very things that worried her—the high risk of his plan, the enormous price tag, the secrecy it required—excited him.

She had to give him credit. Contrary to reputation, David was more steeped in the scientific details than she might have guessed. He was more complex than his critics and the press gave him credit for—than even she had. In the Senate, she'd noticed, strong women seemed to relax rather than intimidate him. Nor was he distracted or act weird when a beautiful young aide came into the room. That was also different from most men in politics.

But in larger groups, unless someone was making a point he found interesting, Traynor could become quickly bored, and sometimes a little manic. When he was frustrated, he would argue both sides of a case to speed the arguments along, which gave the impression he was incoherent or even a little crazy.

What did she think?

"About what?" she said to needle him.

"The plan?"

She was still not sure why he was picking just one option—flow batteries—and not considering more public efforts on the other three they had identified—massive initiatives around wind, huge solar farms, and transforming refrigeration. Traynor seemed to want his opponents to think he was doing nothing on climate.

She looked at him gravely, the way an older sister might at a younger brother. "I think this could blow up in your face. And may even be illegal."

She could see from his expression he didn't know if she was entirely serious. Only a few close friends understood her droll sense of humor. Traynor was not yet one of them.

He gave her a nervous but determined smile. "We still need to try it," he said.

"If we must."

Then he got that she was teasing, and his expression slowly changed.

"I need a glass of wine," he said, "and so do you." He texted his aide Steve Lepler asking that he bring two glasses to Upton's cabin. "And then I want to talk a little more about the discussions earlier today."

KIM MATSUDA, THE NEW "CLIMATE CZAR," HAD STARTED THE DAY by taking the group from the four ideas they had settled on in December—wind, storage, solar farms, and refrigeration—to a single focus: storage, which meant inventing a better battery to hold natural energy. Matsuda had moved them there slowly. She had told the group that morning that the key to slowing global warming required finding a way to capture and store the energy of the sun.

"The challenge," she had said, "is not so much capturing the sun's energy. We know how to build solar panels. The challenge is finding ways to hold that energy for more than a few hours."

She had paused to let that idea sink in and then said: "The nation that solves the problem of energy storage—of building a better battery—will enjoy economic ascendance for the rest of this century."

People had looked skeptical. But Matsuda didn't much care what people thought. That was for politicians to take care of.

"The dominant battery technology today, lithium ion, holds its charge for roughly two days. Maybe less. Think of your cell phone. And most solar storage today is less than that—a few hours," she had said. "If we can develop a battery technology in the United States that will store energy for six months, we can solve most of the problems related to the power grid and auto emissions. And that, may I remind you, is two-thirds of our carbon problem.

"Yet for reasons we can easily solve, the development of such batteries is all but stalled. And that reason is lack of investment."

Upton had been first to raise a question. In part she wanted to model for people that asking questions was part of her role. She was not there to nod adoringly or to keep her mouth shut.

"Isn't there already a lot of investment now in batteries?" She had been reading her briefing books.

"Only in lithium ion," Matsuda had answered. "And the reason for that is simple: other than the Chinese, the world has left battery innovation to the private sector. And the dominant commercial market for innovation right now is in lithium-ion battery technology for cell phones and computers."

But lithium was the wrong storage technology to solve our larger energy problems, Matsuda explained. Lithium-ion batteries need to be replaced after a year or two, which means you'd need to keep replacing your battery infrastructure. "And they're inefficient. A lithium-ion battery keeps only eighty percent of its energy, and that number starts degrading very quickly."

"What will work?" someone asked. And then someone else guessed.

"You're talking flow batteries," said the incoming director of the National Oceanic and Atmospheric Administration. NOAA, which was buried inside the Department of Commerce, was the agency most directly responsible for climate.

"Yes," Matsuda said. "The future is in flow."

It was all in the briefs they'd been given. Flow batteries, sometimes called "liquid metal," worked by moving energy between two chambers, each filled with different metals. They were perfectly suited to big tasks. Flow batteries could be huge—as big as a large room, or the size of a car battery. They could store a vast amount of energy, enough in groups to power a city, and they never wore out. The problem was they didn't hold their charge very long, only a matter of hours. You couldn't keep the energy from summer for use in the winter.

"These batteries last forever. And they discharge a hundred percent of their energy," said Matsuda.

"Maybe there's been so little progress in flow because they can't do what you want," the incoming NOAA chief said. He'd done the reading, too. "How do you know if we poured more money in, we wouldn't just discover there's no way they will hold energy for more than a day or two?"

"Because when there has been investment, the advances have

been dramatic," Matsuda said. Then she had gone through the Australian case. Scientists there had created a molten salt battery that increased solar storage from six hours to twenty-nine hours.

"If we can increase the storage time from two days to a few months, we will have almost solved the problem."

Most of the group knew just enough to know this would be tough to accomplish. They were government people. They prided themselves on their realism. Not their vision.

"And when we improve it to six months, we *will* have solved it," Matsuda said. "At that point, the summer sun will be heating our homes all winter."

"It took the Australians a year to do their project," said the man from NOAA. "And they got the charge to last for two days. That isn't anywhere close."

"Because of money," said Matsuda. "We know flow batteries will work. We just haven't spent enough to get there."

Traynor, uncharacteristically quiet, chimed in: "The amount of money invested in flow batteries worldwide has been minuscule. It's a scandal. A handful of start-ups. A couple of university labs. And all of them, like the Aussies, grossly undercapitalized."

Then Matsuda's tinny voice had become steely. "We're in the same place with flow batteries we were a hundred and thirty years ago with the electric light," she said. "They knew it would work. They just didn't know which filament. We know flow will work. But to get there, we need investment from government. Only governments have the money and freedom to look that far ahead. Only governments—not markets—have the responsibility to save the planet. If we wait for the market to do it, it will be too late."

"How much money?" Traynor's incoming budget chief asked.

"If we increased the amount spent on flow batteries from one hundred million a year to between fifteen and thirty billion, we would have a battery that would solve our power grid problem in eighteen months. I'm confident of that. Maybe sooner."

The expressions on the faces around the room made it obvious most of the other participants didn't believe her.

"Where will you get thirty billion?" Traynor's budget chief said, suppressing a laugh. "Congress will never grant it."

The incoming guy for NOAA added: "There's no political constituency for climate, David. Believe me, I know. I've been working at it for thirty years."

"The oil companies and the car companies will kill us," a congressional liaison agreed.

"We're not going to Congress for this," Traynor said.

"How then?"

"We have the money already, in contingency funds for homeland security, military base security, and other classified budgets."

He had used the magic word. Security.

"Sir," Traynor's incoming director of National Intelligence, Sally Holmes, said, "those budgets are—"

"Discretionary," Traynor said, cutting her off. "For national security. And this is a national security issue."

He looked at his incoming secretary of defense.

"And we have wide latitude there," Traynor said.

The incoming defense secretary nodded. Traynor hadn't left this discussion to chance. He and the defense secretary had worked this out beforehand.

"I agree. We have funds to jump-start this," the secretary said.

"You intend, in other words, Mr. President-elect," the intelligence chief said, "to launch a massive campaign to invest in developing battery technology using national security funds from classified budgets?"

Traynor smiled.

"Same way, Sally, we developed the atom bomb. Or financed the Iraq war. Or got the jump-start on the space race. This is a war, too—to save the planet. Anyone in the room doubt that?"

In private, most members of the Senate believed climate change was now a global emergency. But about half of Washington wasn't allowed to say so publicly. That was politics and money. Not science. The crisis, however, had been ignored so long, it now seemed easier for some people to imagine it would solve itself. It was the worst kind of magical thinking.

Upton, for one, had been enormously frustrated by that mind-set as a senator. It was one of the reasons she had agreed to run with Traynor on a joint ticket. It wasn't any change in her conservatism that had pushed Upton to take that step. It was the denial of facts and reality by the people who were taking power in the Republican Party. It was her fear that in their zeal to crush Democrats politically, they were putting off problems too long. Climate was first on that list.

The room at that point had been a little stunned.

"I have a different question," the incoming head of intelligence said. "Where are all those solar panels going to be? You're talking building massive solar farms. I thought that was one of the options we considered and passed on."

Matsuda had found a solution for this. Traynor smiled at her. Apparently, Upton thought, whatever solution she had for any situation, he loved.

"We don't need to buy land to build massive solar farms. We have the land we need and people won't even notice the panels," Matsuda said.

"Where?" the incoming director of intelligence demanded.

"The medians of all federal highways—thousands of miles of them. And existing roof space on federal buildings. They provide enough real estate to increase solar capture twentyfold," she said. "That is land we already control. They could begin installing in thirty days. Most of those panels will be installed in two years. And we can do that without legislation as well."

"How?" the spy chief asked.

There was already a law on the books allowing the federal

government to install solar panels on federal buildings and high-ways, but Congress, in its wisdom, had set no timetable and provided no funding, Matsuda said. Traynor could sign a classified executive order to get it done immediately, given that this was a national secu-rity emergency.

"There's a lot of solar panels on highway medians now. You haven't even noticed them."

Looking around the room, Upton could see these bureaucrats thinking of a thousand reasons it couldn't be done.

"People will notice construction on public buildings," said the spy chief.

"Eventually," Traynor said. "But how often do you look at the roof of a federal building? Or a highway median? And if people ask, unfortunately, we won't be at liberty to answer their questions."

This was different from the big infrastructure programs Traynor envisioned, rebuilding crumbling bridges or highways, which he wanted people to notice. These would happen under people's noses without much fanfare.

"Where would the money come from for this battery program? And the solar panels?" his budget expert asked.

"Two-thirds of the funds required for the panels and their in-stallation already exist in federal budgets, which can be redirected without congressional involvement under the national security pro-visions," Traynor's incoming chief of staff said. "We've done the math."

"And the battery program? Which is the bigger part of this plan?" the budget expert pressed.

"It's a national security crisis," Traynor said. "That funding will be classified, but it gives us wide discretion."

"And in the process," Matsuda said, "we will create a new do-mestic industry—flow batteries—and revitalize another, solar pan-els. We allowed the Chinese in the last fifteen years to dominate the solar industry because we failed to create subsidies and tax breaks to build our own. But that's reversible. The law requires that these panels be fully U.S. made and U.S. owned. With our own public buildings as the market, we could match Chinese manufacturing rates within a year."

"You'll have to brief Congress, even under national security provisions," said Traynor's budget chief.

"Yes, the Gang of Eight who get our most classified intelligence briefings. But by the time we have done so, we believe we will have moved so fast we will already have made huge progress on the battery program." The Gang of Eight referred to eight Republican and Democrat intelligence chairs, plus the House and Senate leadership, who got special briefings that they could not leak to their colleagues.

It was a lot to process—too much. That was almost the point.

"I just wonder if the political system shouldn't be the proper place to wrestle with this—" Upton began.

"It's had its chance." Traynor cut her off.

Upton didn't like the president cutting her off, but in this case she had the sense it was because Traynor was becoming more comfortable with her. She considered showing her displeasure and decided against it. She could bring it up privately if it became a pattern.

A moment passed before anyone asked another question.

"How long do you think you can keep this battery program secret?" asked his spy chief.

"How long did you keep secret prisons secret?" asked Traynor.

That was an insult—and it stung. Sally Holmes had been an advocate of the controversial classified program to keep Al Qaeda suspects in secret prisons in foreign countries—a story that reporter Jill Bishop had broken in the *Washington Tribune*.

"Two years," the spy chief said.

"I don't think we'll need that long," Traynor said.

Upton ended the silence that followed: "And how do you justify doing this battery program in secret?"

"By succeeding."

Which had led to more silence.

"I have another question," someone said at last. It was the head of NOAA. "Isn't this race for a better battery for cars and power grids something that will go faster if the whole world is part of it? Isn't storing the sun's energy something the world needs? How do we hide it in secret military budgets and justify it as national security when climate change is global?"

"Because these batteries must be an American asset. American made. An American industry."

"Why?" the NOAA chief pressed.

Traynor's incoming defense secretary answered. "Because if our enemies had this intelligence, we believe they would sabotage our efforts to rebuild our power grid and our auto industry. So they could have the technology themselves."

ON THE PORCH, THE SUN WAS SLIPPING BELOW THE MOUNTAINS. Time vanishing. With wine in hand, Traynor was asking Upton what she really thought. He spent a little time making the case for the batteries all over again. He stumbled over some of the technical elements but he understood his crazy battery plan at a conceptual level better than she did. And he made a special case for why rapid investment in start-ups made sense as a way to do it.

"You said you would watch and listen and tell me the truth," he said. "That was our deal, right? Here's my question: If you agree we must do something big on climate, don't tell me what's wrong with this plan. Can you give me something that would be better?"

She gave him a wary look.

"I think you have spent a lifetime beguiling people, David. Venture capitalists, bankers, voters. Now you are trying to beguile scientists and generals. With a secret race to invent a battery that would capture the sun."

"Pretty cool if we succeeded, right?" He grinned.

"The start-up to end all start-ups?" she said, gently mocking him. "Run by the federal government?" She gave him a look. "Using classified budgets for its first-round seed money? You know most of the people in that room don't understand the science of it. They don't know if it's possible or a fantasy. I don't know those things either. Do you?"

"Sounds like sending astronauts to the moon," Traynor said.

"I wouldn't have proposed this," Upton said. "I think the chances of it failing are high. And I think, as I said, it may be illegal."

"I know you wouldn't have," he said, but there was kindness in how he said it. "But how could we not try?"

And to her surprise she felt an electric charge of exhilaration surge through her. The enormity and audacity of what Traynor was proposing, her exhaustion, and the stress of what was coming, all of it was converging. And something else: she was beginning to trust this strange reckless man, in spite of herself.

"The fact that you would doubt it, that's why I wanted you to know about it. And have a hand in it," Traynor said.

He was selling her; they both knew it. But she saw that he also cared what she thought. He wanted her ideas, not just her support.

"Wendy, we really have just one job," he pressed. "To show the public the government can work again. And we start by showing we are trying."

"But this program is going to be classified."

"Not after it succeeds," he said.

She wasn't sure it all held together, but Traynor kept on.

"You think politics is the art of the possible. I think it also has to be the art of the impossible. In order to create faith in it again. If we think about everything that could go wrong, we'll never try anything."

She gave him, at last, a hint of a smile. She couldn't help it. She didn't mean to. He grinned. "What's the worst that could happen?

Really? If we try and fail with this battery thing, we waste twenty billion dollars. The Iraq war cost three trillion. I think the planet's worth the risk."

He wasn't done. "If there's an exposé in the press about how we secretly tried to save the Earth," he said, "well, shame on me."

"Be careful," she advised.

"No," he told her, "be bold. We've been careful too long."

They regarded each other, uncertain allies, not-so-long-ago strangers. But she could see in his eyes he thought he was winning her over. She hoped not. She owed him her skepticism, not flattery.

14

WASHINGTON, D.C.

Friday 15 January

PETER RENA

Rena sat waiting in the attic conference room.

Eight years earlier, he and Brooks had rented the town house at 1820 Jefferson Place not because its uneven floors and perilously narrow stairs suited their growing consulting firm of investigators. They did it for history. Theodore Roosevelt had once lived there with his family. Now, all these years later, the rabbit warren of offices and the low-ceilinged attic conference room were part of the identity of Rena, Brooks & Associates.

Rena felt like he was just beginning to crawl out of whatever funk he had been in the last three weeks. The online attacks had slowed but not ceased, and clients had begun calling to ask if everything was all right—their way, Rena knew, of ascertaining how much was wrong. For her part, Randi had told the dozen or so staff at the firm not to baby Peter; he would hate it. People weren't able to stop themselves, however, and Randi had been right.

He and Vic had still not had a serious conversation, which they would need to have if they were to repair what was wrong between them. Knowing Vic, she would also want to talk it out if she intended to break up. Maybe that's why he hadn't pushed harder, he told himself. Vic wasn't ready to talk. And if he pushed, he might not like the result.

A part of him sensed she was holding back out of sympathy. He was still being slammed online, and Vic was unlikely to want to add to his miseries by breaking up with him while he was so vulnerable. When they did exchange messages, they involved polite queries about how he was holding up—friendly, sympathetic, and no more.

A few days after he returned to the office, Ellen Wiley had arranged a meeting for him with a specialist in cyberstalking and trolls to talk about what Rena could do to respond. Who knew it was a job, counseling people in how to respond to digital character assassination? The woman, who had gotten her degree after being stalked online by an old boyfriend, had said he had two choices.

"You can do nothing. Or you can fight back. But if you fight, you have to do so with all you got."

That, the cyber specialist explained, would require a campaign on his part, including beginning to "live out loud," as she called it, which meant talking about his life and what it felt like to be falsely accused and trolled online. He would also, she said, have to relive the end of his marriage and the story of how he had investigated the general who retired, a man named James Stanhope. Rena would also have to tell the stories of those two events, "the real story," the woman said, to repudiate the cyber version. "You will amplify the whole thing, including the lies, but you'll drown them in the end."

It was unthinkable. He was far too private a person for that. And asking Katie to relive their marriage in public so she could deny he had ever beaten her or abused her emotionally? No.

The only imaginable option was total silence.

That, however, had not made the attacks go away. It also had not silenced them in his own head.

The person he had seen most over the last two weeks was his friend Matt Alabama, who had taken to dropping by most evenings on his way home after prerecording his late-night cable show.

The visits were great, and he looked forward to seeing Matt each day. But he found himself wishing he were seeing Vic instead.

When the cyberattacks were at their peak she had called to ask how he was doing. He had lied and told her fine; she'd said she was glad. There was a long silence then—something they usually didn't mind on the phone—but this one was awkward. "I care for you, Peter, but I am not ready to get past what happened. I am not sure I want to get past it." Another silence. "You have enough to deal with right now."

That had been their one call.

So most nights he talked to Matt, and as much as he enjoyed them, Matt's visits also had made Rena feel uncomfortable. He felt a little handled. Two nights ago, aided with the clarity of two vodka martinis, he had told Matt: "I don't need sympathy. I'm fine."

Alabama, who was from Mississippi and was deliberate in most things, had taken his time answering.

"Hey now, you can't bait me, Pete. You know that, right? No matter what you say, I'm gonna keep coming 'round."

"You are getting ornery and dense in your old age."

"That happens. Don't hear so well either."

"Only what you want."

"It's a lovely ailment."

Rena was smiling faintly at the memory of that exchange when Randi joined him in the conference room. She was alone.

"Where is everybody. I thought we had an assignment from the White House?"

She sat down next to him. "I think the White House is handling the problem elsewhere."

"They've asked someone else?"

She nodded. It took Rena a moment to understand.

"It's me, isn't it. I'm toxic."

"They're just frightened. It will pass."

The White House was required to announce when it hired outside consultants, and even in a denuded news ecosystem, someone would pick up on the fact that the vice president's office was contracting with a man accused on the Internet of beating his wife, killing his unborn children, and smearing a heroic army general.

"I'm sorry," he said.

"Don't even think it. Politicians are professional cowards."

"Not all of them."

"Yes, all of them."

15

ROANOKE, VIRGINIA

STEPH MYERS

Since he had discovered 5Click, Steph Myers had barely been able to resist. It was a new world. It made sense to him. It was like reading the world had been decoded. Like seeing a movie with the director's instructions written in captions underneath.

There was a lot there about this man Peter Rena. So much, in fact, some of it had to be true. Not all of it, of course. The Internet was full of fools and rumors; he knew that. But some of it. There was so much about Rena there, so many details. Where there's smoke there's fire.

From 5Click, he had begun to discover other channels, and a world of people a lot like himself, people who were searching to understand what had happened to the country, people who were asking the same questions he was. He was educating himself.

GAIL HAD STARTED TO GET ON HIM ABOUT IT—HOW MUCH TIME he was spending on the computer at night. She said it made him "irritable" and that he was ignoring the kids. It didn't make him irritable. It made him furious. It opened his eyes.

"You're on that thing all night!" she'd said. "What are you doing there? Porn?"

But he wasn't ready to talk to her about it yet. He didn't know enough. He hadn't learned enough about the forces that had changed everything in the country, so slowly you didn't notice. But changing it for sure. Now working people, like everyone he knew, had so little. Everything about where they lived was dying. Meanwhile a handful of people had so much more, and were getting more every day. People in New York and Washington and California. Blue states. How had that happened? Tell me the truth. Nothing that huge, that sure, happened by accident.

Gail would tell him he was acting like a fool, and give him that look, like she was disappointed in him and in everything he did.

Porn? My god. The only people he could talk to yet about it all were the folks in the chat channels. His fellow questioners.

His life, his calling, was teaching. He taught social studies and democracy to kids at Roanoke public schools, just like his mother and his uncle had. He owed it to these kids—he owed it to himself—not to be a fool.

Not everyone got it. Some people would get left behind in the new world. Frank, his best friend when they were deployed, didn't get it. Steph was worried Frank wouldn't understand and wouldn't get involved when the new world began.

Even Dooley, who had introduced him to 5Click, was struggling to take it in.

"These guys know things," he told Dooley.

"They don't know shit. I just think looking at it is a hoot."

"They do. You're wrong. They know things. Things that connect the dots. Stuff starts to make sense, stuff you could never puzzle out on your own before, but you knew something was wrong. Something was missing. These guys are on the lookout for what's missing. The stuff we're not supposed to see. These guys are decoding it. And they can teach you how. They're teaching me. Things are starting to make sense in a way I could never see before. How people in power are really ripping everyone off. How everything is rigged."

"You're paranoid, man," Dooley said.

"I'm not. I'm learning."

Dooley gave him a look like he was crazy.

"You sound like Gail. She thinks I'm watching porn," Steph said.

"It would be better than this crap."

But Dooley had never been that curious, even back in high school or when they deployed. The fact was Dooley was lazy. He wanted to live in his own little bubble. Fine, Steph thought. Most people did. But when you step out of it and begin to really see, it all begins to make sense. Suddenly you understand so much more than before. You had to put in the work to understand it. It wasn't on the goddamn local news. But when you saw how the world actually worked, it was like getting glasses for the first time. All of a sudden the trees had leaves and the clouds were sharp and the whole world was different.

"You still obsessed with that guy? The one who beat his wife and then blamed it on a general?" As usual, Dooley didn't have the facts exactly right. "What's his name?"

"Rena."

"Still into that?"

"Sometimes."

Dooley shook his head.

"What would the kids in your class think, dude, if they knew you were like this dark web junkie."

Steph was thinking about his students. This was for them.

Dooley shook his head.

16

PORTOLA VALLEY, CALIFORNIA

Sunday 17 January

DAVID TRAYNOR

David Traynor spent the weekend before his inauguration say-ing goodbye to friends out west. Sunday morning, after attending church, he addressed rallies at two of his California companies, the software company for tracking sales and a logistics distribution firm. Farewells to employees, some private goodbyes, and celebrations for the cameras and the evening news—all to feed the public narrative Sterling Moss thought worth reminding: David Traynor was a west-erner, a builder of new companies, a Coloradan and Californian, go-ing to Washington to change things.

After lunch with a group the *Wall Street Journal* called "responsible technology executives"—a not-so-subtle conservative rebuke of Silicon Valley—he and Mariette retreated up Alpine Road to their home in Portola Valley. A wood-and-glass California modern, set on a private hilltop, it was Mariette's favorite, a Shangri-la secluded by valley oaks, bay laurels, and madrones. Secret Service had deemed the house "acceptably secure" as a potential "Western White House"—so long as Traynor didn't move to certain open areas exposed to a neighboring hill, where, he was told, there was "long-gun vulnerability."

That afternoon, he had arranged for private time on his schedule, a few hours for visits with friends he would not see much of over the next four years.

Around four, a black Tesla slid noiselessly up the long drive. Traynor felt butterflies of excitement. He always did when he was about to meet Anatoly. He watched the Tesla stop and the familiar square-shaped balding head emerge from the car. Even in the valley, full of brilliant dreamers and arrogant rule breakers, you didn't meet many minds like Anatoly Bremmer's.

Anatol, the "Russian Bear," seemed to operate on a different intellectual plane than most people, and Traynor always felt a little elevated after seeing him. Bremmer, who ran one of the most successful venture capital firms in the Valley, had a rare gift for synthesizing new information. He might, for instance, learn three seemingly unrelated things in a week, and within days—years before anyone else—be talking about how those new ideas would intersect and alter the future, shifting the purpose of some new technology still years from market, and creating new problems in ten years no governments or even most experts had even dreamed of.

He was the first person Traynor had ever heard talk about "filter bubbles" or "accelerating political polarization," "intensified group identities" or foreign election manipulation. He was the first person to recognize that the platform companies were shifting from the business of targeted advertising to behavior prediction and modification. A lot of financial sages in the Valley claimed they could see around corners to glimpse the future. Mostly they were guessing. Three-quarters of start-ups failed, worse odds than a coin toss. The only real requirement for being a venture capitalist was having capital to venture.

Anatoly was different. Not only did he win more often than other people. The money almost seemed beside the point. It was the ideas, Traynor thought, the flow of human progress that intrigued him. Anatoly had a method, of course; no one that successful was without a process, some craft to guide their intuition. But like a musician who could hear whole orchestral arrangements in his head, Anatoly's mind operated across more spheres than other people's— money, technology, ethnography, history, science, politics, psychology. And that was rare.

He watched Bremmer greet the final Secret Service agent outside the house. Then Traynor rose and met him at the front door. "Anatoly," Traynor said, gripping the other man's hand and putting another hand on his shoulder.

"Meester Prezeedent Eeelect," Anatol said with a slow grin, his accent still, after all these years, thick as a Russian winter coat.

Traynor was always surprised each visit by the Russian's diminutive stature, perhaps about five foot five. Bremmer's presence loomed larger. He was stocky with a square face and hooded eyes, but he was quick to smile. A Russian face, Traynor thought, though he recalled from somewhere that Bremmer was Jewish.

"It's still David, Anatoly. We're friends. And I believe, you are not yet a citizen. So technically you can call me what you want."

"No!" Bremmer declared. "Prezeedent is what you're going to be. So it's what I'll call you." He lifted his wiry eyebrows, "I live in America now. And I am almost a citizen."

No, Anatoly, you are a citizen of the planet, Traynor thought, and you live years in the future.

While still a graduate student in Moscow, Bremmer had started the company that effectively became the Russian Internet. Called, InfoInc, it was the Russian version of Y'all Post, Google, and Microsoft rolled into one. Then, after building it, Bremmer had sold it and moved into venture capital. As the oligarchs and old KGB regained power in Russia, Anatoly began to spend more time in America. Eventually he moved here.

They walked out to the pool, under the oaks, followed at a distance by three agents from Traynor's detail. It was cool in January in Northern California, but you could still be outside. The staff had lit the propane heating towers. They sat in chairs and Bremmer lit a cigarette.

"I will mees you, David. You're one of the grown-ups here. No longer chasing the White Whale."

"You're over my head, Anatoly. That's Moby Dick, right?"

Anatoly smiled. "You, David, will do great things. This country needs you."

Anatoly's voice broke slightly, catching on an unexpected shoal of feeling.

And Traynor felt a little tinge of sadness wash over him. This was just flattery, he knew, but it touched him.

"I wonder if I can really change things," Traynor said. "I worry, sometimes, that I'll be just a transitional figure. One of those guys who breaks the cycle and then is cast out."

"We remember those guys more and more," Bremmer said softly. "The ones who make everything that follows possible." He searched Traynor's face. "This is no time for stewards. Or popularity."

"Don't bullshit a bullshitter," Traynor said. "I could be Jimmy Carter."

Anatoly shook his head. "No."

Bremmer's eyes darted away, and looking into the swimming pool water shimmering in the winter light, he said, "David, you won't see much of me. You can't have an old Russian wandering around the White House."

"I've thought about that," Traynor said.

"Not like this. Not the two of us anymore."

"No."

"Good. Okay. So, you have plans? You're going to change things. I'm glad."

Traynor gave a distant smile. "More than I can keep track of."

"I can guess," Anatoly said. "Entitlements. Infrastructure. Taxes. Climate." Traynor tried not to react. "And you will try *many* things all at once. You've studied why others have failed at them. You have strategies for each one."

The hair on Traynor's arms began to stand up. The man knows me, he thought. "Be careful, David," Anatoly whispered. "Don't want to fail at many things at once."

"If I do many things, it's also harder for my opponents to stop me," Traynor said.

Anatoly nodded, and they were quiet a moment. "Climate will be the hardest," Bremmer said. "The technology is challenging: storage." He drew himself toward Traynor in a gesture of intimacy, animated now by their talk becoming serious.

"But whoever figures it out, they will be the next superpower. The country that dominates renewables will dominate the century." He studied the future president for his reaction. "The rest of the world will need that energy storage, those batteries, to power their cars and their electric grids and their phones and computers. The Saudis will fall back into the desert. And the Texans will become rednecks again."

Traynor said nothing.

"Batteries are the future, Davey. The key to this century. Wind and solar farms to capture the energy. And batteries to store it."

Traynor hoped his expression gave nothing away, but Anatoly said, "So, you are doing something about it. Good." Then he repeated: "Good."

Traynor lowered his voice. "Which technology, Anatoly? Do you have a guess?"

Bremmer shook his head. "You have better experts than me to ask about that. Don't get technical advice from old friends. But remember the equation: Hypothesis. Test. Assess. Test again. Reassess."

It was a catechism of change management they both used: start with a hypothesis. Then test and assess. Create new knowledge. Refine your hypothesis. Test again. And so on.

"Help me with my hypotheses," Traynor said. "What is your guess about which technology will solve energy storage? Which battery?"

Anatoly shrugged. "The Chinese are trying to own solar. And lithium. You can't beat them on cost. So leap ahead."

"Which is hard. And slow. And takes capital."

The winter sun was lowering behind the hills to the west. A ribbon of color, watermelon red, was ripening below a moving cloud.

"Can you go big, David? Very big?"

"That's the plan," Traynor said.

"The Republicans will never let you."

The president-elect allowed himself a tiny smile. "So I can't let them know."

"I'm sorry I can't come to the inauguration. But if you let me, I will call you and tell you what I think of your speech."

"Please do," Traynor said. "And tell me the truth. I need people to tell me the truth."

"I promise."

The two men smiled at each other in friendship and Traynor felt another chilling tinge of sadness. He was, he realized, afraid. Almost as if waking from a dream, he recognized his own fear of failure. And just for an instant the old terror returned, that he had fooled everyone and was a fool himself.

17

WASHINGTON, D.C.

Wednesday 20 January

WENDY UPTON

It always seemed cold on inauguration day, as though God was disappointed, Wendy Upton thought. She imagined God sitting in a corner of her kingdom, arms crossed, expression grim, as she listened to promises of unity her children wouldn't keep.

That image had come into Upton's mind when she attended her first inaugural thirty years ago, back when she was an army attorney deployed to Washington. What else could explain such bone-piercing cold?

It was cold today, too. A numbing, bayonet chill. Her sister, Emily, sat beside her. David Traynor had his back to them, hand on a Bible held by his wife, Mariette, the chief justice finishing the last words of the oath. Little clouds of warm breath burst and vanished as they spoke. Applause, whoops, spreading down the mall from tens of thousands, the cheers warming their bodies and their hearts. Then David moved to the podium microphone and turned to the crowd.

He began with a greeting similar to what Thomas Jefferson had used in his first inaugural in 1801. "My friends and fellow citizens. I come to you today fully knowing the task before me is above my talents." Then a Traynorian twist. "But it is not above our collective will. If we act together."

Traynor had brought her in for the speech—not for its conception as much as for its review, to find holes and anticipate how the Republicans would respond. He accepted a number of her suggestions. The process had been the first in which she began to feel like a partner.

More Jefferson followed. "Democracy depends on the sacred principle of majority rule, also on the majority being reasonable. The minority possesses equal rights, which equal law must protect. To violate that would be oppression. Those are words from our third president. Thomas Jefferson used them two centuries ago in his first inaugural, after our first partisan, highly polarized election. They are worth noting today. They were prelude to Jefferson's first term, one of the most successful of any American president."

She had heard a rumor in the crowd that the speech handed to media before the inaugural was actually Jefferson's 1801 speech, not this one—an apparent mistake but really a prank. Traynor's obsession with surprise, she thought. He gave the media the wrong speech to read ahead of time, so they would listen and be surprised by the real one. Had his people really done that without telling her?

Traynor was coming now to the moment he hoped would define the speech. Upton liked this moment the best, too, for it was full of candor about the problems the country needed to address. David called them "the seven crises." His speechwriter, Will Gersch, had coined the term months ago, but David and Sterling Moss dearly hoped that phrase would define how this speech was remembered. The talking points for discussing the speech afterward instructed that Traynor's surrogates describe it as such: "the seven crises speech."

"We live in a time where the ideas that divide us have led us to neglect our problems. We have seven major areas of need in America we have neglected, that the government has neglected, that we the people have allowed them to neglect. We have let these problems fester until they have become imminent threats to the prosperity, safety, and health of us all—to our future as a nation. Yet these seven crises can unite us. We still have the power to transform these crises into achievements, to turn what was neglect into opportunity, and opportunity into the triumph of ingenuity. We can do this, we can write this new chapter, if we come together. And the world will know. We will know. We have the power of renewal, the power to heal, the power to advance, in our own hands."

Simple, plain, David Traynor storytelling. Define a problem. The problem defines the solution. She was learning his method.

"We all know what these crises are. We have stopped building the things we consume here on our own soil. We have let our roads, bridges, waterlines, and power systems lapse into decay. We have allowed our health care system to become uneven and too expensive, leaving too many behind. With all the best of intentions, we have created regulations that were designed to protect us, but that have become incoherent and make conducting business insensibly hard. Our programs to provide savings for our retirement are about to run out of money. We have let our tax system become too complicated and allowed a few to avoid paying their fair share. And we have allowed corporations to pay almost nothing. We have too long ignored systemic inequities in our policing and our courts and our voting practices. We have neglected the damage we humans are doing to our own planet. The time for neglect has run out. The good news is there is still time to change—if we act as one nation, loyal to our traditions, committed to our common purpose."

The tone of the speech would now shift. What came next was the most difficult section, the transition to his agenda and his accusations. David had struggled with it. The seven crises were a downer, a long straightaway of problems without a lot of cheers. The next section would be divisive, cheers mixed with stony silence. The speech, unlike most inaugurals, was not built for applause lines.

"But diagnosis is easy. Prescription is where we find our differences. How to solve these crises? What are we willing to give up? How are we willing to become uncomfortable ourselves in order to help others, and in so doing build a better life for us all? My answer is we will govern differently than the country has ever been governed before."

Applause here, though people do not know yet what they are applauding.

"I will ask Congress to move on all of these crises at once—starting today. I am sending bills up to the Hill in the next hour that begin to address each of these problems. But they will be unlike any laws Congress has ever seen."

Then he walked through the Scandinavian method of lawmaking—defining a problem and charging the legislature with fixing it by a certain time, without dictating all the specifics or taking on everything at once. Working the problem one step at a time, more money to flow if progress was made, the money stopping if it wasn't.

"This is how we solve problems in our own lives. One step at a time. Not imagining you know all the answers when you start. What begins today is not old-fashioned and often insensible big government. It is a new kind of smart government. This is government that starts small and smart, learns, improves, and changes course as the facts on the ground dictate. Imagine, a government that learns and adapts. Imagine, a new kind of government.

"I am so confident that we can do this, and so committed, that I will make a promise today no president has ever made.

"If we can make meaningful progress on these seven crises—real and dramatic progress in eighteen months—I will agree to serve only a single term in office. I give you my word."

There were gasps in the crowd.

"For that to happen, however, the two parties in Congress—my own party and the other party—must agree to modify certain arcane rules they have followed, rules that for the last twenty-five years have made it too easy for one side to obstruct progress. So, as part of my promise to serve for one term, I am going to ask for a promise from Congress in return.

"I am going to ask that they put an end to these internal rules that block progress. I am going to ask that they, instead, take up new rules for a new adaptive government, rules that will help government do its job of helping the people, while also keeping it from becoming too big, too inflexible, and too rule bound.

"One of these rules, called the majority of the majority rule, holds that a party will not agree to let something come to a vote unless the majority of one party supports it. This sounds like a good thing. It sounds like majority rule. But in fact it is the opposite. In the last eight years, members of Congress have used this rule to stop four hundred and twenty-eight bills or amendments that would have addressed one of these seven crises. All four hundred and twenty-eight of these were supported by the majority of members of the House or Senate across both parties and thus would have passed those lawmaking bodies. But they were not passed. Had they been, we would have reduced the federal deficit by more than nine hundred billion dollars. We would have funded Social Security for another fifty years. We would have rebuilt seven hundred more bridges. We would have reduced taxes for two hundred million Americans."

He offered still more examples of how things could have been better, using math from some consulting experts Traynor, Phelps, and their budget guru had hired.

The speech was designed for Traynor to sound like a translator of government chaos, a change agent who could make this complicated mess simple to understand. And he made the majority of the majority rules, which his enemies loved, sound like tyranny.

The applause was building.

"And so I repeat my pledge to you: if both parties in Congress agree to changes in their rules and get the government moving

again, and we can begin to address the seven crises, I promise in return to serve a single term. We will get these things done, and I
will leave.

"But if Congress does not make these changes, does not agree
to end these hidden rules that make the government dysfunctional,
and does not begin to do its job and address the crises that threaten
our future, I will go to court and challenge them. For I believe, and I
am sure the courts will concur, that these internal rules have broken
our government and are unconstitutional.

"This is a big change. The other side will throw a fit. They will
call me all kinds of names. They will claim I'm a dictator. They will
say I'm violating our system of checks and balances. But don't be
fooled. We must get the country moving again. And some simple
changes like this, which are voluntary rules of Congress, not anything in our Constitution, will go a long way."

Traynor paused. Another key transition in the speech.

"And I must ask something of you out there listening today,
too. You are not just passive citizens. For the government to begin
working again, you must do something. You must take this pledge
with me. You must demand Congress finally begin to solve these
problems. You must demand it of your representatives. The power
to make this change, to make our government work again, is in your
hands. I can ask for it. But you can make it happen. If together we
make a new pledge, a new commitment, a new vow, for a house
united, we can do it."

There was a poetic finish, and the phrase "a new commitment"
again, but Upton barely heard it. She was feeling that electric charge
of exhilaration again. She was letting herself believe.

How was it, after all these years, that speeches could make her
skin tingle and her heart soar? This parade of fools that nearly always disappointed, that was so cynical you could choke on it—how
was it that same parade could lift your soul? She would never know.

She was weeping.

18

TRAVIS CARTER

The Senate majority leader gazed out through the wavy leaded glass window in his Capitol Building office, staring at the White House a mile and a half away, seething.

The last three hours had been a goddamn cluster fuck—like a trip where you miss your flight because you left your passport at home and then find out, when you finally arrive, that your hotel room has been given away.

Carter's own people didn't even have an advance copy of Traynor's inaugural speech. The one Traynor's people handed out was Thomas Jefferson's from 1801.

Sweet Baby Jesus in Bethlehem.

That meant they had no coordinated response.

Fifty-two different senators reacting on their own. The Republican Congressional Campaign Committee shooting out text messages, praying aides might be able to get their bosses on script. It was chaos.

The goddamn liberal press was already saying the GOP had been caught off guard and didn't know what it thought.

How the hell had that happened?

Carter had been so livid he could hardly concentrate on what Traynor actually said. He had sat there on the west steps of the Capitol, freezing his nuts off, the network buzzards training their camera lenses on him waiting for angry reaction shots. One of "Sour Patch Carter's" famous grimaces.

And he had to sit there having no idea what David Merrill Traynor was going to say. A software salesman. Who knew what that amateur in all his gloried ignorance might propose? What war he might start?

During the primaries, one of Traynor's opponents had tagged the billionaire's coterie of Internet boys as the "Let's break shit and see what happens crowd." That's exactly what the speech ended up being.

There'd been a hint of Traynor's plans earlier—that tantalizing flash in December from Aggie Tucker's supposed inside source: word that if the GOP would bend, Traynor would serve only a single term. Without a clear successor, and with a Republican vice president, it was an interesting notion. But then Aggie's source had vanished, and they had no idea whether the one-term idea was a feint of some kind or a diabolical plan. After Aggie's source vanished, Traynor's people had gone silent like a teenage boy hiding things from his parents.

And then there it was. In the middle of Traynor's speech. His promise to serve a single term if Congress gave him what he wanted. If Carter agreed to relinquish most of the tools he had to control the Senate. It was a trap, not a promise.

There had been actual gasps of surprise in the crowd. Carter hated surprises. Surprises in politics were a signal of failed preparation.

The speech had been clever. Traynor had not made the GOP the enemy. He made these so-called seven crises the enemy. He never even uttered the word *Republican*. Nor did he talk policy or politics. He just talked about the crises and how they threatened America's future, and how it was time to finally face them. The picture he painted felt real to people. They recognized what happened when you were sick and it felt like you were on your own to find your cure, searching from doctor to doctor. They recognized the shuttered stores in town, all the products that said MADE IN CHINA and didn't last, and all the crumbling roads and bridges they could see on the highway. Traynor had a way of telling stories. And then, subtly, he had shifted. He had gone from painting a picture that people knew was real to talking about Washington. And he made it all sound as if the party that controlled Congress was responsible for every problem in the country. "Dour men in suits squabbling among themselves, talking about what the American people wanted, as if they actually knew them." And he made it sound as if the arcane rules of the Senate and the House, the rules Carter used to maintain order over chaos, were somehow un-American, a set of lawyer's tricks to impose one-party rule.

That son of a bitch.

He knew he shouldn't curse, even in his head. It was a crime back in Idaho to curse in front of women and children. The law was still on the books. No shit.

And now, when he finally got back to his office from the inaugural luncheon, this news. Traynor's "break shit" gang had already sent fifteen bills up to the Hill. Fifteen.

And they weren't bills at all. Carter had just read the summary from his chief of staff. These so-called bills were like something from a graduate school seminar. They threw all the problems Traynor wanted solved in Congress's lap and gave the House and Senate an absurd timetable to act on them.

Traynor's proposed legislation would allocate money to get started on problems but never defined how the programs would actually work. And he proposed the money be conditional. In Traynor's bill, more funds would be released only if the programs were proven to be effective. If Congress didn't pass something by a certain time, Traynor signaled he would declare a series of national emergencies and reallocate existing money to get started on the problems on his own.

This wasn't legislating. It was extortion.

Carter had always been good at spotting people's weaknesses, but Traynor was an enigma to him. He didn't have a feel for why people were charmed by the man's arrogance. He couldn't fathom why people mistook Traynor's recklessness for creativity.

As far as he could tell, the emperor was buck-ass naked.

They needed to get some grip on the man, find the holes in his swing. But they would. His private polling would zero in on Traynor's shortcomings. People just needed not to panic.

His personal cell was ringing. He glanced down and pushed accept.

"Governor Scott. How are you?"

"I'm worried, Mr. Majority Leader," Jeff Scott, the governor of Michigan, said.

Christ. This was just what he needed. The Blond Apostle from Grosse Point giving him shit.

"About what?"

"About you, Travis."

If Scott weren't tall and handsome, he would be working at a big-box store.

"Oh?"

"The legislature is in session here, but when they are done, I'm coming to Washington. We need better messaging and a more rapid response. I hear Traynor sent fifteen bills to the Hill in the first hour after the transition of power."

"I heard the same thing."

"What are you going to do?"

"As required by the Constitution, we will take a look at them, send them to the appropriate committees, and give them due consideration. It is Congress that makes the laws."

"You can't just shove Traynor's bills in committee and say you're studying them. It sounds like throwing dirty clothes into the hall closet so you never have to look at them."

"Good line, Governor. Can I steal it?"

"You need to come up with Republican alternatives, Travis. Good ones."

As if it were that easy. Scott was as clueless as Traynor.

"You're right, Governor. But that's not as simple as it sounds."

"Why not?"

"He's thrown a lot at us. That raises the bar. We need good answers, not empty ones, or, as you say, it'd look bad for our party."

"You've had decades to come up with answers, Travis."

Carter felt bile creeping up the back of his throat.

"When you get here to Washington, I'm sure we will appreciate your help."

"I knew you'd feel that way. I'll see you in two weeks."

Scott would arrive like cavalry in a John Ford Western, trumpet blaring, banners fluttering in the wind, a packet of half-assed solutions under his arm that he would claim he was already implementing in Michigan. Jeff Scott was interested in helping no one but Jeff Scott and his next run at the White House.

Carter tapped with two index fingers a text message to his chief of staff.

Get Sen. Burke on the phone.

Sane, wise, well liked, Senator Llewellyn Burke. In a moment Burke picked up.

"Lew? It's Travis. I need you to get your fucking governor off my back."

19

WASHINGTON, D.C.

Wednesday 17 February

PETER RENA

Hallie Jobe handed Peter Rena the file and sat down at the small table by the bay window in his office.

"Ishmael Williams," she said.

Ishmael Williams was a kid from Arkansas with a thrilling ability for eluding large men who wanted to knock him to the ground. That wondrous skill had helped Williams come in second place this past season for the Heisman Trophy for college football and made him one of three favorites to compete for the number one pick in the NFL draft two months away. But six weeks earlier, Williams had been with a group of young men, including two of his cousins, arrested for being part of a drug sales operation in Little Rock, Arkansas. Local police had expunged any record of Williams's arrest and placed him in the care of an assistant coach from the University of Arkansas instead. The NFL combine had hired Rena, Brooks & Associates to learn more—no team wanted to draft Williams without knowing the details when this, as it inevitably would, became public later. Hallie Jobe had spent the last two weeks in Little Rock interviewing everyone who knew Williams.

Political work was how the firm had made its name, but the

commercial side of the business brought in more of Rena, Brooks & Associates' revenue. Clients included companies, universities, and foundations that wanted background checks on high-profile college presidents, CEOs, and other major hires. Through contacts that had started in politics, the firm had developed a growing stream of business with sports owners who wanted vetting of athletes, draft picks, and free agents who had controversial histories. An astonishing amount of the work involved allegations of sexual assault and violence against women, or maybe just Rena was astonished by it.

Most people in the firm, however, were more moved by politics and public service, even now. Nearly everyone who worked there had started their working life in public service—the military, law enforcement, or working as staff aides in the House or Senate. It was in their blood.

For the moment at least, Peter Rena was cordoned off from that public service work. It would be better, everyone understood, if they maintained a wall between such clients and Peter.

The warning had come directly from Peter's mentor, Senator Burke, the man who had rescued Rena after his departure from the army. The man who had suggested he and Randi go into partnership. The man who had introduced him to Wendy Upton. A man Peter trusted.

It was a month now into the presidency of David Traynor, and the daring iconoclast was doing better than at least some had expected. His approval rating was slowly rising and the Republican leadership's was dropping. Polls suggested that a good many Americans were still unsure of Traynor, but only a third actually disapproved of him, a number that was low at this point. His approval rating was at 52 percent. But some surprising people had changed their minds. Former president Lee Jackson, who was a Republican, had even written an op-ed in the *Wall Street Journal* praising Traynor and calling him the Happy Disruptor.

Opponents had taken to trying to bait Traynor, famous for his temper, by going after his wife, Mariette, the former Silicon Valley executive. The First Lady had taken on rights for working women as a cause, issues that the firm right claimed were weakening the family. Traynor had kept his cool, so far.

As for Rena, he had almost begun to feel like himself again. The cyberattacks had substantially subsided. Wiley and Lupsa reported that there remained a small but steady drumbeat about him in the dark web. But Peter had ceased to be a person of much interest on the public social platforms. That could change, they said. It was not over. And Rena felt a cold reminder of that when he was not part of discussions involving certain clients at the firm.

Rena had no idea what had happened to his proposal that Vice President Upton create a bridge between herself and her former Republican colleagues in Congress. Before he had become a source of controversy, Rena had proposed himself as the go-between, but that plan, which had Traynor's approval, had fallen by the wayside. Rena didn't know if Upton had found someone else to play that role for her. It had been only a month since the inauguration, and Traynor was still acting with more abandon than most had predicted.

So Rena occupied his time primarily with three cases, the search for a new CEO by a Fortune 1000 restaurant chain, the hunt for the president of a small college, and the vetting of aspiring NFL running back Ishmael Williams.

"My read is this is a good young man," Jobe said. Her voice broke with unexpected emotion. He looked up to see the eyes inside her dark athletic face moistening. "I talked with his mother, his aunts, his cousins. He's got family caught in the life down there, but he's not part of it. He's got a mentor, an old coach, watching out for him. I think the stories are overdone."

Of all the people in the firm, Rena felt he and Jobe were most alike. They were both former military and law enforcement—Jobe a marine and an FBI agent, Rena an army investigator. They were both quiet and watchful. Yet lately Rena had wondered if this idea that he and Jobe shared some kinship was just another foolish notion he had in his head. Hallie was Black, a woman, the daughter of a Baptist minister, someone who had spent her life navigating cultures where she was an outsider. Rena was a white male in the army. She might think that he was a fool to think he knew her—or that she, a Black woman in a white male world, had ever been fully open with him.

How could he be so unsure? What other assumptions had he made—about friends, his colleagues, himself—that he should question? How much of the life he had made for himself was deluded? Even as the cyberattacks had eased, that was something he wondered about. Not having enough to do at the office didn't help. He had always been good at losing himself in his work. Maybe too good. Now that he was cut off from some of it, what was it worth to him?

Jobe could see Rena was not really listening.

"How are you and Vic?"

The question caught him off guard.

"That's direct of you."

"I'm trying to get your attention."

She got a rueful smile from him, instead.

"You'd make a good interrogator. Have you ever thought about a career in investigative work?"

"How are you and Vic?" she repeated.

"Not going to let this go, are you?"

"I don't think so."

"Officially we are not broken up. But we are not together."

"What does that mean?"

"Wow, Hallie."

"I repeat the question."

It was a very marine corps kind of intervention, Rena thought. Very direct. Pinpoint a problem and confront it.

"If I hadn't been a target of cyber bullying, I think she would have already told me to take a hike."

"I'm sorry, Peter."

He realized this was one of the most candid conversations they had ever had about his personal life.

"Very suboptimal."

"We'll see," she said, sounding hopeful. "Good men are hard to find. She might give you a second chance."

Hallie, tall, with high sculpted cheekbones and an intimidating shyness, was in her mid-thirties and still attracted to men who made her father livid and made Hallie, ultimately, miserable.

Rena said, "I think I may have already run through my second chance. Maybe my third, too."

For a moment, they didn't know what to say to each other.

"Give everything time."

"That was one of my mistakes," Rena said.

He tried to blink the thought away. "Tell me more about Ishmael Williams."

20

PITTSBURGH, PENNSYLVANIA

Monday 5 April

DAVID TRAYNOR

David Traynor was now three-quarters of the way to a hundred days.

Today, he thought, would be one of his best.

Franklin Roosevelt was first to use a century of days to measure the presidency. It was July 1933—a presidential term started in March back then, not January—and FDR had sat down for one of his fireside chats with the American people. FDR's use of radio was one of his strokes of political genius. He was the first president to understand that the new medium allowed him to speak to the American people as an intimate friend.

On his hundredth day, that day in July, FDR had looked back on all they had done together, he and the people, a little more than three months into the job.

Today, on his seventy-fifth day, David Traynor would do a little looking back himself.

He was in Pittsburgh to mark the rebuilding of a bridge that had been crumbling for forty years. His administration had rebuilt it in two months, using what they had come to call their "swarm" method, a thousand workers on a site. Traynor wanted to rebuild things so fast that people could see it happening before their eyes and talk about it.

The people, he hoped, would become his advocate.

"You need anything, sir?" asked Steve Lepler, the young man who carried his coat and attended to his personal needs on the road.

"Just tell me when it's time," Traynor said.

Then he was alone in the small changing room for bridge workers they were using as his holding room for the event. There was a second, larger break room next door where his staff was waiting. But the president had asked for a few minutes to himself. He was feeling wistful and a little odd. Introspection made him nervous generally, and self-congratulatory thoughts gave him the uneasy feeling that he might be losing his edge. Despite that, he couldn't deny being a little emotional today, a little proud. Even his wary political counselor Sterling Moss admitted that the polling numbers were good. For the moment, 57 percent of Americans approved of the job his administration was doing, a number that even Republicans couldn't dismiss. He had managed to convince some of the honorable gentlemen and gentlewomen across the aisle to vote with him more than a couple of times in the last two months. He was following his plan of giving Republicans some things they dearly wanted, even before consulting his own party. The bills he sent up to the Hill were also different, as promised, from what people were accustomed to. They gave the legislative branch a deadline to tackle a problem and a place to start—usually within Republicans' comfort zone—and didn't get mired in details. The so-called Scandinavian approach. It was hard to be opposed to legislation so minimal, but it committed the government to doing something. The Senate majority leader and Speaker of the House were having trouble keeping their party in line. The Democrats didn't love it much more—Traynor's proposed legislation seemed too vague to them and gave Republicans too much say—but they had no choice but to back him.

The public was beginning to appreciate this new swiftness, and polls indicated approval cut across demographics. The Traynor administration was ahead of its own schedule, even some of its most optimistic projections.

They'd managed to get eleven laws passed—eight of the fifteen he'd sent up on inauguration day, and three more—while a swamped Congress tried to keep up, with pressure growing not to get in the way of progress.

It was, he was learning, all very Roosevelt. Nina Shirock, the presidential historian Upton had suggested adding to the West Wing staff, had been schooling him on FDR. She was also writing an insider's history of Traynor's time in office.

Shirock had told him that Roosevelt had enacted thirteen major pieces of legislation in his first hundred days. Measures "a stricken nation in the midst of a stricken world may require," FDR had called them. The bills were all things regular people understood. They put Americans back to work, protected people's savings, and sounded like they would create prosperity. Mostly they gave people hope that things were changing for the better.

Hiring the historian was Upton's way, Traynor recognized, of trying to teach him about governing. She put more credit on experience than he did. He had resisted the idea at first. Yes, the past was prelude, he agreed, but that didn't mean not knowing it doomed you to repeat it. But he had relented eventually. His wife, Mariette, had told him he could learn something from an academic and it would make him a better president. He had found, rather than being a waste of time, that he enjoyed having Shirock around, answering his questions and telling him stories.

For her part, Upton had made herself useful in other ways, too, some of which he hadn't anticipated. The vice president watched him and told him in private where she thought he was making a misstep or could do better. Simple, direct, and sincere, she had a way of making people listen to her. She'd shaped his approach to Social

Security and on regulatory reform. She understood Republicans in ways he and his people never would. And she was more skeptical of government than he was, which was healthy. She was helping him get things done. And there were other Republicans like her, she said, who didn't hate government but were wary of it, hiding in the weeds.

"You don't really like liberals, do you?" he'd said to her last week.

"I like them fine," she'd joked. "But I think they worry too much about things they can't fix."

"Like what?"

"Inequality. And morality."

"It's your party that wants to legislate morality, not mine."

"All parties do that," she'd said. "Mine just admits it."

He had not expected a sense of humor. Upton's was droll and easy to miss, but now that he listened for it, he saw it every day.

Upton also had an ability to communicate with a sort of moral clarity, as if she kept her eye on the larger purpose of things, without being sanctimonious. She was observant and chose her words carefully and didn't use too many of them. Their pairing was becoming more of a partnership than he'd expected, even if she remained distant. She was what his sister would call a little bit of a prude.

Steve Lepler came back into the room.

"Mr. President, we're ready."

He followed the young man into the room next door. Sterling Moss was there with Quentin Phelps. They were waiting with his traveling secretary, Danny Mendoza, and some local politicians. They had a fundraiser later. Mendoza handed him a copy of his speech.

Traynor had put more than the usual into this one. Not entirely sure why.

The day after the inaugural, Moss had told him, "Narrate your presidency. People will look to you each day to tell them what you're trying to do."

Moss said he could speak directly to the people on Little Bird and TV, Y'all Post and Hellogram. "You don't need the traditional media much anymore. You can be your own narrator—in first person. You will not believe how large your voice will be."

That's what they were doing today. He was going to narrate his three-quarter mark to a hundred days.

"Tell them how we're doing. Give yourself a grade," Moss said. "Then everyone else will be annotating your version."

Of course, there was much he couldn't say, or wouldn't. That was the whole point of being your own narrator, wasn't it? What you left out was as important as what you put in. He'd learned that back in the start-up days—when you often were faking it so bad you had to omit 90 percent.

But this speech had been hard to write. He had stayed up all night working on the draft his writers had given him, poring over it at a desk in his personal study in the Residence.

"What do you think of it?" he asked Moss, meaning the speech.

"It's sincere," Moss said.

Was that a criticism?

"Yeah, who knew?" Traynor joked.

He felt a little light-headed. "There water?" he asked.

"Here, sir," Lepler said, handing him a metal thermos—Traynor had banned plastic bottles at the White House.

He drank ravenously.

Seventy-five days. Eleven new laws. They'd moved on taxes, infrastructure, and regulatory relief, using targeted bipartisan bills aimed at small problems but promising more—"Iterative legislating" they called it. They'd gone to vulnerable Republicans, asked what they wanted, and given it to them—in some cases over Democratic objections. They'd set up bipartisan commissions on entitlements, on waste, and on duplicative programs. And he'd promised again, in a dramatic speech at Mount Vernon, to serve a single term if the GOP would cooperate. Some fool had called it "blackmail," and even most GOP voices had laughed at that. But it wasn't blackmail. He had boxed them in.

Meanwhile his administration was light-years ahead on its own secret projects. His favorite was the classified battery program. Kim Matsuda had five companies engaged, ramping up at a dazzling pace. Clearly she had had this plan in mind for a year or more. There was no way she could have moved so fast otherwise. He believed they might have a major breakthrough six months from now. When he announced that he had already leaped years ahead on climate change, without working through Congress, for a few billion dollars no one even knew about, it would be the coup de grâce. There would be no telling what leverage he would have at that point.

"Time," Quentin Phelps said.

"Okay," Traynor said.

They moved out of the holding room and headed outside.

The podium was set on a small platform with the bridge they had rebuilt in the background, overlooking the river's gorge.

Downtown Pittsburgh was a picture-perfect background, the three rivers converging at the city center into a single camera angle.

He felt a little dizzy.

There were marks showing him where to stand. The mayor, a gnome-like woman reputed to be so competent even her enemies sought her counsel, was introducing him. Behind her stood the governor of Pennsylvania, the cadaverous grandson of a beloved governor and the son of a popular senator. Traynor thought the man dim.

"Today is not just about a bridge in Pittsburgh," the plucky mayor began. "It is about hope and renewal. It is about promises kept. It is about a bridge to a better future."

"Mr. President, you all right?"

It was the lanky governor. Mike somebody. O'Conner. He had his hand on Traynor's back.

"Mr. President?"

But the hand wasn't on his back. It had him by the belt.

"Sir?"

Traynor must have listed forward and come close to bumping into the mayor as she was talking. Or maybe he had almost fallen. Whatever it was, Mike O'Conner had grabbed his belt to keep him upright.

He didn't feel that good.

"I'm. Ahhh."

Must be dehydrated.

"Aa."

The words kept slipping away as they traveled from his brain to his lips. He really felt pretty bad. His head was spinning.

He tried to explain. "My head . . . I . . . Dizzy . . ."

He was falling again.

"Oh my God."

"Mr. President!"

He heard people screaming.

AMERICANS WOULD LATER HAIL THE EFFORTS OF THE LEAD agent on Traynor's Secret Service detail, Ed Thorsen. First to reach the president, Thorsen's ministrations were caught on camera in their entirety. Thorsen kneeling over the stricken president, gently cradling his head, administering CPR, they would become the iconic images of that day, repeated on a billion phones, on millions of web pages, in the social stream of virtually everyone on the planet.

"Excalibur down," Thorsen could be heard saying into his radio. "Repeat, Excalibur down. Code Nine. I have no pulse."

"Copy."

"I have no external action. Repeat. No shots fired. No external action. I think Excalibur is having a health emergency."

"EMS thirty-five seconds."

They'd positioned first responders, present at any event with the president, out of the TV shot. But given the limited access to the special platform they had built to get the river in the background, the EMS team was stationed on the other side of the holding room and up the makeshift stairs.

The governor, whom Traynor thought so little of, was also attempting resuscitation.

The charismatic mayor, who had been speaking, was traumatized. She held her hand over her mouth and kept repeating "Oh my God."

At a certain point Steve Lepler took his jacket off and placed it under Traynor's head.

Quent Phelps was on the phone.

Agent Thorsen shouted at the president to keep him conscious. "David! Stay with me. Mr. President!"

EMS arrived.

"David, stay with me."

Thorsen told them what he knew and that he'd found no pulse.

LATER, THE WHITE HOUSE STAFF HISTORIAN WOULD NOTE, NO U.S. president, including John Kennedy, had ever died so publicly. And no U.S. president had their death replayed, shared, and viewed hundreds of millions of times online in the first hour after its occurrence, mixed with so much conspiracy, animus, and grief.

PART II

The Tools of the Living

= 21 =

WENDY UPTON

At the moment the Constitution of the United States called for the transfer of power to a new leader, Wendy Upton was in Tucson, having lunch at a restaurant owned by friends.

A cordon of Secret Service agents entered the private room where her party was seated. The detail's lead agent bent down and whispered into the ear of her chief of staff, Gil Sedaka.

"Madame Vice President, I need a moment," Sedaka said, rising from the table. The agents ushered Sedaka and the vice president to an alcove by the kitchen.

"The president has collapsed in Pittsburgh," Upton's lead agent, Leslie Decker, said. "Though this has not been announced publicly, he has just been pronounced dead by doctors at the hospital. It appears to be a stroke or heart attack. We need to return to Washington immediately."

Before Upton could respond, Sedaka suggested, "Let's get you sworn in right here. Now. So there's no gap. So there's continuity of government." The legal term.

Then he whispered: "And no one raises any crazy constitutional doubts about party. Or anything else."

Upton looked at Gil and nodded. She was numb, but the look on Gil's face, anxious but determined, began to help her focus. She was still too much in shock to register any emotion properly, but she was not afraid.

She had never really contemplated being president. People had urged her to run, but she had never allowed herself to seriously imagine what it would feel like. Now she had no time to consider whether she was ready or not. It was simply happening to her.

And so the forty-seventh president of the United States, the first woman president in U.S. history, was given the oath of office by Pima County magistrate Polly Rodriguez at Rebecca's Downtown Kitchen Bar in Tucson, Arizona, at 1:27 Mountain Time, seventy-eight minutes after David Traynor was pronounced dead by doctors in Pittsburgh. A local TV station shot video. A photographer from the *Arizona Star* took photos. The restaurant's patrons, asked to step outside, lined the windows along the sidewalk and looked in. They could see through the glass the familiar pantomime of a presidential swearing in. There was shock, people taking video, and a smattering of uneasy applause.

Sedaka and the new president were led out through the restaurant's kitchen. Her motorcade, now enlarged by the presence of local law enforcement, drove to a secure facility at the airport. There Upton and Sedaka waited. She had asked some people from her old Arizona staff to fly to Washington with her and she didn't want to sit there waiting on the plane. Too cramped. Too LBJ. Gil was staring at her. They had known each other for decades; been young Senate aides together. It was Gil who had urged her to seriously consider Traynor's unlikely VP offer. She'd considered it political suicide. Now she was president.

Gil's expression had changed. Unlike a half hour ago, it was etched now with anxiety. The moment had sunk in, and he was contemplating all that would follow. Seeing Gil's fear, however, seemed to snap Upton into focus. Her mind seemed gloriously sharp, and she felt as if she understood, in that instant, what was required of her. She could see it—the next few days, even the next month—as if they were luminously clear, like the horizon above the ocean on a cloudless day.

"Gil, call the White House historian and find out everything Lyndon Johnson did when Kennedy was killed. Hour by hour, the first few days. And Truman, when FDR died. And Teddy Roosevelt, when it was McKinley." Protocol and precedent, she was thinking. They would reassure the country—and the world—that America had been through this before and survived. That was job one, to reassure the country.

She began making calls through the White House switchboard: first to the First Lady, Mariette Traynor, then congressional leaders and cabinet members. When her plane was ready to return to Washington—any aircraft carrying the president of the United States becomes Air Force One by default—she and Sedaka had the beginning of a plan. Upton had summoned some trusted staff from her former Senate Arizona office to join her, including her closest friend from law school at the University of Arizona. By the time they landed at Andrews four hours later, the White House switchboard had logged more than 40,000 incoming phone calls and 180,000 emails from people around the country.

She issued her first official presidential orders from the air. She would ask Traynor's full cabinet and most of the West Wing staff to remain, including chief of staff Quentin Phelps. Sedaka would become his deputy. The new Upton administration must look like the old Traynor administration as much as possible—for now.

While still in flight, she crafted a brief public statement, influenced by those of the vice presidents before her who had inherited the office while wearing black. It was seven sentences:

"This is a tragic day for people all over the world. The grief Mariette Traynor and her family suffer is everyone's suffering. Their sorrow and their love is our sorrow. Let that sorrow and love unite us. Our task now is simple: to be our best. That is what our country needs from all Americans today. For my part, I pledge to honor the American people, our country, this office, and the memory of David Traynor. May this sad day be remembered in all the days to come for the grace and courage America showed the world."

"Release this now," she said, "but I need to say something on camera when we land. People need to see they still have a president."

Sedaka called Bill McGrath, the GOP consultant in Washington who had helped them fight off the threats made against Upton the year before—another Republican, like Upton, who found himself adrift in a party he barely recognized.

"Yes, a statement on camera when you land," McGrath told Sedaka. "On the tarmac with reporters, something memorable and brief. But take no questions. She should not formally address the nation as president until after David Traynor's funeral. Let the country grieve. When that's over, then she points the way. Not before."

Sedaka was struck by how much confidence consultants—who did not actually have to say these words on camera—always had in their advice.

"I can help draft something," McGrath said, "and send it to you before you land."

After landing and saying a few words on the tarmac, Upton went first to the White House to see Mariette Traynor. The First Lady had been visiting schoolchildren in Washington when she learned of her husband's death. She had quickly retreated to the White House and remained in seclusion. Now the two women met alone in the mansion's private rooms. Upton noticed the First Lady had put on a new dress and fresh makeup.

"We should make a plan," Upton said. "For David's sake."

Four days of official mourning, she suggested, with a state funeral in the Capitol on the final day. Mariette, dazed but still herself, agreed.

"You should stay here, in the White House, until the funeral is over."

For the rest of her life Wendy Upton would remember Mariette Traynor's desolate response.

"You can have this place," she said. "I'll leave tomorrow."

"No," Upton said. It came out more sharply than she wished. Somehow, however, she was sure: as long as David Traynor's body was in the city, his widow, and not his unelected successor, must occupy the White House. The country would never forgive her if she evicted Mariette from her home. "I'm sorry. Please. Stay here until you head to Colorado."

"I've known nothing good here," Mariette Traynor said. This woman, so competent, so accomplished in her life in business, was a public ornament in the White House, and had at times been targeted by people who wanted to attack her husband.

"I hate politics," Mariette Traynor said. "Almost every word is a lie. But I loved David. Now I just want to take his body home."

"Just a few more days," said Upton. "Please."

The First Lady pushed a discreet button on the side table and an aide appeared through a door. The aide was there to escort the new president from the room. She had been dismissed. Mariette rose, signaling that Upton should leave. The new president reluctantly stood but she did not move. Then she heard Mariette Traynor say, "All right."

"Thank you."

The long motorcade next made its way to Quentin Phelps's house in Chevy Chase, Maryland, just outside D.C. It was a gesture, she knew, her going to him. It should have been the other way around.

Phelps, in torn blue jeans, a look in his eyes a thousand miles away, stood in the corner of his living room, as far from this moment and Upton as he could get.

"I need you to stay, Quent. David would want it, too."

Phelps turned away from her, like a boy who couldn't bear the idea of something he'd been asked to do.

"For his presidency to have meaning," she said.

Then, though it was unlike her, Upton crossed the room and wrapped her arms around him. They held each other for a long time, his surprise turning to tears. Before today they had never done more than shake hands.

She felt guilty exploiting his grief. But she did need him. So did the country. For the moment, she believed, her needs and the country's were the same.

But she wasn't really begging Quentin Phelps in order to preserve David Traynor's legacy. She was worried about something else. If Phelps fled from the White House, much of the West Wing staff and even some cabinet members might follow, and that would frighten the country even more. Turmoil was her enemy. She needed Traynor's people around her to project that the government, and by implication the country, was stable. She didn't leave Phelps's house until he agreed.

THE NEXT FEW DAYS WERE A BLUR, ENDLESS AND TOO SHORT. They had to jump-start a new presidency and plan the ceremonial end of the old one.

She also had to win over Traynor's people and decide who among them she trusted. She felt like a stepmother marrying into a large and suspicious family. She found herself relying on an unexpected group—a few of Traynor's top aides, some of her own, and a couple close friends whose judgment she trusted. There were Phelps and Sterling Moss; Gil, naturally; and two others she kept turning to: Senator Llewellyn Burke of Michigan, the calm bipartisan-minded backscenes player; and Bill McGrath, the consultant Gil had called from Air Force One. She also began to include Randi Brooks, the political fixer, who seemed to know what needed to be known about everyone in Washington and who had no problem being candid. She had asked for Brooks's partner, Peter Rena, but Gil had said the former soldier was still "radioactive." Upton never mentioned to Brooks that she had intended to use Rena as a private bridge to Republicans, but that the cyberattacks had quashed the plan. She had never found a consistent or adequate replacement. She had requested that Peter keep it confidential. She assumed Brooks knew nothing about it.

Until Traynor was buried, McGrath had cautioned her that small symbolic gestures were the only kind people wanted her to make. But they should be frequent, so that people knew she was making decisions. She would keep Traynor's desk, "the Roosevelt," built for Teddy in 1902, rather than replace it with the older and more impressive "Resolute" most of her predecessors preferred. The Traynors' beloved photographer, Toni Albion, would stay. So would his press secretary, a glib, witty redhead named Siobhan Walsh.

Mariette Traynor's people planned the funeral, just as Kennedy's family had done for Jack. But the ceremonies inevitably would reflect on her, Upton knew. When Mariette asked an obnoxious Hollywood movie director to help plan everything, McGrath and Moss found common ground resenting him. Hollywood people, they agreed, were usually naive and heavy-handed about politics. Upton still felt like jumping out of her skin at the way people fretted about the symbolism of her every movement. She wanted to govern the country, she thought, not stage a four-day movie—let alone a four-year one.

Traynor's body lay in state for two days in the U.S. Capitol Rotunda to allow Americans to say farewell. A state funeral in the National Cathedral on Wisconsin Avenue. Then the funeral procession wended its way back down to Pennsylvania Avenue to the White House, around the Mall and back up Independence Avenue, a route that allowed an estimated eight hundred thousand more citizens to say goodbye. A horse-drawn carriage pulled the casket, followed by

a riderless stallion. The family trailed on foot, with the new president and the former First Lady, the two most influential women in
the country, side by side, occasionally clasping hands.

The homages to Kennedy's funeral were obvious, but the
procession didn't cross the bridge to Arlington. Traynor had never
served in uniform and the family wanted him buried in Colorado.
So the procession turned at the Lincoln Memorial and concluded its
journey at Union Station. From there a special train bore the late
president's body slowly west. Americans lined the tracks to say
farewell, draping flags on railway bridges, following the train in their
cars where the roads neared the tracks, standing ten deep where the
tracks allowed them. The journey recalled the final rail trips home
of Lincoln and FDR—just as the Hollywood movie director had
predicted. And somehow the pictures suggested that the nation in
grief had returned, at least for a moment, to what were remembered
as simpler times, when we did not hate each other so much.

22

WASHINGTON, D.C.

Monday 12 April

WENDY UPTON

As the country mourned, political Washington plotted. Traynor's aides had wanted the funeral to boost the fallen president's popularity in order to tie Upton more firmly to his agenda. This was still "David's presidency," she overheard Moss declare to Phelps. It wouldn't be "hers until she won herself an election." In private, Republicans urged her to end the most brazen elements of Traynor's tumultuous agenda. One congressman, a pleasant man from Indiana, publicly suggested it was God's will that Traynor had died and that she should abide by that will and put the nation on "a corrective course." He refused to apologize amid the controversy that followed.

The defeated GOP presidential nominee, Michigan Governor Jeff Scott, was omnipresent on television. "The president should now remake her cabinet and appoint an even number of Republican and Democrat members," he declared. "And let them govern by consensus—to finally make good on Traynor's promise of bipartisanship."

Everyone had counsel for her, about everything, from her clothes to a potential vice president. The Internet vibrated like a radioactive pool. "Proof Upton murdered the president with KGB-supplied poison." "Why the new president should refuse to serve and call for a new election." "Six things Upton must do to prove her legitimacy." "Upton associates involved in assassination of Traynor." A cyber forensics team from the National Security Agency delivered a daily report on the conspiracy theories. The briefing included which of the theories were produced by bots rather than real people, which were managed by foreign state-agents, and the virality of each.

"Forget all that," Phelps advised her. "You have to answer just one question, the same one David did. How do you govern when the government is broken?"

They were sitting in the Oval Office the afternoon following the funeral. She nodded to Phelps that she understood. But she recognized what her inherited chief was trying to do. He wanted her to repeat the threats to congressional Republicans that Traynor had made: the GOP leadership had to end its internal rules, which blocked compromise and bipartisan governing. He also wanted her to repeat Traynor's promise to serve a one-term presidency if the lawmakers agreed—and sue if they did not.

Phelps and Traynor had been convinced this threat of an outright war was the only way to break the ropes that were strangling the government, enforcing party hegemony and crushing any hope of congressional compromise. But Upton wasn't ready to make that threat. The problem with David's approach, she thought, was that the obstacles weren't as simple as Traynor defined them. Nor would they be as easy to sweep away. The presidency and the state of the country weren't a company you launched and then sold to someone else— with an exit strategy and money at the end. The presidency was your final moment in public life, your legacy. Your last act. The only exit strategy was history's judgment.

David Traynor had risen to power out of nowhere, a businessman who turned himself into a celebrity and a sports team owner because he was bored and, at fifty, bored again, into a change-management populist who promised to fix broken government. In the few months she and Traynor had known each other well, she had begun to think David's greatest strength might have been his pragmatism. He had been open to suggestions from all sides, in part because he had no interest in the old political feuds and no allegiances to old policies. From his background in start-ups, he believed in experimentation and learning from failure. Had he lived, those qualities would have been sorely tested. Now that he was passing into myth, they seemed like a promise unfulfilled. In the six days since his death, his approval rating had risen by twenty-five points. Americans had come to admire David Traynor in death as they never had in life.

And it was his myth she was inheriting.

Senator Lewellyn Burke's counsel rang in her ears. "Of course, you have to promise to keep Traynor's agenda." Everyone who ever inherited the presidency after a death pledged that. "But the only way you can really succeed as president is if, at some point, you begin to move away from that pledge. Eventually you have to do what you believe. But not yet."

Of course, that had to be true, but it wasn't as easy as it sounded. What did she believe? What did she want to accomplish? Once you are president, that stops being a hypothetical question. And the answer becomes infinitely more complicated.

A day earlier, Upton had summoned the climate scientist Kim Matsuda to the White House. She wanted to know what was happening with Traynor's classified program to invent a new battery that would store the power of the sun, his classified Hail Mary scheme to jump-start a new American renewable energy program in secret.

She knew there was pressure from at least some inside the intelligence community to get their funds back. The odds were high that someone, at some point, would leak the program's existence to the press, framed as a scandal, a reckless and possibly illegal scheme by the Silicon Valley amateur president.

Upton needed to know what was happening and whether there were any signs of success. For Traynor had been right about one thing: the best way to protect the program was for it to succeed. She invited three others to join the meeting: Quentin Phelps, Gil Sedaka, and Cheryl Kingsley from the White House counsel's office. Upton wanted some sense of the plan's legality.

Matsuda sat down on one of the floral sofas in the Oval Office in front of the presidential desk and looked at Upton, her expression betraying her doubts about Traynor's successor.

"Tell me about the battery program."

Matsuda handed each of them a three-page memo. Upton, glancing at it, asked for the highlights. They had made substantial progress, Matsuda declared, especially given that it was only a little over two months since the program's launch. They'd identified five different companies around the country doing the best work on flow batteries, four in California and one in Colorado. All five had begun to ramp up operations.

She mentioned the companies, their slight differences in approach, and how quickly each had grown.

"How is the money coming to them?" Upton asked. In the Senate, her committee work had involved energy and natural resources, so she knew the process of making federal grants as well as anyone.

Some funds came as federal grants, Matsuda said, some in the form of contracts. If one or more of the companies showed real promise, the second phase might involve the government taking an ownership stake. For now, to keep things low profile, none of the original investors in any of these companies had been asked to leave.

Matsuda was not able, however, to tell her precisely how much money had been spent.

The president was now more worried than she had been when the meeting started.

"Are any of these investors foreign?" she asked.

"They're venture capital funds," said Matsuda, with a glance at Quentin Phelps. "Is there foreign money involved? Almost certainly—given the level of foreign money in venture capital."

Matsuda was a scientist, not a financier. But Quentin Phelps knew this world. And Upton had the sense he seemed to know the details of Traynor's favorite program, too.

She asked for more specifics and wasn't very pleased with the answers. Matsuda knew the science here but seemed to have left the companies in many ways to their own devices. The level of oversight sounded thin. This felt like the government throwing money around recklessly, not funding a classified project.

Upton glanced through the memo. It told her little more than Matsuda had just offered verbally. "I'd like more detail," she said after reading it through. "On the science. The approaches of each company. Why they were chosen. The level of security in the program. If it's classified, we need it to be kept secret. Something about the CEOs. And the investors."

Phelps shifted in his chair. "Madam President, I can tell you that in David Traynor's mind this was the single most important initiative of his presidency. Finally addressing the climate crisis was the centerpiece of making government functional again. I think he might have told you this himself. If you want to keep faith with his vision, we need to act on climate and do it now. The program may be two months old, but it was years in the planning. If you are considering pulling out now, after the groundwork we have laid, that would set us back years. I have to say, if you were to step away from this, that would give me pause."

The three sheets of paper that Matsuda had given them were shaking slightly in Phelps's hand. His anger had risen quickly, almost overtaking him, but his message was unmistakable. David Traynor's best friend and chief of staff, whom she had begged to remain at his post to keep her fragile credibility with his party intact, was giving her an ultimatum.

The words of her first mentor in politics, Senator Thurman Morgan, echoed in her mind. He often told her, "Your job as a leader is to not lose your temper. Especially when the people around you are behavin' badly. 'Cause that will only make them behave worse. You need to be the one cool head. Remember that."

Her job was to not get mad.

She couldn't count how many times she had recalled those words in the last twenty-five years, watching people accustomed to having their way lose their tempers, especially when others were attempting bipartisan work and tenuous coalitions. "Your job is to not lose your temper." For the next many months, until her presidency was her own, she would have to hold Morgan's admonition close.

"I understand, Quent. But I'd like to take a closer look. David may have known details that I do not. And now it is my responsibility to know them."

"Of course, Madam President," Phelps said.

"I want a detailed report, Kim. Can you do it in three days? Spare nothing. I'll read every word. Don't overthink it. Just tell me everything you can."

23

RANDI BROOKS

Five days earlier, the day after David Traynor died, President Upton had asked Randi Brooks to visit.

Upton was still living in the vice president's mansion then, waiting for Mariette Traynor to leave the city with her husband's body. Peter was not invited. Though the cyberattacks had died down, her partner was still controversial enough that public figures in Washington were uncomfortable with him in the room.

"Thanks for coming," Upton said.

"How can I help?"

The new president's smile was already weary, Randi thought.

"I need people I can trust," Upton had said. She swiveled her head and whispered, "There aren't that many around."

It seemed a shocking admission, Brooks thought, and she listened with growing surprise as Upton proceeded to ask Brooks searching questions about Washington and about the people around David Traynor. Then she asked something else Brooks hadn't expected.

What kind of president did Randi think she should be?

Full stop.

What a strange query, especially from Upton, this strong, quiet woman who always seemed to know her own mind.

"Can I reframe your question?" Brooks said.

"Please."

"If you could do one thing as president, one accomplishment you would risk everything for, what would it be?"

Upton didn't answer right away, and Brooks said, "Okay, if you can't pick one, make it three."

Upton laughed.

"It's harder to choose once you're actually president," Upton said. "Suddenly the question is real and the answer feels like a commitment."

Randi smiled.

"And now I have to imagine the price I would pay. The deals I would have to make. What am I willing to give up? How much of my soul and for what? It begins to feel like a Faustian bargain."

Randi had never felt as close to this woman as Peter did. Rena and Upton had similar personalities. They were both shy and controlled. Randi was not. She lacked that control and connected with people by being open with them. She wondered now, how many people Upton might be having this type of conversation with. Not many, she figured. The new president was still surrounded by Traynor's people, largely by choice, and there weren't many she knew well. Traynor wasn't even in the ground yet. And there weren't a lot of women in David Traynor's White House. Upton didn't have that many senior people she was close to anyway. In the Senate, she relied mostly on her old chief of staff, Gil Sedaka. Most of her team from back then were young, part of the changing Senate parade.

"You still haven't answered me," Brooks said, surprised to hear herself teasing the new president of the United States. Something about Upton invited candor.

Maybe Upton shouldn't answer it, Randi had thought then. Presidents need to remain mysterious, even to their staffs. Predictability in politics is weakness.

But she had wanted Upton to hear the question.

Upton had given her an introspective look. "That's what the world is asking about me now, isn't it? Who is Wendy Upton? This accidental president. The first woman in the White House. From the wrong party."

The press coverage had been full of slapped-together pseudo-psychological profiles, many of them, Brooks thought, laced with not-so-hidden flashes of misogyny. One profile had called her "an aloof, cautious, and perhaps deeply repressed woman." An influential conservative magazine had warned its readers to remember that "the most important act of her political career was her betrayal of her party and everything she supposedly believed." It made it sound as if she were some kind of adulterous wife.

Even the pieces intended as sympathetic seemed to Brooks to belie sexist double standards she was disappointed but not surprised to see. The *Washington Tribune* had called her "a strong-willed woman who can appear deceptively delicate." A strong-willed woman—as if women were naturally weak so strength should be commented on. Deceptively delicate—as if her looks were a disguise or a trap.

People always called Upton a moderate because she didn't align with GOP orthodoxy, but nothing about Upton struck Brooks as moderate or uncertain. If anything, she thought, Upton felt things too intensely, so much so she was unable to bend to what others expected of her. And apparently Upton had been that way from childhood. When she was sixteen, orphaned by her parents' death in an automobile accident, Upton had sued the government for the right to raise her ten-year-old sister.

Now Upton was an orphan again, Brooks thought, a woman without a party in her own administration. She was not an easy person to know, and that would hurt her.

The country would need to trust her. To do that, they had to feel they knew her. To Brooks, that would be one of Upton's biggest challenges.

THE AFTERNOON FOLLOWING DAVID TRAYNOR'S FUNERAL, UP-ton summoned Brooks again, but this time she invited Peter Rena, too. They were escorted to the Map Room, which was technically in the Residence, free of press and off the formal presidential schedule. Mariette Traynor was still on the train with her husband's body heading to Colorado.

Waiting for them they found Gil Sedaka and Upton and two more empty chairs.

"I have a job for you," the president said after they had settled into them.

"I thought I was damaged goods," Rena answered with a glance at Sedaka. It was Sedaka, Brooks knew, who after the cyberattacks two months ago had put a stop on Upton's plans to bring in Rena and Brooks to vet Traynor's appointees.

"Let's not worry about that anymore," said Upton. "Not for this." A pause to let feelings cool. "Do you know someone named Kim Matsuda?"

"Traynor's special deputy on climate," Brooks said.

"Yes," said Upton. "And what I am about to tell you is classified. Gil has checked your security clearances from the Nash years. As president I am officially reading you into this program."

Then the president told them about the extraordinary secret diversion of billions in classified funding into a major push to invent a new way of storing renewable energy. In a year, if the program were to succeed, they could begin to move the power grid off carbon and accelerate the move of cars to electric as well.

"The whole adventure is wildly expensive, high risk, and high reward. But if it succeeds, it could make up for decades of wasted time." Upton paused again. "I need you two to tell me if the whole thing is crazy."

"Madam President, if you don't mind, what exactly does that mean?" Brooks asked.

"I need to know whether this program is secure."

"From what?" Brooks asked.

"From bad actors stealing the technology. From incompetence. From becoming a scandal that could unravel my presidency. I need a pair of eyes I trust."

Brooks leaned back in her chair. Peter was quiet, listening.

"So, I think I have a couple questions about these batteries," Brooks said.

Upton smiled. "I can imagine."

Brooks asked about the science first, and the president walked them through it with impressive command of the technical details. When she was finished, the president said, "If Matsuda's right, and we add enough solar panels on federal property, in theory we could build a new natural energy power grid. We could jump-start a new domestic industry around battery production and solar energy. And in about five years, we could reduce our carbon emissions by a third. In theory." Upton drew a breath and leveled her gaze at both visitors. "But if it fails, it will mean wasting billions and probably starting a war with Congress. Even if it works, it may be against the law. And, given that I am an accidental president and have no political base of my own, it could get me impeached."

Upton swiveled a glance at Sedaka. Brooks got the distinct impression the president's closest aide hated this project.

The president went on. "There is no justification for doing this in secret if the technology isn't secure from our enemies. And no justification for doing it at all if it can't succeed."

At long last Peter finally said something. Even by his standards the boy seemed quiet, almost stormy. Randi had been wondering when her partner would finally engage.

"I'm not sure we're the right people to help you," he said. "We're not capable of judging the science here."

But Upton waved the point away. "We've already judged the science. I need you to judge the people and the program's security." She waited a beat and added more. "I also need you because you're outsiders. If I ask the FBI to do this, it will leak. And if I ask the national security community, it's their money getting diverted."

Peter gave Upton a piercing look with those dark eyes of his, the ones she had seen so many times convey to people: don't lie to me.

"I'm also persona non grata," he said. "A wife beater. And a liar."

"So I've heard," Upton said, not intending it to be funny.

"You really want me?"

"I trust you, Peter. And without trying to sound dramatic, there aren't many people I can say that about at the moment."

The silence was awkward. Upton brushed something from her skirt. "David could be brilliant," Upton said. "He could also be reckless. Sometimes he was both. I need to know which one this is."

She started to get up but apparently thought of something else, and settled back in her chair. "Until last week, to most Americans I was a curiosity—that woman from the other party, the silent one, three steps back and two steps to the left." Randi felt Upton's intensity and wondered if she also sensed loneliness. "Now everyone knows my name and they're all wondering the same thing: Does she know what she's doing? Help me here to find out if I know what I'm doing."

Then she stood.

"Start tomorrow. Put everything else you have on hold. Consider it an order from an old friend, who happens now to be your commander in chief. You have two weeks. Maybe three. Faster is better. Right now I have a speech to prepare for."

24

WENDY UPTON

Wendy Upton's first presidential address to the nation lasted thirteen minutes.

Lyndon Johnson had addressed a joint session of Congress, so eager was he to demonstrate a government united. Upton wanted something more intimate, but she also wanted real people in the room with her, not just a teleprompter. So she asked friends to join her in the Oval Office, the first time anyone had done that for a presidential address.

"I would give anything tonight not to be talking to you like this. That I am talking to you reflects one of the great strengths of our nation.

"We have lost the man you chose to lead us. Words cannot express our sadness.

"But nor, too, can any words convey the depth of our determination. There is a conviction rising in the country tonight, a will to continue David Traynor's vision. And his vision was good and simple. It was to make our government begin to work again for everyone—and to take on, finally, challenges that our government has put off for too long.

"It falls on all of us now—you in your homes and me in this great house that belongs to you—to make that vision real.

"Some will wonder if our nation possesses the strength. Who see these terrible days in America as a blow that will only weaken a country that often appears divided.

"But those who doubt us do not understand us.

"We are a nation richer, wiser, and stronger because of our differences. Not in spite of them.

"For we are Americans not by accident. We are Americans because we share belief in a common idea and are joined in a common cause. Unlike anywhere in the world.

"That shared idea, enshrined in our founding declaration, is that all people are created equal and thus should be so under law. And as such we should be free and self-governing and share in our sovereignty together. Thomas Jefferson called this idea 'These Truths.'

"We call this idea democracy, and it is America's gift to humanity, our great experiment that has lifted the world.

"Our common cause is that we should all work to make this idea real. To do so, we must understand that our differences unite us and give us strength. E pluribus unum. Out of many, one. Because we are many, Americans of many cultures and free, the only limits to what we can achieve are those we impose on ourselves.

"And so tonight we are tested again.

"Robert Kennedy said tragedy is the tool that gives us wisdom. Let this tragedy make us wise.

"On the first day of his presidency, David Traynor told us of seven crises we Americans have left unattended. On that day, he said, we were resetting our course, taking up the challenge of those unattended crises. It was a moment of renewal and strength."

She went through the issues, staying light on policy, but affirming the fallen leader's promises. They would rebuild the nation's shared spaces—its bridges, roads, parks, and public places. They would change how laws were made so problems were addressed in time, one step at a time, and prudently. They would remake a broken tax system, which had become rigged and unfair. They would confront racial injustice with a fresh and systemic approach. They would, at long last, tackle the problem of the planet in distress, heeding finally the unmistakable warnings, as if God were sending them, burning our forests, unleashing hurricanes of ever greater intensity, rising the seas, washing away our shores. And by doing so she would also return the jobs we had sent abroad.

"And in working together, we will find each other again. We will believe in each other again. We will renew our shared idea and our common cause.

"Tonight, after mourning his loss, we pick up his challenge. We will face those crises with new wisdom, new unity, and a stronger resolve, deepened not weakened by these terrible days of sorrow.

"I pledge to you tonight—and ask you to pledge with me in return—that we rededicate ourselves to David Traynor's vision to renew our great experiment. Let us gain strength by celebrating the shared idea and common cause that unite us.

"After the deaths of so many soldiers at Gettysburg, Abraham Lincoln called on Americans to consecrate the lives of those who died by helping form 'a more perfect union.' Let us today be again and forever at work on making that more perfect union. And let us pledge tonight that David Merrill Traynor did not begin this journey for us in vain. Let his life and his death mark the start of something, not the end. Let the tragedy of his death give us the wisdom to finish his work."

She ended with words from a hymn:

"Shine through the gloom and point me to the skies.
Heaven's morning breaks and earth's vain shadows flee;
In life, in death, O Lord, abide with me."

Then she surprised the production team by getting up from behind the presidential desk and walking to the people sitting in the
room. Viewers at home could hear the applause from inside the Oval
Office; the camera pulled back to show people standing, some weeping, Upton shaking hands, accepting praise.

"You planned that surprise," Gil Sedaka accused her.

"Madam President, may I say, that was just . . . effing awesome,"
David Traynor's press secretary, Siobhan Walsh, announced. People laughed.

People moved to the East Room, where a small reception followed. Two Republican senators, Aggie Tucker of Texas and his
best friend, Richard Bakke of South Carolina, pulled the president
aside. Bakke had always been a rival of Upton's in the Senate.

"We still gonna have a way to talk together?" Tucker asked.

"I think we better," Upton said.

Senator Bakke, a brilliant man whose intellect did not extend
often to situational awareness, asked, "And what about Traynor's
pledge? A one-term presidency? And sticking his nose in our conference's rules? You abide by those, Madam President?"

Wendy Upton had always possessed what her mother had called a
Mona smile, an unreadable curve of her mouth that could be pleasant
but vague—like Leonardo's *Mona Lisa*. She also had perfected
over the years a little frown, which her staff would later come to
call her "Senator Disappointed" face. Both could be ironic. Both
were ways of communicating without words. Upton gave Aggie and
Bakke a Mona.

"Madam President, we're gonna need to know."

"Should I be a one-term president?" she said innocently. "Senators, President Traynor thought that threat would help him achieve
his goals. Will it help me achieve mine?"

She could see the Speaker of the House approaching, followed
by Travis Carter, a man who was relentless and observant and forgot nothing. She needed to escape.

"I couldn't possibly tell you tonight, can I? We just buried the president yesterday and I introduced myself to the country tonight. That seems enough for one day."

"Of course," Aggie said with a bow.

Upton glanced across the room and saw her sister, Emily. "If you will excuse me," she said. "I'm afraid I have abandoned the junior senator from my state to the clutches of my sister, who I think qualifies as an angry constituent. If I do not rescue him, I may have more trouble on my hands than either of you can give me."

And fled before the majority leader arrived.

25

ROANOKE, VIRGINIA

STEPH MYERS

Steph Myers turned off the TV.

"I thought it was moving," his wife, Gail, said.

Steph said nothing.

"Didn't you think so? She seemed sincere. I like her."

Sure, she seemed sincere? They always seem sincere. That's their job, Steph thought. They're actors reading a script. The question we have to decode is who wrote their script.

He'd seen that phrase in the chat room 5Click and wrote it down. That's what you had to do. Decode. Unpack. Not the way he'd been taught in school. Not even the way he taught his kids "media literacy" in his seventh grade social studies class. There was a new literacy now. And he was helping to write the curriculum, a curriculum no school had approved yet. Find your own community. Own your knowledge. Be citizens, not consumers. Read the Constitution for yourself. Recognize our country was born in revolution and will only survive in revolution. Know the militia clause.

He'd been reading things about Wendy Upton. Some of the people in chat rooms knew her in the army or the Senate. They all had questions about how David Traynor died. Not answers, not yet, but questions. Ones worth asking. About things that didn't add up.

"Come kiss the kids good night," Gail said.

"Okay," Steph said. "Be right there."

PETER RENA

Rena and Brooks flew to California two days later.

First stop: to meet Kim Matsuda, the battery program's architect. She had set up shop in a room at the U.S. Geological Survey in Menlo Park, where no one would suspect her of running a classified program. Gil Sedaka called ahead to say they were coming.

She had a gambler's blank face and suspicious eyes. Ellen Wiley had produced a profile on Matsuda for them. Wiley's masterly background biographies were such a special asset of the firm and so richly insightful everyone called them "Wileys." The scientist-soldier had an interesting résumé: the air force, CIA, NOAA—all federal organizations that intersected with climate. Rena suspected a purposeful journey, a conscious managing of her career to figure out how to get the government to confront the climate crisis. Then, once she had the president-elect's attention last year, she convinced Traynor of the daring plan she had devised. He thought she must have magical powers of persuasion and determination.

The woman in front of them was small and thin voiced with a candid and impatient manner. Rena liked her.

She also had an interesting family history, Wiley's file told them:

a grandmother dying in an internment camp in California; a war-hero grandfather; a family schism over the government's treatment of Japanese Americans; an uncle and cousins who ran a group denouncing assimilation. Rena imagined family gatherings and the attitude toward Kim, who had not only assimilated but also joined the same U.S. Air Force that had bombed Japan, and then she had worked for the CIA.

"Upton wants to pull the plug, doesn't she?" Matsuda declared shortly after Rena and Brooks had sat down. She was trying to shock them into some kind of confession.

"She doesn't need us for that," Brooks said.

"Maybe you're just cover."

"I don't know what you know about me," Rena said, "but I bring a lot of baggage these days. I am the opposite of cover."

Matsuda smiled.

"Why don't you tell us about the program?" Brooks suggested.

And for the next hour, Matsuda described the science of the flow batteries, made a case for why the little-known technology might be the most important step the United States could take to end its reliance on carbon, and argued why it was a matter of national security. There was something about the woman, a matter-of-factness, that stripped away the usual bureaucratic posturing and technical jargon. Rena could see how she had persuaded not just Traynor but also others in the government to divert billions in a moon shot to save the planet. He knew embarrassingly little about climate science. After listening to Matsuda, however, he felt a temptation to strap himself to a tree. She was that convincing.

"What do you think?" Brooks asked as they made their way to their rental car.

"I'd be distrustful of us, too."

"You distrust everyone," Brooks said.

"I love everyone," he said. "That's why I worry about them."

She stopped before they reached the car.

"You up to this? You've been moping for the last month."

It caught Rena off guard.

"Then promise you'll let me know if I'm screwing up."

"Don't make me keep that promise."

Had he gotten that bad? A case would help, he thought. Upton's confidence in him had lifted his spirits. This assignment was a signal, if still not a public one, that he was no longer radioactive.

His partner, however, was still worried about him. That shook him.

27

RANDI BROOKS

Tomorrow they would begin looking at the battery companies with Matsuda. This afternoon they had another briefing. They were scheduled for a crash course in spying in Silicon Valley. Gil Sedaka had set it up for them.

The man to see apparently was the head of the FBI field office in Palo Alto. "Jasdeep Bhalla," Randi read aloud from the file, trying out the pronunciation different ways. Bhalla had run the FBI's Silicon Valley office for ten years. "No one in the country," Sedaka promised, "knows more about security and spying in high technology."

Peter had nosed around a bit more. An FBI friend had explained that technically, Palo Alto was a satellite office to the bigger FBI operation in San Francisco, but this was the only FBI unit in the Valley itself. The Palo Alto and S.F. offices were also united by a common grudge, according to Rena's friend: a mutual frustration that Washington's policy on economic espionage in Silicon Valley was naive and inept. "Bhalla is a straight-up guy, but he's pretty cynical," Peter's friend had advised. "For twenty years, Washington has been focused on fighting the last war—against Islamic radicalism—not the new one that Bhalla thinks is hurting the U.S. now."

And what war was most hurting the U.S. now? Rena had asked.

"Technology theft and cyber war from Asia and the former Soviet Republics."

So we weren't just still fighting the last war. We were ignoring the new one, Randi thought. Why was she even a Democrat? she wondered. The entire government just sucked.

Her spirits weren't exactly lifted when she saw the FBI's lone office in Silicon Valley for the first time. If this was ground zero in the fight against foreign infiltration of America's high technology, the good guys were losing.

The Bureau was located on the second floor of a run-down two-story rented building next to the freeway. It looked like a nuclear bunker built above ground by mistake. It was the kind of place a start-up would move to when it left the founder's parents' basement.

Special Agent in Charge Bhalla met them in the lobby.

"Call me Jazz," he said in a travel-worn East Asian British accent.

"You guys trying to keep a low profile?" Randi asked with a glance around the lobby.

"We don't want to scare people," Bhalla said.

He was a jowly, elegant man in his late forties with a weary but friendly look. His thick black hair had distinguished strokes of gray at the temples.

He led them upstairs to a small conference room and introduced them to his deputy, Dave Polansky, a frowning, heavy-boned man with a blond crew cut. The two men leaned against metal desks and stared at their visitors.

"The president's deputy chief of staff says you want a briefing on national security matters in the Valley," Bhalla said. "So . . ."

Another set of VIPs from Washington to get the spy tour, Bhalla's body language suggested. Randi was already worried a little about Peter. She was in no mood to be dissed by a grumpy cop who felt he was wasting his time with them. Not when they had orders from the goddamn president and no time to waste.

"What the fuck does 'so' mean?" she said. Give the boy a shock. "'So I am deigning to give you this meeting, but I think it's bullshit?' 'So I hate it when amateurs from D.C. come out here because it's my patch?' Or 'So I'm going to help you because it's my job?'"

Bhalla looked unsure how to respond. He'd been making a joke, but this woman from D.C., who was taller than he was—and who had a mysterious brief from on high—didn't mess around. There probably weren't that many people willing to get in his face like that. But Randi was in a mood, and she wasn't done. She crossed her legs defiantly. "Or hadn't you thought the joke through that far yet?"

Bhalla raised his eyebrows at Dave Polansky. Polansky smiled back at him. "I was told you'd like her," Polansky said.

"What about this one?" Bhalla asked, looking at Rena.

"He doesn't say much. But he comes highly recommended," Polansky said.

"I'm glad we've been vetted," Randi said. But she felt better now.

"The word *so* means either 'so how can we help' or 'so what the fuck you want?' Take your pick," Bhalla said.

Everyone relaxed, and Brooks began explaining why they were there. Sedaka had instructed them to secure Bhalla's help but reveal as little of the battery program as possible. So Randi explained that they wanted an overview of how foreign powers stole emerging technologies in the Silicon Valley. She called it "Valley Technology Espionage 101."

"And you're not going to tell me why? Or what you're doing here?" Bhalla asked.

"Hell no, we are not, Agent Bhalla," Brooks said. Bhalla shrugged.

Randi glanced over at Peter. He looked amused. Good. She hoped her run at Bhalla might get his juices flowing.

"First thing you need to understand is that this place, the

Valley—from San Francisco to Santa Cruz, and up the East Bay—is now basically a den of spies," Bhalla began. He paused for effect. Bhalla was used to giving this talk, Randi thought. "The Bay Area is crawling with them. And they're almost all invisible."

"Invisible how?" Brooks said.

"The spying here is not undercover cops trying to snap pictures of government facilities through chain-link fences. Or even diplomats trying to sneak gossip at embassy parties."

"Then what is it?"

"The people spying are much more woven into the civilian fabric of the Valley," Bhalla said. "They're part of the academic and financial communities. They're your friends, colleagues, vendors, members of your board, your financial backers, your top scientists."

Some of this had been in the briefing papers Sedaka had supplied them. Bhalla was more emphatic, however, about what the documents had described as simply possible concerns.

"Many of these people don't even think of themselves as spies. They work for companies connected to foreign governments, but everything about their job looks like any other American company. When they pass reports back to corporate headquarters in Beijing or Moscow, they may not know if the person reading it is wearing a uniform."

Randi could see old frustrations rising in the stocky policeman's face.

"And our country rationalizes a lot of this as just 'technology transfer'—which they see as the inevitable cost of doing business in a global economy. But the guys doing it for the other side think of it as war," Bhalla added. "And we're losing it."

He pushed himself away from the table he was leaning against and started to pace. "And that loss will make us a secondary power in the world."

The FBI man was talking with his hands now. "Look, understand something. The new cold war isn't about how many missiles you have. It's how much technology you can keep away from the other guy."

Randi liked Bhalla's passion, just as Rena had liked Matsuda's.

"You see some guy in a Patagonia vest having coffee with his college roommate on University Avenue in Palo Alto. The guy might have gone to MIT and Exeter, might even be a prominent VC here in the Valley. He might have lived in the U.S. most of his life. He speaks perfect American-English. He may even be a U.S. citizen. He has a cute blond American-born wife and three kids. He's as American as you can get. And he could be a hundred percent owned by the Ministry of State Security in Beijing. And his old college roommate has no freaking idea."

Bhalla took a breath. "The venture capital fund he works for is actually a subsidiary of the Chinese spy Ministry. They made him rich. But in his mind, he just reports to a boss. He doesn't really think that his boss is a spy or that the boss considers the Chinese-American kid back in Palo Alto as an asset or a soldier."

Brooks gave the FBI man an encouraging nod.

"Or take some start-up in a promising technology area, one with long-term national security implications. Say they're working on nanotechnology, but there won't realistically be a product for ten years, and it's a long shot this company will get there at all. That's the kind of start-up most big VC firms won't touch. Too much financial risk; the 'exit strategy' is too far away and it's too unlikely anyway."

"Exit strategy," Randi had learned, was Valley Speak for when an investor gets their money out, either by selling to another company or going public.

"The start-up is about to go under. But at the last minute, a new million dollars comes through from a foreign investor. And all the investor wants is a seat on the board. Then that guy turns out to be your favorite board member, your closest advisor. He's like a father figure to you. He knows things about the world you don't. And you feel so lucky to have him."

Bhalla had found his rhythm now. "The VC firm has got an American name, or just initials, DM Capital or something, and its offices are up on Sand Hill Road like all the other posh VC firms. But it's actually Chinese or Russian or Saudi money. And that seat on the board is their eyehole into everything you're doing. And your mentor is really your minder. And you don't even know it."

"How new is all this?" Brooks asked.

Polansky answered. "There was always spying out here in the old semiconductor days during the cold war. Mostly Russian. Guys in bad suits snapping pictures of off-limit sites like Moffett Field or Livermore Labs, zones where Russian and Chinese were banned without a government escort.

"Then the cold war ended and it got quiet. They even put a big GOING OUT OF BUSINESS sign here in the squad room down the hall one day as a joke." Polansky laughed darkly at the government's naivete. "And then the bad guys started up again."

"When was that?" Randi asked.

"Around 2011, after the recession. The Russians were first. They opened up a venture capital firm in Menlo Park called Rusallo USA, which was a U.S. subsidiary of a Russian government VC firm. Lotta money. They were still a bit old school. The Rusallo guys reported to the Russian intelligence guys in the consulate in San Francisco and started using old gimmicks, like high-end hookers for honey trap work."

"Honey trap work?" Brooks asked, as if she didn't know, trying to draw Polansky in; she was beginning to think they might need these FBI boys down the road.

"Ever hear of Cougar Thursday?" Polansky asked. Brooks shook her head. "Sand Hill Road is where most of the VCs have their offices, or used to before they started moving to Mountain View for cheaper rents. The Rosewood Hotel is the most expensive place on Sand Hill. And at the bar at the Rosewood, they call Thursday nights 'Cougar Thursday.' Bored rich housewives looking to hook up with even richer guys from out of town."

You could tell Polansky liked to tell this story.

"It wasn't long before Russian call girls, who are a lot younger and hotter than the bored housewives, started showing up. It's quite a scene."

Now Polanksy was off the metal table and gesticulating, too. "Same thing at the Redwood Room bar at the Clift in San Francisco. High-end hookers bringing idiot executives back to their rooms rigged with cameras. In an hour they have them compromised. The perfect honey trap. American C-suite doofuses ripe for blackmail with a lot to lose."

Brooks raised her eyebrows to make Polansky think his hooker stories were juicy background, and Bhalla tried to get them back on track. "But it's the Chinese who are the real masters," Jazz said. "They have more money, patience, and influence in California than any other country. This is their Nirvana. The only place besides D.C. where the Ministry of State Security has a dedicated unit. They even have a name for their California work. They call it the 'Strategy of the Human Wave.'"

"The what?" said Brooks.

"'Strategy of the Human Wave.' It means using people and money in so many different ways we Americans will never see it coming."

"You need to explain that one," Brooks said.

"The people stealing your technology could be anyone. An entrepreneur, a student, a traveler, a venture capitalist, your employees. Even your best scientist or your boss. They might even be people who never have even been to China. Anyone with family ties there could be used as leverage."

"Isn't this a little racist?" Brooks said. "Anyone from China is a spy?"

"Your liberal guilt is part of what they're counting on," Bhalla shot back. "And my parents are from South Asia. You calling me a racist?"

"Why not?"

Bhalla smiled. "I'm a cop. I deal in facts, not theories."

"You don't know any cops who are racist?"

Now they were irritating each other again. "As a cop who is American and also an Asian," he said slowly, "my professional opinion is that China represents the biggest and most dangerous counterintelligence threat our country has ever faced."

"Then make your case, Jazz," Rena said speaking for the first time, trying to make peace.

"The Valley today is home to about five thousand Chinese front companies, from vendors to VC firms. No other country comes close to that scale of investment or infiltration here. And all of them, I believe, are set up to steal secrets and acquire technology."

"That's just a guess," said Brooks.

"A highly educated one," said Bhalla. He picked up a piece of paper and waved it, as if it were proof of something. "Fifteen percent of the top-rated VCs in the Valley are Chinese," he said. "And another twenty-five percent are foreign born from other countries. That's forty percent of the top VCs who are not from America."

"So what?" Brooks said.

Bhalla and Brooks's détente had not lasted long.

"So in the last five years, the Chinese have invested a hundred billion dollars in financing rounds in U.S. start-ups in the Bay Area. That's about ten times what any other country has put in," Bhalla said. "The Saudis, Russians, French, and Indians are all trying to catch up. So are the Israelis."

"Isn't some of this technology drain inevitable?" Brooks said. She was beginning to think Bhalla had become a cynic. "You can't keep everything secret."

Bhalla was shaking his head. "We're not even trying." He was leaning back against the metal table again, feeling frustrated again rather than impassioned. "Our country is being robbed of its advanced thinking, and nobody wants to face it because we like the money too much. Security is inconvenient for capitalism."

The agent paused, and Randi wondered if the briefing had ended. But Bhalla was just prepping for his final push. "Look, you know why China keeps leapfrogging our manufacturing? Because they keep stealing our cutting-edge technology and putting it in their products. Their jets. Their missiles. Their nanotechnology and quantum physics. Even clean energy. Their government tells them what to look for. Tells them what it needs. Tells them what to steal. It's like a shopping list. And then they steal it here in the U.S. and send it back home. It's not random. It's planned. It's the new war."

"Is China all that different from everybody else?" Randi pushed back. "From us?"

The question roused Bhalla again. "Yes, because they plan! They are way bigger than everyone else. And they look further ahead. They target technologies they think will control the markets twenty years from now. And then they find companies working on it and target them, and then recruit people who work there to start stealing for them."

"How do they do that?"

"One way is through Chinese scientists working in the U.S. There are hundreds of thousands of Chinese engineers now in the Valley. Educated in China or in one of the great engineering schools in India. Then they get a PhD in the U.S. They get a decent job at a tech firm here. They make great money by Chinese standards, one hundred fifty or two hundred K, but that's barely enough to live on here. They feel lonely and underappreciated. And one day a recruiter calls up. The guy who is calling is American and says he is recruiting for a new Chinese company that is starting up in Wuhan and they are looking for engineers who have worked in America. He tells the guy that if he agrees to join the start-up, he will own a share of the new company, and there will even be a signing bonus of six million dollars. They want him to come at the end of the year. The key for this company will be this particular technology and they think he is really knowledgeable about it. They want him to lead the team."

"What's the problem?"

"They never ask the engineer directly, but it's clear to everyone. They're asking him to steal his company's technology. Or there's no deal. We've made a dozen cases like that. More. Not that the government necessarily wants to prosecute."

"Why?"

Polansky jumped in. "The choice of what cases to take to trial is always political," the deputy said. "And Washington doesn't like to make waves."

"I wonder if there is a little anti-Chinese prejudice going here," Brooks said.

"Ever been on a junket to China?" Bhalla asked. Yes, Brooks said she had. "Every hotel room is bugged. And the trips are great ways to collect data, put spyware on your technology, spot potential recruits. You dream it up. They're doing it."

Polansky said, "You know those DNA tests people take to see about their ancestry?"

"Sure," Brooks said.

"The labs are all in China."

"So what?"

"So we believe the Chinese government is using the data to develop antidotes to future pandemics that would treat people with Asian backgrounds but not those with non-Asian DNA."

"Why would they do that?"

"The next global pandemic could substantially reduce the white, Black, and Middle Eastern populations of the world and leave Asians in even greater ascendance."

"You're kidding me," Randi said.

"It's an open inquiry, an actual file, based on source intelligence. There's no doubt they're thinking about it."

Bhalla began to wrap it up. "The U.S. government created this Valley. Most of the early companies lived off government contracts. DARPA invented the goddamn Internet."

DARPA was the Defense Advanced Research Projects Agency, a government group set up to develop technology for national security, and it in large part had invented the web.

"And now all the kids here who think they are geniuses because they are getting rich? They do it by selling private data the government is forbidden from collecting—that Congress in its wisdom allows private corporations to gather and sell. The open web? What an ironic fucking joke. These companies aren't inventing the future. They're hyenas eating off the carcass."

Bhalla took a breath. He nodded to Polansky. The deputy could go.

Then he gave his visitors a darkening expression.

"You got what you needed?" he asked.

"For the moment," Brooks said carefully.

"What the hell are you guys really doing here?"

Peter surprised Randi by almost answering the question.

"If you were a foreign country trying to steal a technology from start-ups that the U.S. government was trying to keep secret, how would you do it?"

Her partner had gone too far, Randi thought, and for a moment Bhalla looked as if he was going to get angry that he had not been more fully briefed. Then he seemed to gather himself.

"Depends on the country. But I would start by putting early-round seed money into a company I think has a promising technology and that fits my nation's strategic needs. Maybe plant someone on the board, someone with a science background, and make sure they have a seat on the technology subcommittee to have access to more technical documentation."

"What if these companies already exist," Rena said, "and you can't get on the board?"

"There's lots of other ways to get inside. You look for targets who are already there. People with family in the old country. People with vulnerabilities—money problems, addictions, gambling, depression, or secrets like a mistress. It's the spy game, only the targets now are civilians, not government people."

Randi could see a change in Bhalla's expression. He was beginning to put the pieces together. Brooks and Rena were investigators from the White House. And now they were asking about how to penetrate start-ups. It didn't take much to figure out the government must be about to make a huge investment in start-ups with technology that was sensitive.

"I gave this same briefing a few months ago to someone named Kim Matsuda. A climate expert. She asked the same questions you are. You guys thinking about some major federal investment in climate companies?"

"You know we can't answer that," Brooks said.

"Look, if I were in charge of the universe and wanted to start this program, I would just buy all the foreign investors out. Of course that would tell them what you're doing. But they probably already know. And at least you could start clean."

He stopped.

"You've been a big help," Rena said.

"Let me help more."

"You guys have too many forms to fill out," Brooks said. "We can't leave that kind of paper trail."

But she was also thinking that Rena was still not on his game.

"You really think it's that bad here?" he asked Bhalla.

"It's so much worse than anyone in Washington seems to comprehend. This is the real war of the twenty-first century. Who controls knowledge? Privacy, energy, natural resources, AI—it's all being invented here—and then stolen and developed by our enemies abroad. It is a war. We're losing. And America doesn't even know we're in it."

28

PETER RENA

If technology in Silicon Valley had become the invisible war, Wendy Upton had given them two to three weeks to find out if David Traynor's cherished flow battery program had become enemy property.

How would they even begin?

Rena would think about it tomorrow. That evening he had someplace to be.

He drove south past Stanford on El Camino Real, the main thoroughfare, and saw RVs lined up on the street right in front of the university. Housing in the Valley had become so expensive, he'd read that tech engineers were living in these campers. They couldn't afford the rents, or they lived too far away to commute during the week, so they lived in RVs parked right on the street during the workweek and drove home on the weekends. The city seemed to tolerate it. When that was how problems were being solved, Rena thought, something was broken. The place no longer worked.

He glided his rental car into the parking lot of a high-rise office complex called Palo Alto Square. Rena saw the names of different law firms on different wings of the building. Apparently, this was a de facto headquarters building for law firms specializing in technology. He went around the back until he found the coffee place where he had been told to go. Inside, he scanned the tables.

In the back he saw the familiar dirty blond hair and a pair of reading glasses perched on her nose. Those were new. When Vic spotted him, she gave an uneasy wave. Then she looked away as he made his way to her. Gathering her thoughts. So she was unsure, too. He detected no sign, however, of joy at her sighting him.

"Hi," he said.

He felt her stiffen as he leaned over to kiss her cheek. He sat down. "How are you?"

"I'm good," she said, but he could tell it came out more curtly than she meant it to.

It had been four months since they'd seen each other. The longest separation since the day they had met. It was spring now, and her dirty blond hair was already streaked by the sun and the freckles around her nose were becoming more prominent. "You look wonderful," but his compliment seemed to make her only more uncomfortable.

"How long are you out here?"

Here. The place you didn't want to move to.

"I'm not sure. It could be a couple weeks."

"I know: you can't tell me why."

Because my life was an unshareable secret, he thought. She made it sound sympathetic, but he knew it was another thing that hurt her. He gave the slightest nod. She gave him a sad, knowing smile.

"Randi called me," she said. "After you did. We're going to see each other." The two women would probably have dinner, Rena thought. She had invited him for coffee.

"She misses you," Rena said. As if he didn't.

Everything fell wrong off his tongue. I miss you, too, he wanted to say, but that, too, he thought, would only make her uncomfortable. He wanted to ask her a hundred things. Was she still seeing whoever it was she had begun dating in December? Was she happy now that he was out of her life? Did she miss him? Vic was waiting for him to say something.

"I miss you, too," he said at last.

"Don't, Peter. I'm not ready for that conversation."

A dozen more things ricocheted through his mind.

What conversation? Breaking up with me? Or reconciling? Or have we already broken up? Why am I here? To apologize? What do you want? Tell me what you want. He said none of it.

"How are you doing?"

"Well. Really well," she said. "What about you?"

She put her hands on the table and leaned forward toward him to signal the question was sincere. She was always mindful of body language and how to make other people comfortable. "I can't imagine what it was like to go through that." She meant the cyberattacks.

They had texted and had a few brief phone calls in December and January, when things were at their worst, but those were courteous conversations, not long ones.

He drew a deep breath. They could talk about this safely, apparently, and avoid a good deal else.

"I'm all right. It becomes something you live with." And he instantly wondered if that were a lie.

"I'm so sorry, Peter. It does seem to have quieted down." She was wrong. There had been a new attack on him today in the dark web, a sign whoever was doing this to him hadn't stopped and perhaps knew that he was in California, working on a government assignment. Perhaps it was someone with a line into the White House.

"It's hard to fathom," she said.

The whole world these days seemed hard to fathom. A world where you can say anything and people believe it.

"Yeah. Hard to understand," he said.

"That doesn't sound like Peter Rena."

"I'm sorry."

Vic pulled her hands off the table. "Don't make me feel protective of you all over again," she said. "It's not fair."

"No," he said. "I'm sorry."

A young man approached the table next to them and a young woman rose to greet him. They exchanged a perfunctory kiss of hello and then a second more tender, intimate embrace. A couple meeting after work, Rena thought, new enough together that every greeting had passion. Living together or newly married?

How would someone observing him and Vic here summarize them?

"How's your dad?" he asked.

"Still enthralled. A pig in mud."

Vic's father was Roland Edmund Madison, the Supreme Court justice Rena and Brooks had helped win confirmation. That was how Rena and Vic had met. She had been her father's guide and emotional translator through the confirmation process. Then she had become Rena's.

He'd like to see the judge, Rena thought, to talk to him about Vic, and then he realized his brain was bouncing from idea to idea. It would be unfair to pull Rollie into the middle of his troubles with Vic, and it would misfire anyway. Despite his profound understanding of humanity and society at large, Rollie Madison could be oblivious to the details of the people around him. To his daughter's feelings in particular. He loved Vic deeply, but Rollie often missed what was happening in her life.

Vic felt Rena's silence. "I'm trying to be happy, Peter. I'm trying to think about myself. I promised myself I wasn't going to talk about my feelings today. So I'm not. I'm just going to say I'm in a good place. I know you're not. But you need to know I'm not the one who can help you right now."

Then she began to cry, and Peter felt himself falling apart again.

"I know you have things to do, Vic. I should let you get to them."

"Peter," she said.

"Yeah?" But he was afraid of what would come next, so he stood up.

"You have to go," she said.

He was making another mistake, misunderstanding her again, hearing her words but not knowing what they meant. He could see it on her face. Should he sit back down? He wanted to, very much. But he also felt ridiculous; and he worried it would make things worse, make her feel more pressured. When he leaned over to kiss her cheek, this time to say goodbye, he inhaled the familiar fragrance of her, and a wave of memory coursed through him. He felt his knees buckle a little. She put her hand on his cheek and whispered his name.

Then she moved her lips by his and looked at him.

"Bye," she said.

He held there a moment, then stood the rest of the way up—and felt light-headed as the blood rushed from his head. He thought the nearness of her might knock him to the ground. A torrent of sensations he couldn't make out flooded through him: confusion, re-gret, longing, loneliness. Love. Self-loathing. He turned and walked away, hoping in vain he might leave that bewildering cocktail of emotions behind.

At the door he glanced back. A wave from Vic. He waved back. And fled.

29

REDWOOD CITY, CALIFORNIA

Saturday 24 April

RANDI BROOKS

Randi Brooks sat in the makeshift office they had set up out of an extra hotel room they'd rented and watched the cars go by on the freeway outside. She was not happy. The anxious part of her brain, the side that registered all that could go wrong, felt like a bucket spilling over. There was no way they could get their arms around the security of the battery project in two or three weeks, starting from a dead stop. And the calm, clinical, problem-solving part of her brain, which was supposed to rescue her, was nowhere in sight.

Now she had a new worry: perhaps there were no solutions. Maybe David Traynor's bold plan to capture the sun and save the planet with a magic flow battery was too loony. What could they tell the president? That her predecessor's secret battery scheme had shown no signs yet of a breakthrough at any of the five start-ups? That the companies had lousy security? That when the whole boondoggle of siphoning billions of classified dollars to the scheme leaked out to the press—as it surely would—it could hobble Upton's nascent presidency? And since she had no party base, who knows what would happen then?

Brooks didn't want to do that. They lived in a country where half the people didn't believe the planet was warming, even though the coastlines were eroding before your eyes and every year the West burst into flames. If Wendy Upton shut this program down, it would set back the effort to address climate for years—again. After what they had learned the last two weeks, she thought the fucking planet couldn't survive that. Something needed to be done. This was something.

They had been in California for eleven days and their time was running out. Randi was dreading a call from Washington any moment. "What have you learned? We need an answer. What have you been doing out there?" They'd met the CEOs and senior managers of the four battery start-ups in California and the one in Colorado. They were poring through personnel records, looking for security risks. They were studying the investors. Everywhere they looked they saw vulnerability, haste, and lack of security.

Kim Matsuda, the quiet, zealous climate scientist, had been with them much of the way, shuttling between their converted hotel room headquarters and her innocuous office at the U.S. Geological Survey in Menlo Park, where she supervised a small team of scientists with secret clearances to monitor the start-ups' progress. From their improvised hotel room headquarters, Rena and Brooks were doing due diligence about project security, which should have been handled better during the first three months. Ellen Wiley had flown out last night from their D.C. office to help them take stock.

Wiley had made copious notes in an encrypted file. They had installed their own Wi-Fi and router and secured the room with jamming technology so no curious neighbors could steal their data and no drones overhead could eavesdrop. They wanted, in part, to impress on Matsuda what real security looked like.

What in the hell had they really learned? In eleven goddamn days? The whole thing felt like a setup. Send her pals out. Find it stinks. Upton can stick a fork in it and say when it leaks that she saved the country a cool $30 billion. Randi didn't like it. She didn't want to be played.

But the problems were real. The five companies getting the classified funding to develop flow batteries had roughly quadrupled in size in two months. There was no way so much hiring at that kind of pace could remain a secret. The alternative energy community here was too small and too close-knit. There was even less chance that all of those people could have been fully vetted.

She was worried about Peter, too. Her partner was no longer lost in the dark lonely place that alarmed her so in January. But he still wasn't himself. She could see that, being with him in the field for hours a day. He would seem fine one moment and distracted another. He took too long to do things. He had trouble concentrating over long stretches. When they interviewed people at the battery companies—their cover story was they were preparing a status report for NOAA—Peter was not the careful listener she knew.

Then there was the whole culture of Silicon Valley. It made her uneasy. No, it appalled her. The kind of start-ups best suited for rapid innovation in new technology tended to be loose and informal. It didn't help that three of the four battery companies out here were cause-driven enterprises run by scientists who probably chanted mantras about saving the world at breakfast. Even the names were idealistic. Cibus, the Greek word meaning "fuel," and Helios, the Greek god of the sun. Ignius, the Greek word meaning "fire." The Colorado company was called Oorja, a Hindi name for "energy." Only one had done anything with the government before, a company called Tolle Industries. Each time they had a new round of hiring, they advertised, which a foreign government could easily see. Given that climate change was one of David Traynor's seven crises, it wouldn't take a genius to connect the dots that someone was trying to ramp up a battery program in plain sight.

And every one of the companies had foreign investors, three of them in the first round of seed money, meaning those investors had special influence. Ignius had seed money from a venture capital firm run by a Russian-born entrepreneur, Helios had Chinese financing, and Tolle began with money from India and the Middle East.

How much risk would Upton be willing to tolerate? The orphan president had her own problems in Washington, where the long knives were already out. There had been unnerving rattlings online demanding a special election—though the CIA had traced the origins back to Russia. Her own country was obsessing over who she would pick as vice president. Upton had persuaded almost all of the West Wing staff and cabinet to remain, but there were stories almost daily speculating about whether she would fill the cabinet with her GOP friends and drive Traynor's people out. Brooks was worried they would have to return with a report about the program being insecure, which it clearly was, and Upton would have no choice but to shut it down.

That was obviously Kim Matsuda's worry. She had poured a lot of her life into this. Built a career working on global warming, making the connections, developing a plan, waiting to rise to the point where she could directly influence a president and propose something bold, dramatic and do it under the cover of national security. It was quite a journey. A brilliant, quiet, determined woman plotting a solitary journey inside her own government to save the planet. Though she did everything she could to appear modest, Kim Matsuda was extraordinarily competent. In the week and a half they had spent with her, watching her interact with these CEOs, Brooks had come to see just how extraordinary.

They had also heard from Matsuda about a frightening condition afflicting people who worked on climate change—a kind of acute, lingering depression. A few days earlier a friend of hers had committed suicide. "I think it's a disease," Matsuda had said. "We talk about it, my friends and I. We all notice signs."

"What kind of signs?"

"Nightmares. Sadness. A sense of failure. We see the data every day—the rising temperatures, the rising seas, the melting glaciers. We're working like fiends to find some way to stop it, and we can't. We can't even persuade people it's really happening. It is unbelievably dispiriting. We feel a profound sense of failure. We know what's really going on. We study it. We dream about it. And no one wants to hear it. They think we're crazy."

That conversation had been after lunch two days ago as the three of them, taking a break, walked around the Stanford campus, which was idyllic in the warming spring. "A lot of my friends show symptoms," Matsuda said. "You can't let it affect the work. Three colleagues this year alone have committed suicide. I dream sometimes I am a guard on the wall of a fort and I have lost my voice and can't call out in warning. And a wave is coming and it is going to breach the wall. I can't make a sound. Then the wall is wiped out."

When Matsuda walked away after telling them all this, Brooks saw her weeping.

AS FAR AS THEY COULD TELL, THERE WERE TWO MAIN VULNERabilities to the flow battery program: foreign investors and recruitable scientists.

And there were plenty of foreign investors to worry about. Helios had first-round seed money from a Chinese venture capital firm called GCM Investments. The Silicon Valley operation was run by a man named James Wei, a naturalized American citizen who had moved to the United States as a child, gone to prep school in New Hampshire, attended MIT, and earned his MBA at Stanford. He was married to a California woman whom he met at Stanford, and they had three children. But he still had family in Beijing.

The second worrisome investor was a firm named Global Partners, a venture capital fund started by Russian-born Anatol Bremmer. He had already been a very rich man in Russia before he immigrated to the United States in 2010 after the economic crash. A series of investments he made in California had turned him into one of the richest men in the world.

Bremmer was considered an oracle-like figure in the Valley. If he took an interest in a company, especially in the first or second round of financing, it was akin to an anointment. Bremmer had put Ignius on the map. He had also been a personal friend of David Traynor's.

Ellen Wiley said she had uncovered press stories questioning whether Bremmer was really the anti-Putin refugee he claimed to be. "He's one of the most respected men in the Valley," Matsuda had protested. She sounded annoyed they didn't know Bremmer's reputation. "The man's like a guru. His backing Ignius is why I noticed them in the first place."

The third most worrisome investor was a prince from Bahrain named Omar Abbad. He was the largest shareholder in Tolle Enterprises, the biggest of the five companies in the program. Abbad's family had oil money, and he was trying to convert the family fortune into a diversified energy empire.

"We're ethnic profiling," Matsuda declared.

It was the same concern Brooks had when they met with the FBI men, Jazz Bhalla and Dave Polansky. But in the last week and a half she had reconciled herself to the fact that these were foreign governments they were talking about. If they were going to ensure the program was secure, better to risk being unfair than naive.

"We're trying to protect your program," Brooks told her.

Brooks remembered Matsuda's file, her family's internment in a camp during the war, her grandmother and great-aunt dying there, her grandfather dying at Normandy, fighting Nazis, the schism in her family. And she had just accused Randi of racial profiling. It stung. Maybe she really had swung too far the other way, too much under the sway of Jazz Bhalla's ethnic and nationalist suspicions.

"Let's move on," Rena said.

The other big worry was employees, Wiley said. "And in many

ways that was a bigger problem to solve." Altogether, the five companies in two months had hired nearly 600 people. No way Peter
and Rena could vet that many. They needed more help.

And there would be more racial profiling, Randi knew. How
many of the employees with access to technical information were
of Chinese or Russian descent—let alone countries that were uneasy allies, like India? Even the Israelis had stolen U.S. technology
before. The answer was nearly 350 of the 600. The whole prospect
gave Randi a queasy feeling. They remembered the stories Bhalla
had told them during their first briefing. Look for people whose
qualifications and talents might exceed their status, people who had
missed out on stock options, who felt they had developed ideas that
they didn't own, people who seemed like they wanted to be very
rich but were still just scientists or engineers for hire. They were the
ones, Bhalla said, who were recruitable by foreign powers.

They had already met a number of foreign-born scientists among
the senior team members who fit the profile. One man in particular, Patrick Singh, had caught Randi's eye. Singh was a Chinese-
raised Fijian-born engineer working for Kunai Sreenivansan at
Ignius. Sreenivansan had struck them as one of the most impressive
of the five company CEOs. He had been committed to flow batteries
since graduate school and had worked under the country's leading
authority on the subject. He had a quiet determination about him
that reminded Randi of her partner, Peter. If any company made a
breakthrough she hoped and thought it might be Kunai's. But the
scientist Kunai put so much faith in, Patrick Singh, was another
matter. Singh was clearly gifted, but he had moved around often
and seemed guarded and full of grievances when they talked to him.
They needed to do a credit check and examine his spending. And
they hadn't had time to do even that yet.

Other potential recruits might be harder to detect. Any employee with gambling debts, financial pressures, hidden drug problems, or other secrets they wanted to keep private. "We need to vet

everyone again and go beyond criminal background checks. We need bank records, more aggressive credit checks. We need to know who might be vulnerable."

They hadn't even begun to make a list, Randi thought, let alone narrow it down.

Matsuda scowled. "I think that FBI agent Jazz Bhalla is paranoid," she said. "He's been on the job too long. He's bitter that he hasn't made more cases."

Matsuda paused, and an expression came over her face Brooks had come to recognize. Kim wanted to make a point, and they wouldn't like it. "I need to say something. The easiest decision you two can make is to kill this program. That's the safe call, right? Limit the risk to Upton. No one ever gets fired for thinking something is a bad idea. They get fired for pushing ideas that don't succeed. But that decision puts the whole world at risk. In the end, all those companies where people get promoted for avoiding risk, those are the companies that fail to adapt and go out of business. And this isn't a company we're talking about. It's the planet."

30

PETER RENA

The meeting broke up and Matsuda headed back to her innocent-looking office at the USGS in Menlo Park. Wiley was heading to the airport and back to D.C.

Then Gil Sedaka called Brooks, using the secure phones they had brought with them. Randi listened and grimaced and muttered a curse. Then she hung up.

"There's a little chatter on the dark web about the battery program. Just speculation. But Sedaka's pissed."

"How many people know about this program?" Rena asked.

"Too many," Brooks said. "What a goddamn mess."

She looked around the makeshift command center. They spent most of their time here when they weren't visiting the battery companies.

"I need to get the hell out of this shitty room," she said.

Rena nodded. They left the room, went down the elevators and straight out to the rental car.

Randi drove. "Where we heading?" Rena asked.

"The Saddle Room."

It was a bar Randi had discovered in an old part of the town, near their hotel. Above a fading yellow front door hung a sign:

THE SADDLE ROOM

THE LAST NEIGHBORHOOD BAR IN REDWOOD CITY.

Randi liked the place, she said, because it reminded her of the Bay Area before obscene wealth changed it. She had taken to coming here most evenings to get away from the hotel, to have some time alone to decompress and mull over the day's work. And to get away from me, Rena thought.

Before they got out of the car, Brooks turned to him.

"It's time, Peter."

"For what?"

She sighed. "Really?"

He didn't know what she meant.

"To look at Kim Matsuda," she said.

"You suspect her?" he said and instantly felt foolish for asking.

"I suspect everybody," Randi said in exasperation. "Jesus, Peter, you taught me that."

It was true. When they moved from being Senate investigators to private consultants, he had counseled her to leave her political allegiances aside and develop a cold eye. It had made her more ruthless. But a better professional.

"Why Kim? Make the case. What did I miss?"

"She's a true believer," she said. "What if this program isn't secure because she didn't want it to be?"

He thought about that. "Why would she undermine her own program?"

Randi was a step ahead of him. "She desperately wants this battery invented. What better way than to create a program and let it leak that the U.S. is doing it. Suddenly all our enemies get serious about flow batteries, too. And instead of one major program you have sparked five or six."

It made sense. And Kim Matsuda was determined and strategic enough to have done it. He should have recognized it himself.

"This leak today, that rumor on the dark web, could it have been her?"

"I think we need to go twice as hard as we have been," Randi said. "Or our only option will be to recommend Upton shut this down. That shouldn't happen just 'cause we did a crappy job."

"If you think we should lean on her," he said, "let's lean on her."

She nodded. "Okay." She slipped off her seat belt. "I need a drink."

People nodded to Randi as they entered the bar. Likable and talkative, she had become a regular in less than two weeks.

It was a small place where people knew each other. The inside was a simple, long, rectangle-shaped room, probably once a part of the Chinese restaurant next door. A bar ran the length of the place on one side. Down the other sat four small tables. The walls were covered with memorabilia, most of it apparently thumbtacked there by regulars—old photos, paper plates with bets on them, tickets from 49ers, Warriors, and Giants games, snapshots of Saddle Room birthday parties. There were more mementos behind the bar, going back decades.

They sat at one of the small tables. Three men at the bar were debating whether the Giants baseball team would ever be good again.

"I'm not holding up my end, am I?" Rena said.

Randi didn't answer.

People had been surprised seven years earlier when they had partnered up. Randi Brooks, the swaggering liberal Senate lawyer, Rena, the Boy Scout–soldier; a Republican but no crusader like Brooks, not really all that political when you got down to it. More a country-and-duty type. From a distance, they couldn't have seemed more different. But Peter and Randi recognized in each other something most people didn't see. They both thought character mattered more than creed. And they both thought honesty revealed character. So did lying. Later they would learn that when they were young, they had each been harmed by secrets and lies: Rena by the lies his family told him, Brooks by secrets she kept from her own family about who she loved.

They had built their careers together cleaning up powerful people's messes and they usually had to remind those people about something power couldn't change: what happened was real, and the only way you ever really ended something was by coming clean. Peter and Randi thought facts were like DNA. When all else was dust and legend, what really happened was still there, waiting to be found.

At least Rena used to believe that.

"Maybe I've been wrong about a lot of things," Rena said.

"What are you talking about?"

"Like what we tell clients."

"What does that mean?"

"We always tell them to come clean, right? Admit what they did. That the public wants to forgive."

"Not always," she said ruefully. Some clients were unredeemable, and they had told them to resign and didn't give a damn what the client said.

"What if we were wrong?" Rena asked.

"About what?"

He shook his head. He couldn't explain it. Or maybe Randi wasn't ready to hear it.

She stared at him a long time. "That's still the business we're in," she said, "finding out what happened."

"Maybe the business is becoming obsolete."

He saw her studying him, trying to get a read on his thoughts, trying to decide whether he wanted her to argue him out of it. Had he really become this uncertain?

He wasn't sure himself. He wished now he hadn't said so much. Then he heard himself saying more.

"When you're young, it's so easy to be sure. You think you know everything. You sort out what you believe. Make your life a certain way. Maybe we decide these things before we understand them."

He could see her concern deepening, but he didn't care. These thoughts and feelings had been flooding him the whole time they'd been out here. He couldn't hold them back.

In the army he'd learned that giving into emotions got you killed. You had a better chance of surviving if you controlled them. Now he felt capsized by them.

Maybe he had been wrong about everything. Or maybe the world had changed. He didn't know.

He could see in Randi's eyes how much he was failing her.

Losing your bearings is a little like losing your mind, he thought. You're the last to know.

"Okay," he said.

"Okay what?"

"Okay, I'm in. Let's look at Kim."

She kept her eyes on him a long while. "You mean it?"

"Ain't we partners?"

Her smile spread slowly. "Welcome back."

He wasn't back, he knew that. She did, too. But they had been honest with each other finally, and if he wanted to be back, he knew she would do everything she could to help.

FOUR DAYS LATER THEY BORROWED A CONFERENCE ROOM FROM Jazz Bhalla at the FBI office in Palo Alto. "No effing bugs," Brooks admonished the FBI man, only half kidding. Rena and Brooks had decided they needed federal surveillance of Kim Matsuda, and they needed Bhalla's help and authority in introducing certain documents to her at this meeting. So Bhalla was read in under special status from the director of the FBI, one of the few people in Washington who knew about the battery program outside the military and Matsuda's team.

They told Kim Matsuda they had more questions to ask the FBI about Silicon Valley spying and would meet her at Bhalla's office. But when Kim arrived, Ellen Wiley was there, having flown back out for this, and Bhalla's grim expression gave away that there was more to this gathering than she had been led to believe.

"Kim, as we look for security vulnerabilities in the program, we have to look everywhere," Brooks began.

Bhalla opened a sheaf of papers. "I have your travel records for the last six months. And your cell phone and location data. We have FISA court approval for these materials." FISA was the Foreign Intelligence Surveillance Act, which authorized a special court to oversee warrants for surveillance of foreign agents suspected of espionage and, in certain cases, American citizens suspected of being involved with foreign individuals.

"We want to go through some of these dates and talk about these meetings."

Matsuda's expression darkened. "I was setting up this program," she said. "Meeting with everyone."

Brooks said, "Then let's walk through it."

Bhalla slid a folder of papers matching his own in front of Matsuda. "I'd like to direct your attention to January fifteenth," Brooks began. "Your cell phone is at the headquarters of GCM Ventures. That's where Jimmy Wei works. GCM is a series A, or first round investor, in Helios Corp. As we've discussed, we have questions about whether GCM is really an agency of the Chinese Ministry of State Security and, in turn, whether Jimmy Wei would then be an MSS agent."

Matsuda's eyes moved from Bhalla to Brooks. "I was asking Jimmy the reasons for his confidence in Helios," Kim said. "Why had he made the investment? I needed to assess for myself whether Helios was a good risk. Jimmy is an astute venture capitalist."

Matsuda's voice was lifeless. "I didn't know you considered him a Chinese spy. At least I didn't on January fifteenth. If he is a spy, his judgment about where to invest his government's intelligence funds is one of the reasons they rely on him."

Her logic wasn't wrong, Rena thought. He also thought Kim didn't seem intimidated by this interview. She was strong and methodical. This would not be easy. It also made it more plausible, he thought, that she might have broken the rules and leaked to scientists in other countries that the program existed so that they might start their own.

"And what did he tell you about Helios?" Brooks asked.

"That he considered the company's founder, Bill Stencel, to be one of the brightest minds in his field. And that he thought Helios was one of a handful of efforts that might make a major breakthrough in the field of energy storage."

"Do you have notes from that meeting?"

"No. And if I did, I would have used a burn bag to destroy them at the end of the day. It's a classified program."

"I'd like to point your attention to January seventeenth, two days later. You took a trip to India. You exchanged emails arranging meetings with several venture capital firms. You also met there with Kunai Sreenivansan, the founder of Ignius. What can you tell us about those meetings, and why did you meet with him in India rather than here in the United States?"

Matsuda paused for a second, thinking back. "He was there on vacation visiting family. I needed to meet with him as soon as possible. And it made sense to meet with his backers if I was going to be there."

Brooks asked, "If you knew about all these foreign investors, Kim, why did you choose these companies?"

"Because they are our best shot for a breakthrough," Kim answered. When Matsuda was angry, she didn't become nervous, Rena noticed. She became quieter. It was an unusual trait and the kind of thing the military looked for when trying to identify candidates for special assignments, like a deployment to the CIA.

"These companies were selected because they were the best choices. And I was trying to see if their foreign investors were okay," Matsuda said.

Brooks asked, "Are you qualified to make that judgment?"

"I was the only person on the project. So qualified or not, I had to make that judgment."

"Was it really necessary to go abroad and display your interest in Ignius to foreign investors for a program that was supposed to be classified?"

Matsuda sighed. "At that point—this is prior to President Traynor's taking office—I was trying to identify for him the best possible partners for his potential plan to rapidly invest in energy storage. The nature of the program, how classified it would be, or whether it would even go forward, was not yet determined."

"But you knew what Traynor had in mind," Brooks said. "Better than anyone."

Matsuda had had enough. She straightened her back and pushed her chair an inch or two away from the conference table. "This is insane. Why would I want to sabotage my own program? A program I persuaded David Traynor to accept?"

"Who better?" Bhalla said.

"Fuck you, Jazz," Matsuda said.

"Kim, we need to ask these questions," soothed Brooks. "We are pressure testing the program. The whole program. That includes the person who runs it. These meetings you had don't prove anything. But they raise questions we need to ask and you need to answer." Brooks offered a sympathetic smile that Matsuda wasn't accepting.

The grandchild of Japanese internment looked at the four people from her own government questioning her loyalty. She folded her arms.

"Please turn to document seven in the folder. Kim, this is a speech you gave in 2017 in Seoul, South Korea, about technology sharing. In it, in the highlighted paragraph, you say, and I quote: 'The race for renewable energy is not the problem of one nation. It is the problem of a shared planet. To reverse the damage of the last hundred years, we must join together in a spirit of peace and trust. We must have a shared sense of crisis. And develop a shared solution.'

"Kim, how can you run a classified program that withholds this technology from other countries, including our own allies, if you believe the technology should be shared?"

Matsuda shook her head and said, "A different assignment. In 2017, I was trying to urge hesitant countries to do more. The goal was to try to pressure the United States Congress, the majority of whose members were officially skeptical about whether global warming was even occurring. Because Congress still holds to that insane position, the goal of this program—the battery program we are trying to build now—is to make so much progress and remain so secret that neither our enemies nor our allies or even Congress know it is occurring until it has already succeeded."

They went on for four more hours. They burrowed into specific meetings. They doubled back over ground already covered. They used the interrogation method Rena had taught Brooks, the one he had been taught by his mentor in the army, Jimmy Kee. It was meticulous and methodical, not confrontational. They went on until they were satisfied they could get no further.

At 6:00 P.M., they finished and Matsuda left. Two of Bhalla's surveillance teams would be following her now. Rena, Brooks, Wiley, and Bhalla stayed behind.

"You really think Kim is sharing technology with a foreign government?" Bhalla asked. He sounded skeptical about what they had just done.

"I think she was sloppy," Brooks said, closing a file. "But you could be sloppy on purpose."

"Meaning?"

"You could let someone into the program you expected might steal technology. Not the same as leaking it to them, but it's close."

"What does your famous gut tell you?" she asked Rena.

"I think we have more supposition than evidence."

Rena's answer seemed to snap something in Brooks. He could see it in her expression. He had told her he would back her on this, and now he was doubting it. "Damn it, Peter, I thought you were in for this? I need you to carry your load."

He couldn't remember his partner ever insulting him in front of other people, even in front of Ellen Wiley.

Bhalla made a show of returning to his office to leave them alone.

What must Kim Matsuda be thinking? Rena thought. She'd spent a lifetime serving a government that had imprisoned her family and they had just questioned her patriotism. Randi was doing what she had to, maybe too fast, but she was right. They were under orders from the president. And she was frustrated because they hadn't made enough progress—and because she was worried he wasn't carrying his weight.

It was Wiley, who had been writing things in a notebook, who rescued them.

"I see five options we need to evaluate," she said.

"Only five?" Brooks said sarcastically. Now Randi was annoyed with Ellen, too.

"One," Wiley said, ignoring her, "is that a major investor is spying on the program for a foreign government. If you think that, or think there is significant risk, remove them. Or if there are too many of them, shut the program down.

"The second option is someone in the companies themselves is a risk, one of the employees, or maybe even a founder. If you find one, remove the company. If it's more than one, maybe you shut down the program."

Wiley's focus was calming Rena and Brooks.

"The third is Kim Matsuda herself. What would we do then? Determine whether the program can continue without her. Which would involve answering the same question—how secure is it on its own?"

Wiley paused. "The fourth is there are so many possible leaks that you can't stop them all. In that case, I think you have to shut down the program. How could you justify using classified money to fund something so insecure? It may be the case that Kim set up this program to be a sieve."

"And the fifth?" Brooks asked.

"The fifth is that there are no leaks or real vulnerabilities that you can prove. And if you can't prove one of the first four options to your satisfaction, maybe that is where you land."

Brooks, who had been standing, sat back down. "But the burden of proof for each of these options is different," Wiley said. "If we doubt an investor, like Jimmy Wei, we can just kick Helios out of the program and recruit some other company in. From what we've heard so far, it's not like Helios has developed anything yet that is worth stealing."

"Okay," said Brooks.

"And if it's an employee, they can be fired—even a founder. All we need is doubt."

"Okay," Brooks said again.

"But for Kim it's different. We'd need proof—that she's either brought someone in to steal the technology or that she is deliberately making it insecure. We can't just kick her out because we aren't sure. It's not fair to her or to the program. And I don't know if it can go on without her."

Matsuda had a small team of scientists working under her evaluating the companies' progress. Could someone from that group take over for Matsuda?

"Anyone can be replaced," Rena said. The look on Brooks's face said she wondered if he was talking about himself.

"I've already made a spreadsheet," Wiley said. Of course she had.

Wiley turned her laptop toward them and went through it. It categorized every employee in their sights: their level of knowledge and a numerical rating of doubt about each of them. It also had a tab for every investor and every board member. Now they would add Matsuda to the sheet. When Wiley finished showing them her work, Brooks turned to Rena. Her expression wasn't hard to read. She was worried about him.

31

WASHINGTON, D.C.

Thursday 29 April

PETER RENA

The president summoned them back to Washington the next day.

They had been gone just over two weeks. Wendy Upton could wait no longer.

A progress report? They had discovered that the program was not very secure. Now they had questions about the woman who had come up with it. It was too early to give Upton a competent report. All they had were doubts—which would probably scuttle the program.

But his two-week immersion in the science of carbon and fossil fuels had changed Rena. He was deeply skeptical of the battery program when they started, though he had kept those misgivings mostly to himself. He thought throwing billions at small unproven start-ups so they could magically invent a new miracle battery would prove a fiasco. Rena had seen that kind of mistake before, a generation earlier, when the military had shifted all kinds of work to private contractors. Billions had been squandered, and the military became less accountable and too dependent on the wrong people.

Now he was beginning to wonder if he'd been wrong about the battery project—at least about the idea of doing it privately. He had spent long days immersed in the climate crisis and now believed only extreme measures could rescue the planet from irrevocable damage. Those measures needed to come faster than the political system could allow. Rena had no idea if flow batteries were the answer. He also didn't know whether Traynor had launched other secret programs, involving other technologies. But after a decade in Washington he knew this: conventional answers were inadequate. And Congress would never fund what was needed.

David Traynor's classified secret plan might produce nothing. It also might be too insecure to be kept a secret. But the logic of it, the need for it, made more sense to Rena than he thought two weeks ago. He felt guilty about how uninformed he had been and how inured he had become to the idea that the planet was warming. He had thought life could go on. Meanwhile, scientists, despondent, were killing themselves because of their failure to convince the world.

They landed at Dulles at 5:00 P.M. They would see Upton in the morning. But tonight Rena had somewhere else to be.

The house was in Kalorama, a wealthy D.C. neighborhood north of Dupont Circle. A police car blocked the road at either end of the street.

When he reached the corner, a uniformed Secret Service officer asked him where he was going. Rena told him. "And what's your name, sir?" The officer confirmed Rena was on a list.

The house didn't stand out. There was no special fencing keeping anyone out. Rena walked up the brick steps to the front door. A young man answered the bell. "You must be Mr. Rena," he said. "He's running late. You can wait in the solarium."

A few minutes later, James Barlow Nash slipped quietly into the room.

"Peter Rena," the former president of the United States said, extending a hand and putting the other on Rena's shoulder. A "shug," as Randi called it, part handshake, part hug, a move that in some circumstances allowed two people to whisper without being overheard, a Washington greeting useful for allies and enemies alike.

"You look well, sir," Rena said.

"A drink?" Nash asked.

"You still like bourbon?" Rena asked.

"I never liked bourbon." Nash laughed. "I like scotch."

"What else did you lie to the country about?" Rena said.

Nash smiled. "I am not at liberty to say."

Jim Nash's love for Kentucky and Tennessee whiskeys was one of many celebrated "secrets" during his two terms in office, though now apparently Rena was learning it was a manufactured lie. A U.S. president could not prefer scotch to American whiskey. The charismatic president's various favorites—from fountain pens to music—were all part of a carefully managed mystique. What was it that he was drinking? Or reading? What was his favorite meal? Aides worked hard to contrive public conjecture about the handsome widower's preferences.

Listening to Nash talk, Rena realized he had already begun to forget the timbre of the man's voice, which had been so familiar for so long. Nash was dashing and graceful and had a gentle, teasing sense of humor that struck people as distinctly American. For a time, James Nash had made the presidency seem fun and that had eased people's growing anxieties. Too much so, critics complained. Even some in his own party wondered in retrospect if he had been more of a favorite uncle and not enough the stern father. In the end, Nash, a Democrat, failed to build on his personal popularity to develop his own party machine. His successor had run a campaign implying Nash's frustrating good intentions were inadequate. Republicans more often than not had gotten the better of him. Yet people still loved him.

Why had Nash invited him here? Rena's friend Michigan senator Llewellyn Burke had set up the meeting. "The president would like to see you." Why? "Ask him yourself," Burke had said. The games powerful people played.

Nash was smiling, an amused friendly press of the lips and glint of the eyes, but it was a subtle smile, offering only about a quarter of the million watts he could show for cameras. "How about a rye? From Pennsylvania? And I won't tell you what I'm drinking," he said.

"Still secretive," Rena said.

"And you're still impertinent."

Nash made the drinks and led them to another room. Crossing the hall, Rena caught a glimpse of Marilyn Kerns, the actress and activist to whom the widowed Nash had become engaged last month, to near total surprise. Nash had kept his private life miraculously private while in office, and some critics called it his most remarkable presidential achievement.

They entered a small den and Nash gestured Rena to two chairs by a lit fireplace. "Why am I here?" Rena said.

"I wanted to talk to you."

"The whole conversation gonna be this slow?"

"Could be," said Nash. "I'm retired."

"I know interrogation tactics. We could speed up."

Nash bowed his head to hide another smile. "You've been roughed up a bit," the president said. So he was here for a talking-to. Because Nash had heard about his being attacked online and not taking it well.

"It's a rough time. The president dying. Not good for anyone."

"I meant you," Nash said.

"A bit roughed up," Rena agreed.

Rena was not close to this man. He and Nash barely knew each other when the president, three years ago, had summoned Rena to the White House. That afternoon he had asked Peter and Randi to shepherd Rollie Madison's nomination to the Supreme Court. Afterward a small bond had formed between the two men. But they had never shared a meal. Indeed Rena had never before been alone in a room with this man.

"Did someone ask you to see me?" asked Rena. He didn't like being talked about.

"Other way around," Nash said. "I told Lew Burke I wanted to talk to you." Nash put his drink down on a small table. "Peter, you know why I sought you out to help with Madison, three years ago?"

"Only what you told me. But I didn't believe you."

That earned another smile. "It wasn't just because I thought you'd learn everything about Madison and keep the nomination on track if something went wrong. Which you did."

Rena had discovered someone was killing people who'd been involved with a case Madison had presided over. He had stopped the man.

"I picked you because you and Randi would make up your own minds about Madison. I picked you for your judgment. To test against my own. I needed someone independent."

That, Rena thought, seemed a hundred years ago.

"I know what's happening to you," Nash said.

"Then you know more than I do."

"Your past is being rewritten. And you're wondering whether there's something to it."

This was strange territory: a therapy session from the ex-leader of the free world.

"No, Mr. President. I don't worry what they're saying about me is true. It troubles me that other people do."

Nash sipped whatever sat in his glass.

"Peter, I'm a politician. Like my dad before me. And if you want to ever get anything difficult done in politics, you soon realize your real business is people—not policy. Not even politics. It's understanding people. How to change their minds, and how they process new information. How to bring people along."

Rena said nothing.

"Folks don't really operate according to logic, at least not the way psychologists used to think they did. They don't operate in a way that serves their best interests either. They're rational in a different way."

Rena wondered where Nash was going with this.

"From the time we're little, we spend our lives figuring out how things work. How to get our parents to do things. How to make them laugh or get our way. How to please our teachers. Annoy our siblings. Predicting how things turn out. That's how we learn to navigate the world. Right?"

Rena nodded.

"So when we're adults, whenever we come across something new, something we don't understand, that challenges what we believe, we look for ways to make it fit the world we know. To have it make sense. Without rethinking everything else. But it's not strictly facts and logic."

Rena nodded again.

"That doesn't make us stupid or crazy or irrational. It makes us human."

"What does this have to do with me?" Rena said.

"You study history. So you know this. People don't like things that challenge everything they've known before. The Catholic Church didn't want to believe the Earth circled the sun. So they put Galileo under house arrest. For a decade. He died there."

Rena felt lost now, like a boat unmoored by the wind.

"I'm not Galileo."

"No, but you upset things. A long time ago you found something out about an American hero and wouldn't let it go. We don't have many heroes. That was hard for people to accept. It is easier for them to blame you. Blaming you puts things right. It took them a decade to do it, but that's what's happening."

"I understand that," Rena said.

"No, Peter, I don't think you do."

"Maybe the world's gone crazy."

"It's done that before. And we're still here."

Rena thought of the sun overheating tiny Earth, melting its glaciers, and wondered how much longer that'd be true.

When the cyberattacks had started, Rena had imagined he would find out who was after him and why. But it had snowballed so quickly he hadn't known where to start. Then he thought it would pass. Time reconciled everything. But it hadn't.

"I don't know what all this means. What are you getting at?"

"It means these attacks aren't actually about you, Peter," Nash said. "This is happening because someone wants to hurt somebody else. They wanted to hurt President Traynor. Or maybe Wendy Upton."

"I don't see how hurting me hurts anyone else. I'm not that important."

"You're close to Upton. You probably saved her career."

Rena thought about that. "Then I should go away."

"No, Peter, you're wrong." Nash's sapphire-blue eyes fixed on Rena. "You need to get up again."

Rena wasn't entirely sure what Nash meant.

"Because when you do, people see you. And it will mean something to them. And when they are knocked down, they will get up again, too, because you did."

Nash drew himself closer.

"That's how progress happens, Peter. It's the only way. When people get up again and keep going, they redefine what's possible for everyone else. And then the people behind them will get up, too, when they get knocked down. Getting up is what matters."

This was Special Forces stuff, the magical thinking they teach patriot-drunk soldiers so they'll follow impossible orders. Just keep going. And your craziness will inspire others. Rena knew. He'd been one.

"I'm flattered you've taken the time, Mr. President," Rena said. "But I'm not a soldier anymore in anyone's army. I'm a guy for hire."

"No, Peter. It's a fight every day. And we never are not in it. We are all soldiers."

Grand men passing along aphorisms, Rena thought. Public figures in the arena, fighting the good fight. It exhausted him.

"When you stop fighting, they win. Understand?"

Rena had believed it all, once. He had imbibed it with the special thirst of the outsider yearning to belong. But that was a long
time ago.

"Yes, sir, I understand," Rena said.

There was a knock on the door and the young aide appeared
from behind it.

"Mr. President?" the aide said. Apparently, Rena's allotted time
was up.

"Yeah," Nash said impatiently.

"Thank you, sir," Rena said.

Nash rose and Peter after him.

"The world isn't really different, Peter," Nash said. "The bad
guys just have better tools. But we'll catch up."

Rena shook the president's hand. Yes, I'm a student of history,
he thought to himself. And the real lesson it teaches is everything
passes. Athenian democracy. Republican Rome. Even life. History's
true lesson is brutality. We only keep the savage human spirit at bay
for so long. It's only nostalgia that endures.

The former president began to walk Rena to the door and then
stopped. "Wait a moment." He went back into the study. He returned
carrying a book wrapped in brown paper. "Take it, Peter," he said.
"And get back up."

Rena looked up at the taller man and felt his magnetic pull one
last time. Then he descended into the spring night.

=== 32 ===

WENDY UPTON

Some days, rising alone in the enormous Residence upstairs in the executive mansion, surrounded all day by aides who didn't know her well and armed agents trained not to look her in the eye, Wendy Upton felt as though none of it was real. She had become the most powerful person on the planet because of a flawed aortic valve. The responsibility was entirely hers, the capability to destroy the earth, the welfare of three hundred million souls, the fears of seven and a half billion. Whether she desired the responsibility was immaterial.

It also wasn't clear who in Washington wanted her to succeed. The American people did—that she now believed. Just as David Traynor had hoped they might for his own presidency had it gone on longer, they seemed to want her to succeed, too. People felt a bond with her outsiderness, with her independence. To most of political Washington, however, she was a mysterious accident. To which party did she belong? In what did she believe?

She had cabinet members who thought their agendas—not hers—should drive her government, because their party had won the last election. She had White House aides slipping changes into federal regulations, hoping she wouldn't notice. She had Republicans whispering through back channels that she should undo much of what Traynor had set in motion. There was even the persistent paranoid conspiracy narrative in the firm right media that Traynor had been assassinated and Upton was involved.

She was uncertain, now, about various old partners in the Senate and House. Politics wasn't personal, she knew that. Still, she was caught off guard by the speed with which old friendships she had considered close had changed.

The oddest feeling, however, was an unexpected sense of peace that sometimes overtook her. In these moments, she felt within herself, removed from the space around her. Yet rather than being unsettling, this sense of being inside herself induced a feeling of serenity, a clarifying confidence she had rarely known before. These moments of quiet certainty came to her most often when she was alone, but in recent days, she also felt it in meetings crowded with people.

She had always felt on some level deeply alone. At least since she was sixteen, the year her parents had died in an auto accident. She had never married, never really been in a long relationship, which of course made some people suspicious. She must either be closeted or repressed. In a sense she was both. Now in her mid-fifties, she felt ready to come to grips with the reality that she loved women, not men. She had finally felt ready to confront that. Then life had gotten in the way. Her presidency probably made facing that exponentially more complicated. She could not imagine announcing now that she was the first openly gay president and had been closeted for years. Sometime in her presidency she hoped to change that. And change the country.

But she was accustomed to feeling that she was on her own. Everyone was alone. Ultimately that is the only truth there is. Loners were just better at accepting it.

What scared her was the thought that she couldn't succeed alone. Her job was to move people to new places, to new ideas, to lead them. And she was only recognizing now how little her life in politics up to that point had trained her for that kind of leadership. Congress, and the life one spent in it as a House member or senator, had become a science of followership, of party-line votes, talking points, dialing for dollars with bullying donors, and fearing the right flank in primaries. Very little of that prepared one to be president. David Traynor, who knew little about politics, and whose career in it was so fleeting, had understood this—how disconnected experience in government was to actually leading.

A month ago, she'd finished reading Nelson Mandela's autobiography. Mandela compared leadership to being a shepherd. Sometimes you led by moving ahead of the flock and showing it the way. Other times you hold back and look for strays, leading, in effect, from behind, waiting for the lost to catch up. How, she thought, could she lead a flock that wasn't yet hers?

She had begun talking on Friday afternoons with the two surviving former presidents, Jackson Lee and James Nash. They were men from different parties, former opponents, and to some degree they reviled each other. But they had agreed to advise her, sometimes even jointly. The meetings had been Gil Sedaka's idea. "Those old goats may know something. And it wouldn't hurt if people knew they were helping."

The only other souls still living who had shepherded the flock. "You will face more palace intrigue in your first six months than I did in four years or Jim did in eight," Jack Lee had told her. The Traynor-Upton administration had lasted seventy-five days, the Upton administration so far twenty-five.

Nash had advised her to study Teddy Roosevelt, a man the Republican establishment had only made vice president to shut him up. The last thing Teddy's party had wanted was for the progressive reformer to become president. Upton could identify. Her presidency was the last thing Republicans wanted. Or Democrats for that matter.

She had decided to shed three cabinet members, each someone

Quentin Phelps disliked. Getting rid of them thus had the double benefit of pleasing her inherited but influential chief of staff and taking her three steps closer toward making her administration her own. One new person joining the cabinet would be Susan Stroud, the former Senate majority leader who'd been deposed last year by Travis Carter and the party's right wing. Stroud would be the new secretary of state. It was a small step. There were many more to come. Upton was a planner, a list maker. It pleased her now that she was beginning to make lists of things that she wanted to do and not just the ones she had to.

There was a soft knock at the door to the Oval Office, and, when it opened a crack, the face of Carla White, her personal assistant, appeared in the narrow gap. "They're here," she announced.

"I'll be right there."

They were meeting again in the Map Room to hide from journalists. Quentin Phelps and Gil Sedaka were waiting, along with the political consultants Randi Brooks and Peter Rena. Brooks looked energized. Rena looked tired.

She invited everyone to sit.

She saw concern on the faces of the two fixers. She asked them to report what they had learned. Brooks did the talking.

"The program is still probably unsecure," she began. "But nothing of value could have leaked yet—other than the program's existence."

"How can you be sure?" Sedaka asked.

"Because none of the companies so far have developed anything worth stealing."

Sedaka broke the silence that followed with sarcasm. "Great."

Gil had been skeptical of the secret climate program from the first, Upton knew, certain the program wouldn't bear quick fruit and that some disgruntled general or intelligence chief would leak its existence. Then she'd be saddled with a scandal—that billions in critical national security funding had been diverted to a crazy secret solar battery scheme that never had much chance of succeeding. Since she went along with it, Traynor's "battery fiasco," as Gil called it, would become Upton's, "because you didn't stop it."

She wasn't quite ready to do that, however.

Quentin Phelps had a different view. He and Traynor together had made millions in Silicon Valley start-ups. He liked the plan's audacity, and he liked it because David had loved it. If Kennedy said "go to the moon not because it's easy but because it's hard," Phelps argued that "saving the planet was even harder, and a lot more important." That's why Americans would forgive her if the plan failed, Phelps maintained. "The public elected David to take risks that were worth taking."

When Brooks finished, Phelps pressed his case again: "Let's say you're right. One of our enemies has learned about the project—one that would make the U.S. a hundred percent energy renewable in five years. Wouldn't they respond by trying to create their own battery program?"

"Presumably," Brooks said.

"Steal what we learned and add to it. Right?"

"Presumably."

"Then that strikes me as a reason to go on—not to give up," the chief of staff said.

"Why?" asked Upton.

"Because if they discover our program, we will have goaded our enemies into jump-starting their own—programs long overdue. They can't take the risk we won't succeed. If we stop now, we lose that chance.

"Remember Reagan's Star Wars program," said Phelps. "The secret plan to build a network of satellites that would bounce any Russian missiles back into the Soviet Union? It never got built, but Reagan thought it was real, and that scared the hell out of the Russians and helped end the cold war."

"No," said Sedaka, "if we waste billions on a battery program that fails, we will just have wasted billions on a failure. And we will have inspired our enemies to leap ahead of us in the process. We will be worse off than if we had done nothing."

"Then let's not fail," Phelps said.

Upton had come to appreciate Phelps more than she had expected. He was more strategic than she had given him credit for when they first met during the campaign. He was more than just David Traynor's organizational man and enforcer, which was how the press caricatured him. In his own way, Phelps was as inventive as Traynor, and almost as relentless.

"If the program isn't secure, and it fails," Sedaka countered, "we'll be skewered for it. And it will leak."

There had already been the rumor on 5Click.

Upton glanced at Rena. She knew about the online attacks on him. They all did. "What do you say, Peter?" she asked.

"Three weeks ago, frankly, I thought this program was crazy. It might still be. But I'm less sure of that now."

"Why?" the president asked.

"Three weeks ago I had a normal person's fear of how bad climate change really is. Now I know better."

"And do you think the program will leak?" Upton asked.

"Eventually, of course," Rena said. "And when it does, all our enemies will know about it and presumably try to catch up, which may be a good thing, as Quentin says. But if it's far enough along, it won't matter. All you were really ever buying with secrecy was a head start."

Sedaka felt the momentum shifting away from him. He made one more charge to take the hill. "If you're right and it does leak— and we have no new technology—we'll be dismissed as fools, and this will be shut down anyway."

Yes, that was the great risk, Upton thought. Discovery, failure, and humiliation. Gil was the only person at the top of her administration whose loyalty she didn't question.

Randi Brooks jumped in. "The two biggest threats to security are foreign investors and employees being recruited by foreign governments to steal technology."

"What will it take to identify and vet the employees you're worried about?" Upton asked.

"More people to help us vet employees faster."

But she saw something in Brooks's expression. The woman would make a terrible card player. "But that's not all, is it?"

Rena answered. "We're looking at something else. When we know more, you'll be the first to know."

The program is more flawed than they were letting on, Upton thought. But for some reason they weren't ready to tell her to kill it. They wanted more time. How much could she give them?

"Won't sending in more people to help do background checks on employees only make the program even more obvious?" Sedaka asked.

"Call it pressure testing," Brooks answered. "We want to raise alarms inside the start-ups on purpose. To see who reacts. And to make any foreign government who might be watching think we're closer to a breakthrough than we are."

"So you want to create a feint?" Phelps suggested.

"I wouldn't put it that way. We need more help. But it's true, making ourselves obvious may help us flesh out who we're looking for."

Upton scanned the faces in the room: a final silent vote.

"Three weeks," she declared. "Then we need to make a final call. Quent, give them what they need." She turned to Rena and Brooks. "But I'll need answers—and signs of progress. If all we have in three weeks are the same doubts, I'm shutting this down."

She rose, signaling the meeting was over, but Rena stopped her. "Madam President, may I have an extra moment?"

Upton noticed surprise in Randi Brooks's reaction to this. Whatever Rena wanted to talk about, he apparently hadn't warned his partner.

Did Randi know, Upton wondered, what she and Rena had talked about privately at times after the election? That he had advised her within days of Traynor's victory back in November that she should open a private back channel of communications with Republicans? That Rena himself had acted as a go-between with Senator Aggie Tucker—until the cyberattacks had made him persona non grata?

Maybe he was carrying some message from the senator now. She glanced at Phelps and Sedaka to signal she would see Rena alone, and when the others had left, she sat down again.

"I wonder if you might be better served, Madam President, if Randi continues on this project with someone else."

This she hadn't expected.

"We have a person at the firm who can replace me. Hallie Jobe."

"Why?"

"It's personal," Rena said. Upton studied Rena's unreadable expression. "I have some things I need to take care of."

Who didn't? Upton thought. The president had died. The country was in mourning, the world in turmoil. The new administration was trying to find its footing. There were extremists in both parties calling for a new election. And Rena had some personal things to take care of?

"This because of those cyberattacks?"

They held each other's gaze, two watchers watching each other.

"I'm not at my best at the moment. You can do better."

She hadn't known Peter Rena long, little more than a year, but she liked him. She even trusted him. Stopping the threat against her last year, he and Brooks had gotten to know her in ways few people ever had. They'd learned her failures and strengths and her most private secret—one she barely admitted to herself—about her sexuality. They'd guessed accurately, too, how much it frightened her. When she was young, she had never heard about "spectrums of identity" or other ways of thinking about how people were different from what was once called "normal." The two fixers' vetting of her last year had taken on a quality of discovery for her, motivating her to confront who she wanted to be, who she was, and to do more to repair her strained relationship with her sister. It had persuaded her to take this leap, this crazy out-of-character act of political free jumping—into another man's political party, into the vice presidency, and now the Oval Office. In part, she was sitting in the White House because of this man and his partner.

So she owed him something. She owed him, she thought, almost anything he asked.

"Does Randi know you're asking this?"

"I wanted to speak to you first."

It was one of those moments of serene clarity she had been feeling.

"My answer to you is no," she said without hesitating. "I need you. I need your instincts. And whatever is ailing you, the best way to regain your balance, Peter, is to find yourself in the task."

For a moment he seemed ready to argue. She decided not to let him. "A year ago, when you wanted to know everything about my life, you told me to trust you. Now return the favor."

She wasn't asking. She was the commander in chief, and they were both soldiers once.

Rena stood. "Madam President."

She held out a hand and he shook it.

"Trust yourself, Peter. I do."

When he was gone, she walked back to the Oval Office, pressed the intercom on her desk, and asked. "Carla, what's next?"

ONCE SHE WAS THROUGH SECURITY AT SFO, KIM MATSUDA FOUND a quiet cubicle at the Alaska Airlines terminal. For all its faults, SFO was the most high-tech airport in the country, and Kim liked it here. There were good places to eat, to sit, to have privacy. She wondered why more airports weren't as clever. She took a look around for a private spot to sit. She kept the text short.

Found something. urgent. Must discuss f2f. Coming to you.

She pushed send, stood up, and melted into the line boarding the plane.

PETER RENA

Rena didn't head straight back to the office. He had to clear his head.

He circled Lafayette Square outside the White House several times, then wandered onto the urban trails of Rock Creek Park near Georgetown.

Request denied. The president had given him an order. *We are all soldiers*, Nash had told him. *I need you*, Upton said.

He was forty-three years old, and he now wondered where taking orders all his adult life had brought him. He had believed all the blandishments about committing one's life to something larger than self. But he had begun to doubt the institutions behind the orders. And in war he had seen the dark side of belief. People did the worst things in the name of creed.

He was also unsure of Wendy Upton, which surprised him. For all its rough edges, Traynor's aborted presidency had been like a shot of adrenaline for the country, energizing everything with a strange mix of hope and apprehension. Since his death, Traynor's ephemeral agenda had morphed into something bigger, a promise of national renewal, one that had to be fulfilled or the country would suffer another blow to its confidence. Was anyone up to it? James Nash could move you with his candid charm, but even that had been insufficient. Traynor inspired people by overwhelming them with his urgency. Despite her decency and her strength, Upton remained a mystery, cautious and remote.

For all their cartoonish excesses, when presidential campaigns ended, we knew, in some odd but intimate way, the strangers we had chosen to govern us. But the country hadn't chosen Upton and didn't know her.

Her command to him a few minutes ago implied he had obligations. To what? To Nash's imagined army in a long struggle toward justice? To a country that no longer believed in its own ideas? To a government that didn't work? Or maybe Upton just needed an errand boy, someone to vet David Traynor's secret climate plan so that she could protect herself politically. Maybe it was nothing more than that.

RANDI WAS WAITING IN HIS OFFICE WHEN HE RETURNED TO 1820.

"Where you been?"

"I asked the president to let me withdraw."

"You what?"

"Hallie could do a better job than I am."

"Peter!"

"She refused me."

He sat down beside her on the sofa. Brooks, at just under six one, was almost an inch taller than Rena.

"What are you going to do?"

"There's nothing to decide," he said.

"Sure there is."

"Let's get to work. Isn't that what you've been telling me?"

"You really asked to resign?"

"It doesn't matter."

He could see it in her face. Randi was thinking about what he must have been feeling all these weeks, and the pressure she had put on him in the last few days about carrying his weight. "You have nothing to prove to anybody," she said. "Especially not to a bunch of assholes on the Internet."

"I'm not trying to prove anything."

"Sure you are."

She waited for him to look her in the eye.

"The point of the game, Peter, is to leave the board better than you found it and also find what makes you happy. It's taken me a long time to realize that doing something that matters isn't enough—even for people like us. You have to find what makes you feel"—she searched for the word—"complete. If you want to not lie to yourself. If you want to live truthfully. Then you have to be able to live *and* to work in a way you can believe in."

Randi in the last year had gotten married to the woman she had been with for several years, named Rochelle, a more public celebration of her personal life than she had been comfortable with before. "It's harder than it sounds. You have to be looking for it. To know it, when you see it. You have to work at it."

Was she talking about Vic? Or was that just who he was thinking about?

"I'm serious, Peter. If you want to stop, stop."

He had told himself the same thing on his walk. But that conviction seemed now to be draining out of him. Or maybe old chords had hold of him again.

"Let's get to work," he said.

"Don't let this go, Peter."

"I promise."

The look on Brooks's face made him want to keep the promise, or at least learn how to start.

Then, as if just remembering something, she picked up her phone. "Did you see this?" It was a text message from Kim Matsuda. Rena hadn't looked at his phone in hours.

"She says she found something. She's jumped on a plane. She's heading out here."

Rena read the message: *"Found something. Urgent. Must discuss f2f. Coming to you."*

"What's f2f?"

"Face-to-face," Brooks said. "And she should have been here by now."

PART III

Experience Is the Name
We Give Our Mistakes

== 34 ==

WASHINGTON, D.C.
Friday 30 April

RANDI BROOKS

Gil Sedaka must have been at home when he got the word.

When they met him at the White House twenty minutes later, he was still dressed in a polo shirt and blue jeans.

"She became ill shortly after takeoff," he said.

Sedaka's office, two doors down from the Oval, was too small for its furniture. The claustrophobic room made everything about the moment worse.

Kim Matsuda was dead. "The flight team on board thought it was some kind of flu," Sedaka said. "They found a doctor among the passengers. But by then, she'd already begun to deteriorate. And the plane was past the point the pilots could divert for an early landing."

It didn't seem real to Randi.

"She probably died in the air, but she was declared at the hospital near Dulles."

"Autopsy?" asked Rena, coldly.

"Her mother's flying in from California for an official ID first."

"We need autopsy results as soon as possible," Rena pressed.

Other clinical questions from her partner followed. What did the airline know? Could they get the names of the flight crew? He wanted to interview them. And anyone else who saw Matsuda on the flight, including the EMS team that met the plane.

Her partner, Randi thought, was finding his bearings playing a policeman, a role he still believed in.

"You think this wasn't an accident?" asked Sedaka.

"Just touching all the bases," Rena answered vaguely. "Randi and I will also need official status. So we can ask questions. Coordinate with law enforcement."

Sedaka took a moment to think about it before nodding his assent. He knew these two, had been with them last year during their harrowing hunt for the person threatening Wendy. And as someone who had handled the infinite spectrum of chaos encountered by U.S. senators, not much fazed him.

A half hour later they were back at 1820 around a table in Brooks's office with Ellen Wiley.

Brooks felt liquidy waves of guilt about Matsuda. It had been her idea to accuse Kim of being disloyal. She'd done it aggressively, to see how Kim would react—and to alarm the senior people at the battery companies, to make them think the assholes from D.C. had *everyone* under suspicion. She'd pressured Kim because she didn't know what else to do.

She had wanted to shake up Peter, too—to have him either all in or completely out, and maybe out was better. That's what she'd thought two days ago.

"This is not your fault," Peter said. "Focus on her message to us. Whatever she knew, she was worried enough someone might be listening. So she wanted to talk face-to-face."

"Which means what?" Brooks asked.

"That she was worried whoever could be listening was pretty sophisticated," Ellen Wiley said. "Someone who could break encryptions if she sent us something electronically."

"That message she sent to us means I was wrong about her leaking," Brooks said.

"Who knows?" said Rena. "Maybe you shook her up, which is what you were trying to do. Maybe she *had* gone over the line."

They had flipped, she thought, Peter now focused and she full of doubt. Her imagination skipped across dark possibilities. Had she triggered Kim's death, terrifying the woman into a heart attack? Or had Matsuda found the real security leak and been killed for it?

What if Matsuda had been complicit in some variation of the scheme Brooks had accused her of, launching the battery program so she could then trigger other countries to start their own? But why would that get her killed?

"We need the FBI to track her devices," Rena said, "so we can see how she spent the last couple days."

They had done that for her devices up to last week, when they had her under suspicion. It shouldn't be hard to get it for the last hours of her life.

"And we need that autopsy," Rena said.

They also needed to get out of here, Brooks thought, out of D.C., back to California so they could retrace Matsuda's steps. She told them that, and Wiley raised a finger to make a point.

"Before you go, I wrote that profile you asked for, Peter. About the general you caught harassing women."

"What's that?" Brooks asked.

"The other day, before we confronted Kim," Wiley explained. "Peter asked me for it."

That would have been after she and Peter had talked at the Saddle Room, after he confessed the doubts he had been feeling.

"I tracked pretty much everything General Stanhope has done with his life since he left the army," Wiley said with a hint of pride that was unusual for her.

The former general's name was James Stanhope, and he ran a company now in Virginia that did leadership training for corporations. Stanhope had retired from the army with full honors after Rena's investigation. That was the irony, Brooks thought. Rather than disgrace the man, Rena had conducted the inquiry in a way that had unearthed Stanhope's history of sexual harassment and also protected him from scandal—and protected the army, too—by keeping his investigation off the books. And for his labors Peter was banished for insubordination.

"Here's the file," Wiley said.

Peter began to read. A look came over his face, one Brooks had seen a hundred times, maybe a thousand. Her partner was forming a plan.

"I'll meet you in California in a day or two," he said.

"I need you there with me now," she told him.

"You told me I needed to take care of myself."

"That was before we knew about Kim."

But it was too late; his mind was made up. He had leaned out the window of his spotter plane, seen something, and was going in for a closer look. "I'll catch up to you," he said. "Promise."

35

ROANOKE, VIRGINIA

STEPH MYERS

"There is a lot of evidence that Traynor was assassinated," Patriot23 wrote.

"True that," answered WillFreedom.

That's exactly what he had been thinking, Steph Myers said to himself.

"So who benefits from that?" Patriot23 typed.

Steph watched the chat in real time. He thought about typing his own theories. Everyone here had an alias. No one could be caught saying these things. Nothing would be traced. You could speak freely.

"Who became president? Duh," wrote someone who called himself TimMcVeighLives.

"You think?" said WillFreedom.

Steph had wondered about that. He'd read a lot about it. There was a lot of info being collected. And there was something about Upton he didn't trust. She was buttoned up like she was hiding something. It wasn't natural. She had never been married. She was like a robot. He hated her. He had voted for Traynor because he would shake things up. Because he told the truth. You could just tell. But this seemed like a coup. He didn't buy all the paranoia, the deep state bullshit. Still.

"Do the math, dude," Patriot23 wrote.

Steph put his fingers to the keyboard and then stopped. And then he typed.

"I'm looking for proof. Got any suggestions? Willing to get my hands dirty. Just need to know the truth."

He was breathing hard. He read it over a couple times. Then, bang. He pushed send. There was his alias for the first time: Truth-NFreedom. His heart raced. But he began to feel freer.

36

NORTHERN VIRGINIA

Saturday 1 May

PETER RENA

Katie Cochran lived in a part of Virginia everyone called the Hunt Country though hardly anyone rode with hounds anymore. It also felt farther away, the clone town homes stretching farther out from the city than Rena remembered. Then around a single curve they vanished and the road became a country highway. The dense forests rushing past the open window of the old Camaro whispered to Rena of the battles fought nearby to hold the angry country together: Grant's bloody chase of Lee in the Wilderness, Stonewall Jackson at Bull Run, Lee's surrender south near Richmond. Rena used to walk the battlefields on weekends, retracing the steps of the infantry soldiers.

He and Katie had been living not far from here ten years ago when Billy Judupp walked into his office at Quantico and it began. Peter recalled that day as he drove. Major William Judupp appropriated a chair, hoisted his pristine combat boots onto Peter's desk, and celebrated his surprise landing with a reptilian grin.

"Got a special one for you, Sherlock. Right from the top," Judupp announced.

Billy had been a third-year at West Point during Peter's first, and they'd been through enough together in the fourteen years since that most people considered them friends. But it was a dry, thin alliance. They'd overlapped in Afghanistan and Iraq, young officers on the rise in wartime. Now rotated home, they were both thriving, freshly minted majors in their early thirties. Billy was assigned to O-ring, the Pentagon's fifth floor, where decisions were made. Rena was at the Criminal Investigation Division, the super cops of the army. If all went according to plan, in seven to ten years they'd be colonels, and by fifty or sooner, one stars. Billy, with his lifeguard good looks and his jigsaw puzzler's mind, was intent on making it happen.

"The fifth floor has chosen someone new to lead CentCom—finally," Judupp said. "So it doesn't take a computer to know they don't want any more problems."

CentCom was Central Command, the U.S. operational command responsible for the Middle East theater. The current commander, General Philip Myers, was being pushed out for talking too candidly to a magazine reporter. His predecessor, Seth Dreyer, had been fired for handing over classified documents to a biographer with whom he was also having an affair.

"The fifth floor doesn't want any more cockups. You've been given the job because you don't cock things up. This one needs a clean bill of health."

"You got paper for me?" Rena asked, meaning written orders.

"You'll get 'em in a day or two. I came down to give you context."

What Judupp called "context," most soldiers called politics.

"Two weeks. Then wrap it up. Something serious. Not a whitewash. But don't kill yourself."

"Katie and I were supposed to go on leave," Rena said.

"Give her the bad news. Take your leave after."

Rena didn't want to share with Billy anything more about his marriage than necessary, but he was afraid Katie couldn't take any more "bad news." She had been sick and heartbroken to have lost three different pregnancies in a row. Rena had been working like crazy, maybe harder because things at home were tense. He knew he was making a hash of it there but he wasn't sure how to fix it; getting away from everything together was supposed to be a start.

"Get this done here, Peter, and you can have extra leave."

Billy was like an irritating brother-in-law who everyone else thought was just great and you couldn't bring yourself to like.

"I'll wait for the file," Rena said.

Judupp's feet came down off the desk, and a lazy salute to the brim of his cap.

"You've got a great reputation, Peter, but you can also be a dog with a bone. We're not looking for any bones."

The next day Judupp's aide came with the orders and the file.

WOULD HE HAVE HANDLED IT DIFFERENTLY IF JUDUPP HADN'T been an asshole? Maybe. Peter didn't know. He resented being told to do less than his best. He needed, at that moment in his life, to do something well.

Two days later, buried deep enough no one was supposed to notice, he found references in General James Stanhope's file to items that weren't there. They'd been removed or sent to appendices no longer appended. Something had been tidied up.

So be it. The United States Army kept copies of everything. You just had to know where to look. From the fragments he could find, all the complaints in Stanhope's file appeared to be from women; Rena could surmise the rest. General James Birdsong Stanhope had, in the grotesque language of another era, taken "liberties" with women in his command. On more than one occasion he had almost certainly made sexual advances toward inferior officers, particularly on long deployments overseas. Such conduct was immoral. It was also a violation of military code—even if the advances were welcome. At least some of the women must have registered complaints; there was never a court-martial. All that remained were traces in the record, like dust particles left behind from a broken glass after the shards were swept up.

Aside from the ghost trail of questions Rena had found, however, James Stanhope was an extraordinary soldier. His talents had fully emerged in the decade of war that followed 9/11, most of which he'd spent in harm's way. Even in theaters where U.S. troops struggled, Stanhope excelled.

His biggest contribution was organizational. At Harvard earning an MBA, Stanhope adapted business innovation theories to the military's traditional approach to making battlefield decisions. The old command-and-control-from-above approach, so ingrained in army thinking, was ill-suited, Stanhope reasoned, to win a war against loosely connected cells of fighters who operated as fast-moving networks. The old way left U.S. commanders hesitant and cautious.

U.S. and allied fighters needed to create smaller teams of decision makers, not unlike terrorist cells, and authorize these teams to act on their own if traditional and timely command-and-control approval was impossible. The army agreed and the differences were palpable. Within a year, Stanhope had revolutionized the future of U.S. battlefield decision-making—particularly for special operations, the military's name for classified warfare.

In eleven years of war, Stanhope also had spent 3,217 nights away from his family, fewer than 800 nights at home.

His last three years abroad Stanhope's wife was dying of cancer. He offered to retire; she told him no, she didn't want her cancer to destroy two lives.

That was the General Jim Stanhope the army wanted to promote.

Rena had found another, less heroic, side of the same man.

At first, Rena had just set out to find what was missing in the file.

But questions have consequences. Once he took the first step, Rena usually took the next—and the one after—until he knew everything he could.

Secrets are hidden for a reason.

It took two weeks to find enough stories, enough women, to know most of it.

When deployed long enough and lonely, Stanhope became infatuated with women in his command. He would make advances. If rebuffed, he backed off. Rena found no evidence Stanhope had ever tried to retaliate against anyone who turned him down. To the contrary, he would apologize for crossing the line—and usually was forgiven. But not always. Rena found no evidence Stanhope had ever forced himself on anyone who refused him, the army definition of rape or sexual assault. But Rena was pretty sure Stanhope had been intimate with at least four women over whom he had power. That itself was a violation of the military criminal code. There was a time when such conduct was viewed as less shocking. Even then, though, these were court-martial offenses.

"What are you going to do?" Katie had asked him. He'd shared with her what he'd been doing, though doing so was also a violation of regulation. He needed his wife's counsel, given that he had been conducting this investigation alone and largely off the books, knowing the Pentagon would not be thrilled. Katie came from a military family. She was his best friend, and they were struggling now, and he needed something to bring them together, especially since he had forfeited their vacation with the assignment.

"I don't know," he'd said.

"It's wrong, Peter," she'd said, meaning Stanhope.

Rena then did something else that pushed the edge further. He'd talked to the general's daughter, Lindsey, herself a soldier, to verify some things and in some way warn her what was coming. A part of him, he thought, wanted her to warn her father. She was shocked, Lindsey said, but not entirely surprised. Her parents did not have a perfect marriage. Her father had been absent for long periods. But she considered him a good man. "Walk him through it," she said. "He'll do the right thing." Then Peter had made a decision he would always regret. He asked Lindsey if she would come with him to see her father. She said yes.

He was off script and acting without approval. He would talk to Stanhope privately, he thought, see what the general said, and then make a decision. A day later he called Stanhope. He was vetting the general, he explained, and had some questions. Stanhope invited Rena to come the next day to the Eastern Shore, where he was renting a friend's house.

Stanhope was shocked to see Lindsey arrive, too.

They sat in the sunroom. Peter explained that his superiors didn't know he was there. He said he didn't know what would happen next. But he wanted the general to know ahead of time what he had learned. Then he went through it, the general's daughter sitting next to him.

Stanhope said nothing, and when Rena was done the general asked only one question: "Why did you bring Lindsey?"

"Is it true, Dad?" Lindsey asked.

Instead of answering, Stanhope went outside. He was gone twenty minutes or so, walking on the beach alone. When he returned, face silted with sweat, he spoke to them standing up and gave a little speech he must have worked out on his walk.

"You had a tough job, son. You did it. You did it the wrong way, but it's done. I am going to tell the president I am turning down CentCom. I've neglected my family long enough. I have grandchildren to love."

Then his eyes moved to his daughter. "I wish you hadn't come here, Lindsey. But I know the reasons. I hope to do better. Major Rena should have known better than to bring you."

Then to Rena: "This was my sin, not yours, Major. I am grateful for the discretion. But you didn't need to do this. I am not a rapist."

Stanhope retired with full honors. The Pentagon picked someone else to head CentCom.

Two months later, it was made abundantly clear to Rena his career in the army was over. After, when Llewelyn Burke offered him a job on his Senate staff, it was the senator's way of announcing to the small circle of people who knew what had happened that in his eyes Rena had done the right thing. It was also Burke's way of sending a message to the Pentagon: sexual harassment would not be tolerated. While working for Burke, Rena met a liberal lawyer from Senator Stan Blaylock's staff, a woman who was just as driven about getting to the bottom of things as Rena was. They worked well together, even if they were from opposing parties. Senator Burke suggested they could do well together offering consulting and problem solving to people in trouble. A private firm like theirs could work as a bridge across parties.

Rena had never told the whole story of Stanhope to anyone. He told his commanding officer what he had found and that Stanhope had decided to retire. He didn't tell him about the trip to the Eastern Shore. Or about Lindsey.

Rena never spoke to Billy Judupp again.

The closest he came to telling the story fully was to Katie, but even then he left out details. It was Stanhope's story to tell, he told himself, and those of the women he harassed.

Senator Burke sometimes told a version of the story—without ever naming the general. In it, Rena was a hero. The general had been grateful and the army saved from a scandal.

Now the story was being retold, in shadowed corners online, as a witch hunt by a man who abused his wife and wanted to find a scapegoat to mask his own sins. Rena knew he had made mistakes; he wondered if there were grains of truth in the lies online. Those are the lies that people believe the most.

37

MIDDLEBURG, VIRGINIA

Saturday 1 May

PETER RENA

The house was made of old stone and sat on the land as gracefully as if an artist had painted it there. It was the kind of house he and Katie had dreamed of owning together someday.

The heavy oak door swung open and inside stood Katie.

She was the same, her features a little sharper perhaps, but only in ways that revealed her intelligence more. He'd wondered if she'd be further altered by time, by a new husband and motherhood. She wasn't. There was the same girlish freckled nose and dirty blond hair. He had never noticed how much she resembled Vic. Her eyes were lighter, an almost colorless blue, not Vic's dark smoky gray flecked with gold. Katie would be thirty-seven in September.

She was alone, no curious little boy hiding behind her legs. Ian was two. Rena had never met him.

Katie offered a friendly but cautious hello and pulled the door inward, stepping back for him to enter. She gave him a light, slightly tentative hug, as if he were a friendly acquaintance she didn't know well, and led him through to the back of the house. "I thought we would sit outside on the veranda, so you could see the countryside."

She filled the silence with talk of the house. "It's pre–Civil War.

We're still restoring it, but the work never ends." She and Darren had bought it just after they married. "It was a wreck but all we could afford." Darren commuted to Reston, leaving early in the morning to beat the traffic. He traveled a lot. Dulles was only forty-five minutes away. He was gone today on a business trip.

Darren was in investments, Rena recalled, but he was unsure exactly what that meant.

She opened French doors to the rear patio, and Rena noticed the soft belly bulge. Katie saw him looking and smiled.

"When?" he asked.

"September."

"Congratulations, Katie."

He felt his hands tingling and recalled the sensation he had the first time they met, when Katie was sixteen, a junior in high school, and had come to West Point to see her brother Kevin, Rena's roommate. When he and Katie met the second time, years later at a party in Washington, Rena was on leave from Iraq, Katie a senior in college. It felt like no time had passed. They talked through the party and saw each other the following day and the one after. There was a lightness to the weekend Rena had never felt before, and he confessed it to the buddy with whom he was staying in D.C. "You're cooked, dude," his pal had said.

Katie had an easy, graceful honesty that people found magnetic. She, in turn, was drawn to his silence. They were young and imagined their differences made them into something more together than they were apart. They could tell what the other was thinking, which seemed to them both a sign of something important. Maybe everything.

That was why Katie had agreed to see him when he called yesterday out of the blue, he thought. She trusted that, whatever his reasons for coming, she would understand them. *I need to talk to you, to ask you about something.*

The last time they'd seen each other was the day their divorce became final. They had agreed to meet at a loud Capitol Hill pub, which was a mistake. They took a walk instead, nearly kissed, and Katie started to cry. "What are we doing?" she'd said. "We're divorced."

Rena's life at that moment was changing more than he could understand. No longer a soldier, he had become a Washington fixer, an accidental profession he didn't know had existed a year earlier. He was in his mid-thirties, and he felt lost. We need to make a clean break, Katie had said. "And start our lives over without each other." Six months later she began seeing Darren, the son of family friends.

THEY SAT ON WROUGHT-IRON CHAIRS ON A VERANDA OVERLOOK- ing rolling hills. And all at once a strange sensation went through him, a feeling of intense belonging followed by stinging loneliness. Seeing Katie in a house like the one they had imagined owning, he felt as if he had returned home, to the city where he had grown up, after being gone for a long time. Then, just as quickly, the feeling fell away, like a wave coming in and going out. He didn't live there anymore. He didn't belong here.

"Ian's taking his nap," Katie said, which meant Rena would not meet him. Another time, he almost said, but that would be a lie and Katie disliked lies, even small ones.

"What did you want to ask me?" she asked. "What's wrong?"

He took a breath. "Partly, I just wanted to know if you would see me."

"Don't be ridiculous."

"We haven't talked in five years. I didn't know if you were still too angry."

She made a face, as if he were stupid. "I wasn't angry, Peter. I was heartbroken." She leaned toward him. "What's wrong?"

"You've seen what's online?"

"You're not letting that bother you, are you? It's garbage."

Rena didn't know how to respond and Katie said, "You always felt too much and said too little." A wan smile; it was a compliment, not a criticism. "That was your charm," she said. "You were always more vulnerable than you thought."

"Online, these people say I went after the general because of us. That I made you so unhappy, it was emotional abuse. And that's why you kept miscarrying." He studied her reaction. "It's true I didn't know what to do," he said. "You were so unhappy. All I did was work."

Katie was shaking her head. "You think I told someone I blamed you for losing the babies? Even back then?"

"No, I don't."

"Well, I might have. I thought it. I don't know if I ever said it out loud. But I was wrong."

"I don't know that you were."

"Stop it, Peter. You think there is something true in what those idiots are saying about you on the Internet? Or that they even care?"

"No," he lied.

"What was that thing you used to say, from that writer you liked? You should always seek truth in your opponent's error and the error in your own truth?"

"Niebuhr," he said. He had forgotten that quote. He couldn't believe she remembered it.

"Well stop trying to understand these people telling lies about you, Peter. That stuff online is crap." She fixed her eyes on his. "It has nothing to do with us. We made each other unhappy, and we didn't know why. Did I lose those pregnancies because of it? God knows."

She took a deep breath.

"What happened between us wasn't your fault. That's your thing—carrying everyone's burdens. If you want to know what made me angry, it was that—you taking everything that happened to us as your weight to carry, as if I weren't there. I thought your guilt was self-centered. You thought your job was to protect me. I thought you should have tried to understand me."

She had never said these things to him before, not quite this way. Or had he just not heard them?

"In the end, I think we just wanted different lives."

But it had been love, Peter thought. Of that he was sure.

She was upset now and tried to calm herself by pouring iced tea, which had been set out on the table before he arrived. Her hands trembled as she drank.

"Listen, Peter. Stop thinking your enemies must always have a good reason for what they're doing. These people don't care anything about you. They're playing a game that you got caught in. I doubt if you are even the person they're really after."

That's what Jim Nash had said.

Then she reached over and took his hand. "Learn to be happy."

Which is what Randi had said.

She squeezed his fingers. They'd been a couple for ten years. But he was a fading part of her now, like a person walking away in the rain until they became a shadow. "Maybe next time you can see Ian," she said. She had even learned to tell small lies.

38

CATOCTIN MOUNTAIN PARK, MARYLAND

Sunday 2 May

WENDY UPTON

The day after she saw Rena and Brooks, President Upton left to spend the weekend at Camp David, the presidential retreat in the Catoctin Mountains of western Maryland.

The lodge and cabins originally had been a camp built for families of federal workers during the Depression, until Franklin Roosevelt's worried doctors during World War II thought the president needed somewhere nearby to get away and relax. Upton took the thirty-minute helicopter flight there Saturday morning to see a couple of friends and do a little business. She invited Quentin Phelps and his family to join her—to forge more of a bond—along with three female senators she had once considered close, two Republicans and a moderate Democrat. Maybe sharing a weekend would rekindle some trust there, too.

After Sunday brunch she met with Phelps to go over a list of possible vice presidents.

"There are some good names here," she said of the list his team had provided. They were all moderate or iconoclastic Democrats—no one from the party's left wing and no Republicans. That, everyone agreed, would feel like an unelected takeover of the executive branch. "But let's get even more unconventional. Look further out-side Washington."

She thought Phelps was catering to her rather than pushing her. She switched topics. "I'm shocked by the death of Kim Matsuda."

"Incredible," he agreed.

"A heart attack?"

"Too soon to be sure."

She sensed there was something Phelps wasn't telling her.

"Which means what?"

"Kim had discovered something. She was coming here to give Rena and Brooks a message."

"A message about the program?"

"That's what they're heading to California to find out."

She hadn't been told.

"Is there some suspicion this wasn't an accident?"

He gave her a worried look as an answer. So now Quent's cher-ished battery project had something else hanging over it, too. Was it really possible someone had murdered the head of the program? What kind of awful mess was this secret battery becoming?

She let out a long breath. "We will talk more about this."

Right now, she had people waiting.

Two other guests had come up for brunch and a talk: Senate ma-jority leader Travis Carter and the chairman of the Senate Judiciary Committee, Aggie Tucker. They were waiting for her by the pool, Carter slightly ridiculous in his khakis and blue sneakers, Aggie decked out as if he had just shopped at REI.

A long time ago, when they were Senate aides, Aggie had been infatuated with her, attracted by her shyness and her strength and her blond hair. Her rejection of him only seemed to have increased his ardor. But the awkwardness between them had melted over the years into a surprising friendship, one that deepened after they were elected senators.

Brunch had been a social affair. This meeting was business. She wanted to deliver a message.

They sat at a small table by the pool. Stewards offered Bloody Marys.

"We've known each other a long time, haven't we?" she began.

"We surely have," Aggie agreed.

"I hope that counts for something because I want to ask for your help."

She glanced at Carter and could see the warning bells clanging in the Senate majority leader's brain, ringing behind his eyes.

"And we're happy if we can give it," Carter answered with a hint of menace.

"When David Traynor became president," she said, "he promised to consult with Republicans first on policy, even before talking to Democrats. It was a bold idea, but he lived up to it."

The Senate majority leader had hated it. It had wooed some of his party members away when Traynor put things they wanted into bills.

"Yes, Madam President, but with all due respect," Carter said, uttering Washington's most universal insult, "David Traynor did not understand how the Senate worked."

When they were in the Senate together, this man Carter had disdained her—a woman who was ideologically suspect and hard to keep in line. Now he was trying to wrap his mind around the inconceivable reality of her being president; and he was hardly the only one. More than a few old colleagues on both sides thought she had cheated her way there somehow, betraying her party for power. What did she believe in? They saw only disgrace, not an effort to rescue her party from losing its way.

"Aggie, when David died, you asked me what I wanted to accomplish? Who I wanted to be as president? Remember?"

"I do."

"I told you I wasn't free to answer that yet—that my obligation was to David."

Aggie nodded again.

"Eventually I will add my own agenda," she said.

She was putting it out there, the tantalizing prospect that they could influence her—that in some way they could shape the White House without having an election. She was, after all, still a Republican.

"So let me turn the tables on you," she went on. "If you were president, if history would remember you for just one thing, what would you want it to be? What would be worth risking everything to do?"

It was a question, but also a message:

Presidents were remembered; senators, usually, were not. If history noted these men at all, it most likely would be only as characters in other people's biographies. Perhaps even hers.

"I'm asking you seriously, Travis: if you had to risk everything, what would you want to accomplish?"

The majority leader seemed momentarily without words.

"I'd want us to be a moral nation again," he said at last.

"Which means?"

"It worries me you do not know," Carter said.

"I'm asking *you*," she said again, trying not to lose her temper.

"We're a conservative country, and a Judeo-Christian one. If we returned to the tenets of Christ, we would know how to solve all our problems."

"What you really mean is I'm not conservative enough."

"If you want to put it that way."

"Conservative enough for whom?"

"The American people."

Good. He had said it.

"Ahh, I think I have you there, Mr. Leader. I'm the only one here voted on by all the people."

It was true: only presidents and vice presidents are voted on by everyone. Travis Carter was elected only by the majority of voters in Idaho.

"But the American people have chosen the Republican Party to control the Senate."

"That's the thing, Travis. You think I'm a political orphan. And I think I have something bigger than party. I have the people, and I intend to keep them."

A new poll that morning found Upton had the support of an astonishing 70 percent—among them not only most independents and Democrats but also nearly half of all Republicans.

She was threatening a realignment. She was telling them that, in the politics she was creating, their party affiliation tainted them at least as much as it gave them legitimacy.

"You have six bills sitting in the Senate, all of them basically things Republican senators wanted that David gave you. If you won't pass them—because you don't want to cooperate with the enemy—I am very happy to see which of us is more likely to win the argument over who's to blame," she said.

"I don't have the votes," Carter said.

"No, you just won't give them to me. If you help me, I will campaign for your reelection. I will campaign for anyone who helps get these things done. I don't care which party they belong to. I have a unique freedom to do that. And I intend to use it."

They had never seen her speak to them this way. In the Senate, she often waited for men to talk before she spoke up—letting them blow off their manly steam. Now she was setting the terms of the discussion, framing the questions, some of which were not questions at all but coded messages.

"Do you intend to intrude on the Senate's internal procedures?" the majority leader asked.

There it was.

Travis's calculus. The majority leader cared about one thing. He wanted to protect his power, which resided in the party's cherished unwritten rules that leadership used to keep members in line—only bringing votes to the floor a majority of his own party supported. His way of protecting his members from being primaried. David Traynor had threatened to challenge those rules all the way to the Supreme Court.

Upton had been silent on the question. Her leverage lay in their not knowing her plans. And she wouldn't give them an answer now. But she had threatened them with war nonetheless.

"Thank you for coming out," she said. "I know it's a long drive. I won't keep you any longer. But before you go, please understand something. David's death has changed everything. His wishes, which were popular, are now a national mandate. That means you need to change, too, or I think you will be run over by this."

She left them sitting by the pool.

When she was far enough away, Aggie let out a whistle. "You know, I was a little in love with her once."

Carter ignored him. "She wasn't asking for our help. She was sending us a warning."

"I believe she was."

"Does she really think having no party helps her? That she can realign the public behind her? That she is above party?"

But there was worry in his voice when he said it.

"Maybe I am going to fall in love with her again," Aggie said. Just to bother Carter.

39

OLD TOWN ALEXANDRIA, VIRGINIA

Monday 3 May

JAMES STANHOPE

William James Birdsong Stanhope was halfway through his seven-mile run when he thought of Peter Rena.

He ran most days around noon, unless someone arranged a client lunch. Then he'd run late afternoon: seven miles. Sixty-five minutes. Five days a week.

He tried not to deviate. Discipline and routine encouraged focus. And fitness ensured mental sharpness.

He ran six steps ahead of Ted Jericho, his former military chief of staff and now his business partner. T.J. was faster than Jim in a flat run, but his aide preferred Stanhope to set the pace. He was a natural number two that way, Stanhope thought. They'd been together nearly two decades, even written a book together outlining the "theory of teams management methodology," which their consulting firm offered corporate clients. Their ideas had melded together to such a degree, Stanhope couldn't remember whose ideas were whose.

They crossed over a small footbridge on the Mount Vernon running trail and into Old Town Alexandria, the village a few miles upriver from George Washington's plantation where their consulting firm, the Command Group, was headquartered.

He didn't know why Rena had come into his mind just now. Running did that; random thoughts just came to you from your unconscious. He hadn't thought of Rena in weeks. Not since the cyberattacks.

By all outward measures, at age sixty-five James Stanhope was enjoying a renaissance. His consulting career, plotted out on a yellow legal pad four years ago, was exceeding expectations. The client list included Fortune 100s and top nonprofits; they had a staff of thirty and more inquiries than they could handle. He and T.J. had just published a new two-part series in the *Harvard Business Review*; there were thoughts of a second book.

But if he were honest with himself, success in business felt like a consolation prize, not redemption.

The media were paying him attention again, which meant the question of his retirement would come up at times, usually obliquely. Reporters tended to make more of things like his commando health regime: one meal a day, four hours of sleep a night, and the seven-mile runs. The public relations firm they'd hired pushed it—part of the Stanhope mystique. Reporters also retold old stories about his intensity, like the day of the Army-Navy Game when he was West Point commandant, and he rappeled from the gymnasium ceiling during a pep rally in full battle dress and war paint bellowing "Beat Navy."

Fact was, in Jim Stanhope's world—least his former one—nothing about his health regimen or his fervor were unusual. He could name a dozen commanders with eating-sleeping-exercise routines as intense as his. Hell, he'd copped his when he was a young lieutenant from his colonel. People just didn't understand. You had to set an example: to get troops to exceed themselves in matters of life and death—to become extraordinary warriors—you had to drive yourself harder than you drove them. And once you did, you had to treat your troops like family. Because they were—your other family. You always had two.

They crossed into Old Town proper toward Fairfax Street and the office. They showered in the office gym and dressed—khakis, dress shirt, and Patagonia vest with a corporate logo of his new consulting firm. He had a meeting at 1400—2:00 P.M. civilian time. He'd spend the remaining half hour prepping.

The Command Group offered "global advisory services and leadership development" to corporate clients, nonprofits, and governments.

Translation: they offered the private sector the same lessons Stanhope and his team had taught the U.S. military about agile, team-based decision-making. It made any business work better in uncertain and rapidly changing environments.

He reached his glass-enclosed office, which overlooked the large open area called "the football" where most of the employees worked, a minimalist space with clean lines, warm wood floors, and unfinished ceilings.

There had been some hard years. Healing, hurting, making amends. But he was better, really, teaching the private sector what he'd learned in the army—and finally being paid properly for it. It was saving Ted Jericho's life, too. And the rest of the people he had dragged down with him.

Stanhope saw Paul Weaver, the guy in charge of client acquisition, heading his way. "General?" Weaver said at his door. "They're here."

A prospective client, a company whose business was being wiped out by an online competitor. Stanhope took the file and glanced at the name, "GenTech." He had no idea what business they were in. "Phil Atkins and Stacey Moss," Weaver said, reminding him of the people he'd be meeting. Stanhope nodded and glanced at the calendar on his phone. Meetings straight till 5:00 P.M. He had a date tonight, a movie; he wished he could leave early, go home, and shower again. "Let's go," he told Weaver.

IN THE PARKING GARAGE A FEW MINUTES AFTER FIVE, STANHOPE saw someone standing by his SUV. A man in a shadow.

The intruder wore a gray pinstripe suit and a calm expression. At ten feet, Stanhope was sure.

It was Peter Rena. He stopped and waited for the shadow to speak.

"You know why I'm here." It *was* Rena. Same voice. Same prickly cool. Stanhope resented this man and feared him. He had been ruined by him. Find out what he wants, Stanhope told himself. Say nothing.

"Yes, you know why I'm here," Rena said. As if he were inside Stanhope's head. That was another thing he remembered about Rena.

He thought about pushing one of the blue panic buttons in the parking garage and alerting 911 but then decided the idea was absurd. Rena might be depicted as deranged. But Stanhope didn't want to appear helpless.

"Not here," Stanhope said.

Rena had moved closer to him, uncomfortably close. "Then let's take a walk. Anywhere you like. But right now."

There was a bench he passed on his runs, just across the street near the little bridge by the river. He headed that way and Rena followed him. What did Rena want? What would Stanhope tell him?

40

PETER RENA

Stanhope had aged well except for his eyes. They had sunken into their sockets a little, which made the man behind the chiseled face look wearier and also somehow gentler. They sat on the bench along the bike path.

"It took me a long time to recover," Stanhope began. Rena's expression told him he had used the wrong word; "recover" was not Stanhope's to use. He was the aggressor, not the victim. "I spoke to them all," Stanhope said, meaning the women he had wronged, "every one of them. And apologized."

"I heard that," said Rena.

That was how the story had been told. After his fall, Stanhope had done what he imagined he could to help fix the problem he'd created. Stanhope was a systems thinker. He had made a list of the women he had worked with, the ones he'd made advances toward and the ones he had not, and he had tried to talk to all of them, admitting he had crossed a line, created an unhealthy environment, and was sorry for it.

According to the story, Stanhope was trying to become a better man and help the women he'd harassed. The general had even told a version of that story to Rena's boss, Senator Llewellyn Burke. An ugliness in him had gone, he told Burke, and he had been reminded of his better self.

Rena had never spoken to Stanhope again. Never seen him again. Until now.

"Are you behind what's happening to me?" Rena asked.

Stanhope was looking straight ahead. "You denied me due process. You blackmailed me, with my daughter there. It was an ambush. You should have let the process play out. Not taken matters into your own hands."

This was a different narrative than the one Stanhope had shared with people like Burke. In this version, he had not been redeemed; he'd been denied justice. Rena saw the logic of it. It was true, Rena had taken matters into his own hands. The military had already turned a blind eye to Stanhope's past, and Rena thought it would again. Rena decided that wasn't okay, but he told himself he had done it in a way that had warned Stanhope, respected his achievements and given the general the choice of whether to fight the allegations publicly or not.

"Those lies people are saying about me online, are you behind them?"

"I forgave you, Rena. I understood. Not everyone felt the same way," Stanhope said.

Some of Stanhope's friends and staff, their own careers tainted, were enraged by what had happened.

"Yes, they told you that a man's life should be judged in full. That you should be remembered for all you accomplished, not the mistakes you made. Convenient for them, too." Stanhope turned his head to look at Rena finally. "And as the years went by, you began to see their point."

"Not exactly."

"Are you behind these attacks?"

"No."

"But you knew they were coming."

Stanhope stood up.

"I think we're done here."

Rena stood, too, and positioned his body in a way to stop the older man from leaving.

Stanhope said, "This is the second time you've ambushed me in my life, and I'm tired of it."

"I ambushed you?" Rena said "Is that your story?"

"Go to hell."

The file Wiley had given Rena had offered him the first clues leading him here. She had discovered that the cyberattacks had actually begun a year ago, during the presidential campaign, around the time Peter and Randi had helped Upton. They had not gone viral the way they had on the eve of Traynor's presidency in December, when they were part of a more sophisticated and orchestrated campaign. But they had already involved Katie. And, most importantly, they had named Stanhope. Who would have known about that? Only people close to Stanhope. They were unlikely to have used his name without his consent. When Wiley had shown Rena the file two days ago, he knew he would be coming here—before heading back to California.

"When you were commandant at West Point, they still taught cadets about accountability didn't they?"

Stanhope didn't move.

"You didn't do this. But you gave it your blessing."

"You are arrogant and out of control," Stanhope said. "You always were. Always going according to your own code of justice."

"Who approached you?"

The most likely person was Ted Jericho, Stanhope's longtime aide. He was the person most damaged by the general's fall—other than Stanhope. But Rena doubted that Jericho had had the technical knowledge to mount a cyber campaign this sophisticated. Someone had come to them with the idea.

Stanhope glared at Rena, but Peter knew he had the advantage. He had studied this man closely once. He'd known almost everything about him. He could easily imagine what thoughts were banging around the general's mind now.

The world also looked more harshly today than it did a decade ago at Stanhope's brand of sexual harassment. And while the general had rebuilt his reputation, he could just as easily lose it.

Something else was probably going through Stanhope's mind, too. Rena had caught him a second time.

"I'm not sorry," Stanhope said.

"It's time to put an end to it."

For a long moment Stanhope said nothing. Then, ever so slightly, he nodded his head.

And without another look the former general walked across the small bridge back into town.

ON THE PLANE BACK TO CALIFORNIA RENA TOOK OUT THE BOOK James Nash had given him. *The Irony of American History*, written by Reinhold Niebuhr. As Katie had remembered two days ago, Rena had been enamored once of the theologian-philosopher's writings, but Rena had not opened one of these books in a long time. Had Nash known? Niebuhr was both a liberal and skeptic of liberals. He believed in the goodness of people but was suspicious of groups.

Rena began to read, and the last three days—the last months even—seemed to connect. The conversations with Randi, Katie, Nash, Stanhope, the concerns of his friend Burke, his self-doubts.

"Nothing that is worth doing can be achieved in our lifetime; therefore we must be saved by hope. . . . Nothing we do, however virtuous, can be accomplished alone; therefore, we are saved by love."

41

PALO ALTO, CALIFORNIA

Tuesday 4 May

PETER RENA

"The prodigal son," Brooks said as Rena walked into the FBI office that afternoon.

"You solved this yet?" Rena asked.

"We're planning the party now," she said. "You didn't get the invite?"

It was good to be joking again.

"This just came in," she said, handing him the autopsy report on Kim Matsuda. He sat down at the small worktable set up for them and began to read. "I'll tell Bhalla you're here."

The cause of death was listed as cardiovascular shock brought on by sudden organ failure. Kim had a flaw in a heart valve, the report said, which could have triggered the cardiovascular event. A sudden virus, the report suggested, could also have done it. So could have deadly foreign agents injected into her body—in other words, poison—a technique lately favored by a host of secret police agencies, including the Russians, Chinese, and North Koreans.

Jazz Bhalla had come out of his office while Rena finished reading.

"So they don't know," Rena said.

"They know her system shut down," said Bhalla. "They're not sure why."

"They can't detect if there was poison in her system?" Rena asked doubtfully.

"It's not always easy to tell," Bhalla said.

Rena had dealt with chemical weapons in Iraq and Afghanistan but was no expert. "I thought they could—if they knew what to look for," he said.

Bhalla took in a deep breath to slow them down. "It's true there's no such thing as an untraceable poison anymore. But if a government wants to kill someone, they can make it pretty hard to find. With some of these toxins, it just takes a microscopic amount. And the bad guys are constantly developing new stuff."

All of Bhalla's practiced laconic defeatism was beginning to rub Rena the wrong way.

"Listen, Jazz. We're talking about a special counselor of the president here. Who might just have been poisoned on a U.S. airliner. It's time we acted as if this mattered."

Bhalla's rubbery face tightened in anger. "Kim has family who want to take her body back to California," he said. "We're going to let them do that. But it will make detection harder."

After all these years, Bhalla had become a bureaucrat, Rena realized, a man who defined himself by going along and then complaining about it.

"Then find a way to do both," Rena snapped.

"I liked you better when you were in a daze," Bhalla said. He got up and headed back to his office.

"Got your big boy pants on today," Brooks said.

She didn't ask where he had been for the last few days.

"I'm sorry for the way I've been," he said. "I'm sorry I'm two days behind."

"No apologies, Peter, not between us. I'll get you up to speed. Then let's see what trouble we can make."

They'd made some progress, Rena thought as he listened, but not enough. President Upton had given the FBI charge of Matsuda's death inquiry, which meant Brooks and Rena were allowed in. They had checked Matsuda's apartment in D.C. and had spent a day going through her computer, which had been sealed in a chain-of-custody bag and sent to Bhalla's office here in Palo Alto. But Matsuda was too careful to leave much of a digital footprint. The computer was empty.

"She leave files in the cloud?"

"Nothing," Brooks said.

"Another device?" Rena asked.

"If she had one, she hid it, or someone took it."

"What about the battery companies? Did you visit them? How have they reacted? Are we watching that list of people we're worried about?" He meant the key investors and the handful of scientists they had identified as vulnerable to foreign recruitment. A long to-do list began to form in his mind.

"It's only Tuesday. We got back here on Sunday. But we are visiting them all. We told them Kim's death is under investigation as potentially suspicious. So they're on notice."

Bhalla returned from his office and sat down.

"How many agents are on this?" Rena asked.

"Enough. We'll get more if we need them," Bhalla said.

Rena closed his eyes a moment to calm himself. He was still on edge. They needed to ramp it up. To frighten people. To make it seem as if the president herself were on a vendetta. And they had no time to waste.

Rena's voice fell almost to a whisper. "Let's assume Kim was murdered and work back from there. She found something that she needed to tell us in person. Who had she talked to? What had she found? That's what we should be looking at."

"Let's not get ahead of ourselves," Bhalla said. "We don't know there was a crime."

"Stop thinking like an FBI agent," said Rena.

"I am an FBI agent," said Bhalla.

"And we're not. We have to walk into the Oval Office with our report. So we're going to reconstruct Kim's last twenty-four hours. Find out what she learned. And maybe how she died." Bhalla said nothing, and Rena asked, "Do we have her phone logs?"

"There wasn't much in them. But sure," Brooks said. She pulled Matsuda's cell phone call log up on her computer.

"Can we print this thing so I can actually read it?" Rena said. "And Kim's texts? Do we have those?"

Brooks opened a different window on her computer. "Yeah."

"And can we geolocate where she was through the day?"

"I started doing that," Brooks said.

Rena retrieved the call list from the computer and began to read it. "Who is this?" he said pointing to the third-to-the-last number Kim had called. There were four calls to that same number the day before she died. Brooks clicked into the list on her computer.

"Someone named Royce Hoskins."

"She also texted that number," Brooks said, opening another tab on the screen.

They should have done this two days ago, Rena thought. But Bhalla was an espionage expert, not a homicide investigator, and this kind of criminal investigation was outside Brooks's legal experience. Rena looked at Matsuda's texts.

The day before she boarded the plane to D.C., she must have visited Hoskins. There was a text to him saying: I'm five minutes away.

"Who is Royce Hoskins?" Rena asked.

Brooks looked at her computer. She said: "Teaches journalism at Berkeley."

"Not that guy," Bhalla said.

"Who is he?" Rena asked.

"A conspiracy theorist," said Bhalla. "Kind of a gadfly. Calls himself an investigative journalist. Writes about the Valley. Sees spies everywhere." Bhalla made a sour face. "Half of what he says is bullshit. He just doesn't know which half."

"Where was she when she texted Hoskins?" Rena asked. They would know that from the geolocation data.

"In Berkeley," Bhalla said checking the data by time.

"Tell me more about this Royce Hoskins," Rena said.

It would take some time to reconstruct who Kim Matsuda had seen and what had alarmed her. But now Rena had a plan. Tomorrow, he would begin to retrace the last hours of her life.

He'd been flying all day and then had run over here. He was tired. And he had somewhere else to be. But he finally knew where to start.

42

PALO ALTO, CALIFORNIA

PETER RENA

Vic Madison lived in a small house in Palo Alto on a hidden lane. She had built a wall around it and inside planted a garden inspired by trips she'd taken to Bali. The garden surrounded the house on all sides. Once you entered the walls, you felt as if you had escaped to another world.

She buzzed Peter in at the gate. Inside, he saw Vic sitting on the small deck overlooking a pond stocked with koi and surrounded by ferns.

Vic rose. Rena wondered what would happen next. She walked up to him and touched his face lightly, just her fingertips, as if he might break. "How are you?" she asked.

He didn't try to kiss her, nor she him. But in that simple tender gesture she signaled affection rather than anger at least.

"Better," he said.

"All better?"

"Getting there."

Vic smiled and sat down again, and Rena wondered what would come next.

"I made us dinner," she said.

"That sounds great."

Then on impulse he came around the table and lifted her out of her chair and held her. He didn't try to kiss her this time either, but she put her head on his shoulder.

"Thank you for calling me," he said.

She tightened her hug and Rena heard Vic sigh. She looked up into his eyes and gave a soft sad smile.

They finished fixing the dinner together and ate outside on a small table in the garden.

"I visited Katie in Virginia," Rena said.

"I know."

"How . . . ?"

Vic put her fork down. "She emailed me. Then we talked."

Rena didn't know what to say. The two women had never met.

"She cares about you. She was worried, and she wanted me to know."

She took a sip of wine. He could see Vic was nervous, too, and Peter tried to take it all in, the two most important women in his life talking about him, both relationships he had managed to screw up. That must be why Vic had called him.

"She said you asked her if everything had been your fault. She said you were stupid, but sweet."

"I must have missed the sweet part."

Vic stretched her hand out across the table and put it on top of Rena's. "And when she lost the babies, you were scared. She said you're scared again now."

Hearing about these two women discussing him, Rena felt strangely defenseless. But rather than making him uneasy, he felt an unexpected sense of release, as if his unconscious mind recognized he could let go of something.

"She seems like a remarkable woman," Vic said. "She sounded happy."

They were quiet for a moment. "I know you can't tell me anything about what you are doing out here. But tell me how you're feeling. That's not classified, is it?"

She added a sympathetic, slightly mischievous smile.

Rena told her about being married to Katie, a subject Vic had never asked about and he had not shared, not this way at least. He told her about the miscarriages, not knowing how to react, and throwing himself into work and about how, as the marriage began to fall apart, he felt guilty and incompetent. It was during this time, he said, he had brought down General Stanhope's career and ended his own. "That's what," he said "the cyberattacks are about." Vic nodded, they didn't need to dwell there.

"I didn't have a lot of models for marriage, and maybe I let that be an excuse."

She waited for him to go on.

"In Virginia, Katie told me she thought I confused loving her with protecting her. That I didn't know the difference. That she resented that. That it was almost a kind of disrespect. Maybe I'm not saying this right."

"I think you're saying it fine. You hadn't known that before?"

"Maybe I hadn't really listened."

Vic smiled again and Rena said, "Vic, I think I was afraid that if you and I were married, I would fail again. I would fail you."

She laid her hand back on his, and he felt an electric charge. But she didn't take the subject any further, and then her hand slowly slipped away.

They talked for three more hours, eating, drinking tea, cleaning up. He told her the story of General Stanhope and the investigation, about the cyberattacks and about confronting Stanhope in Virginia last night. But they didn't discuss their argument in Colorado or the issues between them. Rena could sense that door was still closed. He told himself he would wait to see if Vic opened it.

Before he left, Vic hugged him again and gave him a light kiss on the lips. That was all he had any right to ask for, and all she was ready to give.

When he exited Vic's secret world, he drove back to the hotel by the freeway. Tomorrow he would begin to retrace the last hours of Kim Matsuda's life.

43

PETER RENA

Royce Hoskins was a short, well-built man whose eyes said he had seen tougher people than Peter Rena.

His office, in the wood-shingled journalism building on the Berkeley campus, was crammed with piles of papers, which were perched in haphazard stacks on every available surface. Rena had the feeling of being inside the man's brain.

Hoskins was the second-to-last person Kim Matsuda had seen before she headed for the airport on the trip she didn't survive. At least that Rena knew of.

It seemed from what Rena had read that Hoskins was part advocate, part journalist, part crazy, and two parts pain in the ass. A South African former anti-apartheid activist, he had moved to the United States to become an investigative reporter. His résumé included a string of exposés and a half dozen employers. When no more publishers apparently would hire him, he switched to teaching.

At Berkeley, he ran an "institute" that used graduate students as diggers on investigative reporting projects. The projects took years and usually involved publications in different countries. He had also been working on an unfinished book about corrupt money in

Silicon Valley for more than a decade. Most Silicon Valley executives treated Hoskins as a crank or denounced him as an antitech polemicist.

Hoskins stood behind his desk. He didn't offer Peter a seat. "Who are you exactly, Mr. Rena?"

"I told you on the phone," Rena said. "And I'm sure by now you've looked me up."

Hoskins smiled sarcastically. "You're a kind of investigator," he said, "but the details are a little hazy."

"We're in the same business."

"We're not even in the same galaxy," Hoskins snapped. "You work for private clients to keep things secret. I do it for the public."

"I was working with Kim Matsuda."

"Then why do you want to talk to me?"

"Last thing we heard from Kim is she had something important to tell us that she could only say in person. You were one of the last people to see her alive."

Hoskins didn't look surprised at the news of Kim's death. Her demise wasn't exactly a secret, but it wasn't front-page news either: a little-known government official having a heart attack on a plane.

"Who is *us*, Mr. Rena? Who is it you work for—exactly?"

"We off the record?"

"Off the record?"

"As in, you can't publish what I tell you."

"I know what it means. That's useless to me."

"On the contrary, it'll be enormously useful for both of us."

Hoskins gave Rena a glower, but there was curiosity in it now. He offered Rena a chair, too, remaining standing himself; the reporter liked to play power games. Rena settled in.

"I was working with Kim," Rena said. "We report directly to the president of the United States. And we don't know how she died." Rena studied Hoskins's expression. "Because you're one of the last people who saw her alive, I need to know what you talked about."

At this Hoskins took a seat behind his desk. "She die of natural causes?"

"We don't know yet. That's one of the reasons I need to know what she came here to talk about."

"How do I know you're not here to silence me?" Hoskins said.

Rena sighed. "Record the conversation, Royce. Post it to the cloud or whatever you do to protect yourself. But I don't have a lot of time to waste persuading you."

Hoskins took a moment calculating what he might learn versus what he might risk. Then he took out his phone and pushed a button.

"What did Kim ask you about?" Rena asked.

"She wanted to know about investors in the Valley."

"Which ones?"

"People whose money isn't really what they say it is." Hoskins was still trying to get more than he gave.

Rena leaned closer to the reporter. "Stop playing games, Royce," he said, almost in a whisper.

Instead of antagonizing Hoskins, Rena's anger seemed to make him relax a little. He understood anger.

"You ever hear of the Pandora Papers?" Hoskins asked.

"No."

It was the name of an investigative journalism project that Hoskins's institute at Berkeley was a part of, one of several projects of the International Reporting Collaborative, Hoskins explained. In the collaborative, publications from different countries shared documents and resources in order to conduct more ambitious and expensive investigations than one publication could mount alone. The group had done four projects so far, the so-called Cayman Papers, the Utopia Papers, and a couple of others. They'd uncovered international money-laundering schemes that implicated major banks and some of the world's richest people.

"The Pandora Papers is a new project of the collaborative. I'm an advisor on it. Because of my book." The one Hoskins couldn't seem to finish. "The Pandora Papers is looking at whose money is behind the biggest venture capital firms in the world. Who really owns tech?"

Rena had heard of the collaborative and knew its methods were controversial. They involved leaked emails and whistleblowing employees from financial institutions. But their facts held up.

"It's dangerous work, Mr. Rena. They kill journalists these days—even in the United States. Most Americans have no idea. You call the press the enemy of the people enough times, eventually the public believes you."

"Who did Kim ask you about?"

"So you can hide what she found out and protect the people she was looking at?"

Rena balled his hands into fists. "If I were the man you imagine me to be, would I be here saying please?"

Hoskins took a second to let that spin around his mind.

The reporter would talk, Rena thought. Journalists usually did; they were storytellers, not secret keepers. And Hoskins's curiosity about why Rena was here would be too much for him to resist. But he wasn't quite done resisting yet.

"I find it's best to assume the worst about people until they can prove otherwise," Hoskins said.

"Royce, if what I think happened is true, you're in danger."

Rena said it coolly, like a promise rather than a threat, and as Hoskins's curiosity rose, the resistance finally started to drain out of the journalist's face.

"She gave me a list of names. And asked if any of them were surfacing in the Pandora Papers research or my book."

"And had they?"

Hoskins didn't answer. His last stand.

"If you trusted Kim, Royce, you should trust me."

After a moment Hoskins said, "Three of her names are coming up in our research in a significant way."

"Which three?"

Hoskins gave Rena another look and then opened his laptop. He called up a document and turned the screen toward Rena. Then he read the three names aloud from memory.

James Wei of GCM Investments, the series one investor in Helios. The Russian financier Anatol Bremmer, whose firm was an investor in Ignius. And a name they hadn't focused on much before, Omar Abbad, the Bahrainian prince.

"What do you know about them?" Rena asked.

More than the FBI did evidently. Hoskins had tracked meetings Bremmer had overseas with Russian oligarchs. He had emails establishing that Abbad was acting as the front man for a government group, not acting as an individual investor as he pretended. And Hoskins was convinced, with some evidence, that Jimmy Wei's firm was a front for the Chinese Ministry of State Security.

"Does Jimmy Wei know who he really works for?"

"You think these people are naive?" Hoskins said.

"I think the Chinese might tell a well-placed American only as much as they need to."

"For all I know, Jimmy Wei wears a uniform when he's in Beijing," Hoskins said.

"But you don't know."

"No. We follow money. Bank transactions. Paper. We leave the eavesdropping and hacking to you government people. And we leave stealing people's private information to the platform companies."

"What about this Abbad?"

"He's part of a faction in his family that is trying to get their money out of oil. The family is at war with itself. Cousins killing cousins. Very brutal. Very Ancient World. And Abbad is like a mafia don who leaves no fingerprints. He is trying to move from oil to renewable energy, and some of his family doesn't like it."

"Are you writing that in your book?"

"I will."

"Who interested Kim most?"

"All three."

"She didn't seem more concerned about any one more than the others?"

"I just told you no." The hostile edge was returning to Hoskins's voice.

"And which of these men do you fear most?"

Hoskins gave a strange smile. "I don't fear any of them. But the most interesting is Bremmer."

"Why?"

"Because he's the smartest. And because I learned a long time ago if something seems too good to be true, it usually is."

"Which means what?"

"That Anatol Bremmer is a brilliant man. But nobody gets that rich that fast."

Rena looked at a picture of Bremmer on Hoskins's screen. It showed a fireplug of a man in his late forties with a balding square-shaped head.

"Why are you the only person who seems to doubt him?"

"People have a funny habit of lying to themselves about the people who can make them rich."

Then Hoskins told Bremmer's story: the Moscow-born Jew who became one of Russia's richest people, who fled Russia to get away from Putin, and who became a Silicon Valley superstar.

"You don't believe that he really fled?"

"How did he manage to bring his money with him?"

"Maybe he hid it from the Kremlin."

"You really think he could?" Hoskins gave Rena an incredulous look. "Or that he could operate here, as freely as he does, without Putin's blessing? Bremmer could not be so rich, or appear so independent and critical of Russia, unless Putin is getting something in return."

"How do you know?"

"In what I do, you look at facts and you look at context and see what fits. And you keep gathering facts until you have enough to understand the context."

"And what context fits?"

"Anatol Bremmer used to control the Internet in Russia. Now he influences many of the most important tech companies and technology entrepreneurs in the world. It's a much wider sphere of influence than just the Russian web. In exchange for a little information now and again, that is a good arrangement for both Bremmer and the Russian government."

"You have proof in the Pandora Papers that Bremmer's a Kremlin asset?"

"Let me put it this way: By the time we're done, Bremmer's picture will be on page one."

Were Hoskins's suppositions about Bremmer, if Matsuda believed them, enough to get her killed? Rena doubted it. Nothing had happened to Hoskins. These were informed suspicions, not proof. Either the gadfly professor was holding something back, or Kim had learned more somewhere else.

"What did you tell Kim? Or give her? It had to be something more than this."

Another moment of hesitation and Hoskins said, "You ever heard of Yevgeny Lenovsky?" Rena hadn't. "A Russian journalist in Ukraine," Hoskins said. "Lenovsky was beginning to investigate Bremmer. His publication was firebombed. Then he moved to Paris, where he contracted a terrible cancer. Doctors found traces of a naturally occurring chemical and couldn't prove what killed him. But it was the Kremlin."

"How do you know?"

"You ever heard of Talia Rudin?"

Again Rena hadn't, but he was getting tired of this game.

"She was looking into Bremmer's history, too. She died in Berlin. Same cancer."

"Are you going to write that?"

"Should I be afraid of you asking, Mr. Rena?"

"You should be comforted."

"You're not a comforting person."

"What did you tell Kim you're not telling me?"

Hoskins studied Rena's face. "You have enough," the journalist said. "Go do your job."

"What was the poison you think killed Lenovsky and Rudin?"

With a sigh, Hoskins said: "You ever heard of Unit 21966?"

Rena said no.

"What do you government people do?" Hoskins said with a self-satisfied scowl. "It's a specialized group of Russian intelligence operatives. Their job is to carry out killings and political disruption campaigns, largely in Europe. Our government claims to know barely anything about the unit. Officially, U.S. intelligence just learned the name of the head of the unit a few months ago. I hope to God they're lying. I hope for our sake they know more than they can say."

"What's the point, Royce?"

"Unit 21966 operatives have been linked to polonium, ricin, sarin, and mercury. Lenovsky and Rudin died from a derivative of polonium. Same one. I know it sounds like a movie. But you could look it up." Hoskins leaned back in his chair.

"You worry about yourself being safe?" Rena asked him.

Hoskins gave a strange little laugh. "Sometimes it can be a comfort to be considered a broken-down paranoid."

"I can send people here to protect you."

"Go to hell," Hoskins said. "I'd think they were here to hurt me."

"You really think Bremmer is dangerous?"

"I think all three of these men—Wei, Bremmer, Abbad—are dangerous in the right circumstances. Or the people around them are. The Chinese kill. So does the Abbad family. And we already know about the Russians. Because these men are rich and promise to make other people rich, no one is willing to believe it. That's the real evil, Mr. Rena."

Hoskins's eyes were fierce.

"Did Kim tell you where she was going next?"

Hoskins shook his head. "No. Nothing. I'd never met her before. And she was hard to read."

Yes, Rena was thinking. And he and Randi had read her wrong.

BACK IN HIS RENTAL CAR, RENA USED HIS PHONE TO LOOK UP Yevgeny Lenovsky and Talia Rudin and Unit 21966. It was all there. They were dissident Russian journalists murdered in Europe, suspected to be poisoned by this unit of the Russian secret police. He couldn't find out much about Abbad. He used a secure system to text Brooks, who was at the FBI office in Palo Alto, and told her to find out more. Then he headed off to the last person that, as far as he knew, Kim had seen.

44

PALO ALTO, CALIFORNIA

PETER RENA

Damon Williams was listed in the Stanford University faculty directory as a professor emeritus "specializing in the convergence of psychology and anthropology and the study of place and culture." Rena wasn't sure what that meant. Williams's books had titles like *The Psychology of Place: How Where We Live Changes Us*, and *Utopian Illusion: The Cultural Anthropology of Silicon Valley and the Technology Revolution*. Why did Kim Matsuda go to see him?

"Meet me at the golf course," Williams had said when Rena called from Berkeley. "We can have a beer before I get in nine holes."

The Stanford Golf Course's clubhouse was an old stone building with great arched windows overlooking a small putting green. A trim, balding man with a pixie smile waved Rena over to his table.

"Mr. Rena?" he said, rising from his chair and offering a gentle handshake. "Damon Williams. I'm getting a bite. You want something?"

Rena felt pressed for time but realized he hadn't eaten much since yesterday at Vic's. He said yes.

He'd already told Williams some, that he was working with Kim Matsuda on a classified project. Now he added another fact.

"You were one of the last people to see Kim alive."

Williams's face flushed with alarm. He hadn't known.

"She died of heart failure on an airplane. On her way to see me and my team."

"My God."

"Why did Kim come to see you?"

Williams needed a moment, and when he composed himself he said, "Why are you asking?"

There was no time for being careful. "Kim had discovered something and wanted to tell us face-to-face. That's why she was flying to Washington. Do you know what it was?"

Williams shook his head.

"Why did Kim come to see you?"

"We were friends. We'd met at a few conferences." Williams was still sorting through his shock. "I study how culture shapes social and economic behavior—social capital. What makes one place fertile for innovation and another ripe for economic decline, and how do cultures change? The Valley is not the same place it was ten years ago, let alone twenty."

"What did Kim want to talk about. The last time?" Rena tried again.

"I'm trying to explain," Williams said. "I'd done some papers on why there was resistance to investing in climate work here in the Valley. That is a cultural question, not just a financial one. We'd been talking about how hard it would be to focus the Valley around climate."

"I need to know exactly what you talked about that last time you spoke to her."

"She asked me about certain financiers."

Finally, Rena thought. "Which ones?"

"She had a list. I have it at home. I haven't run it down for her yet." Then it seemed to dawn on Williams that Matsuda would no longer need his thoughts about her list.

"Damon, I need to know what you remember now. Did she ask you about Anatoly Bremmer?"

Williams put down his iced tea. "Yes," he said.

"And Jimmy Wei?"

"Yes."

"And Omar Abbad?"

"Yes."

"Anyone else?"

"I'd have to look at the list. But I remember those three."

"Did she tell you she'd seen a man named Royce Hoskins at Berkeley?"

Williams gave an interested smile. "Yes, she asked me about him."

"What did you say?"

"That he's paranoid but not always wrong. Most people think Hoskins is a left-wing nut. I think he's a good person to have around. You need people asking hard questions when so many people are getting rich."

"Did she tell you what Hoskins had told her?"

"Yes. And I told her she should take it seriously. Not everything he said would be right. But it was all worth looking into."

"What did Hoskins tell her?"

Williams shook his head. "I don't recall the details," he said apologetically.

"Was she more worried about one of those three than the others?"

He shook his head. "Not that she told me."

"What about James Wei of GCM Investments?"

"She asked if I thought he was giving secrets to the Chinese. I said it wasn't that simple. It's not as if he's just a spy. He also runs a VC firm that has to succeed on its own. But they certainly pass on information back to their partners in China. No one really seems to care."

"What about Anatol Bremmer?"

Williams's expression became more subtle. "Most people think he's a genius. Hoskins thinks he's a Russian mole. I think it is possible to be both."

"What does that mean?"

"I think you know, Mr. Rena, coming from a place like Washington."

A place like Washington, Rena thought, said by a man who studied the culture of places.

"Do you think Bremmer is dangerous? That he or the Russians would harm Kim Matsuda?"

"That's hard to say. But the record would suggest all of those men would be dangerous when cornered." Then Williams began to look alarmed, as if the implications of Rena's questions had just dawned on him. "Do you think Kim's life could have been in danger because of what she was finding out?" he asked.

"Do you?"

Williams gazed into the middle distance.

"She seemed sort of alarmed, I guess. She didn't tell me why. She asked me about these men and she gave me a list. I should have been paying more attention to her mood."

Rena couldn't tell if Williams was as muddled as he seemed or, like Hoskins, was holding something back. But the more Rena shared, the more focused Williams became. Rena wanted to test him.

"I'm going to tell you one more thing about myself," Rena said. "My partner and I report directly to President Upton. And I am trying to find out if Kim was murdered."

Williams blanched. "You want to know if one of these men might have ordered her death?"

"Could they have?"

"Do I think people have been murdered in the Valley? Yes. And those killings are rarely investigated as anything more than random.

CEOs dying on hiking trips, working out, getting cancer young. We are statistically abnormal here. And I don't believe it is all stress related. That's why Royce Hoskins is worth paying attention to."

"Damon, I will pay for your lost round of golf. I think you better go home and get me that list."

He followed the professor's car to a Victorian home in a leafy part of Palo Alto called Professorville. As they came into the house, Williams's wife called out, wondering what Damon was doing home so soon, whether he had fallen down or gotten hurt.

"All good, Sally. Just a bit of work."

They went into Williams's den, which was an eclectic shamble of books, magazines, saved newspapers and academic journals, and something Williams appeared to be writing, another book apparently, the manuscript set out for copyediting.

"Here it is," Williams said.

He handed Rena a folded typed list, printed from a computer. A list of people inside the Valley Kim had apparently begun to suspect of espionage—employees in the battery companies, investors, and others she might have talked to along the way. She was conducting her own investigation, Rena realized. By each name Kim had some code of her own making about the person, something Rena couldn't decipher.

Peter was overcome with a sense that he was stumbling in the dark.

"Did you go over any of these names with her?"

"We didn't have a chance. She was in a hurry. I took the list home to study. I said I'd poke around. We were going to talk more."

Rena looked at the names again.

"I hope it's helpful," Williams said, sounding pained now that he had missed signals and not done more. "Let me make a copy for myself. And if I think of anything . . ." The sentence trailed off.

"Yeah," said Rena.

Then his phone buzzed. A text from Randi:

It's happened again.

What has? he answered.

You've been attacked online. And not just you this time. Meet me at the hotel.

45

PETER RENA

They met in the extra hotel room serving as their makeshift head-quarters.

On her computer Randi showed him a raft of new postings in 5Click.

Rena was a fascination again in the dark-web channel. Now, however, in addition to Rena beating his wife, he was being linked to pedophilia. The new posts named Matt Alabama and Randi, too. She and Rena were also identified as special assistants to President Wendy Upton.

Rena's cyber scandal had just become the president's.

Whoever was behind this was trying harder now to make it a news story. Some partisan sites would flog it, then a cable host, hoping to goad a White House reporter into asking the president about it. So it was clear now. James Nash had given him the clue. So had Katie. Rena wasn't the target. He never had been. Upton was.

Rena made a call.

"Are you behind this?"

On the other end of the line, General Jim Stanhope took a moment to register the voice, then struck a defiant tone. "Behind what?"

"New attacks against me."

Another pause. "No. I gave you my word."

Rena weighed the timbre of Stanhope's voice and the nature of his hesitant answer. Was that the pause of a man pondering whether to lie, or one trying to surmise what had happened?

"Who's behind this?" Rena pressed.

"I don't know."

Rena let a little silence help the general begin to consider the implications of what was happening. He'd already caught Stanhope for being complicit in the earlier cyberattacks. The new attacks could harm Stanhope even more were he to be revealed as their source: an ex-general trying to smear the president. His consulting firm would be marginalized to the political fringes.

The same thought apparently was occurring to Stanhope. "You and I are not friends," Stanhope said, "but we've never lied to each other." It was true, strangely; whatever their weird, mutually destructive bond, Stanhope and Rena had always been honest with each other face-to-face.

"I'm telling you the truth," Stanhope said.

And after a moment Rena said, "Okay."

Then he called Wiley. "I'm going to give you four names from the battery project. I want you to see if there's any connection between them and the cyberattacks against me."

The names he gave her were Bremmer, Wei, Prince Omar Abbad, and the scientist Patrick Singh, the sullen but gifted engineer they had worried about during interviews, the most obvious of the scientific figures they had identified whose peripatetic career made him vulnerable to foreign recruitment.

Rena felt like they were casting the first narrow beam of light into a vast dark room. They still had barely begun to vet all the employees they needed to. They were grasping at the few clues they had.

"And see if any of them have a connection to General Jim

Stanhope's consulting company, the Command Group. It's a wide net, I know. But we may be beginning to close it."

"What are you thinking?" Brooks asked after Rena hung up.

"That we've been looking at this the wrong way."

"You think there's a connection between the attacks on you and the project we're working on? How could that be? The cyberattacks started before we were doing this."

"We know the first attacks against me started during the campaign. We just hadn't noticed them back then. They never got big enough. What if that began as a way to hurt Upton through me, mostly from ex-military types who know about Stanhope. Then in December it was more organized, more coordinated. Traynor had won. So there was more at stake. Maybe new people were behind it now, or at least more resources. But it stopped once I was kept out of things at the White House, because attacking me didn't get them anything anymore."

"Okay," Randi said.

"Now the attacks are back because I'm involved with the White House again—which means Upton can be hurt."

"I get it. But why do you think it has anything to do with the battery project?"

"It's just a theory. What if someone in the battery project has connections to Stanhope? And what if that person is attacking me again now because we are starting to pressure them?"

She nodded. "And we don't know who it is?"

"You got it," he said. "Whoever it is, they're worried we know more than we do. That we're closer to catching them than we really are."

"Maybe we finally have a break."

"What did you find out about the dead journalists?" Rena asked.

The two Russian journalists, Yevgeny Lenovsky and Talia Rudin, were separately investigating corruption in Putin's government, Brooks said. "In both cases, they had begun by looking into

Bremmer. Rudin first, and when she died mysteriously Lenovsky took up the cause, convinced she was murdered by Russian operatives, by this shadowy assassination group called Unit 21966."

"How did they die?"

"Unclear. But people are pretty sure Rudin died of some form of a poison called polonium. Put on the steering wheel of her car. Lenovsky's death is more of a mystery. They think it was inhaled in flowers. Both were sick for weeks. Rudin died six years ago. Lenovsky four."

"Any more on how Kim died?"

"No," Randi said.

"Any deaths surrounding Abbad? Or even GCM Investments?"

"Abbad's family feud is pretty bloody. Cousins and even half brothers in the Abbad family have died. Poison. Car accidents. Plane crashes. Take your pick. Abbad's family is all part of the ruling elite of Bahrain. There's a lot to fight over—money, power, family. The infighting is like something out of the Roman empire."

"And GCM?" he asked, meaning the Chinese-owned firm where Jimmy Wei was a partner.

"If the royal family of Bahrain is buttoned down, they're like the Kardashians compared to the Chinese. I got nothing."

Rena pulled out his phone again.

"Let's see if we can light a fire under Bhalla. I'm tired of him telling us all the things he can't do."

Bhalla was just leaving the office.

"I want to see whatever files you guys have at the FBI on three people. James Wei, Anatol Bremmer, and Prince Omar Abbad. If you need clearance, call Gil Sedaka," Rena said. "Do it tonight. Here's his number and his cell. Call him at home if you have to."

"Why?" Bhalla asked. "Did you learn something?"

"I will be by in an hour to pick them up," Rena said.

"Peter?"

"I have another call to make," Rena said and hung up.

"What's that about?" Randi asked.

"You said I told you never to trust anyone, right?"

"You don't trust Bhalla?" she asked him.

"I trust you," Rena said. "And I think we're running out of time."

AN HOUR LATER, THE STANFORD PROFESSOR DAMON WILLIAMS called.

"Mr. Rena, I remembered something going through the list and replaying my conversation with Kim. It had slipped my mind. I was so shocked by hearing about her death."

"Thanks for calling, Damon. What is it?"

"Kim told me she was going to see someone else and asked me if I knew the person. But I didn't. That's why I forgot about it."

"Who was she going to see?"

"A Betsy Mullin. I think it was Mullin. It might have been Mullins. But I thought you should know. Since you asked."

So there was one other person Kim had seen before she got on that airplane.

"I hope that's helpful," Williams said.

"Me, too."

46

ROANOKE, VIRGINIA

STEPH MYERS

Gail stood at the door of the small room above the garage where Steph had his computer. "Go say good night to the kids," she told him.

"In a minute."

"Now, Steph. Come on."

He felt the tips of his fingers bristle. Why didn't she understand how important this was? "Okay!" he said, with a pinch more irritation than was wise.

"What do you do in here?" she demanded. She wasn't curious about the world the way he was.

"I told you. There's stuff going on you wouldn't believe."

"The New World Order, Steph?" she said. Her voice dripping with sarcasm. Sometimes she talked to him like he was an idiot.

He took a deep breath. Delusion is power. Apathy is an opiate necessary for the deep state to operate unobserved and out in the open.

"You don't know, Gail. These people in power, they do things. Messing with kids. I mean people we've heard of."

"You mean people we've met?"

"No. You don't understand. People in politics. People around the president. People who think they're above the law. But they're wrong. People are on to them. People are watching."

She had her hands on her hips and she was looking at him like he was one of the kids after they had painted the cat with permanent marker.

"We're watching them. And we're going to catch them."

"From the room above the garage?"

Someday he would have to sit her down and show her.

"If all that is true, you need to do more than sit in the garage," Gail said.

She was right, he realized. Don't just sit here. Find out for yourself. Track down the truth. Get the proof everyone needed. Then the world would see. America would know. He would be recognized. And Gail would see he was a patriot, not a fool.

47

LOS ALTOS HILLS, CALIFORNIA

Friday 7 May

RANDI BROOKS

"I just want to see the man react," Rena had said.

They were heading to Anatol Bremmer's house, and, as far as Randi was concerned, they didn't have much of a plan. Rena had suggested they "poke a stick in the hornets' nest." She didn't have a better idea. So they were going up there with a stick.

They had spent the last eighteen hours learning everything the FBI knew about Anatol Bremmer, Omar Abbad, and James Wei. Abbad was out of the country. Wei would come next.

So Bremmer was first.

Randi tried to lighten her sense of dread. "I've always wanted to see a house worth a hundred fifty million dollars," she said.

That was how much public records showed Anatol Bremmer had paid for his Los Altos Hills home, the wooded suburb in the southern part of the Valley. "How many bathrooms you think he has?"

"Maybe not that many," Rena said, playing along. "Remember, he did pay double the asking."

That was the story at least. When Bremmer moved from Russia in 2010, he bought the most expensive house ever listed in California, which had an asking price of $70 million. To make sure he wasn't outbid he then paid double the list, a decision that seemed to impress people in the Valley more than raise suspicions and helped raise Bremmer's profile immediately. That, Rena had learned from one of Damon Williams's books, was a clear signal of a culture shifting.

Bremmer met them at the door. He had a square face and piercing indigo eyes, and he seemed different from the science geek he projected in the videos Brooks had watched of him, doing talks about space travel at tech conferences. He was more charming and more intimidating.

He greeted them with a slight bow, an old-world formality. "Welcome to my home," he said, and with a wave of his arm invited them inside.

The house was enormous, the grounds behind it even bigger. This was a compound, Randi realized, a place where Bremmer and his family could be protected, probably by an electric fence and armed guards.

He led them to a home office large enough for its own conference table. The three of them sat around one corner of the table, which gave the meeting a sense of intimacy while reminding them of Bremmer's power.

"Why, if I may, the pleasure of this visit?"

When they called ahead, they'd tried to make him worry. They were working for the president, they'd said, and wanted to ask him about a classified research program President Traynor had started, in which he was an investor.

"You saw David Traynor the day before he was inaugurated," Brooks began.

"Yes. David and I were friends."

"What did you two talk about?"

Anatol paused, taking time to read his visitors' faces.

"I told him he should keep away from me," Bremmer answered.

A self-deprecating smile. "A president trying to heal the country shouldn't be seen with an ex-Russian billionaire."

They didn't smile back.

"Was that all?"

"He told me about the classified battery program. I told him he shouldn't have. David was not good at keeping secrets. Most Americans aren't."

Bremmer's accent was thicker than it sounded in the videos.

"You want to know if I am a leaker stealing secrets for Russia. Do you not?"

Was Bremmer trying to shock them? To gain the upper hand? Randi wondered what Peter was thinking.

"Among other things," she said.

"Everyone wonders this of me. Because I live in more than one culture."

Rena spoke now for the first time. "What does that mean?"

"I am a scientist, for example, but also a businessman. Two different cultures. I am Russian and American. I play chess but love baseball. You see?"

Brooks could sense Rena next to her quickly developing a dislike for the man.

"Which culture comes first for you, Anatol?" Peter asked. "Russian or American?"

Bremmer shrugged. "In Russia, I dream in Russian. In America, in English."

It was the kind of answer Rena would loathe, one that sounded scripted.

Rena said, "I don't believe anyone can be equally loyal to two countries at the same time. Especially when those countries are enemies."

Bremmer studied Rena, the performer becoming the observer.

"My heart breaks because my two countries cannot be friends."

"You don't look like you're suffering," Rena said.

Oooh-kay, time to tone it down, Brooks thought. Peter was going too fast. Bremmer would shut down.

"Why did you leave Russia?" she asked, trying to get between them.

"When I was a boy in the Soviet Union, everything was controlled. The party used to register every typewriter in the country so the censors who opened all the mail could know who had written every letter. Imagine. When the Internet came, we hoped it would change all that. End the surveillance society. The web was not so easy to control—at least back then. That's why I helped build the Russian Internet. Eventually I realized what remained of the Soviet Union would never die. It would seize control of the web and turn it into a weapon. So I left."

It was a good story.

"I know why you doubt me," Bremmer said.

"Why would we doubt you?" Brooks asked.

"Because I have an accent and look like Putin." They were both bald, but Brooks didn't see the resemblance.

Rena leaned toward Bremmer now and said softly, "Where did your money come from?"

"This again?"

"Yes, this again."

"It was 1996," said Bremmer, "and I could see the Internet coming like it was memory, something I had always known. I was twenty-two." Bremmer paused. "But I was a student and had no money. If I were to build Russia its own Internet, I would need financing. Who had money? The oligarchs and gangsters. And since they knew nothing of computers, they had to trust us, even though we were only children and also Jews. My family knew someone at Stoya Bank, which was connected to the government. So, yes, our first millions were, what's the American word . . . *tainted*. They usually are. There's an old saying in the Valley: never look too hard at someone's first million. You will always find dirty money."

"If you already were partners with these people, why did you leave?" Rena said.

"When Putin came to power, I knew he would bring Soviet ways and the cult of personality back. He is KGB. So I gave them the Internet I built for them and came here."

"And kept your money," Rena said.

"I sold my company."

"In the middle of the recession?"

"It was still worth a good deal."

"And here you invested even more wisely."

Bremmer smiled. His first two U.S. investments were record setting. A few million into Y'all Post became a billion with the company's public offering. He repeated the pattern two years later with Little Bird. No one knew where the money came from. In those days after the recession, no one had quite so much of it to spend. His investment firm now had more than fifteen billion dollars in capitalization.

"You think we are trying to steal the technology we invest in? And give it to Russia?" Bremmer said.

"Are you?"

"That would diminish the value of our investments."

"How did you come to invest in Ignius so early, before David Traynor launched his program?"

Bremmer's smile this time was thinner. "I had been telling David for years that this century would belong to the countries that controlled two technologies: renewable energy and space travel. So that's where we were investing."

Rena and Brooks suspected Bremmer wanted to own the mineral rights in space, too.

"Why are you two really here?" Bremmer asked.

Brooks later would think it was almost as if she'd heard something snap in Rena's head.

"To decide whether you should be deported," Peter declared.

They had never discussed making a threat like that.

"You live in a black-and-white world, Mr. Rena."

"It makes it easier not to get lost."

Bremmer rewarded that with no smile at all.

"Did you have Kim Matsuda murdered?" Rena asked.

Whoa now, Brooks thought. This needed to end.

"No."

But Bremmer evinced no surprise at the news of Kim's death.

"Did the Russian government kill her?"

"I have no idea."

"Did Unit 21966?"

Bremmer took an extra moment. "I have never met Kim Matsuda."

"Are you lying to me?"

"This is like the riddle about the man who says he will never lie, isn't it," Bremmer said. "Once he says that, you do not know whether to believe anything he says."

They should go, Brooks thought.

"People who look into your history have a habit of dying," Rena said.

"I have heard those stories, too. They are made up by people in Russia who want to hurt me. I left to get away from all that."

"Or you were sent."

They needed to leave. Now.

"Are you threatening me officially?" Bremmer asked.

"I'm threatening you because Kim Matsuda was my friend," Peter said. "And that should worry you more."

That was when Brooks ended it.

"Okey dokey, boys, that's enough," she said.

She stood up. "Thank you for seeing us, Mr. Bremmer." Peter slowly rose, too.

"WHAT WAS THAT?" SHE DEMANDED AS THEY DROVE AWAY.

"We were poking a stick in the hornets' nest."

Yeah, and that plan had sucked from the jump, she thought.

"I think we're going to get stung," she said.

"I think we're going to see which direction the hornets fly."

48

RANDI BROOKS

Brooks told Rena she would interview James Wei without him.

The managing partner of the Chinese-backed venture capital firm GCM Investments lived in a town called Atherton, just north of Palo Alto. There was something odd about the place, she thought, as they navigated the tree-lined streets. The homes were invisible. It was the third-most expensive town in the United States. The median home price was $6.8 million. But the houses were all set back so far away from the street and camouflaged by high walls and canopies of oak and pine that it didn't feel like a neighborhood. It felt like people in hiding. Witness protection for millionaires.

She'd brought Bhalla with her. They needed the FBI man's co-operation, she thought, and including him would be more helpful in getting it than Rena's exasperated and curt treatment of him. But it wasn't unhelpful for Bhalla to know Rena didn't fully trust him. And it wasn't unhelpful for Brooks to play the good cop to Rena's bad—especially when interacting with a real cop.

Brooks didn't know if they had made a mistake challenging Bremmer—even threatening him with deportation. There could be repercussions, but Peter had wanted to force action and look Bremmer over. She had been curious, too. Now she wondered about Jimmy Wei, the brilliant young venture capitalist who they now suspected might be a spy—or even a murderer.

Wei answered the door in a polo shirt and shorts and led them to a living room. The house was a "C-shape," its proud owner explained. The children's rooms ran down one side, he said, the master suite and the parents' offices down the other. The kitchen and common rooms were in the center. Inside the C's hollow, landscaped grounds sloped down gently to a running brook at the bottom of a small hill, with a pool and basketball and tennis courts just above it.

Wei was utterly American. He had come to this country at age three. His father was a Stanford professor. He had gone to Exeter and MIT; he had a Stanford MBA. He was the sixth-rated venture capitalist in America according to the Halston rating score of the field. She wondered what she was doing there.

They sat in the living room overlooking the yard.

"You said you had questions about Helios Corp. and you worked for the president. I don't quite know what that means," Wei said.

Go slow, Brooks told herself. Be patient. Don't scare him.

"How did you get involved in Helios?"

"We were looking for a new generation of energy storage. Something with a longer time horizon. The market right now is in lithium ion. But that's for phones, watches, computers. We're thinking about the power grid and cars. Ten to twenty years out. So we wanted an alternative storage format, one that leapfrogs lithium. Flow is one option. Helios is one bet."

"There are others?" Brooks asked.

Wei smiled.

"You know what percentage of VC investments survive five years?" he asked. Brooks pretended not to know the answer. "Half?" she guessed.

"Twenty percent," Wei said. "Eighty percent of venture investments fail. You make money on a handful of winners. So you have to make *a lot* of money with those."

"How do you know what to look for?"

Wei had to assume she was playing dumb, but she couldn't tell yet. Interviews such as these, with people you suspected were going to lie to you, were like Olympic wrestling matches, all slow positioning at first, feeling one another out, looking for a slip in balance, a moment to take control. Once you had it, you steadily applied more force until the opponent had no way out. Then, slowly pressing harder, you waited for the signal, the first hesitant sign of surrender, as the thought entered your opponent's mind that perhaps they no longer wanted to fight. Rena called it the moment of capitulation.

"We have ideas about what technology gaps exist," Wei said. "What problems society will need to solve. Driverless cars. Clean energy. Predictive AI. The future of health care. The future of drugs. Preparation for pandemics." Wei paused to see if his visitors were following. A man who was used to making the complex simple. "Then you bet on people you think are likely to arrive at those solutions. But we don't expect them to have the solutions yet."

"No? You're not betting on their ideas?"

Wei uncrossed his legs and smiled knowingly. "Ideas are a dime a dozen. Scores of people come to us with variations of the same ideas over and over. What you're looking for are the characteristics you want to find in a successful founder. Not the perfect solution but someone who can find their way to it."

"Why Helios?"

"I liked Bill Stencel," Wei said, referring to the company's CEO.

"What about him?"

"He's an actual scientist. He's not doing this to flip it and get rich. He is trying to find a better flow battery. I'll take the scientist every time. I can teach them the business end. And I've had my fill of so-called serial entrepreneurs."

Brooks nodded enthusiastically. She didn't want to threaten Jimmy Wei. Not yet.

"Tell us about how much money you've put into Helios."

The question clearly made Wei uncomfortable.

"Why?"

"Why not?" Bhalla chimed in now, adding a little official FBI presence to the conversation. Brooks appreciated his timing.

"What's your interest?" Wei said.

"We're interested in this program. We're vetting the security of the companies," Bhalla said. "But I assume Bill Stencel let you know that."

"Yes. So had Kim Matsuda."

Kim had warned him, Brooks thought? Or was investigating him? "How much money have you put in Helios," she asked again.

"You must know the answer to that. I went through this with Kim."

"And what did you tell her?" Brooks asked.

"Ask her," Wei said.

"Why won't you tell us? Since she's not here," said Bhalla.

"I don't understand why you're giving me a hard time," Wei said.

"How much of the financing of GCM comes from China? What percentage of the fund's assets?" Brooks asked.

"It's not against the law to have Chinese financing in a venture capital firm."

"Do you have family still in China?"

Now Jimmy Wei was becoming uncomfortable. They were in his house, asking questions he hadn't expected. Which was exactly what they wanted him to be thinking.

"Yes, I have family in China."

"Where? We'd like their names," Bhalla said.

"Why? Mr. Bhalla, what's going on?"

"Special Agent Bhalla," Bhalla said. "What did you talk to Kim about?"

Wei was halfway to exasperated. And they were jumping around from topic to topic to confuse him. He didn't like it.

"I can't even remember what you've asked me."

Smart boy, Brooks thought. Everyone was playing dumb.

"So answer what I ask," Bhalla said. "Do you have family in China? Where? What are their names? And then you tell us what you told Kim Matsuda."

Wei took a moment to think about it. "I have family in Beijing, Hong Kong, and Wuhan," he said.

"What are their relations to you?"

"First cousins. Uncles. Second cousins. And so on."

"A lot of family."

"Yes."

"When was the last time you saw them?"

"I go every few months on business."

"Do you have a superior you report to in China at GCM?"

A long pause. "I'm managing partner here in Menlo Park. We are an independent subsidiary of a Chinese company. But we have fellow partners in our offices in Beijing."

"When was the last time you saw Kim Matsuda?"

"I'd have to check my calendar."

"Answer the question, sir."

Wei checked his phone. "The last calendar item was two weeks ago," he said. "But she dropped by the office last week, I remember. Just dropped by. Not scheduled."

"Why? What did you talk about?"

"She asked me how I thought Helios was doing."

"Why did she come by unexpectedly to ask that? Why not schedule a regular meeting? Was she asking about something specific?"

Wei studied Bhalla's expression. "Ask her. It seemed like just a check-in."

"When was your last phone call with her?"

Wei looked at his call list. "This is the wrong phone. I'd have to check my business unit. It's in the other room."

"I can go with you to get it," Bhalla said.

"When we're done," Wei said, hoping Bhalla would forget.

"Did you know Kim Matsuda from before?"

"Before when?"

"Before Helios. And before she began investigating your investment in it."

Wei tried not to react to the word *investigating*.

He had met Matsuda at a couple conferences on alternative energy, he said. But she was a climate person, not a financial one, so their worlds didn't really intersect.

"She's dead," the FBI agent said.

They watched Wei's reaction. If Wei were a trained Chinese State Security officer, he might be prepared for the eventuality of a police interrogation in the United States. If he were simply a naturalized American financial guy, he might be shocked. If he were a spy assigned to penetrate Matsuda's climate program, he would almost certainly know she had died.

The financier didn't react at all at first, didn't appear to understand or maybe he was trying to decide how to react. He just stared at Bhalla.

Then, as if he finally understood, Wei appeared to become genuinely upset.

He put his hand over his mouth and shook his head. "My god. How did she die?"

"How much of GCM's money comes from the Chinese government?" Bhalla repeated.

Wei looked up at the FBI man as if the question were ghoulish. "How did Kim die?" Wei asked again.

"We're still establishing that," said Bhalla. "But I need you to answer my question. How much of GCM's money comes from the Chinese government?"

Wei took a moment to compose himself. "That's not as simple to answer as it might seem. What's Chinese government funding versus private isn't as clean and simple as Americans would be used to."

"So you're a government company," Bhalla said.

"How did Kim die?" Wei repeated. "An accident? What can you tell me?"

Was he genuinely interested? Or trying to find out how much they knew? Randi couldn't tell.

"We'll let you know when we're able," Bhalla said. "So all of your investment in Helios is government investment?" Bhalla said.

Wei said nothing.

"Did you know Kim was dead?" Bhalla asked, switching patterns again.

Wei's face flushed in anger. "Obviously no. And I'm insulted by the question. And I think we're done talking. If you're implying that I had any knowledge of what happened to her, I believe any further conversations should include my attorney."

"You're not being questioned in connection with anything criminal. I just asked you if you knew she was dead."

"You were asking me if I was lying before when I seemed surprised to hear that she was. Don't treat me like a fool, Special Agent Bhalla."

"I wouldn't make that mistake, Mr. Wei."

The two men were staring at each other. Brooks thought they should move on.

"How many times would you say you had met Kim Matsuda in your life?" she asked.

"A dozen. Twenty. Most of it in the last five months." Wei studied Brooks, trying to decide whether she would be more honest with him than Bhalla. "Why are you here?"

"With Kim's death, we need to review the situation involving the companies, including Helios. It's possible that we may require that GCM disinvest. That is why we need to reconstruct what you and Kim last discussed. That is why we need any notes you have of those meetings. That is why we need your candor." She took a moment before adding, "I have just told you the truth. Now we need the same of you—if you want to retain your investments. You have twenty-four hours to provide the information we seek about the source and scale of GCM's funding in Helios."

There was no way they could get a court order to tap his phones. They had no basis for suspecting him. They could follow him. It would take more teams than they had right now. There wasn't exactly a lot of foot traffic on the streets of Atherton. Or even sidewalks.

And Bhalla had become almost as angry as Peter had.

"He didn't seem to know Kim was dead," she said to Bhalla as they were leaving.

"He was absolutely lying," said Bhalla.

49

PALO ALTO

PETER RENA

"We've been called back to Washington," Rena said when Brooks and Bhalla returned. "The president wants to see us."

He showed Brooks his phone. They had to be there at 6:00 P.M. the next day.

Had Bremmer called the White House in outrage after their visit this morning? Were they being summoned back in shame? Could the Russian get results that fast?

Rena wondered if he had ruined things. He was still sifting through his anger at Bremmer. Randi had been right. He had lost control. He kept doing things as if someone else—an unchecked version of himself—was making decisions for him.

What would they tell Upton? That he had threatened to deport back to Russia one of the most influential venture capitalists in America—without either the authority to do so or any evidence? That the president should have accepted his resignation last week because he wasn't up to this?

He could feel Randi's eyes on him, concerned at his performance and what it might have cost them.

"How'd it go with Wei?" he asked.

Brooks lifted her eyebrows to suggest she wasn't sure.

Bhalla said they had pushed him hard, just as Randi and Peter had with Bremmer, and Wei had said he wanted his attorney present. When they'd asked how much money in Helios was from the Chinese government, Wei wouldn't answer.

"I don't like the guy," Bhalla said.

"He claimed not to know Kim was dead," Randi added.

Peter turned that over in his mind. "It's possible, but it seems unlikely," he said after a moment. "The guy's business is to keep track of the health of their investments. It seems a relevant fact."

"I think he's a Chinese agent," Bhalla said.

Rena looked at Brooks.

"And I think," she said, "that we need more than suspicion and intuition."

A *New York Times* sat on the table in the small room. UPTON SIGNS BILL ON CRIMINAL JUSTICE REFORM read the headline.

"She's making progress," Rena said, trying to find something positive to say to calm his partner. The criminal reform bill was an important piece of Traynor's "seven crises" agenda.

"It's all she'll get for now," Brooks said. "Senator Carter vowed in the private party conference this morning, no more bills." That had not been reported anywhere, Rena thought. But Randi still had her sources on the Hill, even from all the way out here in California. Very little happened in D.C. she didn't know something about.

The story below that one was about Upton's continuing reluctance to name a vice president. People in both parties were wondering what she was waiting for. Upton could be sphinx-like. The press was full of speculation.

Rena felt like calling Vic.

"We better figure out what we are going to tell Upton," Brooks said. "Or this whole escapade is over."

It should be over, Rena thought. What had they accomplished? They'd learned Silicon Valley has no control over vital technology. They learned the battery program was potentially full of leaks, but they could prove none of them. They'd learned the start-ups were promising, but promises were all they had achieved. They had made a hash of this. And it was his fault.

His phone was ringing. It was Ellen Wiley. He put her on speaker.

"You asked me to check for connections between those four names and the cyberattacks," Ellen said. "We didn't find one. But we found something else. A company owned by Anatol Bremmer did consulting for Jeff Scott. It was in the FEC filings."

"Why would Bremmer be connected to Scott?" Rena asked. "He was friends with Traynor."

"Maybe this was just a random thing," Wiley said. "Bremmer has a lot of companies and Scott hires a lot of consultants. Especially when he ran for president."

"No, it's no coincidence," Brooks said. "Bremmer was hedging his bets. In case Scott won."

"How do you know that?" Wiley asked.

"Because that's what I'd tell a client to do," Brooks said. "Bremmer was ingratiating himself with Scott as insurance, to protect himself, if Scott became president. I'm sure of it. It would be good business. And good espionage."

"What was the company, the one Bremmer owned, that worked for Scott?" Rena asked.

"An Internet research group called Stratica," said Wiley.

"What exactly do they do, Ellen?" asked Brooks.

"From what I can tell, reputational analysis and cyber analysis," Wiley said. "They scrape the Web for information about people or companies and sell it to clients. It says they also deconstruct cyber-attacks."

"They what?" said Rena.

If you can deconstruct how a cyberattack happened, you could probably conduct one, he was thinking.

"Ellen, can you look for connections between Stratica and Stanhope's company, the Command Group?" Rena asked.

"That may be hard to find," Wiley said. "But, Peter, why would Bremmer have been stalking you? That began before we had ever heard of Anatol Bremmer."

"I think the favor Bremmer did for Jeff Scott was to hurt Wendy Upton by going after me," he said.

"You've lost me," Wiley said.

"Bremmer and Traynor were friends. He wouldn't have agreed to attack Traynor directly. And he wouldn't have taken the risk. But Wendy was another matter. Scott hated her for joining Traynor's ticket, and he blamed Randi and me for helping her."

Last year, they had discovered the person trying to blackmail Upton was a Scott supporter. And they had made the problem disappear by threatening to expose the Scott campaign's association with it. Scott had been furious.

Brooks laid out the rest of the scenario. "Bremmer approached Scott, offering that they do business together. Scott wanted to hurt Upton. But she was popular, and the best way to undermine the credibility of a popular figure is by attacking the people around them. You chip away at them from the sides rather than going head-on. Scott still bristled at what Peter and I had done. And maybe he knew Stanhope. They were both ex-military and would have had friends in common."

Brooks paused. "The only thing I don't get is the attacks didn't get intense till after the election. Why not during the election, when they first surfaced. We didn't even notice them." Then her face changed as the pieces clicked.

"Peter, you realize what happened?" Brooks said. "Bremmer never expected David Traynor to die, or for you and I to be investigating him. We'd never heard of him until a month ago. Once Upton asked us to look at the battery program, we were staring right at him."

That's what he had sensed with Bremmer yesterday. He had sensed the man's culpability and his lies. He just hadn't known yet what Bremmer was lying about. Now he did.

"There's one more piece I haven't told you," Wiley said. "That name you gave me, Betsy Mullin." It was the name Rena had gotten from the Stanford professor Damon Williams, the one Williams remembered last night, the last person Kim Matsuda intended to see before she boarded the plane on her fateful trip to Washington.

"There are more than a thousand people with the name Elizabeth, Beth, Betty, or Betsy Mullin or Mullins in the Bay Area."

So that was a dead end, Rena thought.

"But there's only one who works at GCM Investments," Wiley said.

It wasn't Bremmer who Kim had discovered might be spying on the battery program. It was Wei.

THEY FLEW TO D.C. THE NEXT MORNING. THEIR MEETING WITH Upton wasn't until dinner, so they'd have time to go home and shower before seeing the president.

Somewhere over the Midwest, Brooks asked where Rena had gone the other day when he left mysteriously for the evening.

"I saw Vic."

"What happened?"

"It was good."

"That all you have to say?"

"We gal pals now? Gossiping about my personal life?"

"You're really quite stupid sometimes, Peter. Have I mentioned that?"

"That's what Katie told Vic. They talk now apparently, too, my ex-wife and my ex-girlfriend."

"Do they?" Randi said. He could tell by the way she said it that she already knew. How often did she and Vic talk?

"Vic has stopped seeing that man," Randi said.

The one she had been seeing in December, Rena thought. The one he learned about during the argument in Aspen. How much else did Randi know that he didn't?

"Why didn't she tell me that?"

"Maybe she was waiting for you to ask?"

Rena said nothing.

And after a moment Randi said, "See what I mean. Stupid." But she was smiling when she said it.

WHEN THEY LANDED, RENA HAD JUST ENOUGH TIME TO GO HOME, shower, and change. He'd never dined with a president before, even with James Nash. But this was a working dinner, so he put on a gray pinstripe, the uniform of the Washington aide, a uniform to which he had never quite gotten fully comfortable.

As he dressed he heard knocking at the front door. Rena had on his shirt and pants but no shoes. He had no time right now for a kid canvassing door to door for Greenpeace. But the knocking didn't stop.

═ 50 ═

STEPH MYERS

The trip to D.C. took Steph just under four hours in his truck. Straight up 95 from Roanoke. He found the house easily enough, even though he didn't use GPS. He didn't want anyone tracking him, now or later, even after it was over. Especially after it was over. Cops did that he knew. Got your cell phone data. Then they could see everywhere you had been. So he'd turned the thing off and removed the SIM card, gone old school. Three paper maps spread in the passenger seat next to him. Found a space to park where he could see the house. Got in the backseat, behind the tinted windows. He could do this for hours.

There seemed to be no one home. Then, around four in the afternoon, a kid from next door walked over to the house. He waited to see Rena open the door for her, but the kid used a key to let herself in, and Steph knew then Rena wasn't home. He and Gail always asked Lucy from across the street to feed and walk Rollo whenever they were gone. But the girl didn't come out with any dog, so Steph focused in with his binocs. He could see the kid moving around inside an interior room. She was in the kitchen, he thought. The girl leaned down and picked up a cat. Steph smiled at his instinct to stay in the car and wait. He hoped the guy wasn't out of town overnight.

He dozed awhile. Then a car pulled up and a man got out, taking a suitcase from the back. It was him. Rena.

Well, holy hell.

He waited a minute. Then he got out and went to the back of the truck and got his things. He walked slowly toward the house. A knock on the door. Another. He could feel his heart beating out of his chest.

WHEN THE DOOR OPENED, HE SAW PETER RENA IN SUIT PANTS and bare feet. Steph slid a handgun from his coat with his right hand and pointed it at Rena's head.

"Back up. Inside the house. I'm coming in. You monster."

Rena moved backward slowly and Steph passed over the threshold and moved inside the house. He had done it. He was here. His heart was still pounding.

Holding the Glock in his right hand, he swept the long gun from under his coat with his left. Just the way he had practiced it. An ArmaLite AR-15. How do you like that, asshole? He aimed the automatic rifle at Peter Rena.

The man was cool, he'd give him that. Steph watched as Rena glanced at the long gun and then brought his dark eyes right back to Steph's.

Steph holstered the pistol and kicked his left foot back to swing the front door closed.

"Let's go down to the basement," he said to Rena.

"Why?" the asshole asked, stalling.

"I want to see for myself."

"See what?"

"Don't try to stall me, you monster. I'm here to put an end to it. And save those kids."

"I don't know what you're talking about," the monster lied.

Steph tried to control his breathing. The man in his bare feet seemed eerily calm. Of course he was. He was a monster. He had the devil in him.

"We're going to see your dungeon. Where you rape children. I'm here to verify it. And rescue them," Steph said.

"Point the gun down," Rena said. "Put it on safety. And I will put my hands on my head, and we can go down there. And you can see everything."

"No tricks!" Steph yelled.

"No tricks. The steps down there are steep. You don't want that weapon to go off by accident."

"Shut up."

"Whatever you've read, whatever rumors there are about this house or any other place, they're lies. Put the gun on safety. Find out for yourself. You want to know the truth? Let's find out. You'll see. You've been lied to."

STEPH STARED INTO THE MAN'S EYES. THEY WERE THE COLOR OF black coffee and hooded so they looked sleepily back at you, and Steph knew he was a monster. He pointed the AR-15 at the man's head. The point of the gun shook a little. He aimed it lower so he wouldn't miss.

"Let's go," he said louder and waved the 15 at the basement door.

Holy Jesus! Something touched his leg.

The cat! It had nuzzled his leg. He almost let a round go right there. The cat was fat and gray and had weird gold eyes. It looked like something evil, something a witch or a warlock would have. The cat freaked him out.

Then the monster began to move.

Rena moved slowly toward the door to the basement stairs.

"The light's over here," the child predator said, pointing to the switch. "It's at the top of the stairs. I'll turn it on. Is it okay for me to turn it on? Then I will head down first. And you can follow. You can see everything that way. Verify everything. For yourself. Okay if I turn the lights on?"

The man was so calm it frightened Steph even more. Maybe he should just shoot him right now. He pointed the gun at Rena's heart.

"I'm Peter. Who are you?"

The man was trying to play him, he could see it. The guy had been Special Forces. But he was old now.

"Shut up!"

"I'm not hiding anything," the monster said. "Ask me anything you want. I'll walk ahead so you can see me and know where I am. Just be calm."

The fucking cat was purring. Steph looked down at him. It was unreal. Everything was unreal.

HE WAS AFRAID OF GOING DOWNSTAIRS. BUT HE COULD SENSE that the monster, though trying to be calm, knew he was dangerous. Took him seriously. Knew the gun was loaded.

"What do you want to do?" Rena asked.

He could hear the tension in Rena's voice.

Steph took a few breaths. "Let's go down there," he said. "That's what I came for."

Rena turned and began walking down the cellar stairs, turning the light on as he reached the first step.

Steph thought again about shooting the man right there on the stairs, executing him in the back of the head.

He wanted Rena to walk faster. He didn't trust him.

"Get moving!" Steph yelled.

Rena took the next step. Steph followed but he didn't feel it would do any good to keep yelling.

The damn cat was following them, padding slowly behind Steph down the stairs. He only wanted to see what was down there. But he couldn't imagine shooting anyone with the cat watching.

The basement was small, smaller than Steph imagined it. He had expected some kind of pedophile headquarters down here. Kids in a locked room. This just looked like a semifinished basement. There was a rowing machine and weights and a television set and a washer and dryer.

There had to be another room. A hidden room.

"None of it's true," Rena said. "There's no one here. It's all lies."

"What's in there?" Steph pointed to a door.

"Electrical and furnace."

"Open it."

Rena showed him inside. It wasn't locked. Steph couldn't see any other rooms.

The two men stared at each other.

Then Steph fired into the ceiling and let out a scream.

51

PETER RENA

Rena moved at the sound.

The scream would slow the man's reaction time, and in a second Rena had hold of the rifle. The two men had equal grip of it now, their feet shifting, struggling for advantage.

Rena had only to add to the man's fear. He tried to position his grip and his weight so he could take one foot off the ground. He pushed lightly to move the intruder back, then lifted his right leg, his dominant one, and kicked the man behind the left knee.

One of the man's hands loosened from the gun just enough. A moment later Rena had jerked it free. He aimed it at the young man.

"Sit down on the floor." The intruder didn't move. He was a young man with a close-cropped beard and longish hair. Rena pointed the gun down again at the floor, a sign for the man to sit. Slowly the man did what he was told.

"I won't hurt you," Rena said. "Everything's going to be fine."

The young man closed his eyes and let out a howl that Rena knew was the chant favored by an online group that called themselves The Guard. Then the young man's eyes began to fill with tears.

"The pistol, too," Rena said. "Hold it by the barrel and slide it here."

The young man gave another howl, but this time it was laced with frustration.

Something had gone out of him. Still, he didn't hand over the pistol.

Calmly, Rena said, "Put your hands on your head and kneel down. Please, don't make me knock you down."

The young man slowly kneeled.

"Hands on your head."

The man complied and Rena took the pistol from his coat.

Rena slung the long gun around his back and clutched the pistol in his hand. He stood behind the man and put a hand on his shoulder.

"You a veteran?" he asked.

Something about the way the young man moved.

"Yeah."

Then Rena slowly walked around him so he could look the young man in the eye.

"You read about General Stanhope?"

"I served with guys who knew him."

"Those are all lies," Rena said. "We can call Stanhope right now. He will tell you."

The young man had his head down. Rena saw tears flowing.

Rena knelt beside him. "What's your name?"

Then the young man moved his hand toward his boot. Rena saw the bottom of a sheath there. A knife strapped to the calf. Rena stepped back and aimed the pistol again. "I'll take that, too," he said.

"You going to call the police?"

"No," Rena answered. "What's your name?"

"Stephen Myers."

"Where's your wallet?"

"In the truck."

"I'm going to take your ammo, Stephen. And whatever you have in your truck. And then you should go home. I'm not calling the police. Go home to your family."

Myers shifted on the floor. He wiped his eyes.

Rena could see shame and confusion sweeping over the young man's face, like a fever breaking.

"Promise me one thing," Rena said, "and you can go home."

Myers looked up.

"You can't carry this around. You need to talk to someone. Get some help. There's nothing here. No kids. No monsters. No Satanism. It's all lies."

Myers rubbed his eyes. He was trying to look strong and push away his shame. He didn't say anything as Rena emptied the rounds from the weapons.

Together they walked up the stairs and out of the basement and Steph led Rena to the 4x4 parked down the block. Rena found extra rounds in boxes behind the front seats, and two more handguns. The ID in the wallet confirmed the man's name was Stephen Myers.

"Why aren't you calling the police?" Myers asked. "Because they'd find something? A door you didn't show me?"

Rena shook his head. "If that's what you want let's wait for them and see. They'll be here any minute because of the shot. You can tell them what to look for. But I'll have to make a report. And they will arrest you. Entering my home with a weapon and holding me hostage? Those are serious felonies. Or you can leave."

"And what will you tell them then?"

"The truth. That this was a misunderstanding and I sent you home. But I'll have to tell them who you are. People heard the shot."

"That's it?"

"No, they'll call you. But if they hear from me first that it was a misunderstanding and I sent you home, they won't arrest you. Unless you're still here. Then they'll have to." Rena moved closer so the young man would look him in the eye. "Go home," he said. "See your family. These were lies. You've proven it."

Myers took a long moment. A police siren wailed somewhere nearby. Rena had no idea where it was heading, but it wasn't here. Then Myers got in his truck and drove off, as if he'd never been there.

Rena sat down on the curb. He had sweated through his suit. He needed to shower again and put on different clothes. He would be late.

He'd thought he was going to have to kill that man.

52

WASHINGTON, D.C.

WENDY UPTON

Who came late to dinner with the president? Wendy Upton thought.

Only Peter Rena.

There should be no complication getting here. Drive to the private gate on Fifteenth Street, then straight to the South Portico and leave your car with the attendant. Why was he late?

Fifteen minutes later an aide ushered the fixer into the Old Family Dining Room on the second floor of the Residence. Rena was flushed and perspiring. He made apologies, then whispered something to Randi Brooks, whose expression registered some kind of alarm.

But Wendy Upton couldn't worry about that. They had an important decision to make. Rena's continuing personal dramas had to wait.

The secret battery program she had inherited had turned into a mess. From what she could make out, the two people she had trusted to look into the program for her had found nothing good. The scheme seemed insecure. Its director was dead. And now they had threatened one of the country's most influential investors with deportation.

She had gone along with giving this more time, out of deference to David Traynor's memory and as a favor to Quentin Phelps. But she worried the program was running off the road. The timing was now bad, too. Since her meeting with Travis Carter and Aggie Tucker at Camp David, the Senate had brought two more of her bills to the floor, both of which passed. But Carter had made it clear there would be no more, not for the time being. He was testing her resolve—as well as her threat that she had more political capital than he did. But she could hardly afford a scandal about misused intelligence and a far-fetched secret plan to invent a new battery. Such a scandal would stall and possibly scuttle the rest of her agenda.

The only time she had had for this meeting was over dinner, which she was holding in the Residence, away from aides and the West Wing's public schedule. It was a personal dining room, not a ceremonial one, framed by large rectangular windows overlooking the mansion grounds. She had asked four others to join them: Quentin Phelps and Gil Sedaka; along with the FBI director, Owen Webster; and the head of National Intelligence, Sally Holmes, a Traynor appointee.

Now that Rena had finally appeared, they sat down at the table, the time for small talk over. The stewards arrived with salads and she got down to business.

"It's decision time on this battery program," she announced. Terms of the evening set. "If there is anything new that I should know, tell me now."

She had the sense Rena and Brooks had let her down, that they had gotten caught up in the program's far-flung optimism and lost their objectivity. She wanted them to know there was no more time for negotiation.

Rena spoke first, which was unlike him. "We have learned a good deal in the last seventy-two hours. We still don't know how Kim Matsuda died. But there is more reason now to suspect she was poisoned, perhaps by the Chinese Ministry of State Security. Proving that may be impossible."

Upton stared at the FBI director in surprise. Did he know any of this?

"That's not all," Rena said. "We now believe we know what Kim discovered before she died: that the Chinese government has infiltrated the battery program through a government-owned venture capital firm backing one of the companies. We believe the Russians may have infiltrated the program as well, through one of the most influential investors in the Valley. His name is Anatol Bremmer. We believe he lives in the United States and pretends to be a Putin critic but secretly works with the Russians."

"Why would he do that?" the president asked.

"In exchange for a higher price when he sold them his companies ten years ago. And to protect family and friends who are still in Russia," Rena said.

That was the man who yesterday had called Quentin Phelps, Upton recognized, complaining that Rena and Brooks had threatened him. Upton signaled Phelps with a glance to say nothing. She wanted to hear this out.

"That is why we visited Bremmer yesterday and informed him of our suspicions. We threatened him because we wanted to see how he would react. The same way the FBI might visit someone to apply pressure."

"But you're not the FBI," the Bureau director, Webster, reminded them.

"That's why it was safer for us to do it. We're outside consultants who might have gone rogue."

"A little beyond your brief, don't you think, Peter?" Upton said.

"No question, Madam President. But if we'd asked you first, you wouldn't be able to disavow us, if that is what you decide."

"You have anything to say, Randi?" she asked Brooks.

"There's something Peter hasn't mentioned," Brooks said. "We didn't know it when we saw Bremmer, but we now believe a company he owns is behind the cyberattacks against Peter. And we believe those attacks were designed to hurt you, Madam President. Bremmer's motive for this was to do a favor for Michigan Governor Jeff Scott."

"What?" said Gil Sedaka.

"Scott's people contracted with one of Bremmer's companies during the campaign. A firm called Stratica, which specializes in protecting against cyberattacks. But it would also know how to instigate them."

Upton encouraged Brooks to keep going.

"The first attacks against Peter came during the campaign. But they gained real momentum when you asked us in December to help with the transition. Scott has never forgiven you for joining the Traynor ticket, and the best way to undermine you was to discredit the people you were associated with. We were a perfect target."

Upton had not expected any of this.

One of FBI director Owen Webster's considerable political gifts was a rich baritone voice, which he employed in meetings to make his points seem more persuasive. Webster used the marvelous instrument now.

"Madam President, I believe it's time for the FBI to handle this. From what I can see, these outsiders have turned a secret program into a public disaster."

Not yet it wasn't, Upton thought. But it could become one.

"Are these battery companies going to come up with anything?" she asked.

Brooks was probably not qualified to know, but Upton wanted to hear her answer. Upton had already commissioned a separate team of scientists to give her an independent assessment of liquid metal flow batteries. They had confirmed the conclusion of Kim Matsuda's group: flow batteries were probably the most promising technology for energy storage and they lacked investment. So Upton had decided to explore launching a separate government program to develop them in a classified laboratory in Maryland—just in case

Traynor's start-up program out west had to be shut down. She was also considering using classified budgets to launch three other plans that had been thought promising back in their clandestine climate change gatherings in Colorado during the transition. This had been a Phelps idea, but she was warming to it. Additional programs would make Traynor's bold battery program seem less random and more planned out. David's mistake, she was concluding, had not been his boldness. It had been betting all his chips in one go-for-broke pot. Now, if she had to close it, at least she could let the government try several smaller projects in secure classified labs.

Brooks gave her answer. "It's only been about a hundred days. I wouldn't expect much progress yet."

The FBI director clanked a salad fork on his plate.

"But we think these companies are worth sticking with a little while longer," Randi added. "They were picked for a reason. Of all the companies and labs out there, they have the best chance, the most experience, the best teams. It costs something to start over. You need to appoint someone to replace Kim. Additionally, we would recommend putting Jazz Bhalla of the FBI office in Palo Alto in charge of their security."

Well played, Upton thought.

The director of National Intelligence asked, "But you said you believe the Chinese and Russians have already infiltrated the program?"

"They were always going to eventually," Rena answered her. "All you were ever buying with classified money was a head start. If you shut it down, you are telling them the program has failed. Isn't it worth something for them to worry that they are a success?"

"What do you think the Chinese and Russians know?" she asked.

"That the program exists, and that we're pouring a lot into it," Brooks said.

There was another issue Upton had begun worrying more about

since this all began—the loose culture of big tech and how it en-couraged too high a degree of U.S. technology being replicated overseas. She had asked for and received several briefings on it in the last two weeks.

"What are you thinking?" Phelps asked the president. He was beginning to get to know her.

"Have you ever heard of Brazilian Jiu-Jitsu?" Upton asked the whole group.

Brooks shook her head.

"It is a form of self-defense. You use your opponent's force to defeat him. I learned it in the army," she said. And then she outlined her plan.

53

PALO ALTO

Monday 10 May

PETER RENA

Upton gave them a plane to fly back to California. Rena's first stop was to see Kunai Sreenivansan at Ignius Corp.

The battery company had its headquarters in an old nursery in East Palo Alto, an unincorporated township across the freeway from Palo Alto and Stanford. East Palo Alto had always been poor, the place where Black people migrating from the South came after World War II, then the Vietnamese in the 1980s. Now more new residents were Latino. But East Palo Alto was still poor and predominantly Black. Sreenivansan needed land for his battery factory. He turned the greenhouses into laboratories. His office was a converted bedroom in the old house.

Sreenivansan was tall and broad shouldered and darker than Rena, but the two men could have been mistaken for countrymen, the Indian and the dark Italian. They both had thick black hair, aquiline noses and dark eyes.

The young scientist studied Rena from behind a metal desk purchased from a store that sold used office furniture. They had met only twice before, when Kim Matsuda had brought Rena around as part of the security checks on the battery companies. Rena had interviewed him at length about the company. He knew Rena was thorough and knew a good deal he didn't reveal. There was something a little frightening, Sreenivansan thought, beneath Rena's military bearing and unfailing politeness.

"I need a favor," Rena said. "Tell your board you're about to have a breakthrough."

Sreenivansan looked surprised. "But it's not true."

"Then better not give them any details."

"And if they ask questions?"

"You have a PhD," Rena said. "I assume you know how to dissemble."

"There are rules about what you say to boards."

Rena knew the flow batteries were a mission for Sreenivansan—a lifelong dream from his childhood in India.

"And you'll need to stretch them," Rena said.

"What are you playing at?"

"Saving your company, Kunai."

Brooks was just back from visiting the Helios CEO, Bill Stencel, when Rena returned to the FBI office.

"What'd Stencel say?" Rena asked.

"He liked the intrigue. How about Kunai?"

"He had a little trouble wrapping his scientist's brain around the deception."

"A man who doesn't lie. You two should be great friends," Brooks said.

"You ready for what's next?"

"Most def," she said. She was excited and nervous.

THREE DAYS LATER, THE REST OF PRESIDENT UPTON'S PLAN WENT into action. She had envisioned a way to send a signal to all of Silicon Valley and to technology companies worldwide. The rules about technology transfer and security were going to change. And they were going to use the likelihood that the battery program was compromised as the way to do it. They were going to stage raids on four prominent people in the Valley, simultaneously, for spying.

The ruthlessness of the plan surprised Brooks. She admitted to Peter after hearing it that maybe there was more to Wendy Upton than she'd thought. Behind the president's cautious manner and cool reserve was a rebellious spirit, Randi said. She already knew Upton was quiet, stubborn, and polite, and Randi had never doubted that Upton was strong. But she had not thought the woman quite so daring. The heart of the teenage girl who forty years ago had sued the state to become an emancipated minor and raise her sister still beat inside her.

Messages had successfully been sent via CEOs about technology breakthroughs to all of the companies' boards. With FISA court approval, the FBI had then monitored the communications of key people under suspicion to see if they communicated news of those breakthroughs to anyone—especially back to Russia or China. Now Rena and Brooks were waiting at the FBI office for the Immigration and Customs Enforcement agents to arrive to stage the denouement. The small conference room where they had met Jazz Bhalla all those weeks earlier was now filled with agents in FBI windbreakers. Bhalla drove everyone crazy clicking a pen while they waited. The ICE teams pulled up in front of the small FBI office in separate caravans of black vehicles. Rena joined the caravan heading to Anatol Bremmer's. And they were off.

The radio communication between the teams would be noisy by design. "Lights and sirens. Go in loud and large," Bhalla had ordered. The caravans of SUVs were bigger than necessary, too, eight vehicles each, thirty-two in all. Drones flew over each target's house. They wanted the public and the media to notice.

Jazz Bhalla called in first. They'd arrived at the house of Patrick Singh, the Ignius scientist they suspected might have been recruited by another country, but he wasn't there. Every target had been given a colorful code name, largely for the media to pick up on later. Singh was Mickey Mouse. "We are executing a search warrant of the home," Bhalla reported, on the pretext that Singh had taken work from the office home with him, which was technically a national security violation. Their orders were to make a mess of every place they searched.

Prince Omar Abbad wasn't home either, but they had never expected him to be. A friendly judge had signed a search warrant for the house, an enormous white plaster and glass mansion that looked more like a resort hotel than a residence. But they didn't really expect to find much. No one imagined the prince, code named Bambi, to have brought technical information home from his investment firm's office.

Brooks was in the caravan headed to James Wei's house. Wei had been given the code name Snow White.

Then the radio crackled. "We have a runner." Rena didn't know the voice.

"Lion King is heading out."

Lion King: Anatol Bremmer.

The drone hovering over his house had apparently detected Bremmer leaving. It might mean nothing, a normal trip out. Or it could mean he'd heard they were coming.

"He in a hurry?" Agent Polansky asked from the front seat of Rena's SUV.

"Negative," answered the drone operator. "He's just getting into his car. A black Tesla. But he has a satchel, maybe a go bag."

"Track him!" Polansky snapped.

"Heading toward 280," the drone camera operator reported. That was the main freeway near Los Altos Hills.

"Stay in touch," Polansky said. Then he touched the driver on the shoulder and said quietly, "Go, Bill."

They felt the pulling force of the SUV's acceleration, and the truck listed to the right as the driver turned at speed. Rena hated SUVs. They always felt like they were going to tip over. "Heading 280 south," the drone operator announced.

"Copy that."

"He may be headed to Mineta?" the driver said.

"What's that?" asked Rena.

"San Jose airport. Where the private jet terminal is," said Polansky. "If he's running, he'd go there."

Would Bremmer run? Rena wondered. This elaborately staged trap was designed to find that out. They had designed the coordinated FBI and ICE raid on four prominent Valley executives with foreign ties to send a public signal. A crackdown under President Upton. A shock wave through the Valley. And a cover for the classified battery plan. President Upton was hard on espionage, not a patsy running a naive program—just in case the program was ever discovered by the press and became an issue with Congress.

Polansky radioed to the other SUVs, "It's approximately eighteen minutes to Mineta." He said, looking at GPS, "In ten miles, he may pull off 280 onto 880. If he does that, he's running."

Rena, sitting behind Polansky, tapped the agent on the shoulder. "Our SUV should break off," he said, "and head back to Bremmer's."

"What?"

"It's not him. If he's running, he's not in that Tesla." Polansky swiveled his head to get a better look at Rena. "He wouldn't make that mistake," Rena said. "If he is running, he wouldn't take his own car. He wouldn't be the first out the door. And he wouldn't head to the most obvious airport."

Polansky grimaced.

"Is there another place he could fly out of?" Rena asked.

"San Carlos," the driver said.

"Go there," Rena said to Polansky. "If I'm wrong, let the rest of these cars stay with the Tesla. But send one of the SUVs back to Bremmer's."

Polansky pondered that a moment and then nodded to the driver. "San Carlos, Bill." Into the radio he announced, "Skyline Team, stay with the Tesla. Skyline One is breaking off. Skyline Two, you head to Lion King's house," using Bremmer's code name.

"Skyline One please repeat," someone on the radio asked.

But Rena put his hand on the mouthpiece of Polansky's microphone and shook his head. Then he tapped his ears to suggest they didn't really know who might be listening.

"We're breaking off. Engine trouble," Polansky said. "But remaining Skyline team continue."

The driver turned their SUV around and they headed back toward the 101. Then he got in the emergency lane on the right, lights flashing, and gunned it.

"The Tesla is turning onto 880," the radio announced.

"Pull them over when they enter airport proper," Polansky said.

"Copy."

A few minutes later the radio offered the word. The occupant of the black Tesla was one of Bremmer's employees.

It took them another fifteen minutes to make their way up the 101 to the exit for the tiny private airport in San Carlos.

"Don't park," Rena told the driver. "If he's coming and sees this truck, he'll keep on going." Polansky nodded. "And stay out of sight," Rena added.

Polansky, Rena, and a third agent got out and headed into the tiny terminal. It was a one-story building with a small waiting area and a single person behind a high counter. She looked stunned by the arrival of armed federal agents at her tiny terminal. This was a hobbyist's airport used primarily by weekend pilots. A small tower building sat by itself on the field. There was a third building with a sign that said FLYING SCHOOL and two small repair hangars. Next door was a little museum about the history of private aviation. Most of the planes on the tarmac were small-engine craft, Cessnas and Beechcrafts. There were only a handful of jets that might be capable of long trips.

Polansky went to the desk and asked about flights. Rena went outside and stood at the edge of the building to watch.

About ten minutes passed. Then a Volkswagen Passat pulled in and drove through a small gate onto the little tarmac. It pulled up to a Learjet parked at the far edge of the field.

They were about to lose him.

Rena started running.

Two men got out of the Volkswagen. One of them was Anatol.

"Bremmer!" Rena yelled.

The Russian didn't hear him.

Rena pulled a weapon, something he almost never carried but that Bhalla had authorized for him. He fired over Bremmer's head in the direction of the Bay.

Startled, the man with Bremmer pulled a weapon of his own and squatted in a firing position that suggested careful training. He aimed his weapon at Rena.

"Stop, Anatol!" Rena yelled.

Bremmer's bodyguard set himself.

Polansky and the second agent emerged from the small terminal building, called by the sound of Rena's pistol. They began running toward the group.

Their anxiety, and the bodyguard's, Rena thought, could take this sideways. He stopped, pointed his gun away from the Russians and took his finger off the trigger so Bremmer's bodyguard could see it.

"Mr. Rena, I have a trip to London. I'm sorry I have to leave," Bremmer said.

"Tell your man to lower the gun, Anatol."

Bremmer said something more to the bodyguard. The bigger man didn't move.

From behind Rena, Polansky shouted at them, "This is the FBI. Put your weapon on the ground and lie down, facedown, hands behind your heads. Do it now."

Bremmer repeated what Polansky said, apparently in Russian. The bodyguard stood up, still holding his gun.

"Put down the weapon. Now. Get on the ground. Facedown. Do it now!" Polansky was shouting.

The bodyguard didn't move.

Then Rena put his own gun on the ground, raised his hands, and started walking toward Bremmer.

"Drop the gun or we will fire," Polansky shouted.

Rena kept walking toward Bremmer.

"Rena!" Polansky yelled.

Rena was close enough now that he could speak to Bremmer in a normal voice.

"Anatol, they will shoot him if he doesn't drop his weapon. And you, too."

Bremmer said something more in Russian and the bodyguard finally laid his pistol on the ground.

Rena could hear Polansky and the other agent slowly moving up behind him.

"This is rather unusual, wouldn't you say, Mr. Rena? You could have just called," Bremmer said.

"It was you, wasn't it?"

"What was?"

"You were doing a favor for the other side. Going after Upton. By going after me. But you got caught. And then you went after me again, this time to get me off your back."

"Are you arresting me because people said mean things about you on the Internet?"

"I'm not a policeman. I don't arrest people. I'm just asking a question."

"What are you really doing here?" Bremmer said.

Rena was close now, close enough that Bremmer's bodyguard could have grabbed him and used him as a shield. The man almost certainly had another gun. Rena hadn't meant to get so close.

"Don't come back, Anatol."

"What?"

"Get on that plane, and don't come back. To the world, you are now a Russian spy, not a visionary capitalist. If you try to come back to the United States, you won't be allowed in."

"That's absurd."

"You're not wanted here. Or your company."

"By whom?"

"The president of the United States of America."

That gave Bremmer something that took a moment to think about.

"And what if I refuse?"

"You can be arrested. Or you can be shot for pulling a weapon on FBI agents."

Rena could tell the guns unnerved Bremmer, even his own bodyguard's.

"There are laws. This is America," Bremmer argued.

"And they give the president broad discretion."

Bremmer paused to think.

"That is ridiculous."

"Then stay. Have your company's assets frozen and the firm put on a watch list. Be arrested for espionage. See what case we have. And see how your business fares after the publicity."

"She will regret this."

"It was her idea."

That answer seemed to surprise Bremmer. The Russian apparently thought they'd been bluffing the other day; or that Upton would fold.

"Why are you doing this?"

"Espionage. Treason. Fraud. Trying to interfere in our elections by attacking Wendy Upton. And, also, I just don't like you. You pick."

"You have it wrong," Bremmer said, but he hesitated, his mind trying to process what Rena knew and didn't know.

"I don't think so."

Polansky was next to Rena now, gun still drawn, aimed at the bodyguard.

"But you shouldn't care much, Anatol, if I don't have all my facts straight, right? That kind of thing doesn't matter anymore."

Bremmer picked up his bag and began to move toward the Learjet. Rena put a hand up to keep Polansky and the other agent from stopping them.

Bremmer paused at the foot of the stairs. "You make a habit of collecting enemies, Mr. Rena, don't you?"

"I guess I do," Rena said.

The two Russians boarded the plane.

"I don't like politics," Polansky said as the Learjet lifted off. The small jet was pointed south over the bay and then banked hard left to the east. "We should have arrested that guy."

"We didn't have enough on him," Rena said. "And this is what was supposed to happen."

Inside the terminal, Polansky asked to be connected to the FAA. "I want to know where that plane lands and where the passengers are going next. And if it's on U.S. soil, arrest them."

54

RANDI BROOKS

"Gotta say, Jimmy Wei looked really shocked," Brooks told Rena.

She could still feel the flush in her face. The run-up to the house, the FBI agents with their guns drawn in their FBI jackets like in the movies. Wei in handcuffs. His wife screaming. His yelling for her to call his lawyer.

Randi wasn't a cop. She had never done anything like that before.

Wei was being questioned for espionage. His company and the Chinese government had been alerted. So had the press—all according to plan.

The State Department was signaling to the Chinese government that if they wanted to avoid a scandal, Wei would be allowed to quietly leave the country. If he didn't want to flee, Wei could fight his case in American courts. He had lived most of his life in America, after all, and his wife and kids were all born here. But the publicity of a trial, the discovery that the U.S. government prosecutors would seek, would hardly please the Chinese government. Imagine, the whole "Strategy of the Human Wave" outlined for an American jury and in the newspapers and on cable for weeks. The president had also directed the

Justice Department to open an investigation into GCM Investments. James Wei had a major decision to make. So did his bosses in Beijing.

"I gotta tell you, Peter, he looked like an innocent man," Brooks said.

"Don't be fooled," Jazz Bhalla said. "Like I always say, these aren't Boy Scouts. Even if he didn't think he was a spy, he knew his company was connected to state security."

What a stink it would all make, Brooks thought. The Chinese would start tossing out American companies. The culture of the Valley would be changed, at least for a while. Maybe forever.

But Upton had figured on all that, Brooks thought. She had learned from Traynor to play boldly, but with more calculation.

Peter was quiet, even more than usual.

"Hey," she said. "Can we talk?"

They went outside and began to walk on the old frontage road by the freeway. They were met by the wooshing sound of speeding cars rushing past on the other side of the fence.

"You okay?"

She still couldn't believe someone had shown up at Peter's house with guns. Rena still looked troubled by the incident, but he didn't want to show it, or probably even admit it to himself. She loved her partner, but he was hopelessly a dude.

"There's a lot we don't know," he said. That wasn't what she had expected him to say.

"That's what's eating you?"

"I'd like to know if Kim Matsuda was poisoned," he said. It would take more tests to be sure, but now the pressure to do them had eased. "And did Jimmy Wei have her killed, or did she just learn that Jimmy and GCM Investments were not to be trusted?" They might never know.

And what about Abbad or Singh?

Rena continued. "I know the president was using what we found to make a statement about security and technology—and to save the battery program. But I'd still like to know."

"The greater good, Pete. Don't you think?"

"The greater good always makes me nervous."

"Like Jazz said, these weren't Boy Scouts."

Then she realized that remark, too, rubbed him the wrong way. Peter had been a Boy Scout, an Eagle Scout, and proud of it.

"We saved this battery project, Peter. Something good happened here." But he didn't respond.

He didn't have anything more to say. She knew he wouldn't. She knew him better than almost anyone. But you never really know other people, do you? She had lived probably half of her lifetime already and she was only learning that now.

She put her arm around her partner and they walked back inside.

55

PALO ALTO

Saturday 15 May

PETER RENA

"What did the president call it?" Vic asked.

"Brazilian Jiu-Jitsu," Rena said. "But I'm not supposed to tell." He smiled.

"Then don't," Vic flirted. They were sitting in her Balinese garden.

"I want to."

"Then what's Brazilian Jiu-Jitsu?"

"Some kind of martial art she learned in the army."

"What is it?"

"A way of winning a fight even when you're on the ground with your opponent on top of you."

"How's it work? Brazilian Jiu-Jitsu?"

"I don't know. You use your weakness and turn it into an advantage."

"Is that what you did?"

"I don't really know that either." He looked past her into the garden. "She wanted to use what we'd learned, and the mistakes we'd made to whatever advantage she could."

"And did she?"

He had told her everything. He had broken all the rules.

"Maybe. I'm not really sure of that either."

"You're not sure of much are you, boy?"

"The older I get."

"What I don't understand is why it worked out if some of these people got away. You arrested one man, this man Wei, who the government intends to send to China rather than prosecute. And the other three fled. Including the Russian you let go."

He had told her that, too. He had even told her about Steph Myers. Rena had called Myers yesterday, and they had talked for a while, close to an hour. Myers seemed to want to. They would talk again. Maybe it was helping them both.

"They were supposed to get away," Peter said, meaning Bremmer and Singh. "If they ran, they were probably guilty. At least that's what people will think."

"And how did that save your battery program?"

"The woman who cracked down on Silicon Valley spying would be a hero to the people who worry about technology theft. That would give her license, some level of trust, to keep this program going if it gets found out. Which now it certainly will."

"And why did you tell the CEOs to tell their boards they had made breakthroughs in the battery technology?"

That had also been Upton's idea.

"To see which board members would leak it. We had wiretaps."

Upton was also about to announce her vice president, another iconoclast, a former Republican who had fled his party over its extremism. He was now the Democratic governor of North Carolina, an evangelical Christian who was almost as passionate in his environmentalism as his faith. Another political original. They were hard to find, but Rena thought they might start now to spawn. Upton had taken her time. She must have thought it through. She was always thorough.

Vic studied him.

"Are you sorry you told me?"

He turned to look at her.

He felt safe here in her secret garden, listening to the waterfall, watching the koi flit between the rocks in the little stream she'd built, her invented paradise. Rena slipped out of his chair onto his knees. Brazilian Jiu-Jitsu, he thought.

"Victoria Madison, will you do me the honor of my life and marry me?"

She had not seen it coming.

"You are the best person I know. You are the most beautiful woman I've ever met. And I cannot imagine being happy unless I spend the rest of my life trying to make you happy. I give you my heart, not to give back again. For all the days to come."

Her smoke-gray eyes widened and then blinked a few times; she was trying to stay composed.

He thought he could see what she was thinking. She was wondering, Why now? What had changed?

"I don't say things I don't mean," he said.

"No, you don't."

Vic didn't either.

"Are you going to turn me down?"

"I think you took a long damn time to ask. So I get a long time to answer."

He was still on his knees. He was waiting for her to smile.

"That's only fair," he said.

Then she leaned down, and Rena, hoping for a kiss, closed his eyes.

ACKNOWLEDGMENTS

Novels live inside an author for much longer than the time spent writing them. Some lie waiting for years. Writing, as a consequence, is as much excavation and discovery as creation. Such labor benefits from many people visiting the dig, helping the person with the trowel and brush recognize what has been missed or is just plain wrong.

The Days to Come was made better by various such visitors. The central idea—how a disruptive entrepreneurial president might rethink governing—was shaped with the help of Zachary Wagman, my friend and editor at Ecco, and David Black, who has been my agent for nearly a quarter century. When Zack moved to other excavations at another publisher, I had the great fortune to be placed by Ecco in the capable hands of Norma Barksdale. I am very grateful.

Dan Becker, one of the country's leading environmental advocates, helped guide me through the various possibilities for altering global warming. He was also the one to press the idea that the climate crisis is as much a national security threat as well as an environmental, social, and economic one. Though Dan also reviewed my invented secret plan to save the planet, I alone am responsible for all that is wrong or implausible.

John Gomperts and Brian Roche offered critical advice on the manuscript—John as usual more than once. (Fifty years and counting, JG.) Brian, a lawyer who has tried cases in Silicon Valley, was invaluable in helping me understand how spies in Silicon Valley are recruited. At a key point, Dr. Katherine Klein offered crucial thoughts and criticism.

Many others helped inspire and inform the characters. I am indebted to many journalists who have scrubbed beneath the shiny surface of Silicon Valley, usually against the prevailing wisdom. I also owe a debt to countless scientists and environmental journalists who have written extensively about the climate crisis and how to solve it—while the government has largely ignored the problem or made it worse.

At Ecco, my thanks again to the superb Miriam Parker, as well as to Martin Wilson, Helen Atsma, Meghan Deans, Elizabeth Yaffe, and Lydia Weaver. I am grateful, too, for the long support of the crew at Black Literary Agency, including Susan Raihofer and Ayla Zuraw-Friedland.

The unfailing encouragement of Jon Haber, Bonnie Levin, Martha Toll, and Drew Littman and many others means more than I can say. My thanks, too, for the support of those who have helped me celebrate this work in the past, including Beth Donovan and Luke Albee, Paul and Stephanie Taylor, Mike and Debra McCurry, Eric and Linda Platt. My love to my brother writer-in-arms, Craig Buck; to my mother and sisters, Karina and Beth. And, ever, to my trio, Rima, Leah, and Kira.